GOJIRO

GOJIRO

MARK JACOBSON

THE ATLANTIC MONTHLY PRESS
NEW YORK

Published simultaneously in Canada
Printed in the United States of America
FIRST EDITION

Library of Congress Cataloging-in-Publication Data

Jacobson, Mark.
    Gojiro / Mark Jacobson.
    ISBN 0-87113-396-2
    I. Title.
  PS3560.A27G65   1991   813'.54—dc20   90-49521

The Atlantic Monthly Press
19 Union Square West
New York, NY 10003

FIRST PRINTING

For Nancy—
my own true friend

MEMO

TO

FANS

You know how it begins. Don't you?

There's a vast shimmering sky, empty air. Blank. Except for the dot. The blotch. A tiny piece of fuzz, moving from the right, to the vacant center. What is it? That's the first question. The first question you ask that you already know the answer to—except right then, while you're watching, it's all new again.

Is that how it is for you? It is for me.

You wonder if it's some dark star, a dim flicker in your eye, or maybe a bug—a mayfly. A mayfly!—spending its whole life in just one day, a fragile bit of being, making its faint hum.

The hum becomes a buzz.

And you see the family. The family on the lush hillside, beside the crystal lake, in front of a towering mountain, a diamond sparkle of snow on its crowning top.

The family. The Dad is taking the picture, standing behind the old camera, his head under the black cloth so you can't see his face. There's only his hand, motioning the Boy and the Mom to move this way, that. The Mom smiles. She is beautiful, her skin like heavy cream against maroon satin, her teeth so white.

How often I have dreamed of her, the mother he made, imagined what it might be like to have such a mom—to have a mom at all!

Then you look at the Boy. His clothes are funny: short woolen pants, a blue blazer with the insignia of an academy to which he'd pledged undying loyalty.

Except he never got to be a schoolboy! Never got to wait for a yellow bus,

3

his books held together with an elastic strap. He never got to raise his hand all freshfaced, flushed with the sheer joy of knowing.

"Smile," the Dad calls from under the black cloth. The Boy's fat red cheeks crease. He laughs—*that same high, choking laugh!*—as the Dad comes running to take his place in the shot. They're all together now. The three of them, waiting for the camera's timer to run down. The Boy's in the middle; he has his mother's eyes, his father's mouth.

How long he worked on that! To make them fit together, to make a family!

But the hum is louder now, bigger than a buzz. It's a drone. A dull gnash, anxiety's nag, a ripping, tearing sound. But they don't hear it at all. The Dad puts his arms around the Mom, stands closer to the Boy. Their smiles spread—the shutter's about to click.

And you think, whatever's up there in the sky, it can't touch them. Whatever it is, they'll be safe. Their love will shield them. But the noise keeps on, gnawing, a chainsaw in your head.

The Mom and Dad don't hear it. They keep smiling, looking into the lens: so proud! But the Boy's eyes go. The roar takes them, away from that peaceful hillside and up into the sky.

He worked on it for days! So the Mom and Dad he made would never know what hit them, never have that terror stamped into their hearts. But he couldn't do the same for himself.

The Boy's eyes go. Up and up.

And there they are—Tibbets, his crew. Those gauntfaced newsreel men inside their Superfortress. The light streams into their glassy cockpit as they count backward, tolling the knell for the former times. Buttons down! Thumbs up! The bottom of the plane opens and another world—his, mine, yours—comes out.

Below, they're still smiling, that Mom and Dad. *Smiling, never knowing.*

Even now, at the end of it all, I still can't bear to know *this* was the beginning. Komodo says, "A happy end's worth a sad beginning." But I can't say as I agree. What could be worth shadows seared into stone walls, skin sliding from bones, people jumping from bridges—their minds too filled with horror to see that the river beneath them was on fire? Even now, I want to cry a million tears to douse those raging flames, push those sliding faces back onto the bones, make them beautiful again. Even now, I want to grab that rising Cloud by the neck, choke the fission from it. If it had been up to me, none of this would have happened. But, of course, it wasn't up to me.

So I sit and watch. Like I always do. Like you do. And see the Boy, his blazer singed, steam rising from the brim of his cap, as he stumbles through the wreckage of the City.

"Mother!"

"Father!"

Alone. Alone in Death's world. Disappeared from all he knew, all he might ever come to know, a single figure on the ruined landscape, nothing there except him and Doom itself.

The Boy and the Cloud! That's the part when I break down, when I want to turn away. It's just that he's so brave. How he turns and faces it, walks right into it! He enters Death and comes out the other side!

Through the roiling misery, the burning bodies, the hands writhing from the pyre, the Boy goes out to that hillside once again, to the bluest lake beside the snowcapped mountain. And he begins to call: "Gojiro! Please come in, Gojiro! Please come in. Please heed this humble servant's plea!"

The Supplication! Kills me, the supplication.

"Gojiro! Please come in, Gojiro! Please heed this humble servant's plea!"

And then, looming five hundred feet or more, red eyes twin laser beacons through the gloom, the great Beast is there, sounding his familiar ear-piercing shriek. He extends his massive claw, snatches that Boy from the Heater's maw. Gojiro! King of Monsters, Friend to Atoms.

Him.

Me.

That's what you'd call the beginning, isn't it. Zealous zardpards? You'd swear it, wouldn't you, Gargantuan G Gluttons, followers of the Foremost Frequency?

Sixteen moron movies, sixteen beginnings. And is there a 'tile-o-file alive that didn't love it every time? I wouldn't even care to dig deep into my monster's mailbag to count how many bleating communications I've gotten on the topic. "Dear Gojiro, I was over at the mall and some guys sitting on the hood of the raffle car said you were gonna cut out the beginning. I just got sick. This is a terrible idea! I will do serious physical damage to myself if this happens. Without the beginning my life won't mean a thing."

Shit. I mean, what's a mutant lizard to do?

Got to hand it to ole Shig. Can't say the dude don't have a real grasp of the modern mindset. I hate to say it, zardpards, but if Pavlov had the likes of you around drooling, he could've saved a lot of money on dog food. Like any smart producer-packager, Shig knows the value of Skinner's box, that you'd need a handy beginning, a little touchstone of pretitle knee jerk.

But I ain't here to complain. I'm past complaining now. Past near everything. Everything except the telling. So that's what I want to do: tell. Tell and tell.

Gojiro's story. The real one. From the behemoth's own POV. Who else's story am I supposed to tell? Get up close and personal with Napoleon and Josephine, scoop the inside dope on Waterloo? No, man. This is Gojiro's story, and where's the beginning of *that?*

Komodo, Joe Linear, says, "Why not start at the beginning?" Thanks a lot. Where's the beginning of me? Should I return to those earliest of times I believe myself acquainted with, a misty sixty-six million years ago, to that great hole the comet tore in the dinosaurs' continuum? Maybe I shouldn't even stop there. Why not skip back to the Big Bang itself? What better way to satisfy cosmological longing than to start from absolute nothingness? Maybe *all* stories should begin there, every sitcom on TV, every jerkwater movie. Yeah! Check out Fred and Ethel's primeval antecedents every episode. Exposition's too maligned a commodity in today's overheated information marketplace. Start from the Void, I say, dredge up witty anecdotes to kill time during the slower Devonians and Silurians.

It's just an idea, a narrative tactic. But why push my luck? I might not be a master like Shig, but I do believe I can recognize the integrity of a tale and an audience's tolerance for that integrity. Even if I'm going to die tomorrow, it ain't like I was born yesterday. A judicious hand is necessary, if one wants to tell *everything.* I've got this completist streak, you see. Or maybe it's just that I know that's the way *he* would have wanted it: beginning, middle, and end. I owe him that much, my greenskinned former self.

So, check it out, the official once-upon-a-time regarding that biggest, baddest five-hundred-foot-tall lizard ever to quake a globe: let me say that once he was small, a regulation herp living on a quiet seaside rock surrounded by his fellows. Except then they came in planes, those custodians of the Modern Age, and they busted open the millennium right in his face like an exploding cigar. When he woke up he was somewhere else, inside another skin, alone, forever separate, a most singular red-eyed, multi-ton monster with a telepathic brain inside his giant, addled head. That could have been that, except Komodo, the Hiroshima Jap, escaped at last from his nuclear-induced coma. And the two of them were friends, living on an uncharted South Pacific tract they called Radioactive Island—the same place from where I'm talking now. And then some others came too, poor unfortunates, children called Atoms. And they all lived together on Radioactive Island, this grumpy monster and his ingenious pal and those strange kids . . .

Cut! Hold press. This isn't going to work. I just can't tell it straight out, hip bone connected to the thigh bone. You been through the ruckus I been through, your logic gets scrambled, locution fractured. Besides, if you're a G-fan, follower of the Foremost Frequency, you know all this stuff already. You got the origin story memorized, been doodling it on the backs of schoolbooks for years, etched it into your skin. Shig has seen to that. No King of Monsters could have asked for a more determined, four-walling Boswell—go ahead, ring up a yogurt-eating Yugoslavian, any Bolivian in a bowler hat, a thousand denizens of the Surabaya back alleys, they'll rattle off the leviathan's saga. So what if Shig left out next to everything and changed the rest; Truth in twenty-five words or less, that's his credo. And who's to say, in this day and age, maybe that's Truth enough.

Could be it's only me who needs to hear it told this way, big and messy. Could be it's only me who needs the ever-lurching arc to make sense of Gojiro's life and times. Could be it's only me who has to play it out, step by convoluted step, so as to get the gist of the great Green Machine's most recent super-thrilling adventure and know what really happened in that Valley of the Crossroads.

Komodo says I got to be patient. He warns ten generations might go by before what transpired in the Valley gurgles up from graycurled sub-basements of the mind to emerge in the noonday glare of conscious thought. Even then, Komodo says, it might only be the poets who know it, faraway-eyed handwringers who, in their emotion-wrought imaginations, will point the way to the rest. "The poets are the halfway house," Komodo says. He's romantic like that. Gojiro, though, he was more of a bah-humbug kind of guy. Gojiro always wanted something more concrete, a tire to kick. He would have said later for Yeats and his slouching falcons, get me Joe Friday. Gojiro would have said maybe drummers in jungles got a million years to simmer tales and legends, boil them down to parable and allegory, but the facts, ma'am, the *true facts,* are fleeting, you got to catch them while you can.

Still, Komodo contends, it's inevitable: sooner or later everyone will recognize what Gojiro did. But then again, Komodo believes my story. Like he would.

Myself, I'm not so sure. I mean, how do you think it feels to be unable to shake the conviction that, on an exceedingly bright early morning in the middle of a desolate southwestern desert, you became God, or some rough equivalent, for 0.0247 seconds? You think this is an easy concept to accommodate? Wouldn't you rather confess to insanity than keep on believing in it? Even now, inside this rubberized volcano, merely approaching the outskirts of the idea causes me near thermoregulatory shutdown. But I can't stop thinking *something* happened out there in that Valley. Something that catapulted me across all time and space, beached me up in this place where I am right now, which seems so familiar yet so undeniably different. *Something* happened that separated me from what I once was and what I am now.

Memory says one thing and all sense says another.

That's why I've decided to tell you everything: to see what you think, to see if you'll follow the tale of a former monitor lizard and his Japanese friend, if you'll get even the smallest gist of the world they made, the things they thought—like how for every Beam there's a Bunch, and that Reprimordialization is no walk in the park. To see if you'll believe that for 0.0247 seconds you—along with everything else in creation—were in me, and I was in you.

Listen, zardpards, make up your minds. I wonder what you'll decide. Will you throw down your Crystal Contacts in disgust, renounce the supplication, go off to patronize some other, less demanding superhero, one who is more scrupulous about answering his fanmail? I wouldn't blame you. After all, those parietal tattoos were only weekend jobs; on Monday morning the teacher never knew. Maybe that's the level at which things should have remained: commerce, another cruddy clot of disposable celluloid. After all, it's one thing to sell someone an idea and another to ask them to *believe* in it. That's the catch; that's always been the catch.

"Go on," Komodo says, "tell it." He says there's a poet in everyone, that you never know what chord might be struck. Telling might even reduce full recognition by two, perhaps three generations, Komodo says, with a straight face, which is how he says most everything, boy scout that he is. Great. I've only got to wait six hundred years to find out if you believe my story, instead of eight hundred. What a markdown! I should let Komodo keep talking. Maybe he'll knock off another century or two.

Not that it matters all that much. I estimate I've got about thirty-eight hours left to go . . . make that thirty-seven hours, fifty-nine and five-sixths minutes now. Tick, tick, tick. Hourglass city. It's such a strange feeling, knowing, finally, it's going to end. That the passage of time means something.

Oh, my life!

To think that back through primeval mists, before there was a Heater and a Gojiro, it seemed that time hardly moved for me and my Bunch. Must be that cold blood, but things do go slower for reptiles, you know. That's how it is, being a zard, part of a Bunch whose Line goes back beyond remembering. If I was still among them—my former crew—there's no way I'd be telling this. Because when you're a 'tile there's no need for life stories.

You *were* your life story! Besides, who would you tell this autobio to? The leatherbelly lying beside you? He already knew it. He knew your story as well as he knew his own, every personal detail. If there was a new idea dawning in your head, an improved way to forktongue a fly or slip off a mossy rock, there was no rush to copyright it, study its many facets, come to huge conclusions. Among the zards, there were no geniuses, leaders, heroes. If you had a new idea, chances are everybody else had the same one, and the fruits of that new idea were a hundred thousand generations away, and you didn't care a bit.

But now! I've come so far from my roots, from who and what I once was, even from who and what I was even most recently. I am not myself any longer. I know that. For me, that's the critical something of whatever happened out in the Valley. I'm on the other side of my Eternal Equation now: I am who I am. That's why I have to tell you all this. Because now, divorced from all Lines, remote from all Bunches and Beams, I'm truly one of a kind. Maybe the Evolloo moves slow for zards, but it speeds along at a vicious clip for mutants, faster and faster. So fast that now I, who once had next to forever to think a single thought, to know the smallest detail, have only these three dozen hours to tell everything.

Outside this volcano, I can hear Komodo's hammer. Bang, bang, bang. He's outside with the Atoms, those sad, misformed children who arrived uninvited on our Island of lost souls and stayed to become equal citizens. They're working on my death raft. When it's done, they'll strap me across the bamboo, and, no doubt amid much somber pomp, send me out past the Cloudcover, where my thermoregulation will stutter to a stop and I'll finally be no more.

So listen up, ever-faithful G-fans: I ain't got time to waste. Probably this is just nostalgia for my long-lost Bunch, but, at least for these next few hours, I want my life story to be your life story, and yours to be mine. I know this can never happen, that no one mutant can share everything with another. That is the very definition of who we are—the separateness, the being apart. But still, I wish it. It is, perhaps, my last wish: that when I lie down on Komodo's raft, I won't be the only one in the world who knows my story. Maybe then you'll be better equipped to make up your mind about the sanity of your trusty correspondent here. Too bad I'm not going to be leaving any descendants. Otherwise, maybe your descendants, those poets Komodo is so wild about, could hook up with mine and give each other great ecumenicalism.

Sure.

But still, if you want to tell *everything,* you've got to find the beginning. As I said, that's no cinch. Most likely it'll be best to start from last year or, rather, last year minus thirty-seven hours and fifty-four minutes now, back to that terrible night when Gojiro and Komodo swore the Triple Ring Promise Amendment.

PART

ONE

A DEATH ESCAPED

Komodo could always tell when Gojiro was trying to snuff himself. He just *knew*. The feeling got around his heart like the Tingler, made his chest so tight he couldn't breathe right. Then, if need be, he'd jump through a black hole like a circus hoop, swim across two thousand miles of hostile sea. It didn't matter where from or how far, Komodo would come, never cease to seek until he found. This particular time, though, he wasn't thousands of miles away. He was right there on Radioactive Island, beside Gojiro's volcanic home, trying to teach a sub-beginner genetics course to a clot of real slow Atoms.

Not that the monster tried to kill himself all that often. Suicide's no snap for the invulnerable, you know. Where does the fatal blow go when no blow is fatal? This was the problem, and not a new one. It came up while they were making the first of those King of Monsters, Friend to Atoms home movies Shig stole and spread around the world.

"So what's my weakness?" Gojiro said to Komodo. "Never been no Hero that didn't have a weakness. Not a single paragon of Right who didn't have a heel where to shoot the kryptonite. Got to have a weakness, something to overcome, or how else can I be brave?"

"You make a good point, my own true friend," Komodo said thoughtfully. Experiments ensued. Poison, guns, fire, and flames. Tests were taken that made for tales no Timex ever lived to tell. But not a dent was made, no soft spot was revealed. No physical phenomenon, particular phraseology, or pernicious Pentagon-like ploy had the stuff to lay that greenest leviathan low.

"Has to be *something!*" Gojiro shouted.

1 3

"Don't worry," Komodo said, harried and contrite at what he saw as still another in a series of his failures to find answers to his friend's ever-pressing problems. "It will appear. Your weakness is within you. It will come out."

"Yeah," Gojiro said, "for sure."

In lieu of certifiable shortcomings, they made some up. The sad truth is those films were laced with lies long before Shig ever got at them with his hot splicer. Sure, it looked like that slaverfaced Opposer's sword of glowing PCBs slashed through the monster's previously impervious leathers in *Gojiro vs. Dungeons and Dragons Freaks in the World under the Bed* and it might have seemed like that Southpaw Sludgicle hypnotized the big fella into nearly strangling himself with his Louisville Slugger tail in *Gojiro (8) vs. Hideous Chemical Creatures (6) in the Ballparks of the Night.* But all that was just for suspense's sake, cheap movie logic, setups, so much fish in a barrel. None of those supposed Opposers ever laid a glove on the great Green Machine.

Which made it a bitch if you were trying to commit suicide. "Wouldn't be no big thing if I was a regular movie star," the massive reptile thought. "Any regulation, above-the-title player, they just blow into town, chisel their shallow aspect upon the Rushmore of culture, tip out before everyone gets tired of looking at them. The whole beautiful corpse configuration. But not me! Nooo, I got to live forever."

Being denied death was the irony of ironies. After all, wasn't he the Heater's Child, and isn't Doom what the Heater dealt—the opportunity to end it all with one depressed button? He didn't even have to die completely. It wasn't the *living* that was killing him, it was the *thinking.* What he needed was a little reductive surgery on that burgeoning torture chamber up between his earwhorls. Lobotomy! To be a sedate zucchini, staring thoughtlessly from beneath the fluorescent lights of a Miami Beach hotel, a thin smile on his placido domingo.

That was the plan: blow out the Quadcameral. That was the offending organ, wasn't it? It had to be plucked out. Obliterated. Nothing must be left over. The monster knew if he left a single vestige of his fabulous brain alive, a lone neuron, a solitary synapse, Komodo would be in there with his ever-healing hands, weaving those suffocating gray curls back to life.

Gojiro figured one of those old enhancing mirrors might do the deed. Years before, when Komodo poured the mold for the massive reflectors, the monster couldn't believe it. If there was one thing he didn't need it was a device that magnified whatever was put in front of it by fifty times. More of himself? How much *more* could there be? Fifty tons, five hundred feet from webfoot to cranial dome—wasn't that enough? Now, however, he imagined he could put the special properties of the enhancing mirrors to use. He'd rage a roar of Radi-Breath straight at the silvered glass, and when it came back at fifty times the investment, it'd blow his brain to kingdom come.

It was evil, he knew. Attacking his own matchless Quadcameral mind—was there any greater taboo? The Quadcameral was the compendium of Life's great march from the days of the reptilian, up through the mammalian limbic belt, to the humanoid Neo-Cortex, and onward to that mysterious, yet unspecified, upper zone. The Quadcameral was unique among minds. It was the wellspring of Cosmo, the citadel of Evollooic Thought! The Four-Tiered Oracle! How many times had the monster heard Komodo spout these sanctified phrases? How many times had he invoked them himself? To angle a death ray into the clearinghouse of everything they knew or would know—once it would have been inconceivable, akin to blotting out the sun. But things weren't as they were. The Quadcameral wasn't as it was. The great brain was befogged, degraded, irretrievably stained. No, Gojiro told himself, this would be no violation. He wasn't murdering the Q-cam, just putting it out of its misery.

The plan was an amalgam of junk he'd seen on the Dish: how the cowboy uses a polished beer mug to ricochet a bullet, how the Israelites turned their shields to the sun, blinded the Romans, made them steer their chariots into fiery pits. A nursery rhyme recurred in the monster's head, something about things coming "back on you, like glue."

"I'll stick some Elmer's on this sucker, all right," he snarled. "Seal my fate but good."

Not that it was going to be that easy. The shot had to strike him in the parietal, that third eye a million mystic chanters hope to find but that every zard has, right there, smack in the middle of his head. On Radioactive Island it was universally accepted that (in Komodo's words) "the parietal is the window to the Quadcameral." Now, however, Gojiro planned to use the sacred passage as a conduit to oblivion. It was the only way, the monster told himself. If he missed the parietal's foot-across diameter, the rebounding blast would impact pointlessly into his humongous noggin. Slabs of himself would shear off, but what good would that be, regenerative as he was? What a drag to slash your wrists and watch the wound heal even before the blood hit daylight. The Quadcam was different though; it didn't grow back. That much had been established.

1 5

Adjusting the mirror's angle—no simple trick when your fingers are the size of Greyhound buses—Gojiro pictured his odoriferous decomposing body being found in the solitary gloom of his cell-like burrow, the next day or perhaps the next week, the Dish droning the theme song from "Green Acres." He wouldn't leave a note. What was there to write? "No Thank You" was the best he could come up with, and even that seemed redundant.

But it never got to that. Because you see, just as Komodo knows, in his heart, what Gojiro does, Gojiro knows about Komodo. And, right then, Gojiro knew Komodo was coming. He felt him plug in, sensed him running across the beach at Corvair Bay, heard him wrap his satin pants around the fireman's pole at the volcano's summit and begin the three-thousand-foot descent.

"Stop!" Komodo screamed as he jumped from the pole. "You mustn't!"

"No choice!" Gojiro shouted back. "Please, get away! Here it goes!"

"My own true friend!" Komodo dropped to his knees. "You cannot do this!"

Gojiro didn't look at Komodo; it was one thing he couldn't do. Let Komodo's love through and it would pull him back from death, snatch away its liberation. The monster tried to make his heart a block of dry and smoky ice, all hermetic, like a sub beneath the Arctic cap, an iron lung orbiting beyond the most farflung asteroid. But still Komodo's love came ahead, a relentless, viscous flow, expanding, enveloping, seeping like the H-man through the smallest cracks of the most barred door, across the sill, over the transom.

"Let me go! Can't you see, it's over," Gojiro bellowed. So many times Komodo's all-forgiving love had pulled him from the slough of despond, but now that love seemed the slough itself. What right did Komodo have to hold him now, when death was the only answer?

"Don't try to stop me!" Gojiro shouted. He drew his withery arms close, squeezed his every lid tight. He'd block out Komodo's love, make a barricade it couldn't vault. It was his only chance. Death, full speed ahead.

"My own true friend, you must not!" Komodo screamed, but his voice was a radio thrown out the window of a speeding train.

Suddenly there was nothing in Gojiro's eyesweep but that mental X he'd pasted onto the center of his parietal. A cool sense of precision came over him, a clinical calm. Plenty of times, after watching those old newsreels, Gojiro wondered how those fliers did it, how they followed their flight plan, opened their bomb-bay doors, let the cataclysm descend. Now he knew. It must have been like this, a crease in all emotion, a void where the sum of their supposed charity, the best of what made them themselves, detached and fell away. Maybe, in a wholly different context, with wholly different motives, this was how it once was for him, when he was still a lizard like any other, when he'd wait with boundless patience for the exact right moment to forktongue an insect from the cypress bark. It was a realm where all that existed was the target.

The Radi-Breath left his mouth, white light to chase the spectrum. The sound was a drowning wave.

Then: "Fuck! I can't believe it." The zap charged, but the Ancient Reflex was quicker. The nethermost portion of the Quadcameral, that longest arm from a past that he could neither embrace nor escape, hurled the brimstone tablets of its Law to monkeywrench his designs. That Zardic part of his brain, impulses still triggering millions of years after their incept date, wouldn't allow him to kill himself. Elective death was apparently not an option under his former program. At the last moment, his head veered from harm's way. The blast sailed past his right earwhorl. He felt the singe as it kept going, took a fifty-foot-square divot out of the side of the 'cano and continued on to the Cloudcover, where the impact set all of Radioactive Island jiggling like a fried egg on a sea of shook grease.

"Why can't I die?" Gojiro moaned, a puddle of green self-loathing in the middle of his ravaged burrow.

As always, Komodo was there to comfort him, those long Jappish fingers commencing their soothing work, the high, gentle tenor singing one of those Ellington lullabies the monster loved so much.

"The zard brain overrode," Gojiro said in anguished explanation. "It wouldn't allow it. My used-to-be self. Shit! All my life I search for it, and it hangs in the shadows, on the outskirts. Now you know me, now you don't. But when I'm about to finally get off this idiot world, it's there—like Yale's bulldog, screaming, Survive! Survive! For what? What's it to *it* if I live or die?"

Komodo stayed with him. They snuggled together, the way they used to in the early days, before Gojiro demanded his own quarters down the bottom of the 'cano and Komodo took up his own, in that monk's den deep in Asbestos Wood. Then Komodo asked, "What was it that made you so upset, my own true friend? Was it snakes again?"

"No," Gojiro answered, trembling at the mere mention of the unpleasant incident several months earlier. More than any other recent event, the snake episode showed the ironic anarchy reigning in the Quadcameral. It was a horrible hallucination, a nightmare of vipers for a viper's nightmare. Snakes were everywhere! Wall-to-wall squamata. Slithercity. They coiled across his chest like bandoliers, circled his neck, lassoed about his legs, toppled him with a thud. A Lilliputian army of garters, they lashed him down, began to crawl into his open mouth. The symbolism was disgusting, the pornography of a suburban shrink's couch. The bourgeois humiliation!

Once Gojiro had felt malicious glee in the way previous evolutionary stages of mind remained in the brains of supposedly more modern forms of life. "That's why a sapien can't stomach a 'tile," he'd chortle. "We make their mealy flesh crawl. Well, let them build their Chinese walls to keep us out, it won't help. We're inside, burrowed deep inside their heads. You can't deny what you once were. We're the gargoyles that come to life at night, prowling through their sleep, hissing boo into their soft and downy ears."

But now that same fear was his. He woke with a start that night, his claws springing in disgust from his very own hide. He couldn't stand to touch himself. The merest brush filled him with repugnance. "This is the last straw," he swore then. "Making me haunt myself! What's next? Handing out innocence-banishing apples? Plague Dragons leatherwinging across the ocher moon? Serpents off the port bow?"

Komodo tried to remain calm, analytical. He suggested that the snake experience might be the product of an unfortunate glitch in the Quadcameral, that the internalized fears of the newly sedimented sapien cortex becoming tangled with the reptilian foundation. Almost certainly, Komodo contended, the problem stemmed from a misdirection in the midlevel limbic areas, originating in those sectors most associated with the great cold blood–warm blood battle for land control back in the deep Mesozoic.

But it wasn't snakes again.

"No," Gojiro moaned. "No snakes."

"Then what?" Komodo asked. "What could have caused you to do such a thing?"

Gojiro slammed his fist into the parietal loam. "It's like I got a million boy scouts rubbing sticks together inside my head. I can't take the heat no more! It has to come out—somehow."

"But my own true friend, we still haven't tried everything, we must have hope—"

Gojiro was bawling now. "No . . . no hope, don't you see? I'm at the end of the road. One step forward or back, the gallows trapdoor drops out. It's always been like that, we just wouldn't admit it before."

Komodo wept too. "We can't allow ourselves to think in this manner. We cannot be self-pitying."

"Don't worry about helping me. Help yourself."

"There is no me without you."

"Don't put that kind of pressure on me."

"Please!"

"Stop it. Leave me be." Gojiro turned away. He couldn't stand looking at Komodo, knowing that the earnest Japanese thought their every shortcoming to be his fault. He piled their sorrows on his back, humping them up like Quasimodo. It wasn't fair! Komodo did his best. Komodo was blameless.

It could not go on.

One more look at Komodo—sad Komodo, kind Komodo—convinced the reptile. For so long they'd pledged undying loyalty, a united front. But it was useless; the battle was already lost. Together they were stymied, they dragged each other down. Better that one of them should carry on, and that one should be Komodo. But what chance would he have with a massive Zardic albatross around his neck? On a journey to the end of the night, you've got to travel light.

The clarity of this perception renewed the monster's resolve. If he could shut out Komodo's love, he could do the same with whatever moldy impulses conspired to confine him to the gnawing prank that was his life. Without warning he lurched upward, a great green swell inside that close rubber cone of his volcanic home. Good-byes would be brief, better that way. "Farewell, my own true friend!" he shouted, brave, without doubt. Death was just a breath away.

In the split second it took him to realign the enhancing mirror, Komodo managed more. Gojiro first saw him in that reflector, fifty times his normal size. But the amplification was not necessary. One peek at Komodo made the giant lizard feel shabby, paltry. Komodo didn't need mirrors to prove his purity.

"Ahh," Gojiro gasped.

Down below, Komodo had ripped open the top of his black pajamas, exposing his pale, hairless chest. "A ghost's skin," Komodo sometimes laughed, saying if he'd been a normal Jap he would have had steady work in Nō plays, driving evil lords crazy. The monster looked down, saw the rings— three concentric circles, burned into Komodo's chest as if with a branding iron.

The Triple Rings!

Komodo had already drawn blood. It trickled down, over the circular scars. He held one of those swords Shig walked around with whenever he wanted to look extra cool. Shig was full of that Bushido: sunglasses and steel! But Komodo held the sword like a master, without flinch or flourish. He positioned the point at the exact center of the smallest ring; the weight of the sword alone was enough to pierce his skin.

Then Komodo spoke, his voice resolute and honest, without melodrama. "My own true friend," he said, "I call on you to honor your most solemn Vow. I invoke the Triple Ring Promise."

THE TRIPLE
RING PROMISE,
AMENDED

If you want to figure an absolute zero to all this, those loathsome negotiations concerning what came to be called the Triple Ring Promise Amendment would be the pit to plumb: Komodo and Gojiro poised at the brink of life, ready to cast themselves into the abyss with their own hands, neither willing to back off.

"I won't stop until you do!" Gojiro screamed, holding back a blurt of Radi-Breath.

"You first," Komodo retorted, his sword digging ever deeper.

For Gojiro, the sight of Komodo's drawn sword turned the scene on its hinge; the gleaming blade slashed through the monster's self-possession. Komodo killing himself, too? This was unacceptable. The monster sought death so Komodo could live to seek his destiny unencumbered, not so the two of them could be found, their bodies draped across each other in a manner that might lead a red-faced cop to report "a sordid, interspecies suicide pact." Gojiro would rather die a dozen times—or worse yet, stay alive—than see that happen.

"Don't you get it?" the monster screamed. "I'm supposed to be dead and you're supposed to be alive!"

Komodo tightened his hold around the sword. Blood was gushing now. "Our fates are intertwined into a common Identity. One cannot proceed without the other."

Gojiro gulped. "Wait a minute. Let's talk this over. I know we can work something out here."

The Triple Ring Promise Amendment is what they came up with. They swore it as they once swore the Promise itself, in fire and blood.

In short, the Amendment specified that if the tenets of the original Promise were not fulfilled to the satisfaction of both parties within one year's time, the whole deal was off. The Triple Ring Promise would be null and void. They would be released from everything they ever believed was between them. An extra clause provided that "should, after the one-year period elapses, one of the parties choose to end his life, the other, in all good faith, must attempt to aid him in this endeavor."

"This is gonna be great, you'll see," Gojiro said with attempted animation.

"Yes," Komodo murmured, forcing a gruesome smile. "A fresh start."

"A clean slate!"

"As if none of this had ever happened."

"Yeah! It'll be like we never met!"

"Like we never had met."

Then they looked at each other and wailed. Wailed and wailed. For the longest time, neither could speak.

Finally Komodo brought his face near the folds of Gojiro's hyoid. "Oh, my own true friend. How has it come to this?"

How had it come to where two friends had to bargain each other from suicide?

Gojiro locked himself in his joyless burrow, tried to get a handle on the situation. The grim volcano offered his only privacy on the whole Island, not that being down there was a party. It was a lot more depressing since the renovation. It was the work of those misfit Atoms, based on a picture they found in an old *Playboy.* "A real bachelor pad," the well-meaning but hopelessly damaged children chimed, every eye in their pinnish heads swirling as they installed the chrome, the overheated jacuzzi, and two-hundred-foot-wide revolving bed.

"What? No red vinyl?" Gojiro snorted when he first saw the job. "No hookers in the bathrooms?" It didn't help that he threw up the first time he lay down on the whirling bed. His stomach couldn't take the rotation, which was revved faster than a centrifugal amusement park ride. "I got bedsick," he complained, "I vomited in Lucky Luciano's sheets!"

It was the thought that counted, Komodo suggested.

"Tell them not to think about me! I don't want them down here again, neither. From now on, this is off-limits." Then Gojiro trashed the place. He kicked through every mirror, twisted all the chrome, ripped the pinstripe wallpaper, swallowed the Pepsi machine whole. The one thing he didn't touch was the massive wraparound dishscreen. He just sat down amidst the rubble and began to watch.

That's what he did the night he and Komodo swore the Triple Ring Promise Amendment, too. He watched the Dish. One year of life left, he might as well spend it with Felix and Oscar, Starsky and Hutch. It was a pretty typical night of viewing: "Have Gun Will Travel" reruns from Kuala Lumpur, gavel-to-gavel coverage on the Albanian politburo, a couple of hockey games with everything but the goals and fights edited out. The programs on Komodo's hook-up were nothing if not eclectic. Commercials came from everywhere. Just then a harried young woman was walking down a forbidding city street when three thugs jumped from the shadows and beat her unmercifully with truncheons. "Bitch!" they screamed. Then a bland but jovial announcer's voice came on. "Tired of the wear and tear of city life? Then move! Up to Sherwood Forests! The MODEL model condominium development!" The young woman reappeared, standing in front of a monolithic refrigerator, kissed her husband good-bye, sent her children off to school. "Move up to Sherwood Forests," she said. "I did!"

"Sick," Gojiro commented, restraining himself from Radi-firing the dishscreen. Years before, after hearing how Elvis regularly pumpgunned Graceland tubes, the monster got a little rough on his receptors. After a stern lecture from Komodo, however, he agreed to cut down. It wasn't that hard a promise to keep. Once, the reptile considered himself a merciless critic of the tube-dominated psychoscape. He was always holding forth, making comments like, "Mary Hart! Dixie Whatley! Who are they but jackboot dupes of the culturato-narco-leptic horde! Down with Trapper John!"

But now, he admitted with a grunt, "I just watch the stuff."

How had it come to this? Gojiro thought back, to the earliest of times, the beginnings of what was between him and Komodo. Had there ever been a more remarkable meeting? Komodo, swathed in sheets, stark lights upon his sleep-struck face, in that dismal hospital room in Okinawa. Gojiro, cowering and cold, casked up inside a dead volcano's basalt vault. The two of them so dreadfully alone, forever severed from all they knew, all they were *meant* to know.

Then—across all time, tide, and taxonomy—came Gojiro's plea. Even now it seemed impossible, drawn from mystery's deepest well: "Come in, please come in! Anyone!" A voice in the night, the monster's mayday dot and dash skimmed the stormswept Pacific to be heard only by a single boy in a hospital bed.

"Please to speak again?" These were the words Komodo spoke, his lips never moving, the only sounds in his melancholy room the blips of machinery and the squeak of rubbergloved hands on his skin. "You are a lizard? You are stuck inside volcano—in a place that is not your home, in a body that is not yours, and you think through a mind of which you cannot conceive? You are lonely and afraid? You have no friends?

"I am a boy. I live in a hospital. There is no one here that looks like me. I will be your friend."

More than two decades later, in front of the droning dishscreen, Gojiro wondered—could it really have happened like that? Did a conversation actually take place between a fifty-ton lizard and a ten-year-old boy dug out of a hole in Hiroshima, a boy who hadn't said a word or moved a muscle in nine years? And, did that boy—that Coma Boy, silent icon of a most anxious age—snap free from the slumber that enveloped him, hoist himself from his bed, leave that hospital under the cover of night, and make a most treacherous journey across two thousand miles of sea to where that lizard was?

Or was this just another installment in the series of mental forgeries, one more dollop of bogus history? How to tell? The monster didn't know. Maybe that was the real bond between him and Komodo: a dialectic of lunacy. Whole so-called civilizations had been founded on shared psychosis, why not Radioactive Island?

The monster dismissed these doubts. Komodo wasn't crazy, a liar, or a fool. If Komodo said he escaped his whitecoated warders by crawling out a laundry-room window, and then hopped a tramp steamer going south, eventually reaching Radioactive Island in that small rubber boat, using only a sanitarium sheet as a sail, then that's how it was. If all the rest was madness, at least this was so.

What a scene it was, the day Komodo's tiny boat washed up on the headlands of what would come to be called Past Due Point. It wasn't much of a place then. This was long before the major flotjet influxes and, of course, before the coming of the Atoms. Right then, Radioactive Island was nothing but the 'cano, an igneous lurch from the roiling petrochemical sea, and even that wasn't as big as it would later become, after Komodo perfected his vulcanizing techniques. The Cloudcover was a lot thicker, though, a peasoup no laser could split. You couldn't see a claw in front of your face out there, how dense the viscous draped. Primeval as all get-out, Radioactive Island was an unformed, ground-gurgling world in the midst of being born.

"Lizard!" Komodo shouted when he reached the beach, still in his hospital gown. "I am here! I am the boy you spoke to. I have come to be your friend!

"Lizard! I had a good trip. The sharks were no problem after that one time. Please answer, lizard!"

Gojiro did not answer. He couldn't. It was all he could do to peek his massive green head out of the 'cano's crater, squint into the murk.

"I am that boy!" came Komodo's voice. "The one you asked to come. To be your friend."

Boy? . . . Asked? . . . FRIEND? What an oafish Frankenstein he must've seemed, mumbling "Friend?," the words echoing inside the Gothic acoustics of the vast, new-minted Quadcamerality.

"Lizard!"

Lizard? The monster huddled within the lavaflows, tried to compute the nature of this invader. Dimly, he recalled forms not unlike this *boy.* Were there not boys in his dreams, in that lost and fading world that visited him at night? Bipeds. They made sounds like this *boy.* They threw grass around their scaleless leathers, put bones in their noses, went out to sea squatting in long pieces of wood. There had been reports of them daring to come close to 'tiles, menacing them with sticks. One account actually had them surrounding a solitary basking zard, attacking and killing him. Then they stripped his leathers from his body, threw him in a blackbellied pot, and *ate* him!

"Lizard! I have come. I am your friend!"

What could that boy calling in the fog want? Why didn't he go away? Stop your calling, the frightened reptile silently beseeched, his head a jumble. Nothing seemed the same. Before, it was all electricity. It buzzed, you did what you did. Now there were these *thoughts.*

"Lizard, please, don't be afraid."

Afraid? Gojiro sank lower into the 'cano. Where he came from, there was no such thing as being afraid. Fear had no niche. His kind barely deigned to peer down at the descending links of the food chain. But here—in this place, as this *thing* he had become? Now every step was fraught with doubt. He'd tried to carry on as before, but the great time-honored reflexes failed him. Only two days earlier he'd spotted a small furry thing running through the smoke-filled forest and set after it. It felt good, engaging the ageless predatory geometry, the ever-tightening circle of the hunt. Even the unease of his solitude gave way for the moment. But it turned to disaster. His instinctuals were unfamiliar with the beast's behavior. Given its dirt-brown looks, the animal almost certainly should have gone with a camouflage-based defense. For millennia mammals of this apparent type had frozen cigarstore still, hoping stalking zards would mistake them for mossy mounds or outcropping roots; it was an old trick, the best kind. But instead, this individual began rubbing itself against a swatch of luminous shrubbery. Every time it stroked the bush, phosphor came off on its fur, accentuating its presence. Now, of course, the Max Factor factor in the taxonomic flora-fauna relationship between the blacklight plant and Flounce Fox is well documented, but then, back then, it nonplussed Gojiro no end. The fox's extra legs and eyes didn't do much for him either. Still, he was starving, so he pounced. But the several quick steps he planned turned into one thud, and the furball was crushed beneath his foot, mashed down so as to be indistinguishable from the other little dots stuck between his toe claws. The giant reptile licked off all the spots, but it wasn't like there was a balanced meal there.

Nothing was as it had been. When he tried to forktongue a snaky caterpillar from a branch, he wound up inhaling the whole tree and picking glass splinters out of his mouth for hours. After that, he hid himself inside the 'cano. He would rather starve than hunt again.

And now there was this boy outside, calling for him. "Lizard! I have no friends either. We can be friends for each other. Please!"

If only he could scream back, tell this boy that he didn't need him to be his friend, that where he came from there was no such thing. No, the frightened lizard thought, in my world it's different. Your friend is every other zard, those living and those who have lived, and those who have yet to live. A hundred zards, five hundred, a thousand, all piled up, a carpet of scales, a great quilt of 'tiles, not one inch of ground visible. A thousand zards, ten thousand, a million, maybe more—pressed and touching, closer and closer, so the blood in one as good as runs into another, until they blend into the Enormous One.

That's how it is, Gojiro thought, where I come from. At least that's how it *was* . . .

Gojiro

The boy's shout came again.

And Gojiro screamed, "Here I am. HERE I AM!"

Gojiro noticed the concentric circles on the boy's chest as soon as Komodo came into the 'cano. Three rings—the outermost almost a foot across, the inner half that. In the glimmery light they almost glowed: a heart with a target.

For weeks, the monster refrained from commenting on the strange pattern. It didn't seem right. Komodo, after all, never mentioned *his* not inconsiderable deformities. It was only after a semibucolic jaunt out by Mycotoxin Pond that Gojiro brought it up. Komodo had spent most of the wan afternoon peering into the ever-still waters there, running his fingers over the slight humps of the maroon rings.

"My friend," Gojiro ventured, "do they hurt you?"

"Excuse me?" Komodo answered, lost in thought.

"Those scars on your chest, those circles. Do they cause you . . . great pain? They're . . ."

Komodo grinned, showing his sharp teeth. "Grisly?"

Gojiro was embarrassed. "They do look kind of bad."

"No, my friend, they don't hurt a bit."

"Must have when it happened."

"I would assume," Komodo sighed. "But I have no recollection. I don't remember any of it."

"I don't remember nothing of what happened to me, neither. Just that I used to be one way, and now I'm like this."

"Yes," Komodo said, his voice veering off.

Truth was, Komodo did recall some of his days before he came to Radioactive Island. Every so often, tiny snatches of his life in that Okinawa infirmary would return to him. He remembered the constant stream of fake earnest officials, each anxious to have his picture taken placing a small toy by the bedside of the famous Coma Boy. There was also the conversation of doctors, distant whitemasked men, discussing him as if he weren't there at all.

"What do you make of these marks here?" one doctor said to another, poring over Komodo's torso.

"Yeah, those circles," the other drawled. "Search me. He looks like he's a branded steer off the Triple Ring Ranch."

It drove Gojiro crazy when Komodo told him that. "Cracker navy scum-bags," the monster railed. Making jokes over who the Heater marked! Still, the term stuck.

"These Triple Rings," Komodo said wistfully, "ride upon my chest like a question mark. I sense a great mystery about them. Sometimes I think if I were to find out what they meant, I might learn many things."

"Like what?" Gojiro asked as he hoisted Komodo onto his supraocular ridge, where the thinlegged Japanese liked to ride. From up there he could see over the ragged timber line to the turbid sea.

"Oh, I don't know . . ." Komodo shrugged, his head piercing the dense haze. "Who I am. Where I came from. How I came to be here with you. What we will do next."

"Little things like that."

"Little things like that," Komodo replied with his high-pitched giggle.

The next morning, the heat woke Komodo up. It was like a blast furnace against his face.

"My friend!" Komodo screamed. "There is a terrible fire! We must put it out!"

"No danger, my friend," Gojiro said quietly. He was standing close to Komodo, his back turned.

"But it smells like . . . something from the past. It frightens me."

"Don't be afraid, my friend," Gojiro said. "It's all done, now."

He did it with the growth rings from a crosscut section of a giant metalfi-brous tree he pulled from the ground beyond Reterritorialization Bay. He was careful to make sure he had the perfect trio: one big, one middle-sized, one small. He heated them with his own breath. That was a surprise. He knew something had happened to his throat, but he didn't suspect he'd retained the Heater's fury inside his lungs, that with one bellow he could hurl a city into flames. He held the rings between his claws and roared until they turned white-hot, then he pressed them to his chest.

"My friend!" Komodo shouted, drawing near.

"It's all right." Gojiro turned to Komodo.

"Your chest . . ."

Gojiro's gaze did not waver. "The answers you seek are the answers I seek. This world you live in is the world I live in. What we'll do, we'll do together."

"Yes," Komodo said, "my own true friend."

Gojiro

* * *

That was the Triple Ring Promise. Then.

Those were the Glazed Days, the onset of it all, when they stood on the bonewhite sands of their beach, peered out to the seething Cloudcover and knew: out there was another world, a kingdom that held itself apart from them. Who and what ruled out there made them exiles, fugitives in the countries of their birth. But here, in this dark and ashy tract, they found refuge. Here they were safe. Safe and together in a realm where a twelve-year-old boy and a five-hundred-foot-tall lizard could pledge themselves to each other and be friends.

That's what the Triple Ring Promise said, then.

Could it all have been so simple once, so innocent, a perfect democracy of youth? Or was it just another chimeric "memory," tricked up by nostalgia's ruthless hand? How long did those Glazed Days last, Gojiro wondered, when he and Komodo ran free to spin the full 360 neath the stiffblown banner of the Triple Rings?

Two years, three, five? When did it begin to dissolve? At what point did their Promise begin the creep toward that grotesque Amendment? Gojiro's head ached. The condemning evidence was so exhaustive, the steely finger of accusation pointed so firmly in his direction. His sins were manifold, his record longer than a Nazi's arm. But the litany of iniquity was pitched on a grander scale than any simple rap sheet. The fact was, Gojiro knew, that the Triple Ring Promise had been cosmologized from existence.

Coffee, tea, or milk? Chaos or Cosmo? That was the old joke round the 'cano, back in the days of what came to be called the Budd Hazard sessions. Good ole Budd Hazard! Gojiro liked the ring of the name. It had a downhomey touch, the smell of fatback frying up 'long side the Mahayana. A private gag of a tag: a greenneck called like a redneck, trancing out like a yellowneck. And, during those dark times, before Radioactive Island even had a sun to separate night from day, Budd Hazard filled a need: he pumped up the Cosmo, forged Design.

"Be Budd Hazard," Komodo would say as they clung together in the 'cano's deepest well, the sludge squalls raging outside.

"Okay," Gojiro replied, drawing a breath. There was no effort to it, no psychic's writhe and roil, no incanting exorcist's gory pliers to pull pseudoverities from a recalcitrant beyond. All the monster had to do was open his mouth and Budd Hazard came out.

29

The wealth of information! The generosity of cognizance! First came tales of life on Lavarock, details to fill in Gojiro's misty recollections of his former Hallowed Homelands. Legends and practices of the Zardic Line upon the Precious Pumice were copiously enumerated. Komodo could never get enough. So thoroughly cut off from his own previous existence, he reveled in the summoning of Gojiro's past, illusionary or not. He sat rapt as the monster spieled out uninterrupted sagas of the hunt, whether it be the brutish rush against the foreflanks of a snorty tapir or the intricacies of tonguespearing a hingehung insect from its gossamer web.

"What a paradise," Komodo marveled.

"That it was, that it was," Gojiro said, leaning back, bathed in light and glowing, "a world like no other." But then pain shot through him. "Except it's nothing now. Atomized, blown apart. Wiped from the face of the earth. I alone survive to tell thee, Jack."

In the beginning, Gojiro thought that was what Budd Hazard was about: an afterimage of a life forever lost, a message in a reverberating bottle somehow wedged inside his malformed ear during the Heater's storm. But it quickly became apparent that Budd Hazard was much more than a dry lament. Recollections of Lavarock were the merest germ of what he seemed to know.

There was the night when the fission gales grew fierce and Komodo and Gojiro huddled together inside the volcano of their as-yet unnamed island. "Be Budd Hazard," the frightened Komodo entreated, seeking comfort against the tumult.

"All right," Gojiro said, swallowing hard. The monster closed his eyes and moaned. "The scheme of the Universe," he began, "is embraced within an all-encompassing System called the Evolloo. Everything living, everything that has lived, everything that ever will live is contained inside the unimaginable parameters of the Blessed Blueprint. It is a Vast Flow, a Miraculous Spine of Energy and from it, like the tributaries of a Great River, spring all forms of Life. Those who are Honest and True must learn to walk these Paths so that they may come to know their own Identity and place within the Great Plan—for this is the Order of Things."

Then, snapping from his trance, Gojiro looked at Komodo, saw how the sweat poured from his friend's startled brow. "What I say?" the reptile asked.

Komodo repeated it as best he could.

"Geez . . ."

From that point forward the Budd Hazard sessions took on a new gravity.

Now they weren't just to pass the time, but rather to create the very meaning of Time. It no longer seemed fit for them to receive Budd Hazard's messages walking on the beach or swimming out by the Cloudcover, a half a mile from shore, Komodo balancing himself upon Gojiro's snout. A special section of the 'cano was set aside, decked with fluoro-candles calibrated to best approximate a guru's most conducive thinktank.

Gojiro lay on a massive pile of paisley cushions, with Komodo hovering, poised to record whatever was spoken.

"I can't," Gojiro said as they were about to commence. "I can't find him."

"Concentrate," Komodo said.

"I never had to concentrate before. I'm just nervous, I guess."

"Me too," Komodo confessed.

Truth was, they were more than nervous. They were filled with dread. Budd Hazard beckoned them to a mysterium of obscure Flows, great Forces of Energy extending through Eternity—an Unknown place where they imagined, in their battered, eager souls, they would find the Sacred. At this threshold they faltered. Everything about them—their world, that dank and spewing Island—was without form. By what license did they feel they could even hope to bring shape to that forsaken nothingness?

"We can't," Gojiro tensed. "We are not sufficient."

Komodo paced the 'cano floor. Suddenly, a wild look came over his face. *That look!* Even then he had it, that naive yet undeniable Jap-Mickey-Rooney-discovering-America look, the crazy exhilaration that throws off doubt and pushes forward through the fear. "My own true friend!" Komodo declared. "Budd Hazard speaks to us because he deems us worthy. To refuse him would be a terrible insult. We must seek to know what he wishes to tell us. It is our duty!"

"If you say so," Gojiro mumbled. If it had been up to him, maybe, they would have dropped the whole Budd Hazard thing right there. But Komodo seemed so sure. His face was so open, so hopeful. That was enough. The monster closed his many lids and soon the words rushed forth. The session went on for days; nothing less than the Foundations of Thought were laid down.

Foremost among these bedrocking underpins was the Principle of the Inviolate Binary. "There can be no Bunch without a Beam, no Beam without a Bunch," Budd Hazard imparted, defining a Bunch as "a group of like individuals, what might be referred to as a species." A Beam was a much more elusive concept. "It is the cohering Energy of the world, sourced from the Mainstem, adapted to the individual needs of the Bunch," the enigmatic Muse said. It was in the interface of these two entities that the Universe found its design. "A Beam makes a Bunch a Bunch," Budd Hazard declared. Without a Beam a Bunch would be nothing more than a "disassociated band of biologically similar renegades." On the other hand, a Beam was nothing but "a misdirected font of energy" without a Bunch about which to focus its all-encompassing, aligning force.

"It is the Goal and Obligation of All Life to seek its particular Identity within the Inviolate Binary structure and to live, as distinct yet interrelated forms, beneath the mantle of the Evolloo," Budd Hazard pronounced. "The Evolloo is All."

Gojiro and Komodo listened with an ever-expanding sense of wonder. How sublime it was to hear Budd Hazard's words forge a scheme amid the seemingly unfathomable murk of their world. To witness that swirling hub of Thought shower light throughout the black maw of emptiness. With each new revelation, their trepidations gave way to a giddy joy. It was intoxicating to be in the presence of all that Truth.

"I'm singing!" Gojiro roared. "Can't you hear me singing? I'm singing 'bout Budd Hazard!"

"Who?" Komodo rejoined. "Who might that Budd Hazard be? Where's he been, what's he seen?"

"Who? You ask me who Budd Hazard be? Where's he go, what's he know? *I'll* tell you what Budd Hazard knows! He knows the present and he knows the past. He knows who be first and who be last. He knows what is green and what is blue, and what goes down in the Evolloo!"

"Tell me more, tell me more! Tell me more about what Budd Hazard knows!"

"More? Why not, there's no law. He knows the weather, those of a feather, put *any* words together, and that's what Budd Hazard knows. He knows the jungle, knows the street, knows what bad smell comes from your feet!"

"Oh, please! My ignorance is no joke, it's a sad and sorry yoke. Just tell what Budd Hazard spoke!"

"He knows the secret of the Endless Chain, seen it plain. He knows all Love and what it's worth, and how things work here on Earth. That's what Budd Hazard knows!"

A passion he never imagined overtook Gojiro then. Ideas rumbled within him, then exploded, spread throughout the land. It was as if the Heater itself had detonated inside, its tempest winds blowing his molecules over every inch of this new world he and Komodo called their own. He felt himself cascade down like heavy rain on the forests of the wretched glassine trees, spreading his essence to the beaches, out to the Cloudcover. His particles pinwheeled from the dank skies, settled on the matted fur of all the furtives dug deep in their burrows and onto the creaky wings of the impossible insects struggling through the gales off Corvair Bay. Again and again he came, with the clockwork regularity all things innately understand as symmetry. In no quarter was he unexpected or unwelcomed. He felt connection with everything in this freshout, untried world.

He was Budd Hazard, 'tile for all times, one of the roughs, one of the smooths, a Cosmozard.

Was it inevitable, what happened next? Gojiro reckoned so. He didn't need a goading encounter group of former offenders to tell him that with a personality like his, addiction is not many truck stops down the highway from intoxication. That's what Budd Hazard bred: total dependency. Just as later it got to the point where he couldn't get through a half-hour sitcom without firing up a gluey ball of hardcutting 235, he became addicted to Budd Hazard. He became a Cosmo junkie.

With quicksilver slivers of the Scheme's great jigsaw hot on his clawtips, he obsessed to possess the rest. He declared war on the white areas of his map; no territory would remain Unknown. All levity left him. No longer was there time to stroll with Komodo out by the lurching precipices of Past Due Point. The reptile's every instant was hostaged to Budd Hazard's consuming wigstretch.

"Come to bed," Komodo would say, bleary-eyed from the seemingly endless clocksweeps of transcription.

"Not yet," came the reptile's breathless reply. "I'm on the edge of a great breakthrough concerning the progression of Beamic knowledge relative to the development of a full Bunch as opposed to the individual within the Bunch. Can't you see? We're about to shoot the definitive hole in the theory of the ontogeny and phylogeny of consciousness."

"Perhaps this is the question of a philistine," Komodo ventured, "but is it possible to know too much?"

"Know too much? I thought you fancied yourself a man of science—a philosopher! How can you know *too much* until you know it *all?* You want a Universe mottled with pocks and dings? Don't you want the perfect sphere?"

Gojiro told Komodo he could go to sleep, if that's what he wanted to do. "From now on, worldview constructing goes on twenty-four hours a day around here—just like the world. Get your forty winks. I'll put the transcriber on automatic."

The behemoth grew increasingly withdrawn, solitary. Subtle neuroshifts occurred inside his burgeoning brain. No longer did he have to summon up Budd Hazard. The Muse became a constant, a macro to his program, always there, defining, refining, pumping up Cosmo and more Cosmo. It was as if the reptile had merged with his drug, and it with him.

Then, one night, Gojiro called Komodo into the 'cano. The two friends hadn't seen each other for days. Tension ruled.

"I want to discuss a matter of the utmost magnitude," Gojiro intoned, circles around his red eyes, his leathers sagging. He looked as if he hadn't slept for weeks.

"Yes, my own true friend," Komodo said tentatively.

"It concerns the Triple Ring Promise," Gojiro monotoned, as if he were reading a year-end report. "Recent Budd Hazard visitations indicate this proposition has reached a superannuated circumstance. It exists only within the context of base sentimentality and therefore is meaningless within the ever-march of the Endless Flow. It must be subject to major revision."

"Excuse me," Komodo said, stunned. "Are you really talking about *our* Triple Ring Promise?"

"Yes! In its current form it is hopelessly primitive. We must modernize it, update it, bring it more in line with the current state of Evollooic Thought."

"But . . ." Tears beaded up in Komodo's eyes. "Update our Promise—how is that possible? When we swore it, it was for . . . forever. How can you modernize forever?"

"We must jettison juvenilia!" the huge lizard shouted. "The Boy's Life is not eternal; no moment is frozen in amber. Who are we, anyway, all-for-one, one-for-all fops on a candy wrapper? Later for Puff the Magic Dragon. We must take a more mature view. Would you have our world continue some 'a boy and his lizard' show?"

"It's just as much 'a lizard and his boy'!" Komodo shot back. Then he was crying. "I'm sorry . . . it's just that the Triple Ring Promise . . ."

"I know," Gojiro replied, his manner melting. "I know how you feel—that's how I feel too. But the Triple Rings, what do they really mean? Please, tell me the parameters of our Promise, as it is today."

"That we are together," Komodo stuttered, "that the answers you seek are the answers I seek."

"But what are those answers?" The monster was weeping now too. "Tell me."

Komodo could not. His thoughts had never ventured beyond the marvel of their mutual self-discovery, the ecstasy of their friendship.

"Don't you see?" Gojiro pleaded. "We are allowing our Promise to stagnate, to signify nothing more than the faded loyalty of an old school patch, something to be kept in a drawer—a memento of passed youth. I say our Promise is worth more than that! Deserves better than that! Think of it: *who we are . . . where we come from . . . what we will be*—these answers will not simply come to us. We cannot sit and wait, falsely secure in our blithe dreamworld. Trust is not enough when one craves Light!

"We must seek, set forth on a great quest. And where must this search begin? I submit the starting point rides right upon our own chests. Yes, the Triple Rings! They are our center, the core of all we are. We must *penetrate* our solemn Oath—explode it if need be and bring it back reborn!"

Then, his reverie done, Gojiro looked down and saw that Komodo wasn't crying anymore. Instead, *that look* was on his face. "Yes," Komodo said with quiet emotion, "you are right, my own true friend. This is what we must do."

"Paradise? Here? Now?" Thinking back on these fifteen-year-old events, Gojiro could only shake his massive head. Was there no end to paying for the smallest optimism in this reproachful world, he groused, the phosphor gray Dish light playing over his lax body. All he'd ever hoped for was a degree of meaning, some measure by which to understand what had happened to him, how he'd come to be this thing he was. That didn't seem much to ask, did it?

Yeah, they *penetrated* the Triple Ring Promise all right. They broke right through those pristine diameters with the wrecker's ball of their antic intellect, dissolved the guileless design with a presumptive onslaught more corrosive than any blast of Radi-Breath. Now, far too late, it was easy enough to trace the swath of grievous miscalculation, how so many hot flashes succeeded only in lashing an icy noose around their necks.

The crazed notion that Radioactive Island might be reincarnated as a latter-day, post-Atomic Utopia, happy home to a New Bunch fused with a New Beam, a nirvana in which a mutant lizard and the Hiroshima Coma Boy might glimpse their true Identities—all of it was beyond anything a benighted kabbalist in pointed hat festooned with whirling stars and planets could have conjured. Yet these became the new terms of the Triple Ring Promise, the only conditions by which the updated version could be fulfilled. Just thinking of it ravaged Gojiro. They tossed their Vow into the raging concoctions of Cosmo's test tube, larded its simple beauty with impossible clauses and conditions, and when the fateful bun was out of the oven, nothing remained but that loathsome Amendment.

Swaddled deep inside his melancholy volcano, the whole leapfrog of events weighed on the monster. He thought of Budd Hazard and called out, "Hey, Budd . . . Budd baby. Where you at, man? What's the matter, you don't got no advice for me? No cosmogonic council? No music for a theophanic string quartet? Not an ontological crumb for the hungry heart? Hey Budd—fuck you!"

Of course, there was no reply. There hadn't been for years. Had there really ever been a Budd Hazard? Or was the supposed Muse nothing more than a smirking demiurge, a prank of philosophy perpetrated by one north forty of his mammoth cogitator against another? "Should have known," the monster grumbled. "Jive won't get you Zen."

So many times Gojiro attempted to renounce the Triple Ring Promise, quietly resign. "Maybe there's still a chance for Radioactive Island to become a place of joy and warmth, like Angulome City, Houyhnhnmland, or Mount Daumal," he told Komodo as tenderly as he could, "but it can't happen with me around. I'm a five-hundred-foot-tall cancer! You got to cast my raggedy fate to the winds."

"No!" Komodo shouted, his face wild, his tears flying. "I won't allow it. I won't let you renounce all we know to be so."

"Don't you see where all this crazy Cosmo has got us? Cosmo's Hell's own soldering gun, cementing us in this cell forever and ever. Screw Cosmo. Get Leo G. Carroll in here and cancel his goddamned contract! Don't you get it? We killed our Promise, we overloaded its circuits and blew it out with bullshit."

Komodo would not be moved. "The Triple Ring Promise is what it is. Whatever it says, we shall seek to fulfill it. And fulfill it we shall."

"But we got to face facts," the monster wailed. "We're just two pathetic mutants, victims of an arbitrary force that doesn't care about any kind of aspiration one way or another. The Heater, that's our God, the burning center of our little system. We're nothing but distantly orbiting bits of dust, points in space, remote from the Endless Flow, unconnected to anything, part of no Beam or Bunch . . . never destined to be."

Komodo's eyes grew wide, full of fury and sorrow. "I refuse to accept that!"

That was worst of it, Gojiro told himself, the way Komodo continued to believe. Even now, a week after the hideous near double suicide, he was down in his lab, cooing to those funky chickadees sitting on the branches of that glassed-in Fayetteville Tree. It was crazy how much time Komodo spent codifying the behaviors of those mat-feathered fowls, checking on their manic reproductions, trying to isolate the Instant of Reprimordialization.

Reprimordialization—it was Budd Hazard's central point, and his most perplexing. According to the long silent Muse, Reprimordialization was the "engine of the Evolloo," a continuous, unending series of "invisible Instants" during which Beamic energy cleaved to create new Bunches, thereby springing forth "more life, different and unique." It was in the space of these mysterious Instants, which Budd Hazard called the "realm of Change," that Komodo planted the flag of the Triple Rings, where he sought to fulfill their Promise. In the early days, Gojiro was often moved to tears whenever his friend spoke of Reprimordialization. But now, watching Komodo attempting to isolate the moment when one species of chickadee transformed into another, the reptile saw it as just one more lie of the mind, another cheap trick.

"Cheep, cheep," those crappy birds called from Komodo's lab. The monster hated the sound! Just as he hated it when Komodo would parrot back Budd Hazard's other shopworn koans. "Going on is all! To stand still is defeat! The Evolloo is a vast river, not a mordant lake. A rich man can build a fence around a lake, claim it belongs to him. But no fence can be built around a river. A river is Freedom!" How many times had Gojiro heard that one? "Sure," he'd scream back at his friend, "maybe once we rode that river, that homeboy's Mississippi—but now the silt's built up, the Army Corps of Engineers slabbed their stark white dams in the magic places, and there's no way for a raft to reach the delta where the deep blues play."

Gojiro felt miserable knowing Komodo would never give up, that he'd grow old and gray—he was already past thirty, *a boy no more!*—trying to make sense of the ever-elusive Instant of Reprimordialization. But that's Komodo for you. Most so-called men of science put their faith in the physical, give allegiance to what can be shown and known. They lay a telescope on Uranus, so they know Uranus "exists." Ditto for Pluto. Komodo does that too, he's no metaphysic pisser in the wind; his houses aren't made from straw or wood, he uses brick, lays them one at a time. That's what he loves, to see how things fit together, how they work. But that doesn't mean Komodo believes in things just because they're there and he made them. That's not how Komodo defines belief. Instead, he follows the chain of logic to the point where it breaks down. Then he looks into that Void, and says, "I believe in this."

That's how it was with that invisible Instant of Reprimordialization. The more Komodo failed to understand the workings of the mysterious zone, the more he revered it. All he needed was "the new stim." With the new stim, Komodo claimed, what could not be known would become known, what could not be seen would be seen. Komodo talked a lot about the new stim in those desperate days after the swearing of that hideous Amendment. It became his grail, that single as-yet unglimpsed idea that could jumpstart the dead-in-the-water Cosmo. Every night he'd be down in his lab, making with the beakers and bunsens, hothousing inventions at an unprecedented rate. They were marvelous items too, but when Komodo surveyed what he'd made, his face, once bright with prospect, drooped. "Not what I intended . . . no business being invented, none at all." Then he'd begin again.

Gojiro rued Komodo's disappointment, but he was powerless to help. After all, how easy was it to come up with something completely new, a truly original idea? An old idea throws a rod, you can tow it by the body shop, let Vito swat the fenders with his mallet, beat it to a different shape. Tell him it's a rush job, no problem, he's wild for the overtime. But a new idea, an absolutely new idea? Get out your butterfly net and clear every calendar. A new idea demands Inspiration, and you could wait a thousand years for that. But they didn't have a thousand years. They had less than one. No, the monster moaned inside his gloomy volcano, there was no chance. He was fresh out of new ideas.

Gojiro

He was paralyzed, smothered beneath the lassitude of crumbled dreams. All hope was a shell game. That being the case, when Komodo came sliding down the 'cano pole with that strange letter in his hand, the leviathan was not prepared to put much stock in it.

THE LETTER

When Komodo first pulled that letter out of the pocket of his black pajamas, Gojiro figured it had to be a joke, a warped bid to lighten the heavy weather. That would have been all right; the giant reptile hadn't had a good laugh since he stopped his career as "the Atomic Comic, the world's tallest stand-up."

The monster's comedy career was another of the little "rainy day" activities Komodo whipped up to keep those nutty Atoms from killing one another during inversion season. The reptile would clamber onto the rec-hall stage, wring his withery front claws together, go into his spritz. "Hi ho, neutrinos. *Parlez-vous* protonese?" Then he'd lay a spew of 'tilic titters on the dyslexics. "Okay, okay . . . these two triceratopses go into a bar, see . . ." But it was ridiculous. The Atoms, denser than ingots, thought his every hunk, whether hip or dip, was a riot. "I blow my nose and they're on the floor," Gojiro complained. "Might as well play Bellevue. Laughing-house laughs are no laughs at all. Let 'em go back to pulling wings off flies. I'm finished."

The monster only glowered when Komodo mentioned that in his modest opinion, watching the great reptile blow his massive snout was actually quite humorous.

But the tight expression on his friend's face told Gojiro that the letter was no joke. "We have an offer to go to America," the blackhaired Japanese said quietly.

"Yeah? We win another contest? I told you never to send back those forms, it only encourages them."

"No. This is an offer for work. To make a movie there."

A movie? Gojiro couldn't believe his earwhorls. The mere mention of making movies had been banned for years, ever since Shig's treachery became known. Go to America to make a movie? Had Komodo finally flipped out, blown his every cookie? "I'm retired from show business," Gojiro snapped. "Tell 'em to get themselves another monster."

"I would never burden you with these matters," Komodo blurted, "but this letter . . . I sense a relevance about it, a potential impact on our Promise."

Gojiro tried not to listen. He glued his eyes to the Dishscreen. That desultory blue-gray light was his refuge; it raised no expectations, supposed no soon-to-be-dashed desire.

"This letter—it is from Sheila Brooks."

The name hit Gojiro like a dull tomahawk behind the hyloid. "Sheila Brooks? *Sheila Brooks!*"

Komodo's skin looked ashen. "Yes. She is offering us an opportunity to come to America to make a film entitled *Gojiro vs. Joseph Prometheus Brooks in the Valley of Decision.*"

Of all the madness inherent in the outlandish notion that he should go to Hollywood and share top billing with Joseph Prometheus Brooks, the thing that drove Gojiro to the greatest distraction was Komodo's insistence that it was a good idea.

"But my own true friend, he is a great scientist. One of the most brilliant men ever to live. If there is one person who might fix us, it would be him."

"Fix us?" Gojiro spat back. "Don't you think he's fixed us pretty good already?"

"That's just it. It was Mr. Brooks's creation that brought us to this state, so perhaps he might be able to devise a method by which we could escape it."

If a stray planet had happened to be passing within Gojiro's grasp right then he would have snatched it from its orbit, bearhugged it to dust. Joseph Prometheus Brooks! The inventor of the Heater itself!

Gojiro looked at Komodo in disbelief. It hadn't been all that long ago that the monster had convened a Great Tribunal of the Anti-Speciesist League for the express purpose of putting Brooks on trial, in absentia, for High Crimes against the Evolloo. The meeting ended inconclusively after the two friends engaged in a terrible argument, nearly coming to blows. It was Komodo's refusal to endorse the necessary extreme prejudice that infuriated the giant lizard.

"We cannot condemn Mr. Brooks until we have the complete evidence," Komodo said, acting for the accused.

"You want *proof?* Look at these feet, look at these dorsals, look at these . . . *flanks,* which, thanks to your pal Pro Brooks will never know the sweet rub of a female's leathers. Look at yourself, why don't you."

Komodo would not be budged. "We can't condemn what we don't fully understand. Perhaps Mr. Brooks had no control over events; rather, it was the workings of his unique mind that caused him to act as he did."

"You trying to cop a temporary insanity plea for this fuck or something? Like 'hey, I didn't mean to grab the Universe by the balls—it's just some cupcake I ate.' "

"I am saying that in Art and Science there are ideas that, once created, take on a life of their own."

"Oh, the old Art and Science riff, huh? The old technically too-sweet excuse! Give those willowy boys with paintbrushes the whole canvas, but later for us scufflers down here in the street. I can't believe you're trying to absolve Brooks. I suppose the Heater just sprang from his head, a fullblown, kicking Athena, and all he did was throw the plutonium through the bars at feeding time."

The Tribunal broke up amid Gojiro's charges that Komodo was a "class-worshiping house mutant" who harbored serious and lamentable speciesist tendencies, which caused him to sling the same "presumptive Ptolemaic sludge" as the rest of his "rapacious former ilk."

Now, however, Komodo was going too far. Claiming Pro Brooks, the inventor of the Heater itself, might be a key cog in a potential satisfaction of the Triple Ring Promise—it was enough to make the monster hurl the 'cano toward the Cloudcover like a rubberized snowcone. Except he didn't. He collapsed on the floor instead. Maybe he was right in the beginning. Maybe it *was* all a joke. What else could it be? Talk about your high concept—what comedy could be blacker than *Gojiro vs. Joseph Prometheus Brooks in the Valley of Decision?* The lizard's mind reeled. No doubt about it, if he was to make another of those hideous movies, *Gojiro vs. Joseph Prometheus Brooks in the Valley of Decision* would be one heckuva comeback. "A perfect climax to my motheaten career."

Yeah, the monster thought, chewing over the possibility. Beep that creep Shig, have him line up a meeting posthaste. Get Brooks on the reddest eye, touch him down on Corvair Bay Beach. Pitch a Cinzano umbrella in the cinderfield over by Melanoma Meadow, make it very nice and polite, skimmers on the heads of all the principals, seersucker suits, sprigs of mint in tall glasses, hammer out a humdinger of a deal. Then: get ready to rumble!

Gojiro vs. Joseph Brooks. How long had the monster itched for that matchup? Prayed for it! How long had he snarled what he'd do to Brooks if he ever got him alone, without his B-29s and his white lights? No, forget conditions, ax the handicaps. Let him bring his fissions and fusions, his Super this, Super that. His every exponential pile, the whole militaryfuckingindustrial complex if he wants. Don't matter. "Stick us in a steel cage, Texas Death, no time limit. I'll meet him . . . mess with him!"

Gojiro vs. Joseph Prometheus Brooks in the Valley of Decision. What kind of heart of darkness trip would that be, meeting your maker with the cameras churning?

There was only one small hitch. "He's dead! Brooks is dead!"

The monster's hysteric laughter echoed through the 'cano. "The bastard's dead!" he cackled like a more deranged Renfield. "Deader than doornails." It must have been his hate that made him forget Brooks was dead, had been for twenty-five years. The kind of hate the reptile had, you couldn't locus anything that intense on a rotting box of bones. "Ain't no dead man gonna help us solve the Triple Ring Promise."

Komodo leaned back in his chair, rubbed his chin. "That is so. Mr. Brooks is dead. He cannot help us. But this letter gives me an idea."

"What kind of idea?" Gojiro felt a twinge in his belly. There was something funny about that letter in Komodo's hands. Eerie. Was it the strange, lime green stationery? The monster couldn't put a finger on the feeling.

"I thought, perhaps, *she* can help us."

"Who?"

"Why, Sheila Brooks."

"What are you talking about? I thought you said Science was gonna save us. Sheila Brooks ain't no scientist. She's some sleazebag movie writer."

"She is Mr. Brooks's daughter."

"Big deal. She probably wasn't even born when all this started up."

"Actually, my own true friend, that is not exactly so." Komodo gave a quick smile and opened the thick book resting on his lap. The volume, *Who's*

Who in the Culture Industry, had just washed up on the shore beyond Past Due Point. It squished as Komodo turned the waterlogged pages. "The most recent edition—a very fascinating work. I was gratified to see entries under both of our names. Remarkably, our films appear to be very respected in certain critical circles, especially among the French. Why, right here a Mr. Jean-Pierre Camolli says—"

"Never mind!"

"Anyway, according to this book, Sheila Brooks was born on July 16, 1945."

"Wha?" Just hearing that date knocked air from the monster. July 16, 1945: the day the Heater was unveiled—the very date the planet was forcefed the first dose of what would inevitably land it face-down on a metal stretcher, DOA, in some farflung Milky Way emergency room. July 16, 1945. It seemed the saddest kind of birthday. That is, if you didn't count Komodo's. The tabloids really had a party with that one, how when the Coma Boy was found inside that hole in Hiroshima, a card was in the pocket of his satin suit. One year old today, it said. August 6: happy birthday.

Still, the monster struggled for nonchalance. "July sixteenth, July schmix-teenth—don't mean nothing. Coincidence is thick on the maps of life."

"Perhaps," Komodo sighed. He put the book down, got up, walked around. When he sat down again, he was holding that stereopticon. He must have had the old-time photo-viewing machine tucked deep in the pocket of his black pajamas. He sat on the edge of Gojiro's round bed and looked at the picture inside.

Gojiro turned his head. Whatever happened between Komodo and that stereopticon, it was private.

The monster remembered the day the mahogany photo holder washed up off Pre-existing Condition Inlet, seemingly just another deconstruction amid the flotjet flow. They'd been foraging along the shoreline, looking for electric-blanket remnants to weave into a thermoregulatory quilt, when they spotted the enameled case. From the delicate silk scarves in which it was wrapped, Komodo concluded that the antique viewer had once been the property of an elegant and proper lady. The magnifying lenses that made the 3-D effect possible were still intact, after who knew how long at sea.

"It's got no picture in it," Gojiro noted, about to toss the viewer back and move down the beach to better pickings.

Komodo stopped him. "It is an old item, from another, more genteel time. I will keep it. Someday we may find a fitting image to place within it."

It wasn't until a few days later that those snapshots tumbled in on the red tide. Spring cleaning from a hundred Fotomats, the pictures were shoved in plastic bags tagged "Unclaimed." Gojiro opened a sack with a razored claw and out flew a ya-hoo blizzard of Bermuda shorts posed in front of shiny Buicks, garden hoses squirting, heads cut off. But there were other pictures too, better ones, ones of young couples and families, that looked to have been taken by professionals with waiting rooms, a choice of backdrops, and lollies for the kids. Gojiro imagined that these photos had once sat proudly on the desks of hard-smiling executives or had been pinned to the dashboards of immigrant-driven taxicabs.

Sapiens were so bizarre, the reptile thought, bleary from focusing on the tiny squares. What was the depth of their insecurity that they felt it necessary to record even the most mundane of their insignificant doings? The mountains of photos bugged the monster. He thought of all the times Komodo would pick up a stray magazine, point to a smartly dressed couple in the front seat of a sleek automobile, and sigh, "Do you think my parents could have looked like this?" How horrible not to know what your mother and father looked like, whose eyes you had, whose mouth. Poor, sad Komodo! Reduced to scouring slickpaged advertisements for a clue to his heritage, wondering which of the dowdy models in the Sears catalog might embody qualities of those who gave him life. It wasn't fair, Gojiro thought, kicking his way through the drifts of photos piling up on Past Due Point, that these clods—half of whom couldn't even get their hammy thumbs out of the way—could point and shoot their thirty-six dismal exposures, get them processed in an hour. Why should they have such voluminous documentation when Komodo had none?

Then, one day, as he clawthumbed through Kodak's bland emulsions, the monster came upon those strange photos, anomalies among the myriad visits to Knott's Berry Farm. Side by side on a thick card, the next-to-identical pictures were old, real old, black and white and silvery. Maybe they were daguerreotypes, Gojiro couldn't say, he just sat there looking. They were Japs, the people in that picture. The woman was beautiful, stylish yet inviting—how wonderfully hopeful she looked! The man's eyes were bright, resolute, but kind. A keen mind resided within that handsome head, there could be no doubt of that. The setting was ideal: a lush hillside, beside a crystal lake, in front of a towering mountain with a diamond sparkle of snow on its crowning top.

The next night the monster slipped the photo into the stereopticon, left it on Komodo's tiny desk. Then he waited, worried. He wondered if he'd made a mistake, assumed too much, insulted his friend. It was only after Komodo showed him that little film that was later canonized as the "Opening Sequence" that Gojiro could be sure that his friend was pleased with his gift. For, in the original picture the Mom is not yet a mom, the Dad not quite a dad. Soon they will be, that's obvious enough by the swell of the woman's belly beneath her kimono. It was Komodo who added the rest, the rosecheeked child, the schoolboy with his books wrapped in an elastic strap. He put himself inside that picture, birthed himself to that unnamed couple from the past.

Now, though, so many years later, Gojiro watched Komodo stare into his stereopticon and worried again. "You okay?" the monster asked in a hushed tone.

Komodo did not look up as he spoke. "My own true friend, do you recall a statement made by Budd Hazard pertaining to the Tenacity of Genes and Dreams?"

"Rings a dim bell," the reptile grunted.

"At the time, it seemed a mere aside, a vague corollary to the Reprimordialization texts indicating that even if a Bunch becomes a Bunch in the twinkling of an eye, that moment of change has long been genetically foreshadowed. Yet now, it strikes me that the same is true for ideas, or, in the Muse's parlance, dreams. It occurs to me that some dreams are too big to be experienced all at once, that they must be passed on, piece by piece from generation to generation, until they can be glimpsed in their entirety by a single individual."

"What are you getting at?" This was exactly the sort of talk that made Gojiro nervous.

Komodo peered deeper inside the stereopticon. There was a rising urgency in his voice. "It is so strange, my own true friend, but sometimes I look into this frame and imagine these people are trying to tell me something. A secret that means everything to them—a life's work—something that it is my duty, as their son, to carry on, to impart to my own children.

"It is insane, I know. These people cannot be my parents, it is only an image. Yet I *feel* it, an imploring in their eyes. Finish what we started, I hear them beseeching me. Don't let our efforts go undone. That is why I believe we have no choice but to answer Ms. Brooks's letter."

"Say what?" The monster, greatly moved by his friend's sentiments, had been running a soothing clawhand over Komodo's neck. Now he recoiled.

Komodo looked up, tears running down his face. "I sense that there are others who feel as I do, and that Ms. Brooks might be one of those people, that the work her father started might secretly live in her, straining for culmination."

Gojiro's brain gearground. "Whoa, Nelly."

Komodo didn't stop. Suddenly *that look* was in his eyes. "But my own true friend, don't you sense a yearning to express what is already known to you, yet somehow fleeting, beyond conscious thought? Is it not possible that critical information is passed involuntarily, by means of a kind of Alchemical Heredity resonating from one generation to the next? Is that not how it was in your own Hallowed Homelands?"

"Leave my Hallowed Homelands out of it! This is totally different! What kind of secret you think Brooks's daughter would carry on—a better recipe for the witch's brew, a redoubled toil and trouble? Alchemical Heredity, where do you come up with this crap?"

"I'm only saying that perhaps she might be able to help us. And we might help her!"

"Help *her?* Why should we help her?"

"Because she is in terrible danger! Look at this letter, read what she says."

That letter, the lime green paper! It stopped the monster in his tracks. Komodo began to read it.

From: Hermit Pandora Pictures
To: King of Monsters, Friend to Atoms Productions
Re: <u>Gojiro vs. Joseph Prometheus Brooks in the Valley of Decision</u>

Dear Sirs,
I don't know how to say this—

Gojiro broke in. "What do you mean, you don't know how to say this?"
"No," Komodo said, "that's what it says. I'm reading."

I don't know how to say this. I don't do business. I have no head for it. Bobby says I do, but I don't. The only thing I know is I'm going crazy. I have things in my brain that are driving me insane. I have to get them out. If I don't, I'm going to kill myself. Everyone thinks I'm too nuts to do it, but I'm not. I have a gun. It's in my purse. I'm looking at it right now. You have to help me. You're the only one who can. Please regard this as a matter of Life and Death.

> I look forward to your reply,
> Sincerely yours,
> Sheila Brooks

Gojiro broke out laughing. "Why, it's just some crank letter . . . some loony G-fan mad because his T-shirts didn't arrive on time."

"I don't think so," Komodo said somberly, gripping the lime green paper. "There is something written at bottom that convinces me of its genuineness. A mysterious message. A new kind of supplication."

"A supplication?" So that was it. Gojiro knew why the letter made him so uneasy. Those creepy supplications weren't supposed to get through to him. They were to be flagged on lime green paper by the less deranged Atoms in the Radioactive Island mailroom, and then, according to the monster's decree, dumped into the sea beyond Past Due Point. What was Sheila Brooks doing sending him a supplication, and what was the big idea of Komodo breaking the banning order and bringing the thing down here? "What kind of *new* supplication?" the monster demanded.

But by then, Komodo's visi-beeper was ringing, its eight alarms drowning out all other sounds. He pulled the machine from the pocket of his black pajamas, enhanced the screen. Crag and Slam, those two discipline-problem maladapts Gojiro had long insisted be repatriated to whatever São Paulo shitbox they'd come from, were shoveling mounds of chomping sawtooth flatworms onto the bodies of four other Atoms, who were bound and gagged inside electrified tiger cages.

"Oh no!" Komodo shouted. He ran out of the 'cano, leaving Gojiro alone.

THE BLACK SPOT

The sickest thing about the whole situation had to be what a freak Gojiro was for those Sheila Brooks pictures. *Tidal Wave,* the first one, turned up on the Dish during one of the electronegativity zap-pows that often afflicted the Cloudcover, the kind that really messed up reception. The behemoth was whirling the dials, catching only static, when on what seemed the clearest of channels, *Tidal Wave* bled across the screen.

Right off, the monster sensed this wasn't just the dimbulbed disaster film it pretended to be. It was the look of the girl, how sweet she was, her ponytail behind, how all she wanted to do was ice-skate. She didn't care that the multinationals' illegal krill-spawning project had dried up all the water in the world—she had new skates! She walked across the endless Sahara, determined to find a real pond, not one of those mall rinks where the dry ice scorched your skin and no double axel could be turned.

It wasn't until the part where the little girl journeys to see the Diviner that Gojiro began to get edgy. It was crazy! The monster had seen the thinfaced, popeyed actor they had playing the role a hundred times. He was always frying Boris Karloff's eyeballs sunnyside up or watching some portrait go grotty on a Victorian wall. Campy to the max. But this time, when that old hack poked his whitepowdered head out from behind the heavy wrought-iron door of his sandswept house outside Samarkand, Gojiro nearly jumped out of his leathers.

The face . . . it was so terribly *familiar.* "Hey!" the reptile screamed to Komodo, who was busy with the beakers and bunsens. "Something kooky about this movie, check it out."

"He gave her a potion, told her to dissolve it in liquid," Gojiro explained when Komodo joined him. A tremendous tumbler took up the whole frame. Behind it, shadowy, the girl could be seen, opening the packet the Diviner had given her, dispensing it like Bromo. The whole Dishscreen seemed to shake. Suddenly there was water, water, everywhere. Over England, Russia, Timbuktu, and Kalamazoo.

Then came the Tidal Wave: a rolling wall across the Atlantic, ten thousand feet tall, dwarfing the Empire State Building. And there, cowering in a doorway on St. Mark's Place, crying, bawling, was the little girl.

"She thinks it's all her fault!" a mortified Gojiro shouted. "She thinks she's drowning the world, because she wanted to skate."

"Who's that?" Komodo asked, terrified, as the tall, thin man in black walked up the deserted Second Avenue.

"It's him! The Diviner."

Komodo and Gojiro grabbed each other when the wizened, harsh-eyed man spoke. "So you wanted to skate?" he said, low-pitched and thunderous. He handed the little girl another envelope and told her to wait until the wave was close enough to touch, then throw the powder in the water. "Then you'll skate."

"Throw it, throw it!" Komodo and Gojiro screamed as the little girl stood at the tip of Manhattan, the wave almost upon her, a blinding energy curve of which no Silver Surfer ever caught the crest. The little girl let go. The powder hit the water, stopped the swell solid, turned it to a concave lurch of ice.

That last scene killed the monster. How sweet the little girl looked in her ruffled red skirt, turning her figure eights at the base of that great surge of Doom. And how the robins chirped as the sun broke through the clouds, and the first buds were on the trees.

Back then, neither Gojiro nor Komodo took note of the final credits tacked on to the end of *Tidal Wave.* What could a florid logo indicating the picture was "a Brooks-Zeber Film for Hermit Pandora Productions" mean to them, so far away, on an island Mercator never projected? It wasn't until they read those tabloids, part of the "circulating library" that washed up on the Corvair Bay Beach shoreline every day, that they learned the identity of *Tidal Wave*'s creator.

"Look!" Gojiro shouted to Komodo some time later, reading from the syndicated "Gollywood Agog" column. "No wonder they call the reclusive SHEILA BROOKS 'the Hermit Pandora.' Word is that the daughter of America's late great atomic scientist JOSEPH PROMETHEUS BROOKS will not be present yet AGAIN to accept the scads of kudos her most recent releases, *The Bottom Line's the Swipe of the Scythe* and *Atlantis Came Up This Morning and It Was Anaheim,* both up for Best Picture, are certain to garner. This will be still another disappointment to the Dreamer of the Sad Tomorrow's teeming throng of fans. BOBBY ZEBER, director of the couple's hot-hot-hot pictures, will represent the team, but he does not seem particularly thrilled about it. 'What does it matter, anyway?' ZEBER sighed to your Golly Agog correspondent. To them, we say: 'Come off it, guys! We love you! Get with the program!' "

Alongside the copy was a murky photo captioned "The Brooks-Zeber team." It was clearly not a new picture. They were sitting on a red motorcycle. The man, a brooding presence whom Gojiro took to be Bobby Zeber, sported a fringed leather coat and an upper lip crimped to a Brando curl. As for Sheila Brooks, she sat on the back of the bike, her face turned away from the camera. All you could see was a mass of white hair.

"Brooks's daughter? I didn't even know he had a daughter!"

"Nor I, my own true friend," Komodo put in.

After that, even though he'd sworn, on principle, to boycott Brooks-Zeber products, the monster never failed to find himself rapt whenever the pictures appeared on the Dish. *Tidal Wave* remained his favorite, but he also confessed to liking *Rockefeller's Rocket,* that one about how all the glass towers in the Big City weren't buildings at all, but rather the spawn of seeds planted in financial districts by avaricious dupes of cannibalistic aliens. Gojiro loved it when, at germinational maturity, the buildings developed propulsion systems and flew off into space, interplanetary baguettes to be baked in massive micro ovens out beyond the stars. The sight of the stunned plutocrats trying to make one last hostile takeover before lift-off never failed to tickle the perennially class-antagonist reptile.

"Brooks's daughter, my fellow cineaste," the monster laughed to himself soon after Komodo left the 'cano that day Sheila Brooks's letter arrived. He was feeling a lot better. Komodo's wacko chatter about Alchemical Heredity and that business about facing off with Joe Pro Brooks put the monster into a panic-paranoia red alert, but a major inlay of the hardcutting 235 spruced things up quite nicely. He Radi-fired a heaping superspoon and was soon flying higher than a Chinaman's kite in Mr. Parker's tokebunk.

Yeah, the stupored reptile mused, it was nutty okay, Sheila Brooks writing to them, saying only they could help her. *Life and Death!* What could she be talking about? Life and Death? What could those words boil down to for the offspring of Joseph Brooks? Maybe her career was a mess. Faithful fan that he was, Gojiro had pored over the rampant speculation that Hermit Pandora's reputed nightmare blockage was putting a serious dent into the Brooks-Zeber balance sheet. Might be so, the monster imagined. That most recent entry, *Ants for Breakfast,* no way it was so hot-hot-hot. There was just something *missing.*

"Maybe she's looking for a comeback too," Gojiro chuckled, noting that Sheila Brooks's supposed shortfall of ideas roughly coincided with the ban he placed on the further export of his own rotten pictures. Then, his lids suddenly brick heavy, the lizard dropped off to sleep.

Almost immediately Gojiro found himself back in that dream.

"What? How could I be here again?" he cried within his slumber. It hadn't happened for years, not since those unhappy evenings when the Black Spot Dream had invaded the Quadcameral with numbing regularity. "Can't be just a dream," the monster would yowl to Komodo back then, bolting upright in his burrow. "It's like, alive. A psychotropic tapeworm inside my brain, corkscrewing through the parietal down into the private stock."

Now it was back. Again the monster found himself transported to the Great Promontory he had so long envisioned as his Hallowed Homelands. Lavarock! That's where he was, bellydown on the Precious Pumice, a mere child of a 'tile, quarantined along with his fellow zardplebes. In the distance, he could hear the the slow drawl of the fullgrowns.

"Hear tell there be a variety of us over in Africa," a grizzled eightfooter said, basking in the noonday sun, *V. exanthematicus.* "Said to ovipare in termite nests."

"No shit?" another mature replied.

"Yessir! Termites dumber than a stump over there. Use their formics to spitbuild big bulgy paperthin nests. Then a zard comes along, tears a hole, ovipares, moves on. Couple minutes later, termite comes back, scratches his head, says, 'How come I left this hole here, must of missed a spot.' Builds that nest right back up again, hides that herp's eggs perfect. Termites never catch on, they only see the puncture, not the purpose behind it. In this world, a zard got to take what glitches is given him."

That kind of talk was always going on in the monster's dream. Not that the youngest zardplebe, less than five weeks on the Rock, would think of joining in. It wasn't a junior's place to address his seniors. He was not fit, physically, mentally, or morally. All his basic equipment was installed, he was wired and ready to go, but the most vital juice wasn't flowing through him. He hadn't yet leaped into the Black Spot.

That was the crux: the Black Spot. The nexus of Knowing! Gateway to all Zardic Life! The fixing solution of Identity!

Without a plunge to the Black Spot a zard was not a Zard, couldn't take his place in the Endless Chain. Without the rush of the sacred viscous over his novice leathers, his biologies were nothing more than colorcoded chutes and ladders of DNA, a pointless arrangement of blood and sinew. The Black Spot alone possessed the Big Switch, infused all the standard issue with the Identity of the Bunch.

"Think it's gonna hurt?" one zardplebe asked from the bottom of the juvenile's tangle.

The others shook their heads; they had no idea what the Black Spot had in store. "I heard that if you look on the Spot before you're ready, then you never become an Initiate," one plebe whispered. "You turn into a buzzy dragon-fly or a scuzzfurred goat munching on grass."

"Dee-gusting," the others retched, shaken at the thought.

This chatter only served to make that particular zardplebe of Gojiro's dream more anxious. The youngest and most withdrawn of the group, he'd always been on the outskirts of the clique. The others seemed so much slicker, more prepared to accept the mantle soon to be bestowed. Identity? What could it entail? Who was he to seek it? His apprehension grew as, one by one, his former playmates suddenly broke from their bellydown and went four-on-the-floor over Craggy Ridge. Hours later they would return. They didn't look any different, but they were. Their callowness was gone, you could tell it from their carriage. Now they basked amongst the Initiate, discoursing on topics the youngest zardplebe could not decipher.

By and by a strange incident occurred. A giant silvery bird came out of the sky and set down in the calm waters off where that youngest zardplebe sat. A seaplane! The door opened and out came bipeds, three of them. The fat one, sweat seeping through his soldier suit, was wiping his red jowls with a fluttery handkerchief. The second was smaller, with bushy eyebrows and a sweep of rich brown hair. Elegant in his tropical suit, his gold watch gleaming, his cultivated comportment did not seem affected in any way by the hot and unremitting sun. Then there was that other one. The one in black. Six and half feet tall and ramrod straight, he had the severe look of the most ascetic missionary. He stayed apart from the other two, walking several steps behind. The meager surf lapped over his canvas shoes, not that he seemed to care. He was looking around, his long neck swiveling so as to ensnare the whole horizon, a special intensity to his scan.

What's he looking for? the youngest zardplebe wondered, looking at the dark flamingo of a man. How white his skin was, the color of bone left to bleach in the sun. And his eyes! They were as black as the starless night.

Then they were screaming at one another, the three bipeds. The zardplebe couldn't make out the words, just the frenzy. Suddenly, the fat soldier, more agile than he looked, hurled himself at the man in black, knocked him into the water. The debonair one tried to intercede, to no avail. Finally some other soldiers, a half a dozen of them, pulled the men apart. The fat soldier's shirt was ripped, his hat was gone, his balding head shining in the afternoon glare. The man in black had a cut above his eye, blood stark red as it ran down the nearly colorless cheek.

The soldier, who appeared to maintain dominance over the others of his stripe, kept on yelling, something about how he "wasn't going to let what happened in the Valley happen here." The youngest zardplebe followed the soldier's gesticulating finger. Followed it to a face. A small face looking out the window of the silvery plane. The zardplebe strained, trying to see. There was something in that tiny face, something unsettling, an emotion he didn't know.

Suddenly a forbidding dread filled the air. The zardplebe flicked out his tongue to taste the wind and turned cold. The chemosignal impulsed only death.

"Danger! Danger!" he hissed. Across the ruddy rocks, over the igneous outcrops, through every burrow and den that youngest zardplebe impulsed his warning.

But he was alone. His fellow zardplebes were gone. In the time he'd busied himself with the indecipherable affairs of these sapiens, all his counterparts had been summoned to the Black Spot. He was the only immature upon the Precious Pumice. "Danger. Danger!" The fullgrowns paid no attention. Why should they? They'd been Immersed, in them was a sense of Self and Community built over millions of generations, the product of the most delicate of refinements— so what could a mere zardplebe, the rawest of the raw, tell them that they didn't know already? "They are right to shun me," the youngest zardplebe thought, a single 'tile etched against the implacable blue of the ocean sky. "I have no Identity."

Gojiro

Then the young 'tile felt it, a brutal coercion of being watched. That man in black was staring at him. The man's penetrating gaze had panned over the multitudes of fullgrowns and come to rest upon this single zardplebe. The plebe was overtaken by the most oppressive of sensations. The man and him: their gazes were locking on, a connection was being fused.

"Ahh!" The young lizard's mind convulsed. For at that exact moment his brain was flooded with a competing compulsion. A pulling . . . a tugging . . . something dragging him toward Craggy Ridge. The Black Spot! It was summoning him—entreating him to take his rightful place in the Endless Chain. He sought to follow the sacred impulse, to go off as every other one of his kind always had. But he couldn't. That man's stare—it held him. It wouldn't let him go!

"Come in!" the Black Spot demanded. But that blackclad man's gaze wouldn't yield. It yanked the zardplebe equally, kept him in his place. "Come in!" The lizard felt as if he were about to break in two.

Then, suddenly, he was free! The man in black broke off the stare, turned and walked away, back toward that small face inside the plane.

"Come in!" the Black Spot called again, and the zardplebe, unencumbered, strode off to obey. Only that ancient, unswaying reflex was inside him now, prescribing the most inexorable of courses. All else melted to air. Off he went, unquestioning, over the Ridge, through forested canyons, up an ever-narrowing river. It was thick and airless there. Jaggedy streaks of light serrated down from a sky dark with more than night. Ominous thumps sounded from behind unknown foliages, taxonomically untitled beasts lurked on overhangs of cliffs, but the zardplebe was not deterred. On he went until he reached the headlands of those waters, the center of the Great Stone, the Black Spot.

It didn't look like much at first, just a murky, stagnant pool. A roundish well, set naked on an empty stretch, a hundred feet across, a depression filled with liquid pitch set into the mottled limestone. Then he heard that call again. "Come in! Come in!" That urgent invitation issued from the Black Spot itself!

"Leap!" was the immortal auto-command. The youngest zardplebe readied himself. He came to the very lip of the pool, looked in, saw the blackness there. "Leap!" The word thundered in his brain.

He pushed a foreclaw over the ruddy edge. But then: "Hey, gimme a minute here."

"Leap!"

55

"But, like . . . it's so, you know . . . Infinite."

It was incredible. Faced with the eternal task performed by the untold million links in the unbroken Chain, the youngest zardplebe hemmed and hawed. At the brink of Illumination, he balked.

"Leap!"

And so, finally, he went . . . up and up, higher and higher, to the apex of his leap . . . only to be freezeframed, for all time, in the hottest of strobes.

It figured that Komodo would interpret Gojiro's recurring dream as "a potential central metaphor" in the ongoing attempt to fulfill the Triple Ring Promise. Rubbing his hairless chin, the contemplative former Coma Boy paced the 'cano. "Can it be denied that the Black Spot symbolizes that special Beamic media by which the uninitiate of a prospective Bunch finds his own true Identity within the Evolloo? Is this not the mystic sort of realm we wish to enter? It is my opinion that this vision requires the closest analysis."

Gojiro scoffed. "Hey, park that Sigmund shit at the door. The whole thing seems pretty cut and fried to me. The Heater crushed Newton's apple to sauce; a zard went up, he did not come down. Simple as that."

A light was in Komodo's eyes. "Exactly my point! In the face of holocaust, axioms cease to function, meaning is exploded, history swallowed, expectation shattered. Yet it is into these zones we must go. Imagine, my own true friend, what might we learn should that youngest zardplebe actually reach the Black Spot."

"But he doesn't. It's the same every time. He never gets there."

"That is so," Komodo said gravely and went off to his beakers and bunsens. When he came back, several hours later, he was dragging a large gray box, the first dream printer, prototype of a whole generation of neural periscopes Komodo would develop to see around the corners of Quadcameral plumbing. The plan was to tap into synapsial electricity, render it palpably visual, project it onto a dishscreen. Noting that "all that separates that youngest zardplebe from Illumination is the thinnest gap of time and space," Komodo hoped that through manipulation, it would be possible to somehow influence Gojiro's dream, "change it, so Identity might be revealed."

Gojiro honked derisively. "Man, you go too far! Dreams exist in their own time. You can't change a dream!"

Still, the monster agreed, allowed himself to be hooked up to Komodo's machine. Privacy was not an issue; in those early days, the Quadcameral, everything it thought, was considered communal property on Radioactive Island. So, with the reptile seated 'neath a shocking-pink hair-dryer-type contraption, gator clips hotwired to his every node, they waited for the inevitable return of the Black Spot Dream. It didn't take long. As soon as Gojiro closed his eyes, his dream was playing out on the screen, as clear as any Filipino soap opera.

Suffice it to say that the next few weeks were ridiculous. Every auto-suggestion failed, ditto for Komodo's most ingenious editing schemes. The incident at the Black Spot remained unchanged. In the end, the two friends were reduced to watching the daily rushes of the dream, waiting for the youngest zardplebe to reach the lip of his supposed Identity, then screaming "Leap!" like a pair of demented cheerleaders.

Nothing helped. Immune to their exhortations, the youngest zardplebe leaped, all right, but too late—always too late. Gojiro and Komodo watched the trajectory of his jump, right up to the zenith, only to see the image bleed from the Bomb-whitened screen. "I told you it wouldn't work!" Gojiro screamed, near hysterics. "You can't unfreeze a dream."

"Yes," Komodo said soberly, looking up at the disappearing image of that tiny lizard. "There is nothing we can do. It appears that there are any number of means by which an entity can be brought face-to-face with his personal moment of Truth; however, it is only that individual who can seize Identity, make it his own. It remains to that youngest zardplebe to unfreeze the dream, him alone."

Gojiro saw the look of failure on his friend's face, ripped the wires from his head, stalked off, sat down to watch a hundred hours of sitcoms. What else was he to do? He couldn't exactly come clean, tell Komodo he hadn't tried his hardest to make the experiment a success. He couldn't admit that his whoops of "Leap!" were fake, that he was no more willing to plunge into the Black Spot than that pathetic phantasm in his dream. He couldn't confess that he was equally afraid, immobilized, full of doubt. That Identity was nothing he craved, that the merest thought of it filled him with terror.

Not that it turned out to matter much. For, soon enough, the Black Spot Dream, like Budd Hazard before it, faded from the Quadcameral, never to return.

* * *

Until that night Sheila Brooks's letter came.

The dream was the same as ever. A terrible bad penny come back in its entirety, except now it was worse. The passage of time had annotated the vision in a most distressing fashion. That fat, screaming soldier—only a colonel then— was General Grives, the military head of the Project. Gojiro often ran into the general's porcine image on the Dish, even if they'd recently changed his time- slot from Sunday morning "public affairs" to off-hour religious shows. The dapper one, who else could that have been but Victor Stiller? Stiller: calculating accelerator of particles, the most politic of men, advisor to presidents. He'd given up science, they said, become an owner of things. Maybe he owned everything.

And, of course, the man in black. Joseph Prometheus Brooks.

So it was Brooks all along! Brooks whose steely gaze had panned the Lavarock horizon. Brooks who singled out that youngest zardplebe among the great tangles of 'tiles and turned him stockstill with his deathstabbing stare. "No!" Gojiro called out, once again inside the dream. "No!" he yelled to that zardplebe when Brooks's stare fell upon him. "Don't look! Turn away! Don't let his pestilence into your brain!"

But it was to no avail. The dream kept on, unchanged.

Then there was that other positive ID: the small face in the plane window with the unknown, yet vaguely unnerving expression. Maybe it wouldn't have held up in court, given that she couldn't have been more than two or three years old at the time. But Gojiro was sure. It was Sheila Brooks, and on her face was fear—not fear a youngest zardplebe would ever recognize, but the kind Gojiro knew all too well.

"Sheila Brooks—inside my head for years!" the monster screamed in his sleep.

The dream wound on toward its inexorable conclusion. Once again the reptile reached the crucial position, poised on the edge of Identity. Again Gojiro tried to make his mouth move, to summon up a shout, offer heartfelt encourage- ment. But it came out weak, barely a squeak: "Leap."

It didn't help, not at all. The youngest zardplebe hesitated as always, jumped too late . . . too late to avoid the crack of Doom. Up he went into its angry face—only to *come down again!* Yes! The youngest zardplebe hurtled down through that Cloud, saw the taut black surface below, coming up to meet him.

Gojiro heard himself yell as the zardplebe plunged. A bellyflop into the

Black Spot! The dream had unfrozen. But why was he surrounded by green, not black? Lime green!

"Ahhhh!" The monster shook himself awake. Lime green . . . that letter! The one from Sheila Brooks! What was Komodo saying about a *new* kind of supplication?

The monster thrashed out of his burrow, lurched toward Komodo's desk. What *was* Sheila Brooks doing sending in a supplication? He grabbed the letter, held it up to the Dishscreen light, read through. It was exactly as Komodo said, except for the end—the part he never got to. There, written in a hand that might have belonged to a nine-year-old, was "Come in, Gojiro. Please come in, Gojiro, BRIDGER OF GAPS, LINKER OF LINES, NEXUS OF BEAM AND BUNCH, DEFENDER OF THE EVOLLOO. Please come in, please heed this humble servant's plea."

Gojiro read this and fainted dead away.

THROUGH
THE CLOUDCOVER

It was near dawn when they left their island. In the metallic sky above, the stretched-canvas moon creaked down on pullies and out came the sun they'd made.

The sun was their first great public-works project. The idea for it began in something Komodo once said, about how even though those Okinawa white-coats always referred to that dank hospital ward as "his" room, he never got to fix it up the way he wanted. It made Gojiro mad, hearing that. Everyone should get to fix up his room how he wanted, the reptile declared, and, since Radioactive Island was their room, sort of, they ought to get cracking. A sun would be the place to start, Komodo suggested. That way they'd be able to tell night from day.

At first Gojiro protested. "Later for the 'let there be light.' Let's live by night, slither surreptitious on a roulette wheel of life. Each to his own Eden, I say." But, after stubbing his toeclaws on steel-drum boulders a couple hundred times, the reptile agreed that they had to have a sun.

They used a wrecker's ball for the core, discarded beach reflectors and shards of broken bottles from the top of sugar-plantation walls to make it shine. Gojiro forged the sphere with his Radi-Breath, sealed it with his spit, then shotputted it up into the dull sky. But it didn't stick. It tumbled like a junkyard meteor into the sea, sending up a steamy fog that took three days to clear.

"Now we'll never have a sun," the monster said dejectedly. "How we gonna hang it?"

Komodo rubbed his hairless chin. "On a hook," he said.

"On a *sky*hook?" Gojiro smirked. "Hey, you can't fool me, there ain't no such thing as skyhooks."

But Komodo was right. They searched the forlorn firmaments of their world and, sure enough, in the gritty air above Asbestos Wood, suspended over the razortipped treeline, they found a skyhook. "Only here," Gojiro muttered as he launched the sun into the sky once more. On the twenty-fifth try, it stuck.

Still it wasn't right. "It's so small," the reptile moaned. "It looks like a manhole cover up there, a medallion round a record producer's neck. You can barely see it."

Nodding grimly, Komodo went to work with his beakers and bunsens, whipping up a multiglassed optical that when accurately adjusted afforded their sun its proper prominence.

Together they stood on the rapidly growing beach at Corvair Bay and marveled at what they had made. "We have a sun," Komodo said, staring into the dazzling disk, "a center to our sky."

"Yeah," Gojiro replied. Then he told Komodo to stand back.

"What are you going to do?"

"Just stand back," Gojiro repeated, and with one great whooshing leap he catapulted his massive body upward until he hovered face to face with the gleaming globe. He grabbed the sphere and held it tightly to his chest. Komodo had to shield his eyes from the ensuing explosion, but when he looked again, he saw that their molten sun was now embossed with three concentric circles.

"Now it's really ours," the monster said, thumping back to land. "I always wanted to carve my name in the sun."

They'd hoped for so much new under their sun! A Bunch! A Beam! The founding of a longest Line! But now, backpaddling toward the Cloudcover, Komodo resting on the monster's belly, it seemed to Gojiro that their sun radiated all the majesty of a fifteen-watt bulb hanging naked in the hallway of a new but already shabby housing project. How pitiful that it should have to peer down on such a sorry state of affairs: the two of them, skulking away without even saying good-bye.

But what other course of action was there, after Gojiro awoke from that Black Spot Dream and read Sheila Brooks's letter? None. None at all.

"Okay!" the monster had screamed to the still sleeping Komodo. "I give in. Let's go to America, let's see this Sheila Brooks—but we got to go now! Tonight!"

An hour later, carrying a sack not much bigger than the one Komodo held when he first arrived on the Island, the monster and his friend were tiptoeing across the bleached beach beyond Radon Seep. They couldn't chance running into Shig. You never could tell when the severe post-teenager would turn up, peering from the synthetic thicket, the day-for-night glinting off the sheer drop of his no-eye shades. Be seen by him and there would be explanations to make, incurring who knew how much guilt.

Then there were the Atoms. A gaggle of those grinning spasticates could stumble from the steel-trunked forest at any moment, nipping at Gojiro's pedal extremities, whining for him to put them up on his shoulders for a dragon ride. So many evenings he'd endured that humiliation, being made to jump over the counterfeit moon like a common cud chewer. News of their departure could not be broken to those wretched kids in any civil fashion. Hideous tantrums would ensue, the more epileptic Atoms spincycling into most soulrenderingest of thrashes. Komodo wouldn't be able to take it. He'd seek to soften the pain of parting with a splash of pageantry, organize some brass-band Busby-Berkeley-goes-to-the-Special-Olympics bon voyage extravaganza that would involve at least two weeks of rehearsals and wind up, without doubt, in the anarchy of pointed heads being shoved into the bells of tubas. It was a vicious thing to do, Gojiro knew, stealing into those Atoms' funksmelling dormitory, lacing their nightly IVs with an extra helping of Thorazine, but he saw no other way. Without immediate action, there would be no action at all. Inertia-city. Now was the time. If all went well they would be in Hollywood in a week.

"Bridger of Gaps! Linker of Lines! Nexus of Beam and Bunch! *Defender of the Evolloo!*"—again and again those horrid locutions swarmed inside the monster's head, contrails of gluey semiology, spinning their Sargasso-like net. It didn't take any elementary Watson to figure who the weaver of that web was. It was like one of those turgid 1950s teleplays where the private eye gets all pent-up about a particular murder only to find every clue pointing to the shaving mirror.

"The chickens," Gojiro anguished to himself as he swam through the murk, "have come home to broast."

Gojiro

The 90 Series! That was the fate-sealing blow, the self-starter for this most forbidding journey. What a horrorshow it was that first night as the monster, his mood mean and desolate, reeled about the 'cano under the influence of rotgut 238, and then, resounding in the Quadcam: "Gojiro . . . Please come in, Gojiro. Please heed this humble servant's plea."

"Huh?"

"Gojiro, come in, man. This is Tyrone Everett of Philadelphia, Pennsylvania. Be waiting on the 90 Series! You got to give it up, that 90 Series! And, by the way, I be needing some transportation, okay? And none of that ten-speed shit. One of them mountain bikes! Please come in, Gojiro."

The sound slapped the reptile end over end. What was a supplication doing inside his head? "Known I shouldn't have messed with that 238," he croaked to himself. "Swill pulls the cruelest of coats!"

But it came again. "Gojiro, come in! This still Tyrone! Telling you, man, you got to reveal it! You got to reveal it now! The 90 Series!"

Then: "Whoa!"

Like teleportation, Gojiro wasn't down the 'cano looking to lick the last cranny of a microwave anymore. He was in a small, unhappy room in the south section of Philadelphia decorated with torn Earth, Wind, and Fire posters. He wasn't inside his own body either, he was a small-for-his-age nine-year-old black kid wearing high-top Cons. He saw a woman, his mother, cowering by the cold radiator. Then there were footsteps on a staircase, a door smashing open. "Jimmy!" his mother screamed, terror in her eyes. "You get away, don't be coming back here. I'm calling the police!" Much as he wanted to turn away before Jimmy's fist hit his mother's mouth, he didn't. Instead he rushed toward Jimmy, trying to strike him, to rip his eyes out of his head, anything to keep him from hitting his mother again. He knocked the big man sideways for a minute, then saw him scowl, lash out. The pain from where Jimmy smacked him across the face was terrific. It was the first time he'd ever felt *physical* pain like that.

Then, like nothing, Gojiro was back inside that vulcanized volcano again. A moment passed, and the voice returned. It was quieter now, full of sobs. "Gojiro . . . Come in, Gojiro. Please heed this humble servant's plea. Be Tyrone again. I don't mean to bother you all the time, I mean, I know you got all them other supplications on your desk too. But I *got* to have that 90 Series. Just got to! Please!"

Gojiro stayed very still. In a low, disguised tone he said, "You got the wrong number, man. Sorry." After a distant whimper, he heard a click and Tyrone Everett of Philadelphia, Pennsylvania, was gone.

Gojiro lay down on the 'cano floor, drained. But there was no rest. More came. First it was a trickle, then a flood, a hundred shrieking state hospitals inside his Quadcameral brain, all of them wanting the 90 Series. "Gojiro," they called, "come in. Please heed this humble servant's plea! Wake up! Reveal the 90 Series now!"

It seemed like his body was fractioned out in a billion slivers. Just as he'd been instantaneously set down in Philadelphia, he was in Guatemala, in a dark jungle. Soldiers were dragging away his family, shooting them before his eyes. Then he was in Cambodia, in a barbed-wire-fenced pit, given a bowl of rice swarming with maggots to eat. And then, in the Sudan, he was an eight-year-old carrying an AK-47. And in Beirut, stealing food from pockets of the dead and decomposing. And in Winnetka, Illinois, they wouldn't let him borrow the car.

"NOOOOO!" he screamed, rolling around, holding his head.

Komodo came immediately. "My own true friend! What is happening to you?"

"There's millions of them! Inside! Wanting me!"

"Try to speak, to tell me what you feel."

Gojiro started to answer but another wave came through, wrenching him everywhichway.

"Beat it!" he screamed at an unseen assailant. "Don't touch me with those wires . . . I didn't shoplift that candy bar . . . Don't take my mother away, she didn't mean what she said about the government . . . But all the other kids have one . . . You mean I'll never walk again?

"THIS FREAKING 90 SERIES, WHATEVER IT IS, IT'S KILLING ME!"

In lieu of more precise information, Komodo did what he thought best. He pulled out emergency medicinals from the pocket of his black pajamas and rammed half of Pakistan through Gojiro's parietal. And soon the voices in the monster's mind merged to a faraway clamor, then to the wash of the local news, street noise, easy to ignore.

It wasn't until a week later, while watching the late-night Dish, that Gojiro and Komodo found out anything about the 90 Series.

"It's me!" the monster shouted, looking at the fuzzy transmission. He was standing on the parched beachfront of Corvair Bay, all the Atoms looking up at him, their goony eyes swirling counterclockwise. Gojiro recognized the footage immediately. Komodo had shot it at one of the misfit kids' birthdays, years ago, when the monster would still turn out for those things.

"Hola, zardpards! Yo, yo ho, and hi-ho!" Gojiro listened to that image of himself say. "Calling all Green Scene fiends! Check this out, 'tile-o-files! Talk is not for me, you know. I don't like talk at all—action is the louder thing. But now I have no choice. So listen up."

"What the hell is this?" Gojiro stormed. "That ain't my voice. It's . . ." Komodo swallowed hard but was silent.

"It's Shig! Putting on some crazy accent. Making me sound like a mush-mouthed Chinese waiter!"

On the screen Gojiro's picture kept talking. "Loyal zardpard fans, do you possess some wonderment why there have been no new exciting, ultrafantastic adventures of your favorite King of Monsters, Friend to Atoms lately? Could others of you, collectors of the very philosophic Gojiro Crystal Communications who have had much edification from numbers 1 through 89, say: why? Why, after 89: none other? Never 90? Never 91? 92? Well, I say to you it is not because I do not love you anymore, or that I am too much partying down with my swinging Radioactive Island joyboys and galpals. Actually I am in grave danger! It has been with great risk that I even send you this message."

"What is this crap? What's he trying to pull?"

"Shhh," Komodo motioned, his attention on the screen.

That voice Shig put into Gojiro's mouth went on. "I have been placed into that most terrible spell by the evil zombie see—zombie do Opposer. Yes! That same pencilneck geekster I personally refried in that cool cooking adventure *Gojiro vs. the Depthless Society Beast in the Achromatic Casino.* Can you believe it, 'tile-o-files? That crumbum came back! He sneaked up on me when I was playing poker with my monster friends and used his Stultifying Art Ray on me. I had two aces looking up and two eights turned down too!

"Zardpards! This ever-bad Opposer has caused me to fall into a deep trance. I cannot wake up. And I must. I must awake and give you the 90 Series! Listen now, this is the important thing: the 90 Series is everything! *It is all that counts!* I must reveal it to you so we all will be saved! *It is the only way.*

"But there is trickiness. The 90 Series is a hidden thing. No one knows it except yours trulyest. Except I forgot. This evil ray has made it fly from me. You must help me remember! Only by hearing the 90 Series from *my own lips* will I be awakened. *Help me to know what I know so I can tell you!*

"Yes, *you,* Timmy and Tommy, *you* Billy and Bernice, *you* Debbie and

Dwayne! Only you can do it! But there is only one way to reach me. You must supplicate for the 90 Series through a Gojiro Crystal Contact Radio!"

Then, in some real cheesy "trick" photography, a pair of what looked like plastic earmuffs appeared on the head of that phony Gojiro. "Save me! Save yourself!" the dubbed dummy implored. "Supplicate for the 90 Series! Get your Gojiro Crystal Contact Radio today! Only five dollars!"

The screen went blank, and Shig, in his normal voice, said, "For your special Save Gojiro, Save Yourself offer, send five dollars, plus postage and shipping." He gave a post office box number somewhere in Fiji.

"Fuck," Gojiro exhaled.

Resolutely paddling out to the seething Cloudcover, onward to their no doubt fateful meeting with Sheila Brooks, Gojiro now regarded the 90 Series as just another cinch in an ever-tightening noose around his neck. Not that he would call it a tremendous surprise. He'd been girding himself for some new gambit on Shig's part.

Gojiro's growing apprehension that Shig followed a private agenda, some sort of master plan aimed at boxing him into some unknown yet horrific corner, commenced several years before during one of those beachcombing jaunts he and Komodo often took to pick through the flotjet flow.

"Look at this," the monster said, quizzically, eyeing the steady stream of lobby cards washing over his semisubmerged clawtoes. "These stills—ain't they from *Gojiro vs. Anti-Syncopators on the Street of Forgotten Cool?* Yeah—here's a shot of me rescuing that stack of Chick Webb records from that Electronic Sampler Beast."

Komodo examined the garishly colored photo. "Yes," he said, biting his lip. "But here the title of the film is given as *Gojiro vs. the Square Grabbyhands of Jump on Fifty-third Street.*"

"Fifty-third Street? Ain't Fifty-third Street. It's Fifty-second Street! What's going on here? We never made any lobby cards for any of those movies."

"There was no need to, because—"

"Because *they never played anywhere!*"

They weren't supposed to play anywhere, either. The movies were just another pass-time, one in a series of activities Komodo worked out in hopes of providing those unfortunate Atoms a few moments of mirth before their inevitable demise. "Many of the children display superior technical abilities and would make excellent crew members," the kindhearted Japanese explained to Gojiro, attempting to get the reluctant reptile to star in those old scenarios the two friends conjured up during the heady Glazed Days. Assured perpetual over-the-title billing, the monster could not resist. So the movies were made. But they never—ever—were intended to go beyond the Cloudcover.

Yet here Gojiro was picking up a dripping poster for a movie supposedly entitled *Gojiro vs. the Most Nasty Internal Cells inside the Heavy Heart* but which, from the accompanying stills, was readily identifiable as *Gojiro vs. the Buzzsaw Teratomas by the Bad-news By-pass*. At the bottom of the sheet, in balloonish handwriting, it said, "Playing all this week, Centerville Simplex, theaters one, five, nine, twelve. Free RV parking."

It wasn't until several months later, when the Gojiro—King of Monsters, Friend to Atoms movies first began turning up on the Dish, that the monster became aware of his international celebrity. "I can't believe it!" he cried. "Shig stole those jerk movies! All over the world they're looking at my swollen supraoc, laughing at my mutated face. God, I'm so embarrassed!"

Then, not for the first time, Gojiro felt like crashing across Vinyl Aire Meadow, knocking down every tree in Asbestos Wood until he found Shig's hideout, and having it out with the weird boy. But that was out of the question. The reptile's shameful memories defeated him. He couldn't say a thing.

It was only with the advent of the 90 Series, however, that Gojiro began to glimpse Shig's ultimate scheme. Of course, the monster was well acquainted with the contents of the other eighty-nine so-called Gojiro Crystal Communications, not that the dictums, in his opinion at least, amounted to shit. Maybe they did at one time, but not now. Once, in another form, they represented his personal interpretations of the Great Teachings of the Evolloo, as revealed by the prophet Budd Hazard. At least that's how the monster billed his lecture series to the Atoms back in the days when he retained some hope that those abnormals might psychically upbootstrap themselves and become Initiates in the New Bunch he and Komodo dreamed of founding on Radioactive Island.

"Do 'em some good to catch a smack of the Cosmo," Gojiro told Komodo as he mounted the rec-room podium to deliver the opening lecture, "The Evolloo and You, a Young Mutant's Guide to the Unfathomable." "Couldn't do no harm," he added as he faced his drooling audience.

For six, sometimes eight hours, Gojiro talked, carried away by the beauty of the Design he loved so much. But the Atoms, the ones who stayed awake, were less than rapt. They threw gummy spitballs at the blackboard, smearing Gojiro's diagrams of Beam-Bunch matrices, and their renditions of Anti-Speciesist chants had neither rhythm nor resonance.

"It's pointless," Gojiro said, throwing up his claws. "I have lost my dreams for them. They have no grasp, no scope."

So imagine his chagrin when, one evening, he saw the Atoms sitting in orderly rows and reciting in unison the Communications Shig made up. "Now repeat," Shig barked, his spiked pointer screeching across the blackboard. "Gojiro Crystal Communication 42: either you are in the Evolloo or you are not." And the Atoms, even the impossible stutterers, all repeated "Gojiro Crystal Communication 42." Ten times they said it. Then they went on to Number 43.

To Gojiro, this was obscene, abhorrent: Shig had taken the vast-reaching teachings of Budd Hazard, the splendor of the unknowable Evolloo, and reduced it to rote. "I won't allow it," he stormed at Komodo. "I won't stand by and listen to him make fortune cookies out of everything Sacred. You hear what he did to the lecture on Fate? Wait a minute, I got it here. Yeah. Gojiro Crystal Communication 27: 'The Evolloo covers Fate like paper covers rock, like rock smashes scissors.' "

Komodo raised his narrow eyebrows. "You must admit, my own true friend, there is a certain ring to it."

"Ring? There's a certain ring to ring around the collar! Doesn't it bother you that the only songs they know by heart are hamburger jingles? I've had it with this *Reader's Digest* of a world. Isn't it our charge, as followers of the Evolloo and Anti-Speciesists both, to renounce this undercut of wonder?"

Komodo was troubled. Certainly he agreed with Gojiro. Yet while his own true friend's methods had so resoundingly failed to motivate the Atoms, Shig's short course had gotten results. Now, instead of the tumult that formerly accompanied dinnertime, the Atoms marched into the dining hall and spoke a grace asking for "good fortune of all Beams and Bunches."

"This is some progress, isn't it?" Komodo asked.

Gojiro did not agree. "Standing in a straight line is no progress," he rejoined. "Don't you know maladapts will goosestep to the smallest smack of supposed structure? Especially maladapts! I liked it better when the oatmeal was running out the sides of their mouths."

Gojiro

It only got worse when the tide pools bore evidence that Shig had packaged the Communications (price, $1 per Comm, "#1–#89—collect 'em all") for the growing mass of G-fans. Apparently Shig was not content to have Gojiro—King of Monsters, Friend to Atoms be just another outsized pseudo-saur battling in the box-office wars for the minds and spending money of hero-lusting twerps and twitchers. Not that every other so-called superguy on the shelf didn't come complete with a marginal moral spiel, perhaps a dim Arthurian hustle or some Valhalla-in-space knockoff. But the Comms, as debased as they were, spoke to more than that. Gojiro thought of his fans, the alienate pizzaeaters from Toledo, the turned-out bellies from Bangladesh, Paramus pimplefaces sucking on the poison pacifier, and began to quake. Shig's Comms, stylized hokum that they were, nevertheless held out the chimera of world critique, the intimation of *Weltanschauung*. A little bit of that, the monster knew, was more than a dangerous thing. The notion of his Cosmo-needy followers plugging into that purloined, jerryrigged philosophy chilled the behemoth no end.

"He's trying to turn me into a Jiffy Pop Godhead," the monster agonized, his brain on fire.

"Get out!" Gojiro screamed as those 90 Series supplications invaded the Quadcameral. "Leave me alone! Haunt Odin, bother Wayne Newton, see if he'll punch your ticket. Who you think I am, some cold-blood Ann Landers? Don't they got no gypsy ladies in storefronts no more?" But it was no use. Whole colosseums of yowl besieged him, the seeming babel of their pleas falling into a common rhythm, coalescing into a wrenching harmony of need. "90 Series now! 90 Series now!" they chanted.

The reptile bashed his giant head against the 'cano wall seeking relief, but there was none. Supplications surged from every corner of the globe, each one transporting the monster into the tortured mind of the supplicant. "Borneo!" he cried in torment. "They're eradicating my culture in Borneo!" Then: "Patafreakingonia! Brigands stole my goat!" And: "KwaNdebele!—ain't there no end to misery in this world?" No matter how much anguish torrented into the monster's Quadcameral, there was always room for more.

The worst of it was he had no idea what they wanted, what was being asked of him. That was the most galling aspect of Shig's 90 Series spiel—the lunacy about how Gojiro supposedly possessed the key to Salvation, if only he could remember it himself and tell everyone else.

"Shig's unbelievable," the reptile railed at Komodo. "First he makes up this bogus, cut-rate notion of the Evolloo, perverts every tenet, then he tells the little buggers out there that unless I validate the lie, make the valorizing duck come down by saying this 90 Series secret word—*which I don't know the first fucking thing about!*—the world is going to come to an end.

"Goddamn Shig! Can't he forgive? Can he really hate me that much?"

"I don't feel he hates you," Komodo said quietly. "He's not like that, not really."

"Oh, sure, he's Joe Quality of Mercy all right." It was only then that Gojiro noticed Komodo's tears.

"My own true friend," Komodo sobbed, "again my negligence and stupidity cause you pain."

"Ain't your doing."

"But it is! I have played my part! That machine, the one called Crystal Contact Radio . . ."

"Those earmuffs Shig's selling? What about them?" All at once, it hit the monster. "Wait a minute. It's them that's putting those supplications into my head, right?"

Komodo lowered his head. "Yes, I'm afraid you are right." Eyes downcast, Komodo told what happened. How one night several weeks before, almost without being aware of it, he arose from his lonely bed, walked to his lab, and made the Crystal Contacts.

Now if there's one thing you got to understand about Komodo's man-of-science scene, it's that some things come easy for him and some don't. Patterning a neon tattoo, punching up a new injector for an electro plasti-car—those were cherrytopped pieces of cake for Komodo. It was only when it came to what he called the Quadcameral communication samples that his method became erratic. That's when, after weeks of frustration, he'd suddenly find himself sleepwalking to his lab, feel a half-conscious obsession overtake him. More often than not, he'd wake up, feverish and exhausted, on the laboratory floor, his bunsens still roaring their blue-green fire. Then he'd look at what he'd made, shake his head, melt it down, obliterate it from his sight. "This has no business being invented," he'd cry. "It's not what I intended at all."

It was as if the one thing he *really* wanted to invent, he couldn't.

To hear Komodo tell it, that was the basic situation that night a few weeks before the 90 Series trouble started up. "As I was working," Komodo told Gojiro, "I had the strongest sense that I was close, that what I'd been seeking was right there, in my hands. My thoughts skipped with light assurance from point to point, factors coming to me faster than my hands could record them. But then, when I stood back to see what I'd made, I knew it was *wrong*. As wrong as all the others!"

A mordant look came over Komodo. "If only I had smashed it like the others. Destroyed it as it should have been destroyed. Then he wouldn't have—"

"Wouldn't have what?"

Komodo couldn't speak.

"Don't tell me," the monster said with soft resignation. "Shig stole it. He was in there with you, he knew what it was, and he stole it."

Komodo stood up straight, looked Gojiro in the eye, and bowed sharply from the waist. "It is to my everlasting shame, my own true friend, that I did not tell you this until now."

Gojiro felt the air go from him. "Oh, boy."

The very next morning, Komodo was up on Dead Letter Hill, erecting that spire. He made it from what was left of the Eiffel Towerette that the fifty-thousand-watt TalkRadio Beast wore as a headpiece during *Gojiro vs. the Casey Kasem Creature on a Journey to the End of the Dial*. At the top of the spire, Komodo installed an advanced-generation Crystal Contact receptor capable of attracting the 90 Series supplications, rerouting the ever-more-urgent pleas from Gojiro's besieged head.

Tired and worn from his ordeal, it took Gojiro several days to summon the will to even look up Dead Letter Hill. When he did, he couldn't believe it. The entire cliffside, once teeming with the typically grotesque Radioactive Island flora and fauna, was bald, empty. Around the spire's base, the soil was bleached a dour white. Every day the blank spot spread. It was an awesome and terrible sight.

"That 90 Series," Gojiro gasped, unable to turn his eyes away. "It's sucking life from the ground."

Komodo nodded grimly.

Suddenly, Gojiro felt a clutch at his heart. "Tell me about this 90 Series. I mean . . . I know it's Shig's doing and all, some arbitrary revenge plot. But look at all that . . . pain up there. All that *need*. Who do you think it's *on?*"

"*On?* I do not understand your meaning, my own true friend."

"You know, like, who's got to take the weight? Who's responsibility is it? Anyone's?"

Komodo rubbed his chin thoughtfully. "I think it is *on* whoever feels it."

It started under the guise of an evening constitutional, except that it was after midnight and Gojiro was not in the habit of taking such walks. "Just a little stroll, stretch the old hindquarters," he said to himself, intending to go by Corvair Bay and skip a couple of recapped tires across the turbid sea. Soon enough, however, he found himself at the base of Dead Letter Hill.

That's when he heard the whimper. A murmur, a small whine fighting to distinguish itself from the swash of nightsounds. Better check it out, he thought, and he started to climb. It didn't take long, maybe three or four upward strides until the spire came into view. By then, though, the whine had turned to a wail, a million blaring sirens. Those supplicants! Howling in the night!

The monster withered neath the din. At the outset of the 90 Series, he'd tried to convince himself that it was all a hoax, that the supplicants never really existed, even that they were being generated by Shig himself, product of some offshore ventriloquism. Now this notion seemed impossible; these screams could be not counterfeit. Building, ever building, they became a mother's cry to a lost child down an empty stairwell, an urgent shout that gains in wretched authority with every unreturned echo until it becomes the terror of every mother searching for every child everywhere, the shriek of the wildebeest staring into the hyena's bloody jaws on the Serengeti, the moan of monkeys seeing their offspring fitted for an organ grinder's costume and cup. It was insane, standing there, feeling those pulsations swirl about that spire as if it were a maypole of despair. Gojiro stepped back, aghast. Could all that have once been inside his head, all that *need,* all those unanswered prayers?

Gojiro fell to his knees and began to weep. "I'm sorry!" he screamed into the agitated air. "But it ain't me! I ain't the one you want! You got to believe that." His voice rose, became just another supplication in the seething darkness.

Then he heard that tick. It wasn't loud, but just as a gouge in vinyl cuts across two hundred years of time to truncate Beethoven's fury, it soon became all Gojiro could hear. He went forward till he found the sound. It was coming from a large plastic box attached by a heavy cable to the bottom of the spire. Inside were numerous tape decks, all turning, hundreds of cassettes. They'd run to the end, then—tick—turn around, go the other way. Each tape bore some sort of recorded message, Gojiro could tell, but it was hard to make out any single one amid the bawl. Right then, however, enough of the tapes tracked simultaneously for the reptile to hear "Yo, this is Gojiro! I am sorry, I cannot come to the Crystal Contact Receptor right now. I am still in the terrible grip of that Narcolepto Opposer. But have no fear, I will return your supplication. I will return all supplications! I will fulfill the 90 Series! Have *faith* in that, loyal zardpards!" It was the same pathetic imitation Shig had used on that movie trailer.

"Bastard!" Full of frustration and wrath, the monster cogwheeled his every appendage through the pandemonic atmosphere. In his rage, he never noticed how close he was to the spire until his great tail clashed against its base and held there.

Gojiro jerked at his posterior peninsula, but it seemed welded in place. "Shit!" Years ago, he assumed, he possessed tail-detachment capability. But now, likely still another product of his unfortunate encounter with Joseph Prometheus Brooks's nucleus-smashing brainchild, the lizard's backdragger was fixed solid. It stayed glued to the spire. A dull vibration was creeping up his dorsal ridges, vertebra by vertebra, nerve ending by nerve ending. Soon it was in his neck, an inch from his head. Physical contact with the spire had allowed those 90 Series supplications to surge back into him.

Just stay perfectly still, he told himself. Don't say a word. Stonewall. That was the key. Komodo said as much during that conversation they'd had about where the weight of the 90 Series fell. "Perhaps," Komodo said, "it is like a glance across a crowded room that is never seen and therefore cannot be returned. No love can grow from that." When the impulse came, though, it wasn't like before. There weren't thousands of supplications, no graspy horde, no inconsolable throng. There was only one, a single supplicant: Billy Snickman.

How, out of all the teratogenic syndromics, the run-of-the-mill victims of divorce, and the sad ones who keep their sadness hid, how in the world did Gojiro choose Billy Snickman? Or was it how did Billy Snickman choose *him?*

Truth was, at the outset, Gojiro figured being transported into Billy Snickman's skin wasn't all *that* bad. Not that the kid's life had been free of violin music. As Gojiro whizzed through the pathetic pages of the thirteen-year-old's luckless dossier, the usual hurt and heartache ruled. His father was a black-lunger, sixth generation in a Kentucky mine. The bosses made everyone sign a release the day before the full extent of the epidemic became known, then moved the company to Atlanta, diversified to textiles and poultry. A month later Billy's dad got shot in a bumper-pool dispute. His mom took him out west, but the car broke down in Arkansas, where they hitched along the road until the wrong pickup stopped. They found her body in a drainage gully, and Billy began his career in foster care. Sixteen families in three years. He was withdrawn, they said, a retard. Billy didn't mind the labels. He made up little poems about those sixteen families and sang them to himself. The one he liked the best was called "Forget That House." It went "Forget that house, forget that door, tomorrow it'll be another color, not there no more."

When he was twelve, Billy ran away again, but is it really running away when they don't chase you? His big break came while hiding inside the trunk of a Buick about to cross the California line. He coughed at the fruit-inspection stop and was found out. The driver smacked Billy around, accused him of trying to steal spare tires, but his clubfoot won him sympathy. The local paper ran a story; the driver, a feed and pesticide dealer looking to make a name in local politics, made a show of adopting Billy. After that he lived in a raised ranch house, eating wordless dinners under a cut-glass chandelier with his new parents, who, until him, were childless. He got his own room. It wasn't until the feed dealer, in the midst of his campaign for county clerk, broke Billy's withered arm with a hard hit in a father-son touch football game and screamed at him, "Get up and walk it off, you pansy," that Billy ran away again, this time to craggy mountains in back of Barstow where he lived like a wild wolf child, sleeping in interstate rest stops, stealing food from motel dumpsters, singing his poem-songs in the sunbaked arroyos.

It was a typical enough catalog of woe: a drag, but no Ethiopia. And after living Billy Snickman's life along with him, Gojiro readied himself for what he knew would come next. What would this Billy Snickman want? An organ transplant for the wheezing dog he found that night in Needles? What would this bottomfeeder of the genophenic pool request—a request that would never be answered, or fulfilled.

"Come in, Gojiro. Please heed this humble servant's plea," Billy Snickman rasped. "I only got one question."

Gojiro swallowed hard. This wasn't going to be so easy, after all. To deny a million supplicants, that was a breeze. You could look into a million needy pairs of eyes and they'd never lay a glove on you. Numbers like that added up to an administrative problem, nothing more. Maybe that's how those men in that B-29 approached their mission, thousands of feet of air between them and eternal pain. Gojiro wondered: suppose the only way to detonate an A-bomb was to strap it to a soldier's body on a time release, send him to the center of the town, make him walk around, eat in the greasy spoon, take a book out of the library. Then would there have ever been a Bomb?

"I need to know this one thing," Billy Snickman said. Gojiro girded himself. It was strange; usually the supplication was blurted out, a slurred invocation followed rapidly by a behest for the monster to come step on wildeyed drinking parents, or to blow dry rot from decaying bones, or to provide a life's supply of Mars bars. But this Billy Snickman was deliberate, careful.

Finally, the boy said, "I need to know—*who are you?*"

After that, it was pretty much a blur, a smear of lurching emotions. First came the schizoshock of hearing his own voice say, "I am Gojiro, Bridger of Gaps, Linker of Lines, Nexus of Beam and Bunch, Defender of the Evolloo." That was followed, almost immediately, by the panic of trying to deny that he had said it. Not that it mattered. Billy Snickman was gone. Gojiro could not raise him again.

Then came the worst of it, the way Gojiro went running to Komodo, screaming that the spire was defective and more drastic methods had to be taken to banish the 90 Series from his brain. "You got to cut it out," the monster screamed, "whatever part of the Quadcameral that takes in the supplications! Cut it out or I'm gonna die!"

"But . . . what happened?" Komodo was stunned, horrified.

"Don't matter, just do it. Please!"

Two hours later, Komodo was climbing up a ladder he'd leaned against the monster's massive noggin. Toolbox in hand, white smock over his black pajamas, miner's lantern strapped to his forehead, he began his forced entry of the parietal. It was a terrible thing, Gojiro knew, demanding his friend pierce the parietal loam and descend, boot-first, into the fourth chamber of the Quadcameral. Insisting Komodo make that obscene incision, defile what he held Sacred, knowing his friend would never deny his request—it was the king of sins! But what else could the monster do? He couldn't let Billy Snickman come back into his head, not with what that boy knew.

"Whatever happens," Komodo said before he began the surgery, "might not be reversible." One false move, he pointed out, one mistaken slice with his garden shears, and they might be saying good-bye to each other for all times.

"Chance we got to take," the lizard shot back. "Cut it out!"

Then Komodo was inside Gojiro's brain, and there was the sound of something popping, a wire being cut. This was followed by a soft sob, and the track of a single tear from Komodo's eye, falling through that Quadcameral, from the tortured realm where the 90 Series had been to the highlands of the Neo-Cort, down through the muddy flats of his limbics, tumbling like a solitary silver pearl of dew from leaf to leaf until it was lost among the dense mists of so long ago.

These were the recollections Gojiro carried with him as he and Komodo reached the edge of the Cloudcover and looked for the exit that would take them through to another world. Komodo never asked why Gojiro changed his mind concerning Sheila Brooks's letter, nor did he inquire further about the strange supplication scrawled at the bottom of it. For that the monster felt relief. How could he explain? Was there any explanation? Why *did* he answer Billy Snickman's question as he did? How had that reply wound up in Sheila Brooks's maniacal invitation for them to make *Gojiro vs. Joseph Prometheus Brooks in the Valley of Decision?* The monster didn't know, didn't want to know, but there was no denying it. This was one supplication that had to be answered.

"Steady as we go, keep starboard-bound," Komodo, the able mariner, said, gentle in the monster's ear.

It would be no easy trick, escaping the Cloudcover, that grayish Astrodome that encased their world like a tarnished platter surrounds a cooked goose. It was nothing solid, no jut of geology with weight and properties. Instead, it was an angry wall of heat, a sheer blare, a space-age Styx. So much had come through that fevered curtain, but nothing had ever gotten out.

The warp. Komodo kept talking about the warp. It was there, he said without apparent sentiment, he'd seen it all those years ago, the only other time they'd been out this far, the only other time they'd sought to escape their land. Gojiro closed his eyes. He had no desire to see that scene of still another of his crimes, where those waters once raged, the spot where the swirling death-pool dragged Komodo's beloved down.

"There!" Komodo screamed, gesturing left toward that growling tunnel. "Go there!"

The monster clenched his jaw, sprang ahead. "Hang on! We're going through!"

Then there was no horizontal, no vertical; all plain geometry was out the window. The churn shook them like fries in overheated oil. Then the sea went flat, an eerie calm, only to shatter out again, a spew of watery shards.

"It's like trying to crawl out of a drain!"

"I'm slipping," Komodo cried, the tiller rope bucking madly in his bleeding hands. He tried to dig his heels into Gojiro's drenched leathers, but they were too slick.

"Hold on," Gojiro called, craning his neck to snatch his friend up safely in his mouth.

Again the ocean exploded. "We're going over!"

Over and over they tumbled, a great log cascading down the most slicked of shoots. And when they stopped, they were right side up on the most tranquil of seas.

PART

TWO

THE HERMIT
PANDORA

Komodo traveled as Professor Takamoto, a visiting lecturer from the Herpetoholographic Institute of New Chiba-chrome City. Gojiro, shot up with a special shrinkage potion that contracted him to a mere nine inches, stayed inside Komodo's carry-on bag, posing as a specimen. In this fashion, they made their way across the Pacific, hopscotching from a Caroline to a Gilbert to a Hebride. Before long they were circling the smogsky over LAX.

"Who can tell," Komodo sighed as he peered through the plasticine window down to the El Segundo tract houses below, "what this world will hold for us, my own true friend?" Gojiro didn't know, couldn't say. He couldn't say anything. Over Hawaii, he'd devoured Komodo's in-flight chicken cordon bleu, gotten sick, and been swimming in his own juices ever since.

Some hairiness ensued at the airport. Waiting in the customs line, forcing near face-breaking smiles to each passerby, Komodo noticed a sign referring to animal quarantine.

"What's that mean?" Gojiro asked with alarm as he peeked from the bag. "They gonna stick me in a pound?"

Unsure of the answer to his friend's question, Komodo moved quickly. He broke off a section of an emergency shrink pill and crammed it into Gojiro's mouth. Then, with the monster further diminished to less than an inch, Komodo stuck him on the front of his shirt. The customs inspector, clearly no expert when it came to reptilia, knew nothing of the morphologic dissimilarities between the alligator and monitor types and waved Komodo through as if he were just another Izod wearer.

A moment later, approaching the rent-a-car desks, there was more trouble. Due to complications Komodo attributed to rapid altitude shifts, the shrink drug became unstable. Without warning, Gojiro began to blurt in every direction. His head ballooned, his back leg grew seven feet. That linoleum floor was cold; he felt the blood of his ancestors down there. His tail surged outward, wrapping around Komodo's neck. Before the necessary corrections could be made, three Hare Krishnas and a bag hustler fled the main concourse in terror.

Shaken, Komodo ran out the door and hailed a taxi. It was just as well. Renting a car would have probably been a bad idea. Sure, Komodo had practiced saying, "Oh, are you not the trying-harder company who only carries the fine family of Ford cars?" But really, aside from an occasional spin in one of the three-wheeled plasti jobs that served as all-terrain vehicles on Radioactive Island, Komodo had never driven a car. He had no clue as to California geography either.

Taking a taxi avoided those potential problems. But when the driver, a young woman, turned and asked, "Where to?" in a deep, noir-affected voice, Komodo froze. It was the woman's appearance that did it, the way her long, knotty white hair seemed to lunge from beneath her cap, the ghostly pallor on her face, and the tilt of the black sunglasses she wore shoved tight against her eyes.

"Ms. Brooks?" Komodo gasped. Could it be that Sheila Brooks had anticipated their arrival and, for reasons known only to herself, affected this cabdriving persona? "It is so thoughtful of you to greet us at the airport. We never expected it."

The cabdriver giggled. "Pretty good, huh?" she said.

"Pardon?"

"My facsimilation." As it turned out, the woman was only dressed up like Sheila Brooks. She was "a Brooksian" she explained as she edged the yellow cab onto the teeming freeway. "You know, like, we're into Sheila. We try to vision with her Vision, dream the Sad Tomorrow, see the End. It's very constructive. Sheila Brooks has changed my life. I never miss an Eschat-out."

"Excuse me?"

"Eschatological Outlet Session. Jim—Jim Dust-to-Dust—he's my Annihilation Terminal, you know, sort of our group leader, a really together guy. He says it's really important to unburden your Apock Vision. You know, we midwife each other's End Day intimations, enfold them to our own. It's nothing heavy. We just get into our Sheilaness, know what I mean?"

Komodo nodded. Words were impossible for him right then.

"Good. I didn't want you to think I was a Satanist or something, like my parents do. They threw me out of the house when I got into Sheila. They don't know anything. Sheila's not about Evil, she's about getting rid of your Evil." The woman, who couldn't have been more then twenty, turned to look at Komodo. "You into Sheila?"

"Into her?" Komodo pulled at his suddenly sweaty collar. "I don't know. I hope to see her, my friend and I. We hoped she might be able to help us."

"Wow! You really sound into her. Maybe you could come to one of our meetings. We eschat at the Dull Medulla—you know, that club downtown. You'd dig it, I'm sure."

Gojiro couldn't believe it. So this was what "fans" were like! No wonder any number of zardpards and 'tile-o-files were more than happy to embrace whatever chicanery Shig spewed out. Apocalypse Anonymous, Armageddon on the pyramid scheme. Sapiens would believe anything!

The monster felt terrible for Komodo; this conversation wasn't doing him any good. The reptile had never seen his friend so nervous. It had been building throughout the journey. Just the day before, waiting to change planes in who-knew-where, the two friends found themselves staring at a young well-groomed couple. With them was a young girl wearing a blue frilly dress. The parents were holding hands, beaming at their daughter. It wasn't anything you'd really notice, just natural, in the way of things. The woman and the man kissed lightly, but within that slightest touch was a passion that spoke of much more. The man got up, lifted the daughter in his arms, hugged her. Then he took his briefcase and went off. "Tomorrow night!" he shouted over his shoulder, waving.

Something that happens a million times a day in a million airports, right? But immediately Gojiro felt Komodo's gyros scramble. Uneasy on his feet, he had to lean against a vending machine, his breath coming hard, in spurts. It killed Gojiro to see his friend suffer like that. So many times before, not completely kidding, he'd downrated the extent to which the Heater worked its surreal elasticity upon Komodo's person. "Compared to me, what's your beef?" the monster mocked. "You ain't a hundred times your supposed size, you ain't got feet for days. Ain't like anyone can tell what you are by *just looking*. You open a sushi bar in Shreveport and what's the worst—they make fun of how you say your *r*'s?"

Now Gojiro regretted those not-so-gentle jokes. This was Komodo's first time amongst his erstwhile Bunch since those dim-perceived days on Okinawa.

And it was obvious, regardless of his outward appearance, that he wasn't one of them and never would be again. It was one thing to be Bunchless on Radioactive Island; that was a world of freaks. But here—everywhere Komodo turned was a reminder of all he'd lost, what he'd never regain. It wasn't fair! Why shouldn't Komodo have been that man with the wife and the daughter, that man who was about to board an airplane, be hurled into the void of space, yet was so assured of his place he could turn and shout, "Tomorrow night!"

"This is it—235047 Neptune View Lane," the cabdriver said, apparently ignorant of the fact that she was stopping in front of her idol's home.

Komodo gave her a twenty-dollar bill and, remembering his lines, said, "Keep the change."

"Thanks!" she said, handing Komodo the address of the Dull Medulla, telling him to come by. "You look like you have some great nightmares." Then, somewhat quizzically, she asked, "You don't wear pajamas all the time, do you?"

"You sure this is the right place?" Gojiro said, poking his head from Komodo's satchel. "You'd figure big Tinseltown types would have a doorman with a bearskin hat. This joint looks abandoned."

It was true. Set alone atop a hill overlooking the ocean, the house that corresponded to the address Sheila Brooks gave in her letter appeared to be ripe for the gentry's rape. All along the barely visible sidewalk were crumpled cigarette packs and pieces of shattered glass. The tall cement wall was cracked in spots by creepers, overgrown with palm fronds. The iron gate hadn't been painted in years and was nearly rusted away in some places. The only things that looked new were the half-dozen or so shiny locks drilled into the gate.

Locating a small squawk box, Komodo pushed a cracked plastic button. An ear-splitting gnash emitted. "Naaaaaaa."

"What's this thing's problem?" Gojiro sneered. He could feel himself getting into a pretty bad mood.

Komodo rang again, and this time a shriekish message came out. "Voice-activated! Intone now."

"Excuse me," Komodo said into the box. "I am Yukio Komodo. I wish to please speak with Ms. Sheila Brooks."

There was no answer.

Louder this time: "Please, I am Yukio Komodo of Radioactive Island, to see Ms. Brooks." With that the locks turned in their tumblers and the gate slid open with an Inner Sanctum creak.

"Geez," Gojiro said as they stepped into the courtyard. For sure, no Beverly Hills landscaper was getting any richer off this spread. It looked like someone had thrown a wild party there in 1962 and forgotten to clean up. Off to one side of the two-acre enclosure was what looked to be a half-finished swimming pool. Now, though, it was no more than a mosquito breeding ditch with a caterpillar tractor stuck in the bottom. A weatherbeaten, blindfolded clothes-store mannequin slouched behind the tractor's controls. In the center of the yard was a cracked and mottled statue of Saint Sebastian, but instead of arrows, rusted golf clubs were stuck into it. The lawn was solid kudzu.

So this was the Turret House, so called because of the roundish protuberances at its two seaward corners. The domicile loomed large in the Brooks-Zeber legend. When Bobby Zeber first moved in, twenty years before, it was a boardinghouse. Just out of Brooklyn, a hardnosed city kid who wanted to be a movie director, Zeber paid seventy-five dollars a month for the room at the top of the left turret. It was in that room that Sheila Brooks was said to have had the first of the End of the World nightmares Zeber translated into films, creating the vast Brooks-Zeber empire. That's where the couple stayed—along with the other tenants, two old cat-ladies and a country singer—long after *Tidal Wave* was breaking all box-office records. It was good, living with "real people," Bobby Zeber was quoted as saying. But soon the old ladies were dead, and the country singer crossed over. Bobby Zeber bought the place and erected the giant fence, leading to much speculation as to the exact variety of beatnik Xanadu happening behind those walls. There were reports of hivelike installations of isolation tanks that doubled as bomb shelters, one unit for every fifty square feet. Looking at the joint now, though, none of that seemed feasible. It was just too beat.

The house's heavy wooden door was ajar; after getting no response to his knocks, Komodo leaned in. The foyer was ripe with a thick scent of mildew and animal hair. "Ms. Brooks?" Komodo called out timidly, but there was only the sound of the ocean. A quick scan of the hallway, which opened into a large dark room that had most likely been the parlor of the boardinghouse, revealed no sign of life. Three large Spanish Inquisition–style banquet tables—seating for at least fifty—dominated the gloomy room, although it was difficult to imagine that anyone had ever eaten there. On the walls were stray op-art paintings and dozens of acid-rock posters stuck up with peeling Scotch tape. High stacks of yellowing newspapers and piles of greasy motorcycle parts were scattered everywhere.

"Ms. Brooks?" Komodo called out again, a little louder. The wood floor, which was partially covered with somber, thick-piled Oriental rugs, heaved with every step. A dim shaft of light coming from a small stained-glass window was the only illumination. "I thought this was California, not Transylvania," Gojiro said, peeking from Komodo's bag. Right then, two cats sprang from a breakfront and ran yowling in opposite directions.

"That tears it," Gojiro shouted, lurching toward the door, nearly pulling the case from Komodo's hand. "Let's book!"

"Please! You know what we must do," Komodo whispered, trying to be the brave one.

That was when they heard a groan from the next room. "I need an eight-letter word for 'ersatz curd enzyme,'" came a pinched, wheezing voice.

Komodo went toward the voice. He turned a corner and was immediately blinded by a blast of light. When his irises adjusted he saw a tall, bony woman. She was standing in front of a large picture window, holding a folded newspaper. The glare streaming in the window blurred her outer edges.

"I'm close. It'll fall into place—with just this one word."

"Ms. Brooks?" Komodo said tentatively.

"Got it! Velveeta! They ask that one a lot," the figure said. A moment passed. Then the woman slowly began to turn around to face Komodo and Gojiro. It seemed to take an eternity. Neither of the two friends knew what to expect. The few recent photos of Sheila Brooks they'd seen in magazines or on the Dish had been taken at extreme long range, between the pickets of fences or across crowded streets, and with that large floppy hat she always wore, not much could be made out. But it was her all right. The shock of recognition nearly blew Gojiro out the back side of Komodo's bag. Sheila Brooks: that same face in the window of the seaplane in the Dream of the Black Spot, the little girl with the fear on her face.

Gojiro saw what twenty-five years of fear does to a face. It was all red, white, and black. The red was a haphazard streak of ruby lipstick applied, roughly, to the outline of her wide mouth. The white was her hair and skin—her cheeks seemingly colorless and the texture of hospital tile, a sheen of frostlike desolation down to the jutting point of her chin. And the black. The black was those glasses, wraparounds and more: the glacial slick of the lenses surrounded by suctioning rubber sidepanels extending from the upper reaches of her invisible eyebrows well down to the bridge of her prominent nose.

Sheila Brooks stood there without speaking. She wore a fuzzy pink bathrobe held closed by a patent-leather belt. With her eyes tucked up behind those gruesome glasses, it was impossible to tell what she was looking at.

"Excuse me, Ms. Brooks," Komodo ventured, "my name is Yukio Komodo . . . of Radioactive Island . . . I've come . . ."

Sheila Brooks did not answer. A long, pointed tooth slipped into view and bit into the smear of her lower lip. Then, pivoting on the heel of a blowsy bedroom slipper, she turned to face the large window once more.

"Some greeting!" Gojiro said with disgust. "No manners. None at all."

"Perhaps she did not see us," Komodo offered.

"Then what the hell was she looking at?"

Komodo moved forward. "I will speak to her."

Quicker than he wanted, he was standing beside Sheila Brooks. Outside was the ocean's great expanse, nothing else. How long they stood there, side by side, mute, framed in that latticed window, peering at the boundless sea, was hard to gauge. It seemed like forever.

Sheila Brooks's voice broke the spell. There was an urgency in it. "Why do they do it? What's in it for them? Why do they keep coming back for more?"

"Pardon?"

"The waves."

Gojiro slapped his forehead. Had they come all that way for this? Komodo was in trouble, the reptile could tell. Any moment, it seemed, he would pass out, crash through the window, and fall to the surf below. Gojiro stiffened his leg and kicked at his friend through the bag. "Wake up!" he hissed. "Find out what she knows and let's blow this pop stand."

That got Komodo going. He took the lime green stationery from the pocket of his black pajamas. "We have come in response to your letter."

Sheila Brooks craned her long neck defensively. "Letter? I don't know about any letter."

"But Ms. Brooks. It came to us at our home."

Sheila thrust her arms down on either side of her body, clenching her elongated fingers into bloodless fists. "Must be some other Sheila Brooks. There're hundreds of them. Look in the phone book. I'm not lying."

Komodo began to sweat. Again he presented the envelope. "But it has your signature, your address."

Sheila Brooks's lower lip began to quiver. "Couldn't have been me. I haven't written a letter in years. Not since boarding school. I'm a terrible correspondent. No one's ever gotten a letter from me. Ask anyone."

"Please, Ms. Brooks. You must listen. We have come across the ocean, traveled many days—"

"I can't help that!" Sheila Brooks's voice was beginning to crack now. "You know, you just can't walk in here and start talking to me. You've got to make an appointment. You've got to wait six weeks in the outer office, another three in the inner office. Even then I'll be too ill to talk to you. I'm a sick woman."

"But Ms. Brooks, that is part of why we have come. To help you."

"Help me?" This came out as a squawk.

"Yes . . . in your letter. You said it was a matter of life and death. This is a great coincidence, since, for my friend and I, this situation is likewise a concern of life and death."

"Life? Death?"

"Yes. I must talk to you about your father."

"Life? Death? . . . *My father!*"

Komodo reached to touch Sheila Brooks for the first time, brushing his hands lightly by her shoulder. "Yes," he said, beginning to unfold the letter, "it says you wish us to come to this place so that we might make a film entitled *Gojiro vs. Joseph Prometheus Brooks in the Valley of Decision.*"

"*Gojiro vs. Joseph Pro . . .*" Her mouth dropped open, hung there a moment.

But then, staring down at the oversized watch on her bony wrist, she pulled away. "Can't you see what you're doing to me? You're throwing off my entire schedule. I've been looking at these waves for thirty-four minutes. Those four extra minutes could be fatal! I've got to stop. It's my therapy! You just can't barge into someone's house and interrupt her therapy."

Sheila Brooks turned from the picture window, pitched her gaunt body across the room toward a trio of television sets. A hard plastic cowl was affixed to each set. Peering into those formfitted funnels effectively blocked out all other stimuli except what was on the screen. Sheila shoved her head into one of them.

"Ms. Brooks, please."

"Not now!" Sheila screamed from inside the gray hood. The sound of a game show Gojiro recognized as "Family Feud" droned in the background. "I'm in therapy! You can't even conceive of how expensive treatment like this is. A team of doctors at UCLA work around the clock to keep me in psychic alignment. One half-hour of vacant landscape alternated with one half-hour of saturated reality. I can't deviate! One more second of looking at those waves and who knows what might have happened. I told you before: I'm a very sick woman. You can't conceive how sick. Now, please, go away!"

"But Ms. Brooks, you must understand what is at stake."

But she was gone now. She would not answer.

"I have not come alone!" A zipper opened above Gojiro's head. Sunlight flooded over him. He felt Komodo's hand reach down, grasping for him.

"What's the big idea?" the monster yowled. Komodo was filling a syringe with the shrink antidote; he planned a demonstration, right then and there. "You're crazy!"

Then, from the other side of the house, came the sound of a door opening. "Hey, Sheil," came a voice. "The gate was open, you open the gate?"

Immediately Komodo threw Gojiro and the needle back into the bag, out of sight.

"That's the second time this week! Voice-activated, my eye! The other day a chipmunk opened it. I didn't even know they had larynxes."

It was a rueful, authoritative voice, nothing less than one might expect from Bobby Zeber. After all, wasn't Zeber supposed to be the diabolical Brooklyn Svengali, bad hat of the Hermit Pandora story? The way the tabloids had it, he kept Sheila locked in a closet with a Betamax strapped to her head. "Terror's own whipcrack," they called him, "a slaver in a town of slavers who happened to luck into the best slave."

Gojiro, casual fan, was familiar with this characterization, but did not necessarily agree with it. There was that time, before all the public appearances stopped, when Zeber and Sheila were interviewed on the Dish. Sheila couldn't speak, not a word. Zeber was chatting like mad, covering for her, distracting everyone with his street-hewn good looks. But then came the question: "Could you tell us, Sheila, what Bobby really does for you." Sheila blanched and said, "Well, he keeps me . . . safe. Gives me the safe place." That got to Gojiro. Basketcases like Sheila Brooks needed safe places, he knew, someone to keep them safe. From then on, whenever he watched *Tidal Wave* and saw that little-girl version of Sheila Brooks skating blithely beneath that melting wall of ice, Gojiro imagined Bobby Zeber was there too, holding an umbrella over her head, warding off the falling drops so she'd never know what deluge hit her.

However, right then, as he came from the dark hall into that sunbursted room, Bobby Zeber didn't fit the fierce protector image, not at all. Throwing his leather case onto a chair with a grunt, there was a weariness about him, a smack of defeat. You could see it in his eyes. They looked dead, like the windows of buildings in bad neighborhoods seen from passing trains, dark holes with the glass crashed out.

"I don't know about that circus script," Zeber was saying. "You know the antigravity scene? That jerk Mazwell gives each Bazami brother a soliloquy to say as they fall. It must be a half-hour from when the Flying Rhombus collapses until they hit the floor. It's going to be a problem . . ."

Zeber stopped when he saw Komodo. "Who are you?"

Sheila, keeping her head pushed deep within the television container, shouted, "I thought he was you."

Suddenly pantherlike, full of barbed tension, Zeber planted himself between his wife and the intruder.

Komodo bowed sharply at the waist. "May I introduce myself?"

"That's a start." Zeber's voice was hard, edgy.

Komodo bowed again. "I am Yukio Komodo of Radioactive Island. Mr. Zeber . . . I cannot express how unworthy I am to have such magnificent artists as your wife and yourself invite me to this great country to potentially collaborate on a film. It is an honor that far exceeds my meager talent."

Zeber did half a double take. "I come in late or something? Sheila, is there some reason I don't know what this guy is talking about?"

Komodo began to speak, but Sheila Brooks cut him off. "I wrote him a letter!"

For the moment it was as if Komodo was not in the room. Bobby looked at Sheila with an even gaze. "What kind of letter? What did you write in this letter?"

Sheila fell into a chair, her long legs flying out from beneath her. "I don't know!" she wailed.

Bobby's voice grew very quiet. "What do you mean you don't know?"

"I don't know . . . I don't know if I remember."

Bobby turned to Komodo. "Pardon me, Mr . . ."

Another sharp bow. "Komodo!"

"Mr. Komodo, would you mind excusing Ms. Brooks and myself for a moment."

"Certainly." Komodo bowed again, a couple of times.

However, as he turned to go, Sheila Brooks screamed out, "Show him the letter! Show it to him!"

For a moment Komodo did not know what to do. Bobby Zeber seemed quite intent on getting him out of the room. But, following Sheila's instructions, he produced the letter. Unfortunately, he forgot he'd resealed it in that special Cloudcover-proof sleeve. It was a little something Komodo churned up from a tideload of vinyl slipcovers. Zeber took one tug at the envelope and it shot out of his hands, careening around the room with the zest of a Spalding Hi-bounce.

"Wha?"

It wasn't until it had knocked an Oscar from the dusty mantelpiece that Komodo was able to snare the ricocheting letter from the air. "Oh! I am so sorry," he said softly, mortified. "I am an amateur inventor. This covering is one of my less successful efforts."

"Sure thing," Zeber said. Gingerly taking hold of the letter once more, he began to read it. He seemed to take a few passes before he got the gist. He alternately blinked and looked up at Sheila, who was half turned away, wringing her white hands.

"*Gojiro vs. Joseph Prometheus Brooks in the Valley of Decision* . . . oh, sweetheart," Zeber said mournfully. Sheila was crying real bad now. "Baby . . ." He went over, put his arms around her. The two of them stayed like that a while, Sheila crying, Bobby soothing her. Gojiro poked his head out of Komodo's case and studied the scene, wondering about the circle Zeber's arms made around his wife. Was that the circumference of the safe place? What went on in that zone? Did gravity reign, or did you just float?

Komodo had no etiquettal angle on the situation. His head was spinning. He was about to go when Bobby Zeber left Sheila's side, extended his hand.

"Mr. Komodo, I'm sorry I didn't offer you a more congenial welcome. Of course I am familiar with your work. It is certainly . . . interesting, in its field."

That was good for another half-dozen manic bows from Komodo. He was getting out of hand with those bows. Every time Komodo flung himself forward, Gojiro got thrown around inside that sack; by this point he was feeling pretty sore.

Bobby Zeber smiled but didn't take his eyes off Sheila. "As you can see, Mr. Komodo, this isn't the best time to talk. I didn't see any car outside—can I call one for you? Where are you staying?"

"We are . . . not staying anywhere. We just arrived."

An odd half-smile came over Zeber's face. "You just got off the plane and came right over here? Don't you have any luggage?"

Komodo blushed and held up his bag. "Only this."

"You travel light, Mr. Komodo. Well, my office can make a hotel reservation for you."

"That is most kind of you, Mr. Zeber . . ." Komodo managed. He didn't know what else to say.

Komodo was about to leave when, from across the room, Sheila wailed, "He says he can't wait. He says he's got to know now. He says he didn't come alone."

Again Bobby Zeber was puzzled. "Didn't come alone?"

That was when Shig came through the door.

HOME AWAY
FROM HOME

That Shig, he was nothing if not a take-charge guy. A smoothstepping razor in his dress-white linens, moving with the eerie grace of Nureyev's own android, he bowed sharply to a blubbering Sheila Brooks and nodded to a uncomprehending Bobby Zeber. Then, without apology, he hustled Komodo and Gojiro out the door, through the Turret House's still-squawking front gate.

"This way, please," Shig said, placing a chauffeur's hat over his impeccable flattop as he held open the rear door of a stretch limousine. Then he got into the driver's seat and pushed a button that rolled up a soundproof partition between himself and his two passengers.

Gojiro scrambled out of Komodo's bag. Shig's servant act always got to him. "He makes out like he's just some lackey playing a salaam game, and all the while he's puppet-stringing us along. Dammit!" The shrunken monster threw himself at the limousine partition. But the glass had obviously been swabbed with Komodo's reinforced Gardol shield window cleaner, and the reptile, given his reduced size and strength, could do nothing but bounce and bruise.

Forty minutes of listless freeway watching later, Shig turned off into a canyon and proceeded over a succession of yucca-choked dirt roads. "Where's he taking us?" Gojiro whined. "We come a million miles, for what? To have *him* lead us around by the nose?" Moments later, they passed under an overgrown archway and stopped. Shig jumped out, dutifully trotting around to swing open the back door. "They have been waiting."

Komodo and Gojiro, now stabilized at six feet and able to bipedal, tumbled out of the car and into the scratchy late-afternoon sunshine. "Who? Who's been waiting?" They looked around and saw no one. Off to the right was a large stand of date palms and behind that a huge, looming house. The air was still, hot.

A cockatoo's shriek cut through the quiet. Then a trumpet's clarion: "Bap-bap-bap-ba-da-bap-ba!"

The monster's ears pricked up. He never mistook a James Jamerson bass line. A familiar voice rang out, "Calling out around the world, are you ready for a brand new beat?" The sound was all around, deafening. "Cause summer's here and the time is right for dancing in the street!"

The first egghead came out from behind a huge topiary hedge that looked to have once been cut in the general shape of a giraffe, but that now was grown into an indistinct horticultural blotch. "They're dancing in Chicago, down in New Orleans." Crudely fashioned from papier-mâché, magic-markered horn-rims ringing its big button eyes and a pleated white skirt wound around the middle, the egg was obviously supposed to resemble Billie Jean King, the tennis player. Knotty legs covered with pink spandex, the egg held its racquet like a guitar, strumming across the catgut crosshatching. "Can't forget the Motor City."

Other eggs emerged from the bushes, arrayed in haphazard formation. They carried a large replica of the American flag constructed, like an ornate car-wash sign, from small metallic streamers. There was Al Capone, Mickey Mantle, Dolly Parton, Abraham Lincoln. Together they no-lip-synced, "Every guy grab a girl! All we need is music! Sweet music!" The Davy Crockett egg had a live raccoon on top of it.

"Oh, shit! I don't believe it!" Gojiro shouted. "How'd *they* get here?"

It was the Atoms, all right, at least three dozen of them. Any doubt was removed when the inevitable squabble broke out, Dick Clark ramheading John Travolta, Billie Jean burying her racquet deep into Al Capone's dome.

"They created these crafts for you during our journey across the sea," Shig said tautly, "to welcome you to our new home."

"New home? What's he talking about, new home?"

Before Komodo could answer, the Atoms pecked through their eggshell heads and shouted, "Welcome to our new home, Mr. Komodo and Gojiro!" Then they stormed forward, hurling their ruined bodies at Gojiro, knocking him to the yellowed lawn, licking and slobbering all the while.

"Welcome to our new American home," they kept screaming, over and over.

Gojiro

Home. Now there's a concept that's taken a touch of abuse in my little life and times, Gojiro thought. No more than right then. The American home Shig had picked out for them was a ten-acre parcel of nonstop disaffection. Once nothing but an oasisless desert, the land had been settled by some lowrent migrants, but those predustbowlers were chased out in the early teens by the agents of a big producer who wanted to build a castle for a particular starlet he couldn't get off his mind. What resulted was the kind of joint God might have thrown together if he had enough bread and bad taste. Five or six dozen rooms, the style was mostly Spanish, with gables and buttresses slapped on here and there. Maybe the Alhambra got more inlays, maybe not. Too bad the starlet became a nun and moved back to Texas, leaving the producer to spend the rest of his life in the place, by himself, crying. The press, unendingly maudlin, dubbed the place "The Taj Mahal of Tragic Heartbreak," Traj Taj for short.

After the producer died in the late 1950s, the place fell into disuse. Sure there was that band of hippie squatters who ate the kidneys of the young caretaker couple, and that rock band that painted the mansion purple, but they only used the place for parties, so you can't count them. In fact, including the two failed cults and the short-lived seminars run by insurance companies, it could be said the Traj Taj had never maintained a meaningful population.

Now this was to be their crib. Shig had already done some remodeling, ripping down the highest minaret and replacing it with a stone chimney that continually belched smoke rings, three at a time, concentric. It wasn't the first time Gojiro had looked at those three rings and seen nothing more than the filigree of a most fanciful jail cell.

Still, it was almost worth it all to lay eyes on Ebi again. It was the worst part of sneaking off Radioactive Island, not being able to say good-bye to Ebi. How horrible it had been for the monster, especially as he swam by that fateful spot just inside the Cloudcover, to think of Ebi asleep in that delirious dormitory right beside those mutantous children.

It wasn't that Ebi wasn't an Atom. She was—Komodo's tests proved that. "Her cellular breakdown is accelerating. She can't have long," Komodo said the very night they left. "We . . . may not see her again." But that's how it is for Atoms, they got an hourglass sewn inside them, and it don't take Dr. Kildare's abacus to chart how their meter be running down, running down.

There was a time when Komodo thought he could do something for Ebi.

For all the Atoms. He imagined his destiny might entail somehow curing these orphans of the Heater's storm, offering a modicum of medical shelter. Every time another of the ravaged children washed through the Cloudcover, clinging to whatever flotjet, Komodo would dig deeper into his Nightingale bag searching for a new remedy. He made studies, charted the torque of their every twitch, plotted the way the malignancies spread across their faces like coffee stains. Tubes went in, tubes came out, but it was no use, the pestilence stayed. Try as he might, Komodo couldn't erase the condemning print of the wrong finger on the wrong button from those Atoms. Their Mendels were too messed, the bisects of their half-lives too frenzied.

That was when he started wearing those black pajamas all the time. It is not a commonly known fact, but Komodo was not always such a dour dresser. Time was he'd snatch all varieties of natty sartorials from the cresting surf off Corvair Bay Beach. Plaid sports coats, checked golf slacks, vented guayabers, jaunty Bavarian hats with feathers in the brim, the occasional blue blazer, all these were part of Komodo's wardrobe. It was only after the Atoms began to appear that he went to the black pajamas. There was always one of them to mourn.

It killed the reptile to see Komodo's disappointment, the way every time an Atom died, he'd come loose from his pacific nature and smash up his beakers and bunsens. "I cannot save them! I am useless," he'd sob, hiding his face in shame. Sometimes it seemed to Gojiro that the only justification for the Atoms' existence was that Komodo might find a way to heal them, and, in this way, heal himself. It seemed unfair, the way those hapless children remained remote from all help, impervious to any savior's redemption.

Ebi, however, was a different story. Gojiro couldn't contain his delight at seeing her there, digging in the underbrush behind the Traj Taj. How beautiful she was!—her skin the color of groundnuts, her hair an ebony sheen, her marvelous whitetoothed smile. So many times Gojiro looked at her and found it impossible to believe she was like the others. But she'd start rubbing those luminous eyes, which sometimes couldn't see, pulling at the webs between her fingers, and he'd know: Ebi was an Atom, same as if she'd come in on the tide walleyed from Megaton Night, India, or twistspined from Luminescent Creek, Arkansas.

When Komodo saw Ebi, he wanted to run to her, to hoist her in his arms. But he suppressed the urge. He didn't pick Ebi up like he wanted to, he didn't hold her close to him. Gojiro had to look away. His friend's restraint was heartmangling. But Komodo could never break an oath. When he swore, so long ago, that Ebi would be treated like any other child affected with this terror, he had meant it. He stuck to it.

"Mr. Komodo," Ebi said, looking up from her digging. Her face was open, full of wonder. However that acid burned the blackholes of the Heater's honeycomb through her marrows, she never let on.

"Come see this," she exclaimed with that soft eureka in her voice that Gojiro always found so enchanting. She was holding up a sausage-shaped six-foot-long segment of velveteen strangler vine. The tubular trash was all over Radioactive Island. It grew so quickly that Gojiro would wake up with it lashing down his entire lower body. He'd have to bite through the thick strands to free himself, no picnic since those vines were sourced from fireproof drapes and the crap tasted worse than a month's diet of styrofoam, not to mention the wiggly stringslugs it left between your teeth that had to be beaten to death with sticks.

"Why, it's a specimen of *Velvetinus vinus* number seventeen," Komodo said, with no small interest.

"Yes," Ebi said, excited yet thoughtful. "I found this growing here."

"Here?" Komodo rubbed his chin. "Could that be possible?"

They stood there for a moment, just the two of them, investigating her find. For the first time since arriving in America, Komodo seemed himself. Just being with Ebi, having a problem to decipher, reconvened his equilibrium. Back on Radioactive Island, doing botanicals with Ebi was among his greatest pleasures. In the beginning, nature trail walks, weeklong forages into the jungles past Vinyl Aire and Melanoma meadows, had been open to all Atoms. However, the ones who did show up either quickly lost interest or went face-first into the grinding underbrush (*Treadmillus turftoeus,* short-blade type). Only Ebi persisted. Komodo was so proud when she took over as chief taxonomer and set about identifying the varying components of the Island's burgeoning ecosphere. In a few short years, she'd already specified and named fifteen thousand brandnew species of Insta-Envir, which is what Radioactive Island flora and fauna in its recombinant postflotjet stage is called, if you don't know.

That was Ebi: head of herbages, appellator of birds and beasts, as morally diligent a scientist as the discipline allowed. One incident in particular stands out. Not long after designating her three-thousandth species, Ebi decided she couldn't keep all the classifications and categorizations under her pillow anymore. It got too lumpy. She needed a more orderly record-keeping system.

With Komodo's help, she rigged up small monitors and placed them in close proximity to representative examples of wildgrowing flora and fauna. Each screen featured a crawl detailing the particular species' flotjet antecedents and various integrative adaptations since it first appeared on Radioactive Island. However, it wasn't too long before the monitors began to be vandalized.

"Down with nametags! Radioactive Island isn't an aluminum-siding convention!" said the graffiti scrawled across the screens. It was a big scandal. A few days later, however, the screens were removed by Ebi herself. She said she understood the vandal's objection, that the assigning of potentially demeaning labels was "antithetical" to the credo of Radioactive Island. "Here, everything is equal, we are all part of an interlocking system that in time will come to recognize its collective personality. It is not right for anyone to have to carry ID if they don't want to."

She said she would continue to keep taxonomic records privately, for posterity. Komodo, inwardly beaming, congratulated Ebi on her statement, remarking that ethical pursuits and the scientist's zeal are often difficult to reconcile.

Still, it was a puzzler how growth considered native only to Radioactive Island was busting out of the trucked-in Traj Taj topsoil, no more than fifteen miles from the starstrewn pavements of Hollywood Boulevard. It wasn't only the velveteen vines, either. A quick perusal of the coconut palms revealed a startling transmutation. None of the lowslung coconuts retained their smooth green exteriors. Each was covered with thick bark, into which was carved a face. They might as well have been growing in the trees ringing Little Albert Swamp, where the souvenir coconuts gaped down from their treetop perches with mocking mother-of-pearl eyes and sneering mouths full of shark's teeth. In fact, the entire grounds of that old producer's house were beginning to take on the pungent Kodachrome hues associated with the world within the Cloudcover.

"Extraordinary," Komodo said.

"Terrific!" Ebi enthused, scurrying about with her camera, documenting the phenomenon. She got a great time-lapse shot of a metal-edged spun flower *(Tulipus fiberglassus puertoricanus)* just as it broke through the brown earth. However, it wasn't until Komodo saw Bop, one of the saddest of the current Atoms, stumble by, running after his pet pig, that the source of the Insta-Envir bloom became apparent. Seems that when Shig herded the Atoms onto the SS

Gojiro

Adamski (one of those flying dutchmen that regularly pierced the Cloudcover with the pipes and cigarettes of the absent crew still warm in their ashtrays), the orders had been no pets. That Bop, though, he couldn't live without his pig; he smuggled the tumorated thing under his shirt, right next to his hump. Now it was loose, and all the Atoms were after it, which was some sight. Komodo got to it first. He turned the porker over, examined it.

"Look at this," Komodo motioned to Ebi, indicating the layer of dried toxi-waste on the pig's swollen feet. "Slops—the animal's feed has embedded in its hooves and the residue has somehow taken root here."

Ebi immediately recognized the danger of the situation. "Why, if this is so, we will be guilty of loosing invader species! These forms are adapting to the host landmass."

Komodo was alarmed. "If the Envir can spread this quickly, it will likely engulf the entire state of California!"

Gojiro found no small irony in the circumstance. He remembered the time, back in the earliest of the Glazed Days, when the flotjet first swarmed the beaches of Radioactive Island. "What's that," he asked Komodo, sighting a mass of plastic bags, "jellyfish with their guts ripped out?"

"I don't know," Komodo said, poking at the items with a stick. "But someone keeps sending them."

That was, of course, just the beginning. From that point on, it seemed like every beer can ever thrown from a speeding pickup, each pack of Kools crushed neath a smack freak's sneaker, all the wallboard from electric field–infected timeshares had been issued a one-way ticket to Radioactive Island. Each morning more refuse was on the horizon, flowing in on the tide, then clumping hard and solid on the shorelines, like yesterday's Dodge Dart pressed inside a wrecker's tight square.

There was nothing to do but sit and watch. "It's like everything they don't want, they're palming off on us," Gojiro said, demoralized.

Komodo looked up. "Perhaps you have something there, my own true friend," he said.

"Like what?"

"Do you notice how these objects, which otherwise would remain distinct from other objects—never blending in—as they are made almost exclusively of nonintegrative, unbiodegradable materials, are actively meshing together on our shores? It is almost as if what no longer fits into the world beyond has come here to find refuge."

"Oh, great," Gojiro groaned. "You saying we got an Ellis Island for the exhaust of the modern world going here? Like we should offer political asylum to every recapped tire or something?"

Komodo was suddenly filled with emotion. "I can only think of my own journey here," he began, his voice quivering, "how I was driven by some inner compass, synchronized to the beat of your heart. It was amazing to me that some nights, when I no longer could keep my eyes open out on that raging sea, I'd awake and not be hopelessly lost. I was only closer—closer to this place, to you. It was as if there was nowhere I belonged but here. Until I came here, all around me I felt nothing but rejection. Rejection by those men in the hospital. Rejection by the ships that passed and somehow refused to see me. Rejection even by the clouds, and the sea. But here was acceptance. Perhaps that is why these things come here. To be accepted. I feel we should welcome them to our land."

"Welcome them to our land? Look around. They *are* our land!"

It was so. Rather than simply washing up and littering the beaches of Radioactive Island, the flotjet had merged with the existing structures, knit itself into the various chains of being lurching into motion on the previously ash-strewn and empty tract. It didn't look like any jungle Sheena ever swung in, that was for sure.

Gojiro couldn't take it. "I can't watch the sea no more," he screamed. "It's like looking into the wrong end of a cornucopia."

Komodo was not dissuaded. The next morning he was striding into the incoming surf carrying a sign saying "Welcome to Our World, Unindigenous Deconstructions." Gojiro refused to participate. He hung around singing mocking songs, such as "This land is our land, this land is your land . . . pieces of crap." He steadfastly refused to allow that a waterlogged leisure suit had as much right to his world as he did.

But then, of course, the first of the Atoms were on the horizon, and nothing was the same again.

With this in mind, the monster could not resist a hearty "go around, come around" as he watched Komodo fret about the potential mass introduction of so-called invader species to the scenic Los Angeles County ecoscape. So what if constricting *Velvetinus vinus* number seventeen reblocked the Brown Derby? Those burgers were never what they were cracked up to be anyhow.

It turned out to be a false alarm of sorts. A speedy survey revealed that while the Radioactive Island–type Insta-Envir held sway within the Traj Taj grounds, not one instance of perimeter spillover could be authenticated. After some deliberation, Komodo and Ebi attributed this phenomenon to what they called the "precondition" of the Traj Taj grounds. Pointing out that even though widely disparate sectors of unreal estate—some bloodstrewn battlegrounds so small as to only accommodate a barrel cactus and stripmined tracts dozens of square miles in area—had managed to pierce the Cloudcover over the years, these pieces of tortured land had one thing in common. They were all previously part of a coastline somewhere, whereas the Traj Taj lay in the hills, several miles from shore. More than likely because of its cheerless history, that old producer's spread was probably ticketed for Radioactive Island integration, Komodo contended, but its landlocked geography prevented disassociation from the mainland.

"Give it a chance," Gojiro spasmed upon hearing what he took to be another of Komodo's far stretches. "If what you say is true, it won't be long before whole districts of Paraguay and Afghanistan come crushing up on Corvair Bay Beach. Just because they're inland today don't mean they got to be tomorrow. When them Bomb-boys get to gerrymandering, there ain't no subdivision that can't be made."

"Oh, Gojiro," Ebi said, giggling in her perfect way. "You always look so funny when you're mad."

That stopped the monster's tirade. One smile from Ebi and he'd get goofy, start swinging his leg, aw-shucksing all over the place.

So, at least for a moment, things felt nice and easy around the Traj Taj—just Komodo, Gojiro, Ebi, hanging out. Until, that is, they noticed Shig standing there. He always seemed to come out of nowhere.

"An invitation has arrived," he said, formally.

UNDER
ALBERT BULLINS'S
BIG TOP

It was with his heart in his hyoid that Gojiro, holding steady at six feet and snuzzled within the silk sheets on that old producer's bed, watched Komodo fumble with his cummerbund. Poor Komodo! He'd been on edge ever since Shig brought around that invitation to Albert Bullins's sixtieth birthday party, and this monkey suit wasn't helping things.

"These people are very sophisticated," he said, attempting to straighten his black tie. "I am certain they will immediately sense I am not one of them and shun me."

"Who the hell are they?" Gojiro blustered, trying to set his friend at ease. "Nothing but a passel of trickledown dysfunctionates, the spawn of squint-eyed Okies and smarmy rag hondlers. You think *they* know which fork to use?"

Komodo continued to tug at his tie. Gojiro had never seen him look in the mirror so much. It was ridiculous! As far as Komodo was concerned, the proper attire for this affair might as well have been a bubble helmet and suction shoes. Albert Bullins was president of National Pictures, last of the major Majors, and his soirees were stone legends. According to the columns, this one was the biggest A-lister of the year, with thousands of H-wood's sharper articles booked in solid. No wonder Komodo was sweating. Talk about a coming-out party, this was some kind of a scene to make a Bunchic debut! Gojiro shuddered at the thought of Komodo in that alienate habitat, sans a playbook, with only the vaguest input on the native Emily Posts.

But there was no way they could have ignored that invitation. Embossed with florid goldleaf script, it had been taped to the Traj Taj gate, crammed in a plain, unmarked envelope. Scrawled across the card was a single word—"Please!" It was in the same handwriting as the supplication at the bottom of the letter Sheila Brooks had sent to Radioactive Island.

"She continues to attempt to contact us," Komodo said severely. "It is almost as if she does this against her conscious will. I must speak with her. She *knows something,* I can feel it." He was splashing on half a bottle of cologne, for chrissakes.

The monster grunted. The Old Spice fumes were near to blowing out his olfactory bulb. *Knows something.* Gojiro lived in dread of what Sheila Brooks knew. To tell the truth, until they reached that gloomy Turret House, the monster had held out a wan hope that the appearance of his lamentable reply to Billy Snickman's solitary supplication at the bottom of Sheila Brooks's letter had been nothing but a mad coincidence, still another puckish hoax engineered by his ever-mischievous Quadcameral. However, one look at the Dreamer of the Sad Tomorrow and the monster knew: he was in deep shit. Who knew what calamities cultured behind the macabre mask she wore? Hermit Pandora indeed! Why not lock her up in her own box, toss it in the river, and cordon it round with cops to keep the Houdinis away? It would be a public service, saving the world from those sunblasted Brooksians, lounging in their fey bars, passing their coarse Apock Visions to the right like some twisted bridge game. What card would Sheila Brooks slip him, the reptile wondered. No way it wouldn't be the Hangman; there seemed to be none other in the short deck she played. Maybe once they needed four horsemen to herald Kingdom Come, but now there was only Sheila Brooks, a most singular National Velvet.

Know something? *Of course she knew something!* But how could Gojiro tell Komodo that whatever that might be was the last thing he ever wanted to find out?

Still, the monster attempted to keep an upbeat posture concerning Komodo's attendance at Albert Bullins's party. What with the downward tick of that merciless Amendment, the reptile felt compelled to take the long view concerning his friend's future. I'll soon be dead, Gojiro told himself, but he'll have to live on. A dim prospect, to be sure, but it was possible that these people—these fastmouth, sleekgeek cine-scum—might turn out to be Komodo's Bunch after all. If that was so, then he better start getting used to them, hadn't he.

"Knock 'em dead," Gojiro exhorted, maintaining that the Bullins party would be an excellent learning experience.

"Yes," Komodo answered, buffing his shoes, "I am sure there will be many fascinating people there."

"Some brilliant minds."

"Some truly sensitive artists."

"Without doubt!"

"Do I look all right?"

"Great! Fabulous! Molto debonair," Gojiro answered, swallowing hard.

It was terrible to see those gray hairs intermidsted through Komodo's lacquerish crew cut. They were a desolate reminder of all those years lost on Radioactive Island, years spent pretending to be a boy, when he was nothing but a man. Even so, it was no lie, he *did* look good, as good as any headwaiter at the Osaka Hilton.

Komodo held it together until he heard Shig rapping on the door, announcing it was time to go. Then he grasped Gojiro and began to weep. "But my own true friend," Komodo sobbed, "I'm afraid." Gojiro held his friend close for a while, scouring his Dish memory for potential behavioral tips. But they'd already seen *Valley of the Dolls, Beyond the Valley of the Dolls,* and *Way Beyond the Valley of the Dolls.* What else was there to know? So the monster said, "Look, if you get in a tight spot, go Jap. Right to *The Nutty Professor.* Give 'em the teeth. Buck 'em out big. It never misses!"

Komodo mustered a crooked smile. "Oh, my own true friend, what would I do without your suggestions?"

The Bullins party was to be held in a voluminous yellow and white striped tent set up out back of the studio head's digs overlooking Sunset Boulevard's seaward snake. Komodo, with Shig posing as his private secretary, got there way too early. But how was he to know? The invitation didn't specify a time, and since all the doleful birthday parties he threw for those decomposing Atoms always began at seven o'clock, he assumed this one would too. The tent was empty when he got there, except for several slight, taciturn young men nestling pink linen napkins into crystal glasses set on the two hundred tables fanned across the lush grass.

Komodo was almost about to leave when a large antique automobile entered the tent and sped toward him. "Duke!" the man behind the wheel was yelling. "Duke Kalalau!"

It was Albert Bullins. Komodo recognized him from his tabloid pictures. Infinitely more picturesque than the current clean-and-sober, snap-in, snap-out number-crunching studio head, Bullins was not shy with the sleaze shutterbugs. The limelight was his life. He was the son of Sam Bullins, an original Hollywood privateer who was famous for swearing he'd live to spit on D. W. Griffith's grave and doing so. With this bloodline, Bullins played the oldtime mogul number to the hilt. In a town of mineral-water drinkers, he was the only one fat enough to pull it off. A lifetime in the business, he showed no signs of slowing down. Rain or shine, he stuck to his regimen of couching six starlets a day in his massive office, then swimming a lap. The item that caught Komodo and Gojiro's attention, however, concerned an award Bullins once received from the National Large Caliber Stalk and Kill Association attesting that he had shot to death the last white rhino in Sumatra. There was a picture of him chowing down at the Extinction Certification dinner. The caption read, "Wouldn't want to eat it every day, guess now I won't have to."

Dressed in tuxedo pants only, Bullins continued to call out from behind the wheel of the massive car. Obviously, he had mistaken Shig for the famous Tahitian surfing champion, Duke Kalalau. Shig turned around. He was wearing those special mirrored contacts that automatically revealed to the reflected individual the most despicable aspect of themselves, the one they always sought to conceal. Komodo, utilizing rosy fibers, had been trying for exactly the opposite effect when he first made the lenses; he threw them out when he recognized his mistake. Shig, however, never dull to an opportunity to further his forbidding affect, pulled the contacts from the trash and stuck them in his eyes. Boy, he could bale. At the gate to Bullins's house, a single glower turned the hardcase sentry, a practicing Sicilian, into a tearful hulk. Apparently he'd been cheating on his wife and now felt the need to confess his sin to whomever would listen. Bullins, however, had no trouble looking at Shig. Obviously, whatever conscience he once possessed had long ago been loaned out, subleased, or diversified so as not to be a factor.

"Love your 'tacks, Duke baby," Bullins said to Shig, grabbing his hand, putting the old pumperootie on him. Shig growled. He hated to have anyone touch him.

"So, Duke-o, how's it hanging? All ten of them, huh? We really laid down some pipe with those bobbysoxers that time over in Wiamea, didn't we?" It was only after Shig tensed his hand around his razored saber that Bullins realized his misidentification. "Whoa! No small sticker you got there, Pancho," he said, jumping back, his bared, ample stomach heaving. "But if you're not Duke, who are you?"

It was Komodo who answered. "I am Yukio Komodo. This, sir, is Shig."

"Just Shig? What, you only got one name, like Mantovani?"

"Excuse me, sir, but he prefers to be known that way," Komodo said.

"Whatever," Bullins said, losing interest. He perked up again when Shig barked, by way of a more formal introduction, that Komodo was the director of the Gojiro—King of Monsters, Friend to Atoms series.

"That so?" Bullins remarked, his brown, bagged eyes bulging. "Hey, my grandchildren are bugs about . . . what's his name? Gogyro?"

"Gojiro."

"Yeah. Just bugs about that Gozero. And those headphones . . . what you call them?"

"Crystal Contact Radios."

"Great tie-in. Like I said, my grandchildren . . . they're just bugs."

With that, Shig dug into a leather sack he carried and handed Bullins one of those supervulcanized models of Gojiro in deep mantis stance. Back on Radioactive Island, these replicas were the subject of much controversy. "Great," Gojiro railed when he first saw the models, "now he's putting out blowup dolls of me, just like any other porno star! Does it come with any vibrating parts?" Komodo was deeply embarrassed by such talk, and he attempted to put a stop to the production of the dolls, to no avail, of course.

"Give it to those who love him," Shig said sternly, shoving the toy into Bullins's girth.

"Yeah, sure," Bullins said, opening the front door of the gleaming automobile he'd driven into the tent and tossing the Gojiro doll onto the cut-velvet seat.

"So how you like it?" the mogul chortled, tapping the car's rich maroon hood. "Bearcat, nineteen thirty-six. Thought I'd show it off a little. You know, sort of a centerpiece for the party. It's my new little treasure. Didn't cost me shit either! Just traded Prince Baggala a pair of Joan Crawford's old panties. Can you believe that? I still got two pairs left. Ann Sheridan too, if you're interested. That Baggala, what an idiot. Just between you and me, you can take the burnoose off those guys, but they're still a bunch of blanketheads. Know what he had under the hood of this baby? A Ford four thirty-seven. A Ford! And he calls himself a sportsman."

Bullins stopped and put his arm around Komodo. "So . . . what's your first name again? Yukio? Where you hail from, Yukio?"

Komodo was about to say Radioactive Island but stopped himself. It wasn't a conversation he was prepared to have. "Well," he said, shakily, "I was born in Hiroshima."

"Hiroshima!" Bullins bellowed. "That a fact? I was out that way once. Picked up a Zero over there. Gora K-44 Sacred Blossom, too. Not too easy to find a kamikaze in cherry condition, let me tell you. The people I got it from though, those bumpkins, they were using it as a planter, chrysanthemums growing right out of the cockpit. Took me weeks to get the dirt out of the upholstery. Good little buzzbomb, though. I'd like to take it up, strafe the VA hospital, give those old boys a heck of a flashback. So, you're a Hiroshima man. Mind if ask you a personal question?"

Komodo was wishing he hadn't tied his tie so snugly. "Yes, certainly, Mr. Bullins."

"Please—Albert! Now, tell me, how come Hiroshima gets all the ink? It's always Hiroshima this, Hiroshima that. Correct me if I'm wrong, but Nagasaki took quite a hit too, didn't it? I've seen the films. Burns, peeling skin, the whole burrito. But you never hear anything about it. You're a Hiroshima man—how come Nagasaki always gets passed over?"

Komodo was bollixed. Yeah, maybe he should have hauled off and slugged Bullins there and then. Except that wouldn't be Komodo. It was a longstanding problem, his inability to get mad over the horrors of his past. There was the time he quietly asked Gojiro if he would please refrain from taking Radi-Breath practice on a crosshaired blowup of Harry Truman. Truman's decision had been complicated, Komodo claimed; you couldn't condemn the man without knowing all the facts. Hearing that, Gojiro flipped out, screaming that Truman was nothing but a pipsqueak trying to show Stalin he had an atomic weenie. Nevertheless, following the incident, the monster had trouble working up the same hatred for the doughty little haberdasher. The fun went out of it. He had to substitute pictures of MacArthur and Tibbets. From then on, except for disputes concerning Joseph Prometheus Brooks, Gojiro abstained from conversations about Bomb-related celebs with Komodo. He didn't want any more of his targets taken away.

Forcing a smile, Komodo turned to Bullins. "Perhaps Hiroshima has a better press agent?"

"Better press agent! I love it." Bullins slammed Komodo on the back. "Let's get ourselves a drink, what do you say?"

Now Komodo very definitely does not drink. Never did, not even once. In fact, you might say Komodo is viceless. Addiction- and substance-abuse-free. That doesn't mean he gets as reproachful as a salt-lake Mormon and lays on you the heavy tsk-tsk-tsk. Komodo's libertarian, he never once got huffed over Gojiro's rampaging habits. He knows too much about pain and its abatement to point fingers. But still, going with the when-in-Rome schemata, he took Albert Bullins's highball, grasped it in his sweating palm, and splashed the stinging liquid down his throat.

The effects were next to immediate. Whatever adhesives had kept Komodo so tightly wrapped all those years began to unstick. Faces smeared sideways, the grass beneath his feet turned over a new leaf, and the striped tent above his head swirled like a hypnodisk. The next half-hour or so was a bumper-car tour, the liquor insulating the rebounds. At one corner of the tent, a purplenosed man told him Jimi Hendrix wasn't dead but was actually a gardener at Graceland. Then a tweed-suited matron with a wide, musky mouth took Komodo aside to point out another, younger woman, who was affecting an extra-snooty carriage. This second woman, Carrie Coast, whose name Komodo was supposed to know, had recently sued her husband for divorce, asking millions in alimony. "She hires linebackers from the Rams to throw her down the steps and then, one time, Jack raises his voice and he's slapped with an extreme cruelty. It's a disgrace," the woman reported, with a phone operator's bland whine. Komodo didn't know what to say. It was still another stim for which he had no ready react. "A scandal," he finally responded, full of outrage, but the woman was already gone, telling her tale elsewhere.

It didn't matter. Hardly anything did. The booze and the women—so many women, their smells and skin so deliriously close to him—had him floating, vortexing left, right, all in time to bombastic rhythms laid down by that 175-piece Stan-Kenton-from-Hell orchestra. The tent was crowded now, a teeming hive of life's own glitter. Everywhere were cyberslouching men in loosefitting retro clothing speaking in a military/corporate patois appropriate to certain frat hip off-world colonies. It didn't take long for the word to pass as to who Komodo was. Burnished gladhanders angled toward him, beadeyed to slice off a corner for themselves. Turk Mincefeld, the producer, came over to ask if Komodo was interested in a certain Kafka property he "owned." "But forget Czechoslovakia," the epaulet-bedecked Mincefeld said. "Cold weather is no-go.

I say we put it in Phoenix. *The Baileys and the Bug*—is that delicious or what?"
Komodo nodded, said he found it a challenging concept.

The attention wasn't *that* surprising. After all, as Gojiro himself often
noted, with a sick pride that instantly mutated to disgust, hardly a week went
by that several of "his" pictures weren't in *Variety*'s top fifty at the same time.
Not that they were ever number one or anything like that. The rungs were
reserved for the Brooks-Zebers of the industry. Number twenty-nine, number
thirty-two, that was more like it. But they were *always* twenty-nine, thirty-two.
Worldwide, that was a lot of repeat viewing. "*Gojiro* has hydralegs," the trades
said. The pictures might close in Bandung, but a week later they'd be giant in
the Sulu Sea. What exactly Shig did with all the money wasn't a question either
Komodo or Gojiro had worked up the gumption to ask.

Yeah, Komodo got asked to lunch, more lunches than he could eat in a
year. Komodo's not that big an eater, you know. A crisply diagonaled sandwich
perhaps, a few grapes, that's about it. Meanwhile, the warming, lavalight-like
slog of the liquor (he quickly mastered the seemingly essential behavior of
snagging drinks off passing trays) kept him earnestly shaking hands with all
these would-be partners, thanking them with an embarrassed smile for their
interest.

Others threw faster-breaking curves. "So, tell me, what's the monster to
Komodo and what's Komodo to the monster?" asked a widebellied, black-
mopped man. The pocked face was not unfamiliar. A pinchy Brit; his "critic"
hustle—billed as rapier wit, but actually nothing more than a cache of regim-
micked public-school rankouts—often turned up on the Radioactive Island
Dishscreen.

"Excuse me?" Komodo replied uneasily.

"You heard me," the critic bellowed. "We are confronted by some variety
of monster here, are we not? I only seek to ferret out exactly what variety of
bugeyed thing it is. You are his creator, you ought to know the brand of the
beastie. Is he the guilt-ridden Lugosi who lies awake through the daylight hours
staring at the inside cover of his coffin, racked by the consequence of his crimes,
or is he the stoic, clumping Karloff?"

"Well . . . he's more of a monitor. A varanid, actually."

"Ah! Not mineral, not vegetable, but animal! A reptilian. A Moby Dick with
scales." The critic winked to a sallow, bleach-headed woman. Watch me work,
the look said.

Komodo swallowed a mouthful of vodka. A tense grin came over his face.

Moby Dick wasn't exactly unknown to him. Several Cliff Note paraphrases of the venerable allegory had washed onto the island over the years. It remained a firm favorite, Gojiro often springing surprise quizzes based on the text during his Anti-Speciesist lectures, even if he felt the author missed the boat by not telling the story from the point of view of the whale.

"Something like Moby Dick," Komodo threw out, "but there are differences, of course. For instance, Gojiro is green. Moby Dick was white."

"Yes!" the critic pounced. "White! That royal preeminence of hue! The color of the kings of Pegu! The rulers of Siam! The Caesarian overlords! White of the Prairie Steed, milky chargers with the dignity of a thousand monarchs. White like the northern bear and treacherous shark, whose whiteness only serves to heighten the intolerable hideousness of their brutish nature. White like the Albino! A whiteness that repels men, that sends them away, a whiteness of the world uncharted, a world unknown and never to be known! The whiteness . . . of the Whale.

"As you say, Mr. Komodo, Moby Dick was white!" the critic concluded. "Now, your chum, that large and saggy fellow, what's his name—I forget. What color did you say he was?"

There was a smattering of snickers from the knot of chiseled profiles. Front-runners all, they gravitated toward the slap of public flogging. And probably, Komodo being Komodo, he would have just let it all go. But the booze was in him. Besides, the way that fatuous jerk was talking, making uncalled-for remarks about the classic fold of Gojiro's leathers, it kind of ticked Komodo off.

"Green. I said Gojiro was green," Komodo retorted, geniality masking his passion. "But not the green of the vast unknowable, certainly not. Not the green of the windswept sea, nor the green of the most fertile lichens growing in the emerald forests, nor the green of the sturdy pine. Just the opposite. The green of Gojiro is the green that is too well known. It is the green of the slick left by a malfunctioning motorcraft in a previously pristine lake. The green of the dacron weave, the green of the garish paint chip in a homemaker's catalog, the curious green of a jungle resurging from defoliation, the green in the faces of those whom cartoonists imagine live on Mars.

"You are right. Gojiro is not the color of the snowhowdahed Andes, their eternal frosted desolateness reigning at great altitudes. His is the color that God never splashed upon the spectrum. He is the green of men. The green we have created.

"That is the greenness of Gojiro!"

Gojiro

* * *

When Komodo was done, he could have been anywhere. Everything was going by itself. He never imagined he would say such things, certainly not in front of the suddenly cheering crowd now gathering around him. It was only when a hand touched his shoulder that Komodo felt his feet on the floor once again.

"A very elegant argument, Mr. Komodo. A lot of people around here wouldn't have minded knocking the shit out of that asshole." It was Bobby Zeber.

"Mr. Zeber," Komodo gasped, bowing quickly. The lightheadedness was gone, replaced by a dull throb in each temple.

Zeber smiled tersely. "I admire a man who arrives in town cold and three days later steals the scene at the hottest party of the year." Under the halogen floodlights of Albert Bullins's tent, Zeber looked quite handsome, dashing even, in his evening clothes. The weariness he displayed back at the Turret House was gone. He looked younger, moving with a kind of blasé self-assurance that denoted years of being truly big. "I've been trying to call you. But you don't seem to be staying anywhere. My office phoned all the hotels."

"We have taken a house."

"A house?" Zeber frowned. "That sounds kind of permanent."

Without the booze's buffer, Komodo was back to square one. He could feel Zeber's sharp brown eyes studying him. "Please let me apologize," he blurted. "It was a terrible breach for me to appear at your home unannounced. I can only hope my impetuousness did not cause you or Ms. Brooks any discomfort."

"Don't worry about that. In fact, your visit seems to have been a tonic for Ms. Brooks. I came home yesterday and she was cleaning up the house. I nearly died of shock. That's the first time I've ever seen her do that."

Unsure if this was a compliment or not, Komodo bowed again. "Will Ms. Brooks be here soon?"

Zeber's face tightened again. "What gave you that idea? Sheila doesn't come out in public. She hasn't in years."

"But . . . she must, I have urgent matters to discuss with her." Komodo dug into the pocket of his dinner jacket. He would show Zeber the invitation he had received, make clear to him the gravity with which his wife obviously regarded the situation.

His top lip curling, Zeber spoke before Komodo could find the card. "I'm terribly sorry and embarrassed about this, but there's no way—no way in the world—that Brooks-Zeber can make a film like the one Sheila mentions in her letter. It can't happen. It's the *last* thing that could ever happen. I think it would be better for everyone if we just forgot about the whole thing, okay? Of course, I will more than recompense you and your staff your out-of-pockets and attempt to make right all other inconveniences you've incurred."

"But . . ."

Zeber slitted his eyes, went into his modified Brooklyn street act. He was very good at it, had used it to intimidate a thousand executives. But somehow, this time, it came out mournful, full of hurt. "Look Mr. Komodo, you seem like a nice guy, but there's one thing you got to understand. Sheila . . . she's just not, how can I say this? She's not like you or me. She's another kind. Failures of communication, misunderstandings, come up. This letter she wrote you is one of these misunderstandings."

The orchestra's upper-register-intensive version of "How High the Moon?" blared into Komodo's brain. "Mr. Zeber. I must urge you to reconsider. The film itself is not paramount to myself and my friend. There are other matters of great importance that must be addressed."

"What other matters could there be?"

"As Ms. Brooks says in her letter, matters of life and death."

Maybe Komodo said that too loud. The tent seemed all ears; any info scrap pertaining to the enigmatic Brooks-Zeber team would be quite a plum to pick. Bobby Zeber noted the encroaching knot of poorly faked nonchalance, unfurled a surprisingly boyish smile. Then, clasping Komodo's hand, he said, "This isn't really the time or the place to talk. Why don't you come by my office tomorrow morning. I really think we can settle this."

That might have been that, but just then a slim waiter, obviously an aspiring actor hoping to be noticed by the great Bobby Zeber, came over. "The gentleman in sector two, sixth left table, wishes you to join him, Mr. Zeber. He says to bring your friend."

There were other people at the table, but Komodo only saw the silver-haired old man with bushy eyebrows. "Yukio Komodo, meet Victor Stiller," Zeber said flatly. Komodo was stunned, amazed. Drawing himself up, he delivered his deepest, most deferential bow. "Mr. Stiller. It is a great honor to meet you, sir. Your work has made a tremendous impression on me."

Stiller smiled engagingly. There was a playfulness in his dark brown eyes, a look of absolute serenity, self-satisfaction. He looked as if he'd never had a sleepless night in his life. "Only in the most beneficial of ways, I hope," he said, his well-mellowed Euro accent as comfy as an old fairy story.

"You are a great thinker," Komodo said with ultimate sincerity, his heart racing. Could he actually be talking to the famous Victor Stiller—the great pioneer of nuclear physics? Stiller was there from the start, from the first battered neutron, the initial accelerating particle; he was a fission and fusion colossus whose fabulous career spanned every critical pile from Ulm to Amos Alonzo's Chicago squash courts out to that fateful Valley. Komodo felt his palms clam up. What an opportunity this was—to engage the brilliant Stiller in a discussion of the most profound subjects of the Universe!

Stiller creased his sunkissed brow. "Bobby, I like this Mr. Komodo of yours. He has a very refreshing point of view. These days most people barely remember that I ever set foot inside a laboratory. They think of me only as a paperpusher, a colorless bureaucrat." By this, Stiller no doubt was referring to his more recent fame as a fixture in the cabinets of three different presidents and his authorship of the Stiller Doctrine, a far-reaching policy that was described by opponents as "never too many missiles as long as someone's making money to make them." It was this hardline pro-proliferation stance, coupled with the scientist's astounding rise from a near-penniless physics student, son of a shoemaker from the Bluthgeld ghetto, to his current status as one of the richest men in the world, that often prompted Gojiro to go into the sort of rage the monster usually reserved for Joseph Brooks himself.

These aspects of Victor Stiller's notoriety, however, were far from Komodo's mind right then. "I have read your essay on orbital electron capture and beta decay," the awestruck Japanese told the old scientist. "It was very inspiring."

"You flatter me unmercifully with this ancient history. But the truth is— and please don't tell anyone this, Mr. Komodo—I agree with you. Still, I am retired from science. Or was it science that retired me? Who can say? True thought is a vast and uncertain terrain one enters only at the greatest of risks, for very soon even the most promising minds are humbled, humiliated. Inventing an idea is difficult enough, but maintaining it, allowing it to flourish, that requires courage and a very thick skin. Today, I have neither. I am just an old man who finds it amusing to come to these galas and ogle at the beautiful young things."

Stiller smiled at the couple seated to his right. "May I present Ms. Conapt and Mr. Dance."

Helene Conapt and Ty Dance, H-wood's current rising couple, turned in tandem. Punched from the same cookie cut of Aryan friskiness, the sexy pair, hits as homicidal fraternal twins in National Pictures' recent series of eroto-slasher films, had been lost in each other's next-to-identical blue eyes. "We just got married," Helene Conapt said with an unexpected screech, displaying a gold band wider than anything Johnson and Johnson ever put out.

"They've just returned from their honeymoon," Stiller said with a grand-fatherly glow.

"We went to Two Bunch for cosmo rehab."

Komodo thought this quite marvelous. "Such a wonderful idea to renew your philosophical beliefs on the occasion of your marriage. Congratulations."

Ty Dance looked at Komodo with wary confusion. "We just got our earlobes redone, that's all."

It was then Komodo noticed that Victor Stiller was staring at him.

"Mr. Komodo, have we met before?"

Komodo felt his heart seize up. "I don't think so. I'm a stranger in this country."

Stiller squinted behind his gold-rimmed glasses. "You're certain? You have the most familiar face. Didn't we meet many years ago? Have you ever been in Budapest? Or perhaps Vienna?"

Komodo shook his head nervously.

"Not even as a child? Somehow I remember you as a boy. A boy from long ago."

It was Bobby Zeber who came to Komodo's rescue. "Mr. Komodo is a film director. You ever hear of Gojiro, Victor?"

Stiller raised his thick eyebrows, shook his head.

"Never heard of Gojiro?" Helene Conapt grated. Then, to Komodo, "Wow. You're the one who makes those Gojiro movies? They're great. My little brother, he really thinks the monster's real. You can't talk him out of it for nothing."

"You make children's films?" Stiller said. "An important task. A noble and daunting responsibility."

Komodo smiled uneasily. "Yes. Well, actually, many children see them, but much of the audience is quite a bit older."

"They're monster movies," Helene Conapt explained eagerly. "Everyone likes monster movies."

"A monster?" The concept seemed to amuse Victor Stiller.

"Big green ugly thing, but fun." Ty Dance tossed in.

Stiller smiled amiably, taking in the byplay, then turned to Komodo. "Tell me one thing, sir. Do your films have happy endings? To me, that is essential. I can't abide doom and gloom, worlds in disarray. It makes me uncomfortable, as if some insufficiently disguised transgression is about to leap upon me. To deny the viewer a sense of comfortable completion connotes an unforgiving attitude on the part of the filmmaker, I feel."

Bobby Zeber put down the glass of club soda he'd been drinking. "Maybe it's a good thing to make some people uncomfortable, don't you think, Victor?"

"Oh Bobby, don't start in."

Zeber turned to Komodo. "Victor doesn't care for the films Sheila and I make. He only profits from them."

Stiller did not answer, addressing Komodo instead. "What are your views on this? Do you feel, as Bobby seems to, that in this day and age an unhappy ending is somehow intrinsically more honest than a happy one?"

The flare of tension between Victor Stiller and Bobby Zeber made Komodo want to disappear. Yet this was *Victor Stiller* asking *him* a question, an intriguing one at that. Instantly converting to an ever-eager schoolboy, he sought to construct a closely reasoned exegesis that would both stun and delight his master. "Why, I believe in the earned arf," is what Komodo said.

The earned arf. It was Gojiro's term, invented back in the days when he and Komodo first considered the narrative structure of those scenarios that Shig eventually turned into the King of Monsters series. At the time it was Komodo's idea to have the movies end happily, since the more reality-tenuous Atoms might not be able to stand the strain of a downful denouement.

Gojiro was against it. "Enough with this obligatory final-frame iconography. I ain't taking no arfs that ain't earned," he declared, in reference to what he deemed the repulsive practice of certain Dishscreen wallahs who truncated their shoddy sagas with the family dog barking at a particularly stupid joke made by one of the numbnuts characters, thereby triggering a spasm of laughtrack hilarity that fabricated a totally unearned sense of well-being. This didn't mean the monster was against the happy ending—quite the contrary. He felt that any story that didn't end happily, *truly* happily, was no story at all.

"We must speak of the nature of the storyteller in today's changing world," Komodo said as he stood under Albert Bullins's tent, hoping to do justice to Gojiro's argument. "Perhaps at the outset of the Modern Age it was enough to hold a mirror before the face of the world, to document the predicament into which we were heading. Now, however, it's too late for that. The situation is there for all to see. It is the job of the storyteller to seek the Way Out. He must keep on talking, inventing incident after incident, stalling for time if need be, until an ending that is both happy and True springs to sight. That does not mean that I despise endings that appear to be sad. To me, no ending is truly sad unless it produces a false closure to the story. Then it is a bad ending, and, by necessity, sad. No matter what the circumstances of the tale when the storyteller stops, the story remains valid as long as there is a promise of a next episode, a maintenance of at least the *potentiality* of a happy ending. This is the *earned arf,* the goal of Art in our times, I believe."

When Komodo looked up, he saw that Victor Stiller, whom he was desperately trying to impress, did not appear to be listening at all. The old man's attention was affixed to the perfect sweep of Helene Conapt's breasts. It was Bobby Zeber who seemed immersed in Komodo's words.

"The earned arf . . ." Zeber half laughed, a strange disassociation passing over him. "So you're an optimist, Mr. Komodo?"

"I prefer to call myself a pragmatist," Komodo answered, his gaze meeting Zeber's in a form of uncomprehending concordance.

Zeber shook his head once more and turned to Stiller. "Mr. Komodo is very interested in Sheila's father."

The faintest tremor seemed to shoot through the old scientist's previously impeccable bonhomie. "Oh?"

Zeber cocked his head, as if exploiting an unseen advantage. "It is Mr. Brooks, really, that you wish to speak to, isn't it, Mr. Komodo? That's what you told Sheila, right?"

The sheltered moment he thought he shared with Bobby Zeber shattered, Komodo fumbled about. "Well, yes . . ."

Stiller glowered at Zeber, then smiled in Komodo's direction. "But Mr. Brooks is . . . dead."

"Yes. I know that," Komodo sputtered. "I think what Mr. Zeber means is that if Mr. Brooks *were* alive, there would be many pressing matters that I would hope to take up with him, matters of extreme importance."

"But he's dead."

"Yes, alas." Suddenly, Komodo began to choke up. "It was a terrible loss. Of course, no one can be certain of these things, but I would say that Mr. Brooks was the most brilliant of all men."

"That is true. He was, as you say, the most brilliant of men. The most brilliant mind civilization has yet produced. We were boys together, you know—"

"At Göttingen!"

"Yes, Mr. Komodo. That's right."

"When he arrived you were his protector, his only friend!"

Stiller smiled benevolently. "How do you know that?"

"I have made a special study concerning the lives of the great twentieth-century scientists and how they contributed to the first Atomic test." This was true enough. Komodo didn't miss a word of the Bomb books that happened to float in as part of Radioactive Island's circulating library. He was familiar with the unique working relationship that existed between Victor Stiller and Joseph Prometheus Brooks, the way Stiller served as the so-called interface between the spectral Joseph Brooks and the world at large. "Brooks created the Beast, but Stiller sold it" was the famously cynical comment concerning their partnership.

Komodo's interest melted Stiller. "It's true, I took charge of him. When he arrived at the school he seemed so lost. He was only thirteen years old. I was only seventeen, but already it was clear to me that he was the most capable mind in the school. I couldn't allow the autocrats to squeeze the life from him. We became friends, yes. I believe I was the only real friend he ever had."

Stiller took off his glasses, rubbed them with a monogrammed handkerchief. "I'm sorry. I've become very nostalgic. Mr. Komodo, you take me back to days I haven't thought about in years."

Komodo smiled ear to ear. "Could you just speak, talk about this great genius? Any information at all would be invaluable to me."

Stiller looked at Komodo quizzically. "But there is so much . . . Did you know that he once was determined to quit physics and become a musician instead?"

Komodo nodded politely. This was not a new story.

"He was quite a clarinet player, or so I'm told. He left the school, went off to Paris. I remember going to that Hot Club, where he played in a band with some black men."

"Sidney Bechet."

Stiller looked up. "What's that?"

"He played with Sidney Bechet."

"Was that the man's name? It's so long ago now. Anyway, I went to this place and tried to talk some sense into him. I demanded he return to his work.

He wouldn't listen. He said he was looking for something he couldn't find in science. Something more. It was quite irrational. There was nothing I could do, nothing any of us could do. It seemed such a waste."

"It was only his wife, Leona, who could make him return to science."

Again Stiller stopped, frowning this time. "That's correct, Mr. Komodo." The scientist's tone turned deliberate, remote. "She was an American girl in Paris, an art student. She was very beautiful, flamboyant, in her way. So different from Joseph. Yet from the very first time she saw him, she wanted him. It was an obsession. We were so worried. She seemed so odd, always making strange comments, spiritualist nonsense. We thought, if he goes with her, we'll never get him back. Science will suffer. But it was her; she did it. She was the one who convinced him where his destiny lay."

Komodo swallowed hard. Stiller's sudden coldness told him not to ask any more questions. How he hated himself then. Why hadn't he kept his mouth shut, allowed Stiller to speak at his own pace?

A strained moment passed before Bobby Zeber said, matter-of-factly, "Did you know, Mr. Komodo, that it was Leona who chose the Encrucijada Valley as the Bomb site?"

Komodo turned. "No. I didn't know that."

"It's true. She'd been out there before, years earlier. She was going out west with her family and the train broke down. Maybe she was fifteen, sixteen . . . anyway, she wandered away from the train, went over a ridge and into the valley. She convinced Brooks that the test had to be made there and nowhere else—"

Stiller coughed. "Mr. Komodo isn't interested in these old wives' tales, Bobby. The Valley was chosen for the test because it met every specification. It was unknown and self-contained—"

Zeber kept talking to Komodo. "That's where they were married, Joseph and Leona. Victor knows that, he was their best man—"

"Bobby—"

"That's where Sheila was born, in that valley."

"On July 16, 1945 . . ." Komodo said softly.

Then Komodo felt Stiller's eyes on him, as if the old scientist's stare was trying to bore into his head. "Mr. Komodo, are you absolutely certain we've never met?" The way Stiller looked at him was frightening—that scientist's brain, which once contemplated the power of the Universe, was beginning to kick in. Komodo could feel its heat. "We have met. I'm certain of it. It's coming to me, just give me a moment."

It was as he sat girding himself for Stiller's next word that Komodo felt the first low frequency, the initial trembler. Automatically his eyes went to the source. Albert Bullins's 1936 Bearcat! It was exploding! A fireball shot forth, dense smoke filled the tent.

Komodo rose to tell the others to take cover. But when he opened his mouth, no sound came out. It was madness! Across the table, Victor Stiller was still trying to decide where he knew Komodo from. Bobby Zeber shook an ice cube from a tall frosted glass into his mouth and out again. Komodo watched the ice descend; it took a while. Everything was happening in slow motion . . . slow motion and no sound. Helene Conapt moved her hand over her siren's hair. Ty Dance flicked a crumb from the collar of his white sailor shirt.

Then Komodo felt his head turning, as if some unseen force was pulling him, drawing his attention. There was no choice in it at all! He looked across Albert Bullins's tent, through the idle talkers and hard smilers to the other side, where he saw her.

If anything, she looked more harrowed than she had at the Turret House. The fact that she'd apparently made an effort to dress, prepare herself for this public appearance only made it worse. Makeup bleared across her pallid countenance as if applied by a spin-art operator, white hair staticked from her skull like it was trying to escape. Her unwieldy body was draped with a satin outfit reminiscent of the film *Forbidden Planet,* her long, parched legs shooting like stilts beyond the hem of her red skirt. Put together with those gummed black glasses, it was an arresting sight.

"Ms. Brooks!" His shout came out distorted, like the electronically disguised voice of a government witness. She saw him now, moved ahead.

They could have been anywhere. Amongst the teeming masses of a Calcutta railway station, deep in a great rain forest, on the far side of the moon. It didn't matter; nothing did except that they be together. Faster and faster they went, flung forward like paper ghosts strung up on wires in a children's show. Faster and faster, until all they saw was each other's face.

But then it was over. That strangest crease had opened—it was now shut tight. Clocks began to tick once more. Wham! The roof blew off Albert Bullins's car. Made a major boom, too: they heard it all through Bel Air, the papers said the next day. It seems that the Gojiro doll Shig gave Bullins—the one the mogul casually tossed into the Bearcat's backseat—was equipped with one of those Chinese New Year miniblasters Komodo once worked up to satisfy the pyro-lusts of certain boy Atoms. Remote-controlled, detonatable from a hundred yards, those bombs could stop your heart, as Gojiro found out that night when some brat Atoms imbedded one inside his ear as he slept. The payload on this particular doll had obviously been anted up. It not only shot through the roof of Bullins's car but ripped a hole in that big top as well, kept going, returning to earth several miles away, smack between two ready-to-rumble sets of Bloods and Crips.

What a scene! Guests were flung left and right by dozens of bodyguards barging through the crowd, looking to throw their bulky persons across the torso of the client paying them for this service. Through it all, Komodo stood looking at Sheila Brooks and Sheila Brooks looked back at Komodo. They tried to make their mouths move, to speak what was on their minds. To say, "What just happened, did it happen for you too?" But then Bobby Zeber was there, wanting to know if everything was all right.

THE FAYETTEVILLE
TREE

Gojiro wasn't about to stay inside that dreary old mansion with the Atoms. Bunk down in there and forget sleep, what with the brain fevers and all-night whine. It was a lot better to lay a pallet under the milky LA sky in the Zoo of Shame.

Not that the Zoo accommodations were exactly deluxe, being nothing but a twenty-foot strip of ground inside a chicken-wire pen populated by that miserable medley of quaggas, moas, sloths, ivory-bills, and the rest. But the conversation was better. Outside of an occasional whimper, those desolate beasts never made a sound. Yeah, the monster decided, the Zoo of Shame wouldn't be that bad, as long as he avoided eye contact with the dodo.

Peeking between webby claws, Gojiro winced as he remembered when that pathetic bird had come into existence. It was back during those bold activist days, when the great chants of Anti-Speciesism resounded on Radioactive Island. How thrilling it was to shout "Two, four, six, eight! Speciesistic crumbs—get ready to reparate! Reparations for the forcibly extinct now! The checkerspot butterfly will rise again! Buffalo Bill is swill!"

The struggle intensified after a book entitled *Strange and Unusual Animals* washed up. Flipping through the elaborate woodcuts, Gojiro was angered that the book made no distinction between beasts killed off by humans and those that existed only in fantasy. Passenger pigeons were pictured alongside unicorns, centaurs, and—of course—dragons. "So they think they're the arbiters of reality," the monster railed. "That they can play mix and match with the great patchquilt of existence? They call it Manifest Destiny, do they? I got some Manyfist Destiny for their face!"

Mark Jacobson

The reptile's plan was simple, sweeping. Komodo, by means of his green-thumbed beakers and bunsens, would rewhelp representatives of extinct Bunches. Then the formerly obliterated would be transported en masse in a "Repatriation Ark" to the UN General Assembly, where, at a hastily convened Tribunal on International Speciescide chaired by Gojiro himself, the dispossessed would be able to confront their excluders. This procedure was to be repeated in all the great capitals of the world. "Imagine," the reptile chortled, "a herd of long-retired rhinos, their horns liberated from the dark wood drawers of Chinese apothecaries, charging down every Elysées."

Komodo was unsure. "But my own true friend, wouldn't this be tampering with the order of things?"

"Don't you mean the *dis*order of things?" Gojiro shot back. "We'll be righting wrongs, partner, aiding justice! Get to bioengineering, we got miles of niches to restock 'fore we sleep."

Of all the reanimation jobs Komodo mixmastered from his widebrimmed beakers the dodo was the most sublime. There was only one problem. Instead of the undying gratitude the reptile expected, the dodo's Necco wafer–like eyes said only, "Why?" It was then that the monster perceived the grievous error of the plan. Fired by rhetoric, they'd coathangered an entire warp-of-time menagerie back from oblivion, belched them up, robbed of habitat, in a world where they saw not a familiar nut or berry.

"What have we done?" the lizard moaned. How could they have neglected one of Budd Hazard's most fundamental teachings, the Principle of Adherence and Disadherence in Beamic Fluidity? The precept was quite clear: without the conjuncting pull of a living Bunch, Beamic ions rescrambled, became free agents, scattering through the universe. Quite obviously, the Beam that once infused the dodo Bunch, thereby connecting it to the Mainstem of the Evolloo, had long since dispersed. Perhaps that immortal energy now served a crew of screaming Bahian monkeys or had become nothing but a disassociated sheen off the coast of Mars—the monster couldn't say. One harsh fact was indisputable, however: within the Evolloo, there was no right of Return. The disappearance of forms was as unconditional as their advent. Besides, if the dodo had been so easily scuttled, didn't this speak to the calcified Maginot of the bird's Line? Extinction, by whatever means necessary, obviously suited the Evolloo. Probably that's why people were invented, Gojiro thought; as the grimmest reapers charged with the task of routing expendables. Dirty job, but someone has to do it, and those sapiens, they were pro.

1 2 2

"Stand aside!" he screamed to Komodo, readying a fatal blast of Radi-Breath to hurl at the re-created beasts. But the resolute Japanese would not move.

"Don't you understand? We created freaks. We got to get rid of 'em."

"No!" a distraught but firm Komodo said. He stood between Gojiro and the doleful reconstitutes, a father superior in black pajamas, sheltering his imperfect children. "Perhaps we should not have given them life, but it is not our place to destroy them. Their fate is now beyond our hands, except that we may try to make them as comfortable as possible."

Gojiro fell to his knees and slammed the Island floor with his clawfists. He knew Komodo would not move from that spot, that he'd take the first shot of Radi-Breath himself rather than allow those jittery obsolescents to feel the singe. Still, the problem of what to do with this passel of unnaturally selected losers remained. For a while it seemed the animals might make good pets for the Atoms, but this idea was abandoned after they woke up one morning to find the dodo dressed in white boots and a miniskirt, a flashing sign around its neck saying "Dodo au Go-Go."

After that, the high-security Zoo of Shame was incorporated as a living shrine to the mysterious workings of the Evolloo. Back on Radioactive Island, in a mournful spirit of spent solidarity, Gojiro often passed a week or two there, shrunk down, mutant among the mutants. Which is where he was right then, in that makeshift zoo pen Shig set up behind the Traj Taj, trying to avoid the dodo's gaze.

"Knock it off," the monster shouted at the moony bird. "Why don't you go imprint yourself on a lawn jockey? I ain't your ma."

"Excuse me, my own true friend?"

"Nothing." The monster hadn't seen Komodo standing there, outside the Zoo of Shame confines. "How was the party?"

"Oh, fine. Very . . . interesting." Komodo looked beat, at loose ends. A good deal of time passed before he was able to relate even the barest outline of the events that had occurred under Albert Bullins's tent.

"Geez," Gojiro sighed, shaking his head as Komodo spoke. But then, attempting an air of unconcern, he said, "No reason to get all pent-up, at least about Stiller thinking he knows you."

After all, the reptile reminded his friend, it wasn't completely out of the question that *someone* would finger him as the erstwhile Coma Boy. Hadn't a copy of that old *Life* magazine floated right by them just a few days before, as they were swimming out to the Cloudcover? "Coma Boy—conscience of our age?" the cover line beseeched, the white letters slung above Komodo's Heater-struck visage. How many people still had that old issue moldering in their garages, thumbed through it at garage sales? The Coma Boy of Hiroshima wasn't exactly a nobody. Time was, a million beatniks carried posters with his likeness during candlelight processions. The UN named a week for him, thousands of school children were touched by his plight in their *Weekly Readers.* Even now, his sobriquet was invoked on quiz shows, the answer to one of the higher-priced choices in the Fabulous Forties and Fifties category. Yeah, the Coma Boy had once cut a moral swath, okay; there had to be one person in Hollywood who'd remember a face once thought to be the conscience of the age.

It made sense that it would be Stiller. Stiller had been there, right inside Komodo's hospital room. The scene was well documented in that old newsreel that kept turning up on the Dish—*Time! Marches On!*

What a nightmare . . . Komodo forced to see those murky images of Red Cross workers scouring the broken city for survivors, to watch them come upon a flattened house where, with block and tackle, they pulled a tiny, seemingly lifeless boy from a hole in the ground. "In the wreckage of atomic fury," the merciless Voorhees boomed his narration, "a young boy found! Where there was only Death, a child alive—alive and apparently unhurt. Just stunned. Stunned into a coma!" Then, they cut to Okinawa, into that miserable hospital room, the camera tight on Komodo's wide open, supposedly unseeing eyes. How awful it was that first time! To see Komodo stare at that screen, to peer into his own face, hear him say, "My God, it's me."

It seemed so long ago, Gojiro had almost forgotten. To recall his friend's beginnings now made the monster nervous. After all, if today's headline might be made to read, "Coma Boy Alive!" could "King of Monsters Also Alive!" be far behind? Nevertheless, Gojiro continued to insist that Stiller's near ID didn't mean a thing. "What could happen? The army gonna dun you for the hospital bill? You're *dead,* remember? It's official: they said you're dead. Besides, he ain't gonna remember. The old fart's totally Palm Springs now; he's been cooking in Sinatra's Jacuzzi so long, his brain is poached. He's just got you mixed up with the Astro Boy."

Komodo shook his head sadly. "No," he said, "if Mr. Bullins's car hadn't exploded at that moment, Dr. Stiller would have placed me then and there."

Without another word, Komodo got up and walked over to where Shig had installed that Fayetteville Tree. "Four new species in the last twenty-four-hour period," he noted flatly, devoid of the excitement with which he customarily greeted further editions of the North Carolina chickadees living among the Tree's glass-enclosed branches. "An unprecedented increase. Ebi is correct. These are extremely fecund environs."

"For sure." There wasn't much else for Gojiro to say. Once Komodo peered into that Fayetteville jar and began thinking about the Instant of Reprimordialization, conversation was useless. The sight of those crappy little birds flitting about the gnarly neobonsai always seemed to transport Komodo into a meditative realm. You might say that as old Darwin had his finches and Galápagos pine, Komodo had his chickadees and Fayetteville Tree. However, to tell the truth, the monster had grown increasingly weary of his friend's ever more arcane search for the key to what he called "the vast enigma of the Reprimordial change."

Not that Gojiro hadn't once admired—even envied—the cosmological boldness of Komodo's original conception. The earnest Japanese first hit upon his insight in the middle of a typically laborious exercise aimed at placing Budd Hazard's mysterious koan, "Reprimordialization is the hand on the Wheel, the Engine of the Evolloo," within the context of the Muse's doctrine of Beam/Bunch collective self-awareness. Komodo was moving through the dry contingencies when he scribbled two formulas on his worksheet: $P = I$ and $P + AT = I$.

"That is Prewire equals Identity, Prewire plus Acquired Traits equals Identity," Komodo blurted, *that look* on his suddenly animated face. Then, defining Prewire as initial Beamic input and indicating Acquired Traits to be the sum total of a Bunch's ongoing experience, Komodo asserted that the two equations were cyclical and eternally linked.

The key was the interplay between the two formulas, Komodo explained. "Even though nearly all of a Bunch's time is spent within the $P + AT = I$ paradigm, this statement can be said to be meaningless. True Identity can never be *absolutely* glimpsed by a group in the midst of acquiring traits. Immersed in the Great Flow, their passage is eternal, ever changing; they cannot stop and look at themselves. Luckily, an unconditional determination of Identity is not crucial to the growing, healthy Bunch secure within its Beamic framework. It is only during *Crisis*—a condition that Budd Hazard defines as the Crossroads of Life and Death that every entity must face sooner or later—that a Bunch must conjure a *reconfirming vision* of itself and its place in the Universe or, failing that, cease to exist."

It was at this critical moment, Komodo contended, that the symbiosis of his two equations came into play. "A Bunch can only continue within its P + AT = I configuration so long," he declared. "At some point the acquisition of traits will become a burden rather than a boon. Development turns to decadence as an entity moves too far from its original perception of itself. Yet the goal cannot be the restoration of days gone by; that has been proved in our failures with the Zoo of Shame. The Evolloo is an endless forward-moving river. The goal of all Bunches is forge ahead to a *new* understanding of their nature."

This could only happen, Komodo said, "through *willful, symbolic reconnection* to the Mainstem." It was then that, like yesterday's skin, the used-up, overloaded P + AT = I would be discarded to be replaced for a fleeting moment of searing clarity by the P = I. It was at that point—when a Bunch internalized who knew how many eons of acquired traits into a new reincorporated Self—that the Evolloo lurched ahead, and Life pushed on. Komodo called it the Instant of Reprimordialization.

That's what the Fayetteville Tree was all about. From the moment he saw the twelve-foot tree-inside-a-bottle bobbing like Brainac's live-action paperweight in the waters off Indemnification Shore, Komodo understood its value as a Reprimordial laboratory. To him the Fayetteville Tree, with its stunted limbs and equally stunted population (owing to the proximity of the Philip Morris Company to the town that gave the Tree its name) was "the perfect container—a closed, controlled, yet totally natural habitat with which to study the immortal branching of the Blessed Blueprint."

This was due, in part, to the remarkably rapid rate of species diversification among the Tree's aviary populations and the ease with which this differentiation could be discerned. The chickadees were color-coded, so to speak. When the Tree first appeared, there were only three primary population types— yellow ones, blue ones, and red ones. But then, overnight, came orange ones. Purple ones. Green. Green-yellows. Burnt siennas. It soon became necessary to crib taxonomic nomenclatures from the large-size Crayola boxes to accommodate the influx. However, Komodo's DNA X rays revealed these color changes to be more than feather deep. There were morphologic changes as well. Every fresh-mixed hue of chickadee represented a distinct animal, a wholly unique Bunch.

Gojiro

Komodo viewed the ever-prolific Fayetteville Tree as a beacon of hope. "Oh, my own true friend," he said to Gojiro, "once again Budd Hazard's law has guided us. Reprimordialization is indeed the Engine of the Evolloo. New life is being created each day in this seemingly forlorn jar." Then, when the monster only shrugged, Komodo said, "Do you not see the great opportunity presented us? Our Promise calls for the establishment of a New Bunch to live upon our Island. If only we can isolate this Change, this Instant of Reprimordialization, then perhaps we might peer into the means of our own salvation."

After that, Komodo set up his cameras like some Muybridge gone Captain Video—720 at the height of the investigation, one long and wide lens for every half degree in his circular surveillance pattern—around the bottle containing the Fayetteville Tree. Each unit was equipped with Komodo's customized high-speed shutter, up to ten thousand frames per second, capable of producing the slowest of mo. Whatever happened in that tree, Komodo was taking no chances on missing it.

But it didn't work. Every morning Komodo would come out to the Zoo of Shame and count the new species pacing herkyjerky on the Tree's dungcaked branches. There were always more; one representative of the somber-browns had crossed with a showy orange to produce a toffee. New forest-greens abounded. However, when he developed his films, nothing could be seen. No moment of conception, no Instant of Reprimordialization.

"I don't get it," Gojiro fumed, barely resisting kicking the glassed-in tree. "One minute we got 57 varieties, the next there's 58 and it's like all invisible?"

Komodo rubbed his chin. "It is very puzzling."

Shortly thereafter, Komodo suggested that the Instant of Reprimordialization might "reside in a hidden zone, a realm out of time, out of space, a zone that cannot be recorded."

Gojiro rolled his eyes. "Wow, you mean like another dimension or something, where Vaseline's on the lens and the Stockhausen music starts up?"

Komodo only shook his head. But he did not give up. Not Komodo. Call it dementia, call it faith, but as mentioned before, Komodo's innate capacity for believing expands when he's confronted with the apparently insoluble. The more that Instant of Reprimordialization resisted his attempts to render it part of the temporal world, the more he became convinced not only of its existence, but of its sacred indispensability.

In place of the photographic record, Komodo substituted the Reprimordial Scenario. Much of this hinged on a shadowy reference once made by Budd

Hazard to "a special Breed inside a Breed, those who journey to the outside of What Is: the Throwforwards." The engendered imagery was full of awesome terror: two small and insignificant entities, emissaries of a Bunch so overloaded with Acquired Traits as to be struck autistic, moving toward each other, ever closer. They don't know why they go, or how, only that they must, because deep within them lies the preservation of their race. Closer and closer they come, until they enter the voidscape of Change, that private domain where they must meet and create something New, separate from what had gone before. Just thinking of such a trek made Komodo and Gojiro weak. Sometimes they'd look through the thick glass at the Fayetteville Tree, scan the feathered faces there and wonder: which ones are the Throwforwards? Which one of the blue-greens possesses that one extra chromosome, that as-yet unimagined adaptation that will become kinetic only when linked with the exact opposite chromosome hidden in the helixes of a light-yellow—and when you put them together, you got an aquamarine. Which were chickadee Adams and Eves, the ones who would push the outside of What Is, come into that void that is out of time, out of space and, once there, create new Life?

"That chartreuse over there, he's got a randy look," Gojiro said quietly after crossing the Zoo of Shame to join Komodo in front of the Fayetteville Tree. "I take him and that magenta. Give me four to one, you got yourself a bet." Komodo did not respond. He looked pale.

"My own true friend," he finally said, his face a haunted mask. "It was like a dream . . . a frightening, yet somehow beautiful dream. I felt Mr. Bullins's car explode, and then it was as if all time had stopped and I was transported to a vast and distant place. It was a moment of suspended will. I went toward her as if I were being pulled by an unknown force, as if I had to reach her—as if everything depended on it. Oh, my own true friend, can you understand what it might be like to be in such a place?"

And Gojiro shuddered, because he did. He absolutely did.

The horror played inside the monster's head always, a vicious loop.

The morning tide would be heavy on that long-past day, they knew. It never failed that whenever a Heater was shot off, whether thrummed deep beneath Nevada or cracked open like a glowing crown above Novaya Zemlya, Komodo and Gojiro felt the preseismic smack like a pair of old codgers rocking on a wooden porch who can tell, sure-nuf, next Tuesday it's gonna rain. It welled up in their lymphatics, raged fetid blisters on their skins and leathers. Then they'd start bawling, crying and crying. It was a signal to watch the shorelines, since Komodo's research indicated that the density of the flotjet flow was in direct proportion to the worldwide explo of Heaters. Whenever the fissions and fusions were busy, the shorelines of Radioactive Island bulked up big.

"Come on, my own true friend," Komodo said that early morning, "we must go out to greet the newest immigrants to our Land."

"Some fucking alarm clock," Gojiro groaned, picking at the Macy's parade–sized tumor ballooning from the side of his jaw. "How come they always got to blow these babies off before dawn? They ashamed to face the light of day, or they just want to knock off early, beat the traffic?"

The two of them trudged out to see what the current brought them. "There! What's that?" Komodo gasped from his perch on Gojiro's supraoc.

Squinting, Gojiro saw a ragged piece of land, singed and sawtoothed at its circumference. On either side were two barrel cactuses, and in the center a tall palm, its fronds dry and brown. Beneath the palm, barely visible, were two unmoving figures. Gojiro swallowed hard. People!

"Hurry," Komodo screamed, grabbing his medicine bundle, "we must attend to them!" A moment later, Komodo astride his dorsals, Gojiro was butterflying through the heavy sea.

The tract steamed and smoked and was hot to the touch. Komodo had to wear syntho-booties just to walk upon it. "They are alive! Help me! We must get them back to shore." That was when Gojiro saw them for the first time: a boy in his middle teens and a somewhat younger girl. Even as they lay there—silent, brownskinned, remote—it was clear that they had come from the same womb.

It was Shig and Kishi. Brother and sister, escaped from the Heater's grasp on this hummock of palm desert, the first Atoms ever to come to Radioactive Island.

She was only fourteen then, six years younger than Komodo, but you'd never know. The Heater had aged her, twisted her features, turned them into the face of War, a thousand years of War. They got her back to shore, laid her down right there. Komodo pulled out his remedies and went to work, utilizing techniques picked up during all those years of keeping his Coma Boy ears open back on Okinawa.

"Your sister needs a transfusion," Komodo shouted to Shig, but he just sat there stunned. Somehow, he'd avoided serious damage. Shock and exhaustion seemed his only maladies.

Komodo could waste no time; he rolled up his sleeves, jabbed a needle in his arm, ran a line to Kishi's. Gojiro turned his head when the tubes went red. He couldn't stand to watch Komodo pour himself into this unknown girl. More than blood was going in there, he knew, from the very first. It took what seemed like hours, and Komodo's face went white. Gojiro feared that his friend was being bled dry. But just when it appeared Komodo had nothing more to give, Kishi began to stir.

From then on, Komodo cared for her. He brewed medicinals in his beakers and bunsens, but mostly he did it with his hands. His hands divined where Death lurked, doused it out, dispersing the darkest swarm with the lightest touch. For six weeks he tended her. Then, one day, she smiled, and the next she walked, and you could see she was more than a girl. She was next to being a woman, a very beautiful one. She had the whitest teeth, and the blackest hair, and the brownest skin. Komodo had kneaded the Heater's terror from her, brought her back to life.

When the feeling first began, Gojiro imagined he was only jealous. As jealousy he could accept it, try to overcome it. Besides, it seemed perfect, Komodo being in love with Kishi, her loving him back. Why shouldn't the two of them stroll the meadows of Vinyl Aire, stand serenaded by the dissonantly clashing rocks off Ba-lue Bo-livar Shore, Komodo holding her hand, in the most chivalrous of courtships.

It made sense, Gojiro thought, that Komodo should no longer wish to ride upon his back, that the two of them would cease to soar behind their sun. Hadn't he himself railed against the lie of eternal boyhood? If his life with Komodo was to become no more than a yellowing page, a bittersweet turn of time, then so be it. He wouldn't be one to try to push the past beyond its proper limit. What was would be.

As weeks turned to months, Gojiro saw Komodo less and less. He was always with Kishi. Sometimes Gojiro would hear him, telling her his poems, singing her his songs. The same songs they once sang down the 'cano to get them through those long, long and lonely nights. It was no big thing, listening in, Gojiro told himself, watching them through the spread of Insta-Envir. Komodo was happy, finally. That was cause for mutual celebration.

He just wanted to see what love was like. Some details stood out. How they'd laugh and then fall silent, then laugh again, the joke being beyond speech.

Everything they did had an unconscious dynamic. They'd be lying there, then they'd jump into the water and swim, then they'd be lying on the beach again. There was no windy philosophy between them, none of the overheated intellectuality that so often bullied his own relationship with Komodo. That made sense too, the monster thought; Komodo no longer needed to forge artificial meaning from his fractured existence. "He doesn't need Cosmo anymore, his world is complete," Gojiro said to himself, watching the lovers.

It became his life, sneaking in the darkness, thirsting for glimpses of them. It seemed that he spent his every moment peering over the top of the 'cano, spying. It was then it started up, that gnawing inside him. An unknown sensation, inundating, frightening.

He tried to discuss the compulsion with Shig, for all the good it did. Even then the bizarre teenager was what he always would be: sullen, forbidding, obscure. Yet it seemed right that the two of them attempt some kind of relationship, so Gojiro tried. "I'm having trouble dealing with my attachments," the monster offered one afternoon as Shig practiced his swordplay on Corvair Bay Beach.

"Me too," was all Shig would say, stopping only to pluck a pair of Ray Bans from the water.

Obscene, seemingly unthinkable thoughts began to seize the reptile's brainscan. He could think of nothing else but Kishi. It was as if his mind were impulsing a hideous message, daring his unwilling body to carry it out. He'd close his eyes and see her, then wake himself, horrified, revolted at his fantasies. "This is hell!" he screamed.

One night he saw them in the moonlight, Komodo's arm placed so gingerly around Kishi's back. "In *our* moonlight," Gojiro muttered, dragging himself back down into the 'cano. He was a miserable thing; his leathers were without elasticity, his hyoid hung.

"I'll leave. I'll make my own way in my own world," the monster exclaimed, his head filled with jaunty pictures of himself as a vagabonding Tom Joadish sort of zard, hitching and hoboing along the windswept highways and byways, a hard travellin' song on his lips. He tossed a few personal items in a bag, among them that most primitive napkin holder fashioned from a distributor cap that was the first present Komodo had ever given him. He would go with no hard feelings, leave with only joy in his heart. His own true friend had reached happiness, and wasn't that the true goal of the Triple Ring Promise?

I forsake Radioactive Island with a free and easy mind, he told himself, hoisting his bindle onto his shoulder. He paused on the beach to peer out into the distant Cloudcover, wondering what adventures lay on the other side.

But it was no good. Before he could place a foot into the foaming surf, that sensation was looming once more, commanding him. "Komodo, I need help! Komodo!"

But his friend did not answer.

That's when he knew it was more than jealousy. Whatever malignancy consumed him, it exceeded any of the seven deadlies, was more than all of them squared. It was something utterly compelling, something beyond all self-control.

So he killed her.

He thundered across the land, possessed by an impossible demon. "I want her!" he bellowed, crashing through the contorted vegetation, ripping the tops from trees, mashing everything in his path. "Now!"

He caught up to them on the beach out by Past Due Point. Komodo knew. He sensed the madness welling up inside his friend. He and Kishi were already in the water, aboard that same inflatable raft that had carried him to the Island all those years before, feverishly pulling at the starter rope of a corroded outboard motor. "My own true friend! Please stop! You are not yourself!"

And, you know, maybe it holds up in court and maybe it doesn't, but Komodo was right. Gojiro was not himself. In fact, as far as the monster knew, he wasn't even in that water thrashing out toward the Cloudcover. He wasn't anywhere near Radioactive Island. He was in a zone, seized by a bizarre hallucination. Inside a crazy world he'd never seen, never known.

He was in the middle of a great valley, its reddish walls lurching high above. He was little: a tiny zard again. And everywhere around him was Death. Giant animals—saurs? Were they really saurs?—fell to either side of him, lay writhing on the smoky ground. But he couldn't stop, not for a moment. He had to go forward. *As if everything depended on it.* "Doom behind!" an undeniable voice inside his mind called out. Ahead: *her.* Her and a million more like her. A billion more, as many of her as could be seen in opposing mirrors, an unbroken chain snaking to infinity.

Then he saw her—Kishi! In the bottom of that boat, out in the water.

Water? What was Kishi doing in a boat? There was no water here, in the middle of that great red-rimmed valley where Death ruled.

Something was happening to Kishi. She was writhing at the bottom of that boat. Komodo was hunched over her. Komodo? What was he doing here, in this valley, in this desert?

It was only then that he saw the situation, what he'd done. Possessed to get to Kishi, he'd raged a savage whirlpool out by the Cloudcover. The torrent threw Komodo and Kishi from that little boat, slapped the two of them tight to the centrifuging sides of that terrible vortex. Round and round they went, holding hands. There was no sound inside that swirl. Numbed and helpless, Gojiro watched them go. Round and round. Komodo and Kishi, Komodo and Kishi.

When he finally heard that scream, he was certain it was his. His own horror at what he'd done. But it wasn't. It wasn't him at all. It was a baby's cry. "Waaaa!" A freshout baby's cry. It was the last thing he knew.

When he woke up, he was on the beach, alone with the anguish of his deed. There was only one thing to do. He dragged himself back down the 'cano to prepare. He fired up a crosshatched section ripped from an old smelter, gridironed it to his chest. Down and down he forced the white-hot pattern, until the Triple Rings could no longer be seen.

Then he heard Komodo sliding down that greased pole. "My own true friend! What have you done?" Komodo shouted. "Your Triple Rings!"

"I thought you were dead! I thought I killed you!"

Komodo looked a hundred years old. "Please! Let me help you, this is terrible!"

Gojiro recoiled from his friend. "Leave me alone! How can you bear to touch me . . . after what I've done."

"Lie down!"

Komodo put his welder's hat over his head like a shroud. He worked with his plasti-cosmetic torch, blazing away, scaling, contouring. "There," he said, "good as new."

Gojiro felt his Rings. "Good as new," he croaked. "How good is that?" He couldn't look at his friend. He didn't have to see Komodo's face to know: Kishi was dead. He'd murdered Love.

That was when he heard that cry again. The same one that broke the silence inside that whirlpool. "Waaaa!"—that little baby's cry. Komodo smiled then, because beside him was a child.

* * *

133

That was it, the final turning point. When and if the definitive history of Radioactive Island is ever written, that maelstrom will be the demarcation, the exact spot the Glazed World stopped and everything else began. Sure, Komodo tried to tell him that Kishi, like all the Atoms who would come after her, was going to die anyway, that she was dying that very day. As if that absolved him of anything! There was no forgiving this. Thank God for Shig. Who could blame him for pouring on the malevolence like he did, never letting up. At least *he* was sane.

Gojiro never told Komodo about that crazy compulsion. Not about the weird valley, the jutting red cliffs and the Death all around, none of it. To talk about it was to relive it, to be that deranged creature once more.

Now, though, out back of that sad producer's mansion, in the Zoo of Shame, Komodo was saying strange things. How did he put it? That he "pulled" toward Sheila Brooks? That he had felt himself transported "to a huge and distant place"? That for that "frozen" moment it seemed that "everything depended" on him reaching Sheila Brooks?

Gojiro tried to make sense of it. Back on Lavarock, he recalled, there was talk of something called "the pheromone." What a pleasure it was for that youngest zardplebe to sit upon the great Stone listening to the Initiates talk of that mysterious airborne chemosignal and how it triggered your inborn reflexes, directed you to your Chosen One. How wondrously racy those full-growns made the pheromone sound, and how spectacular to do its piquant bidding! How, once it came into your body, there was nothing but sex—tailtip, snoutjoust, and backscratch, and when you shake it all around, the next link in the Line been laid down. Later, of course, in the stream of supposed "scholarly journals" that washed up on Radioactive Island, the reptile came across an article entitled "The Role of the Pheromone in the Reproductive Cycle of the Common Southsea Monitor Lizard." Made the monster so mad. As if those hornrimmed fieldworkers really figured it was as simple as your cloacals come coldcreeping, then bong!—time to breed. What did those assholes know about love?

When Gojiro looked up, Komodo was still pressing his face against the container of the Fayetteville Tree. Was it the pheromone his friend felt under Albert Bullins's big top, the monster wondered. Komodo seemed too wrought up to talk about the incident right then. Besides, that dodo was getting antsy, smacking his cracked beak against the rocks again.

"Dodo didn't get a treat," Gojiro mentioned.

"Really?" Komodo said, jumpy, spreading out a handful of Moa Chow. "I could have sworn I gave him some . . ."

The Atoms were raising a ruckus, their high-pitched voices shearing through the smoggy air. They'd been restless since setting foot in America. Something about the place hacked up their maloccluded helixes. Just the day before, ten of them found their way onto the Ventura Freeway, tied frying pans to their faces, and ran out waving whatever hands they had, screaming that they were invaders from an angry red planet. Those nutty kids! What they wouldn't do for a chain reaction. Back on Radioactive Island, they loved to knock down endless lines of dominoes and blow ping pong balls around with hair dryers. Here it was the freeway. The results were predictable: squealing brakes, front end–rear end, a State Farm feast. Shig arrived just in time, getting the Atoms off the scene while the cops were still trying to strap Breathalyzers on the whiplash screamers.

"Always something with those wackos. I think their dosage is going to have to be reevaluated," Gojiro noted idly, casting a gaze in the direction of the noise. Then: "Oh wow . . ."

It was Sheila Brooks, staggering from the Insta-Envir.

THE DINNER GUEST

She followed a Home of the Stars map so out of date as to still list the Traj Taj as a major attraction, parked her little red Corvette outside the iron gate. Probably most visitors would have run away when they saw those fifty-foot mother-in-law tongues lurching over the fence, but she never even noticed. All she saw was the late-afternoon sun glinting off the shark teeth of the cocohead palms. To her, every one of those lurid faces said, "Come in."

She couldn't have gotten more than ten feet inside the gate before the turf jerked beneath her feet, sending her flying into a crowd of fiberglass daffodils that embedded spiky plastic shards into the furry Dale Evans chaps she wore. That's when Al Capone and the others surrounded her. Henry Kissinger gnawed on her leg, Billy Graham offered her a controlled substance.

Ebi saved her. She came running through the creeper vines and scattered those eggheads. The others, they sensed something about Ebi, deferred to her. And really, that's what had Komodo and Gojiro so flummoxed. It wasn't just that Sheila Brooks was coming out of the Insta-Envir, but that she was coming with Ebi—the way Ebi, so small and brown, was pulling Sheila Brooks, so big and white. "Help me!" the little girl shouted, "I think she's going to faint." Which Sheila Brooks did, right then.

"Let's get her into the house!" Komodo screamed, his voice tinged with hysteria. It wasn't easy carrying Sheila Brooks. Over six feet tall, her lank body seemed only to elongate as it folded over Komodo's slim shoulder, her wild white mane streaming down nearly to the floor. Still, Komodo managed to transport the groaning Hermit Pandora across the Traj Taj's vast ballroom and set her down on one of the long couches.

It was several minutes before she came to.

"Oh, Ms. Brooks!" Ebi said with delight. "We are so pleased and excited you have come to visit us. You cannot know how long we have waited for you and how welcome you are!"

Sheila Brooks craned her head around. "You are? . . . I am?"

"Yes!" the Atoms shouted.

There was nothing left to do but invite her to stay for dinner.

Komodo sat in his usual place at the head of the long, narrow table. He never felt at ease with this patriarchal positioning, but this was how the Atoms liked it. Sheila sat at the opposite end, likewise by demand.

Dinner was the usual slop scene, splatter left, splatter right. Immediately the Atoms began chanting for the Burger Train. "Burger Train! Burger Train . . . sixteen coaches long!" It was useless to protest. So, smiling like a ninny at the uncomprehending Sheila Brooks, Komodo laid the Lionel track around the edge of the table. Onto each flatcar of the toy midnight flyer, he laid a steaming hamburger, then he whirred the transformer dial. As the doublediesel engine began its circular creep, the Atoms whistled a disjointed version of the theme from *The Bridge on the River Kwai*.

It was a straight Russian-dressing roulette trip, based on an idiot sabotage movie. According to a chance program, the train crunched to a halt in front of one Atom's placemat, and then another's. The trick was to snatch your burger off as quickly as possible; you never knew at which stop on the train's culinary passage the boiled meat would blow up. This time it happened in front of poor Bop. Wham! Saturated fat erupted, forty feet or more, geysering up to the vaulted ceiling of the Traj Taj dining room. A solid sheen of mustard, followed by a second surge of ketchup, showered Sheila Brooks as if she were a nonrepresentational canvas.

"Oh my God!" Komodo shouted, running toward Sheila with a wad of napkins. Crinklecut pickles gummed both lenses of her glasses. A roll stuck to her head like a shrunken pillbox hat. "I knew we shouldn't have played our silly games! Are you all right, Ms. Brooks?"

A tension gripped the room. Every Atom hung on the reply.

Sheila Brooks peeled off the pickles, looked around at the expectant, misshapen faces. "I guess so. Sure. I'm okay."

"But your wonderful clothes, they are ruined." Several Atoms came over with gooey napkins and despite good intentions only ground mayonnaise deeper into the suede nap of her quisenberry-dyed buckskin vest.

Sheila managed a gruesome smile through the ketchup. "Don't worry about that. I have a dozen outfits like this. I don't pay for them. They send them to me for free because I'm famous. I try to give them to the Goodwill, but the designers threaten to sue. Besides, that was . . . fun. Yeah! That was great!"

The Atoms went into an uproar. "Hooray for Ms. Brooks!" they shouted. Some of them started dancing on the table. "Ooga-booga," they chanted; Sheila was "one of us."

The rest of dinner was more relaxed. The squirm food caused only minor difficulties. Squirm food was a nutritional measure worked up by Komodo in an effort to get the Atoms to eat. As befitted their postholocaustal neoferal tendencies, few of the unfortunate children would consume anything if it simply lay on a plate. They preferred to hunt and gather, or at least chase. Komodo, after much dietary R&D, managed to concoct a menu of syntho-veggies and mock meats equipped with a spittle-proximity escape mechanism; when an open mouth got close, the food bolted away. Several of the clumsier Atoms sustained fork wounds as they attempted to pin their prey, but this could not be helped. It was the heat-seeking seaweed that almost got to Sheila. Some slob Atom dropped a piece of it onto the floor and it began lacing itself up her leg like Caesar's sandal. Komodo, however, was able to slice the weed off with his pocketknife before her circulation was affected.

After dinner, the Atoms brought out their potholders: an inevitability. Originally conceived as Monster Day presents for Gojiro, the potholders were another arts-and-crafts project gone awry. In the beginning, even the grouchy reptile had to admit it was kind of cute, each and every Atom independently turning out the same exact design, an off-angled profile of Gojiro, fire raging behind. Except they got carried away. They kept making the things, churning them out like Helen Keller's assembly line. Then they'd bring them to the lip of the 'cano and rain the ratty things down on the Monster like a polyester inversion. "Make 'em quit," he roared, knee-deep in potholders. "Don't they know I got hundred-inch-thick skin and nothing in the oven?" Attempting to save the situation, Komodo suggested that the Atoms sew their potholders together into a quilt, which they could then present to Gojiro. To avoid the fight about whose potholder would go where in the finished project, Komodo put them all in a giant drum and spun them around. But when he dumped them out, there it was: a football field–sized replica of the smaller potholders, that same off-angled profile of Gojiro, fire raging behind. Komodo couldn't fathom the math of how it had turned out that way. Gojiro could only shrug. How do you fight obsession like that?

There was no such hassle when the Atoms presented their potholders to Sheila Brooks. They sat her in a velvet chair at the front of the mansion's ballroom, then lined up in painful imitation of a department-store Santa Claus scene. One by one, the Atoms did their best bow and said, "Thank you, Ms. Brooks, for inviting us to your wonderful country." Sheila Brooks accepted each potholder with an exaggerated nod of her head, putting each one on the neat pile in her lap. "This will really help me in the kitchen."

"Are you a thrifty home economist?" Ebi asked.

"Uh, sure . . . I try to be," Sheila said. She did, after all, spend hours a day poring over the supermarket ads, circling the best prices, scrupulously cutting out coupons. However, the idea of actually getting into a car and going to a wide-aisled, fluoro-bright market filled with gleaming wagons was psychically out of the question, so she just threw the coupons into a drawer.

"Perhaps you will cook for us sometime," Ebi suggested.

Cook? Sheila considered the concept. "Well, I made a meatloaf once. You know, from a recipe on the back of the oatmeal box. I was going to make mock apple pie, too, except I ran out of crackers. I dunno. I got out of practice after Bobby said I was nuts to try following the thirty-day budget-stretcher menus in *Woman's Day* when we had twenty million dollars in the bank. So mostly we order in . . . you know . . . the studio sends the catering truck over. But . . . I could try. I could try to cook for you."

"Hoorayyy!" the Atoms yelled.

It was about then that Lapu-lapu, that fishboy, started having a fit. Something was alive beneath his Ban-Lon shirt, circumnavigating his belly again and again. Komodo reached under his collar and pulled out a threeheaded frog. It was Crag's work, couldn't be any other. That kid! Him and a petri dish were a dangerous recombination. Komodo tried to harness the boy's bio-gen talents, but it was no use. He created things only to destroy them. That's what happened this time. The frog slipped from Komodo's grasp, and Crag crushed it flat against the marble floor with a shovel.

"Ah-ha," Komodo said, turning from the quivering blotch. "Bedtime, my little friends. Let's be on our best behavior for Ms. Brooks."

To Komodo's amazement, this worked on the first try. It was too strange how eager those Atoms were to "be good" for Sheila Brooks. Suddenly as docile as sedated members of a police lineup, they made their way up the ornate staircase. "Good night, Ms. Brooks," they intoned.

Sheila waved wanly.

Just then, Ebi broke out of the line. Had she ever looked prettier, happier? She moved so lightly, her long nightgown skimming the cool Italian tiles. Then she grabbed hold of Sheila Brooks's limp hand and asked, "Can Ms. Brooks come upstairs and tuck us in?"

"I . . . well—Ms. Brooks, how do you feel about that?"

Sheila Brooks shuffled her outsized feet. "I dunno . . . I mean, if that's all right."

"Oh, Ms. Brooks!" Ebi exclaimed joyfully. Then, standing on tiptoes, Ebi put a kiss on Sheila Brooks's whitecaked cheek.

The notion of anyone tucking in the Atoms was ridiculous, of course. Once, after much medical research, Komodo had customed a special bed for each of the luckless children, to fit their individual handicaps. But it was a waste. They threw themselves on top of one another and slept in a jumble, zardic style, which is exactly what they did right then, under the chandelier of the Traj Taj's master bedroom. From the pile came the shout: "Story and song! Story and song!"

"I usually tell them a story," Komodo said to Sheila Brooks, who was pressing herself against the thick velveteen wall paper. "Do you mind?"

"No . . . I don't. I like stories," she said, wringing her long fingers.

As with the potholders, if the Atoms weren't tired of something the first time, they never got tired of it. So there was only one bedtime story, told over and over. It was an old tale of Evollooic survival, the one about the wicked king and the antlers.

"Once upon a time, in a sad kingdom very far away," Komodo began, in his most sonorous voice, "there was a bad king. This king didn't like anyone, but there was one group of his subjects he hated more than the others. These people were proud and fierce, and they stayed to themselves and would not bow down when the king passed by. One day, the king sent his soldiers and made all these people come to the palace.

" 'You must prove your love for your king,' the king said.

" 'How might we do that?' they asked, for they did not care for the king in the least.

" 'By growing antlers,' the king proclaimed.

"The people protested. How could they grow stubby bones from their skulls? 'It is asking the impossible. Please have mercy.'

"But the king did not have mercy. 'Antlers in six weeks! If you love your king enough, you'll be able to do it. If not, I will have every last one of you killed.'

" 'Six weeks!' the people cried. 'How can we manifest such a massive adaptation within so short an interval?' They did not know what to do. Some of them tried to fool the king. They tied wire hangers onto their heads, covered them with papier-mâché, pretended these were antlers. But the king was wily. He sent his guards to destroy these people.

"There was one small boy and one small girl in this kingdom, and they did not want to die. 'Maybe we can save ourselves by taking the king's advice,' the little girl told the boy. 'Perhaps, if we concentrate on how much we love our king, we'll grow antlers on our heads.'

" 'But I *hate* the king,' the boy said.

" 'It doesn't matter,' the girl replied, 'we have to survive. If it takes loving him to do it, we must.'

"The little boy didn't know if this was possible but said he'd try. Every night they went to bed thinking only of how much they loved the king. Every morning they woke up and checked their heads. But no antlers appeared. 'It's no use,' the boy despaired. 'I can't control my hatred.'

"Then, only one day before the king's deadline, the boy and girl vowed that they would love the king as they had never loved before. They would love him as if he were more than himself, as if he were All Things, as if without him and the love of him, the world would cease to be.

"The next morning both the boy and girl awoke with the first bumpy ends of antlers sticking out of their heads. They went to the king's castle and were examined by the court scientists. These great men conferred for some time and agreed: antlers had grown.

" 'You are spared!' the king proclaimed. 'Your families are spared as well. But tell me, how did you do it?'

" 'We vowed to love you with a love greater than any that we could conceive of, more than Love itself,' the little girl told the king, who was very pleased.

"So, by and by, it came to be that the little boy and girl, whose antlers grew bigger and bigger, were married and had children. Their children had antlers too. Eventually there was a whole community of people with antlers in the kingdom. And soon enough, they declared war on the rest of the people, the ones without antlers, and wiped them out. The king was the last to go.

" 'What makes you think you have a right to do this?' the now elderly king asked with his dying breath.

" 'On the basis of our superior love,' the girl said, as the boy rammed his sharpened antlers into the king."

It was something Gojiro swore he'd never do again. But still he skulked away from that Zoo of Shame, suctioned up the creaky old drainpipe, skittered across the terra cotta roof, stopping on the wirewoven skylight overlooking that master bedroom. Was it the same as the spying he did back on Radioactive Island, all that time ago? The monster didn't want to ask himself. All he knew was that he couldn't resist.

As he peered through the window, the monster felt himself seized by another hallucination. This time, however, there was no panic in it, no possession. Instead, he felt himself become another beast, a flying zard, an archaeopteryx riding the hot Santa Ana winds, into the Los Angeles sky. He circled the Traj Taj, looking down to see a family—a mom, a dad, a passel of kids, the station wagon parked outside, same as any town, any place.

Then the light went off, and he scampered from the roof. He got back to the Zoo of Shame just in time for the song to begin. It was the second half of the nightly ritual. After telling the story, Komodo would take out his pocket synthbox, lay his calloused fingers on the tiny keyboard, and ask the children what they wanted to hear, even if he knew the answer would always be the same: "Heartbreak Hotel." It was Komodo's best number; his aching, choirboy tenor had a certain way with the phrase "Down at the end of lonely street, at Heartbreak Hotel."

THE BRAIN IN THE
BASEMENT

"Cute kids," Sheila Brooks said, finally.

Until then they'd just been standing, mute, in the middle of the drafty ballroom, as if waiting for a spectral orchestra to strike up an angular, tonelessly modern waltz.

"Yes," was all Komodo could say, as stiff as Greenland. Face-to-face with her in that grandiose, cavernous room, he felt cornered, trapped.

"Are they all yours?"

"Mine?"

"The kids. Are they all yours?"

"No, not exactly."

"They're adopted?"

"Well . . . not formally."

Sheila Brooks tugged at the more accessible portions of her unruly coif. "Then . . . they're foster children?"

Komodo seized on the term. "Foster children! Yes, you could call them that." Then, feeling the ball in his court, he asked, "Do you have children, Ms. Brooks, you and Mr. Zeber?"

Sheila pressed her hands together, forcing the chewed skin around her nails whiter. "No. I can't . . . have children."

"Oh, I'm sorry. I didn't mean to—"

"It's not *biological*. I'm not barren or anything. I took tests. There's nothing wrong with my *flesh*." She hit herself hard on the forehead with her palm. "It's up here! That's what stops it. Brain cells. They tunnel down and

143

murder it, right in the womb—psycho-abortion. The doctors won't admit it, but that's what happens. I know." Then Sheila Brooks turned her back, stared out the thirty-foot-high French window. She was sobbing now.

Komodo's throat tightened. How different this was from that moment beneath Albert Bullins's candy-striped tent. Back there, it was as if his every ion were charged, directed. He could have walked through any obstacle to her. He knew it was sinful—she was another man's wife!—but, whatever had come over him during that uncommon instant, he wanted it back. It did not come. He could only stand, glued to his spot in that hideous room, listening to her sobs echo amidst the painted stars upon the vaulted ceiling. He was starting from absolute zero, as if the right words, the entire language he needed to express his thoughts hadn't yet been invented.

"I'm awful," she said, blowing her nose with a honk. "Coming over here, laying this on you. It's just that . . . kids . . . I dunno. I walk through nurseries, see them lying in their plastic cribs, with their little feet and little hands, all of them, just starting out and then it takes over—what's gonna happen. The squealing brakes, the microbes eating away, the bad water out of the tap, tornados tearing off the roof of the school . . . And the kids—they know. They *know I know*—who I am. They see me coming and they run."

She let out a wail. "I don't know why I'm telling you this. It's just that *your* kids—well, with them, I dunno, it didn't happen. I don't know why. I looked in their faces, and the horror, it didn't start up. It was like . . . you know what I mean, whatever was gonna happen to them, it already did. It was different. Like . . . comfortable."

She took a breath. "That one, the one who kissed me, what's her name?"

"Ebi. Her name is Ebi."

"Ebi."

Grasping at etiquette's thin straw, he asked if she'd like to see the house.

They made an ungainly couple, moving through the gloomy mansion together. It was more than the height discrepancy; there was significant differential in their bipedal formats as well. Komodo, crisp and compact, walked with a straight-lined precision that no fashion model with the Britannica balanced on her head could hope to duplicate. Sheila Brooks, on the other hand, locomoted with complete physical obliviousness. Her step was shot through with a cartoonish segmentation, each wideslung leg swing accented by an outward heel flare. This was compounded by a radical forward crane of her seemingly extra-vertebraed neck, which caused her large oblong head to precede the splaying footflap by a good yard. Needless to say, her posture left much to be desired. Despite this shambling display, however, her stride remained quite lengthy, so much so that she only required one step for Komodo's every two. He attempted to compensate by doubletiming his gait. But then Sheila went faster too, causing Komodo to speed up further. In this way they traversed the shrouded corridors and cold marble staircases, faster and faster, neither one of them willing to call attention to the ever-escalating pace.

Finally, halfway down a dismal hallway, Sheila Brooks stopped to look at a painting of the sad producer's long-lost love. There were dozens of the portraits in the house, all done by the old producer himself. Apparently, it was the way he'd passed those years alone. Each painting was dated, enabling Komodo, a student of such things, to trace the artistic trend. It was interesting to note how, in the earliest works, the pert-faced subject was almost always seated beside a sunlit window, much in the Vermeer style. The later pictures were darker, grieving, as if the window had been shuttered up with bricks.

"She is quite beautiful, don't you think?" Komodo offered tenuously, recounting much of what the real estate brochure imparted in regard to the Traj Taj's legend.

"Really good skin," Sheila noted.

"It is a sad story," Komodo said. "But the children enjoy looking at the paintings. Many of them have copied the works in finger oils. They have an ardent appreciation for art."

"My mother was a painter," Sheila Brooks said bluntly.

"Oh yes," Komodo replied with sudden excitement. "I am aware of her work."

"You are?"

"Absolutely. Her portrait of your father standing in the middle of the Encrucijada Valley is . . . shattering. Of course, I have only seen reproductions, shoddy ones at that, but sometimes I cannot even bear to look at those. It is almost too beautiful, too powerful. I'm certain seeing the original would be a great experience."

"I never saw it."

Komodo shuffled his feet. "You've never seen your mother's painting?"

"I've never seen any of what she did."

"But you should."

"What for?"

"Because . . . because you are a great artist yourself. Your films are very compelling."

"What's that got to do with it?"

Komodo couldn't stop himself. "Where I came from there is a theory, sometimes referred to as Alchemical Heredity, or the Tenacity of Genes and Dreams. This means that, just as certain physical aspects are passed from parents to children, it is possible for thoughts, ideas, *dreams,* to likewise be inherited. Perhaps it is simply a personal folly, but I believe that there are dreams that, left unfinished in one generation, can be completed, or at least carried on, by the next. In fact, it was by virtue of your parentage that I felt we should come—"

"I don't want to see my mother's dreams," Sheila Brooks said sharply. "It doesn't matter anyhow. She's dead."

Komodo's head slumped. "Oh, I am sorry."

"She died the day I was born."

Again, Komodo felt himself falling, down and down. Shame straitjacketed him. Then he felt someone standing behind him.

It was Shig. "Please forgive me," the severe neoteen intoned, the hallway's Caligari shadows only exaggerating his macabre aspect. "I heard a noise and thought I would investigate. We are in a strange country and cannot be too careful."

Shig's head pivoted like a surveillance camera in a convenience store, first scanning Komodo, then Sheila. "Mr. Zeber is ill?"

"No," Sheila said faintly. "Why?"

"I only hoped he could have accompanied you to enjoy our hospitality."

"Ms. Brooks just happened to be passing by," Komodo said.

"I see." Then Shig stared at Komodo. "Perhaps you might wish to check the laboratory; I noticed the door ajar." He bowed and withdrew.

"That was the guy who came to the house. Who is he?" Sheila Brooks asked.

"A longtime associate," Komodo answered.

"Really creepy."

Komodo turned away. "Ms. Brooks, would you mind coming with me for a moment? There is something I must attend to."

Shig was correct. The door to the makeshift laboratory Komodo had set up in the basement of the mansion was open. That could mean only one thing:

146

Atoms had been in there. It was a serious problem, the little misfits sneaking in, guzzling every liquid, getting sick all over the place. There wasn't much that could be done to stop it. Back on Radioactive Island, even with the latest intelligence equipment flotjetting in like a paranoiac's trade show, security had been difficult. Here, it was impossible. Spastic as they were, many Atoms nevertheless possessed startling aptitude when it came to breaking and entering. They could turn every tumbler, pluck out any electric eye.

Sheila Brooks saw him first, pinned up there on the ceiling like an overweight moth. It was that Bop again. Obviously the unfortunate boy had wandered into the lab, gulleted some spare helium pellets, blown up to twice his normal size, floated upward, and become wedged between a pair of ceiling beams. "Do not be alarmed, Ms. Brooks. The boy is not hurt. It's a chronic problem." Komodo climbed a ladder, defused the pellets, and carefully guided the boy down to avoid a potentially disastrous propulsive exhaust.

"On your way," Komodo said, giving the resuscitated Bop a kindly tap on the backside.

"What is all this stuff?" Sheila Brooks asked, surveying the array of blue-sparking static tubes, twelve-foot Tesla coils, multidialed torque engines, blip machines, and fish-eyed mirrors. Komodo, unhappy without his toys around him, had managed to slapdash the entire lab from several beginner-level Gilbert chemistry sets he found in the multigabled attic of the mansion. He could transform any room into a set from *The Bride of Frankenstein* in no time.

Uncertain of his next move, Komodo grabbed a pair of steel-rimmed glasses off the workbench. "Try these," he suggested with forced conviviality.

"What are they?" Sheila asked, suspiciously regarding the cheaters.

"You'll see! Try them on!"

"I don't know," she said, indicating her electrician's-tape-encrusted goggles. "These aren't just for fashion, you know. They're prescription." But then she reached out. "Well . . . okay, just for a minute."

Komodo's heart began to pound as Sheila reached with both hands behind her head and began to undo the catches of her glasses. *Spall-lurt* went the suction cups as they separated from her face. He'd never seen her eyes; he didn't even know what color they were.

They were green. An emerald sort of green, maybe a bit darker. A verdant sort of green, showered through with gold. Komodo felt dizzy, as if he'd walked into an intoxicating cloud.

"So?" Sheila asked after placing the thin-lensed, clear-view glasses on her face.

"Do you feel the small button on the inside of the right temple wing? Push it when I tell you to." Then, in a most uncharacteristic pose, Komodo put his thumbs into his ears, wiggled his fingers, and stuck out his tongue. "Now!"

"Wow! It has instant replay!"

"Sixplay capacity for each event, expandable by a factor of twelve. It can store two hundred individual events. It comes equipped with audio echo as well."

Sheila pushed the button again. "This is great! You could make a fortune with these."

Komodo scratched his head. "Oh, I don't know. I just make them up for fun. To play with. I have a Braille one, too. Some of the children cannot see."

"Do something else!"

"What?"

"Sing something, like before."

Komodo blushed horribly, then, in a reprise of one of those solitary talent shows he used to put on for Gojiro back in the old days, he grabbed hold of a pole, whirled around, and sang a couple of bars from "Jailhouse Rock": "And the whole rhythm section was the Purple Gang!"

"Great!"

"No."

"Really! You're a terrific inventor, you know."

Komodo blushed. "I try hard and someday hope to invent some truly useful things such as the deep-sea hippodrome, the spectromarine copter, and the electric dining car runabout."

"Who invented them?"

"Tom Swift."

Her eyes lit up when she laughed, turned even greener, deeper. Her lips seemed thicker, almost plush; a small, inviting crook appeared in them, especially the lower. "That's silly," she said.

"Yes, I'm very silly," Komodo said giddily. It was his only joke, and it had worked!

"What do you do with these things you invent if you don't sell them?" Her eyes seemed serene now, a deep mist on an isle of pines.

"Oh, I usually destroy them, cannibalize them for parts to make other things."

"But why? That's such a terrible waste."

"Waste? I don't think so. I don't really have all that high an opinion of my work. Nothing I've yet created merits preservation. Sometimes I feel I am close to creating something of value, but just as I reach the crucial stage I experience . . . a failure of inspiration. Besides, it would be an unforgivable vanity to use additional resources solely to produce these mental doodlings."

"But if you keep breaking them up to make other things, what are you left with?"

"The last invention, whatever that may be." He shrugged. "But probably I'll wind up just destroying that too."

The idea upset Sheila Brooks. "You shouldn't sell yourself short. You are really a very gifted person. Bobby said so, after the party. He was real excited. I haven't seen him like that for a long time. He said you represented an unbelievable opportunity."

"Mr. Zeber sees opportunity?"

"It's how he talks; he can't help it. He hates that corporate thing. It's part of what I've done to him—always making him take care of the business crap, hang around with those jerky studio people, while I stay in the house. It wasn't how it was supposed to be . . ."

She trailed off for a moment, then continued with a quick smile. "Oh yeah. Bobby really thinks you're great. He said that special-effects guy—Tim Tuttle—he does our pictures, he's supposed to be the best or something. Anyway, he told Bobby he couldn't figure out how you do it. He said, 'Either that Komodo is the most innovative FX guy since Méliès or he's using a real monster.' "

Komodo tugged at the collar of his black pajamas. "Well, er, that's very . . . flattering. But—"

Right then a six-foot-wide shaft of blue-white lightning bolted through the room. It came from the other side of the wall, leaving a smoldering hole there.

Sheila Brooks jumped two feet. "Agggh!"

Komodo ran toward the next room. "Stay here, please, I'll be right back!"

He didn't think she'd follow him, but she did. *"What's that?"* she screamed, pointing at the pulsating gray mass, some fifty feet round and high, sitting in the center of the immense spare ballroom.

"This? Oh, it's nothing. Just a brain," Komodo replied, attempting informality as he ducked under another shear of razored light on his way toward a control panel on the other side of the room.

Mark Jacobson

"Why do you have a giant brain in your basement?"

Another bolt shot from the protruding frontal lobes, igniting the thick drapes at the other end of the shuttered room. "It's not exactly a brain," Komodo explained breathlessly, running to subdue the flames with a foam-spurting extinguisher. "It's a simulacrum."

Komodo never intended to bring that inflatable Quadcameral model with him to America. They were already resident at the Traj Taj when he noticed it, wadded up in a corner of the left pocket of his black pajamas. He couldn't resist puffing it up to its true scale. Now he regretted the installation. Why hadn't he lied and said it was an indoor tennis court, why did he have to tell her it was a *brain?* After this, Sheila Brooks would have every justification to deem him less than a serious individual, a mad scientist of a certifiably demented stripe. If she fled right then, he couldn't blame her.

However, when he finished stamping the fire from the drapes, Komodo saw that Sheila Brooks was not only still present, but was striding toward the model. Her arm was stretched in front of her, palm out, much in the manner of a sleepwalker. She was heading straight for the parietal opening.

"Ms. Brooks! No!" But it was too late. Komodo felt a pitch in his stomach as Sheila Brooks sank her hand deep into the loamy aperture. She was in up to the elbow before voltage recoil set in. Zam, she skittered backward on her heels, a gawk's moonwalk. When Komodo reached her, she opened her eyes—greener now—and said, "It's alive."

"Not . . . exactly," Komodo grimaced as he helped Sheila Brooks to her feet. "It is composed of a synthetic neurological material. A fiber."

"It thinks?"

Komodo grimaced. "Not completely, not yet. This is just a crude sketch, a hollow, woefully insufficient prototype. It cannot even be considered to approach the living ideal. But it can reproduce elements of the thought process."

"Intellectual dacron, the mind boggles. Can we go inside?"

"Inside?"

Sheila Brooks kept looking at the brain. "Yeah, I want to go inside, is that okay?"

Komodo was sweating. "Yes . . . it is possible."

* * *

When Komodo took Sheila Brooks into that Quadcam replica, it was the first time he'd entered the great model in years. He used to go in there all the time, to sit and contemplate, imagining himself in a kind of sanctuary, a realm apart, a holy place. How he loved those moments! Within that dense and humming place, he felt renewed, as if the shroud surrounding every riddle of his life might give way. "When I am in there," he once told Gojiro, "I feel most close to myself."

However, after the abhorrent operation that banished the supplications from the monster's tortured mentality, Komodo ceased to visit the huge schematic. It lay fallow, used only as a base for ring-a-levio-playing Atoms. The wild children delighted in sliding down the parietal tube, setting it churning like a revolving barrel in a fun house.

Now, riding the small lift up through the contoured folds, Komodo attempted to explain the rudiments of Quadcameral morphology to Sheila Brooks. Speaking loudly so as to be heard over the cerebral drone, he focused on the time-tiered structure of Evollooic sedimentation, chronologically delineating what he called "the ages of the Mind." The deepest seated of these layers, or the "primary cognitioner," was the so-called Reptilian Complex, a holdover from the Quadcam's earliest issue. Next came the thinner, emotion-wrought limbic layer, developed with the fall of the Sauric Empire and most closely identified with the cruder mammalian populations. On top of that, Komodo announced tour-guide style, was the primates' burgeoning Neo-Cortex, which reached its fullest flower in the portentous advent of *Homo sapiens.*

"A mistake often made by the humanoid host is to assume that the older segments of brain are somehow vestigial, that they exist only to perform the most menial of tasks and are subservient to the Neo-Cortex," Komodo explained as he led the pliant Sheila Brooks through the model, holding an umbrella over her head as a shield against the occasional jet sprays of neural fluids. "Just because a cameral form is more recent does not assure superior development. This misconception can result in serious difficulties, as the nether-situated lobes seek to assert their presence in the face of attempted override by the upper regions. Much seemingly pointless contradictory behavior results from these intracranial conflicts."

Sheila Brooks touched the breathing walls with her fingertips. "Far out."

Following well-marked pathways, they reached the forwardmost section of the Neo-Cortex, where Komodo invited Sheila Brooks to sit on a small ottoman-shaped polypous outcropping. "This is a pleasant spot," he said, pulling a foldout candle from his pajama pocket and lighting it. "I've often stopped here to reflect."

"Kind of clammy," Sheila Brooks allowed. "You make this from a kit?"

"Kit?" Komodo thought of the gluesodden replicas of battleships the Atoms turned out with such delirium. "No, this is more of a *projection.* An *idea* of the New Mind—the Quadcameral. It cannot be more than that."

"Why not?" She hardly noticed the synapsial vessels which hung loose from their contacts and had begun to entwine themselves in her wild mane.

Komodo sheared the vessels off with his pocketknife and continued. "To comprehend the New Mind, one must be able to think with one himself. The sort of brain in which we sit right now represents an entire other way of being. It is my belief that adaptations inherent here are so remarkably *different* from the current mind that those who attain them cannot rightly be counted within the same species as those who have not."

A sawtoothed spark of electrostatic energy serrated across the neural chamber. Again, Sheila Brooks didn't seem to care. "But who's going to get this brain? Anybody? People collecting tolls or selling insurance? Mary Kay agents? Or is it just gonna be those enervated guys, the ones with the giant heads and no bodies in the comic books?"

"Prediction, in these matters, is a hazardous game. However, this isn't to say individuals exhibiting fundamental elements of the New Mind do not already exist, even if they might not yet be aware of it."

Sheila Brooks rubbed at her cheek. "But how can they have it and not know it?"

"It is possible that the initial possessors of a new trait may *never* become aware of their difference, at least not in their own lifetime. Palpable cognizance of Quadcamerality and its particular capabilities may not become accessible for hundreds of generations."

Komodo cleared his throat. How could he explain this to Sheila Brooks without an exhaustive survey of Budd Hazardous cosmologics, an avalanche of jargonized terminology? Yet he was seized with a need to make her understand. "What I am saying is that often there is a passage of time between the inception of an organism's change and the perception of that transformation. For instance, one of the most commonly accepted schemes of the mind, which we might refer to as the Tricameral or triune brain, has, according to many studies, been extant in the *Homo sapiens* species for several thousand years. This, of course, is an eye blink in the scope of the geologic clock, but, in the life of the group, or Bunch, in question, it is a considerable period.

"Let us examine how the *Homo sapiens* have adjusted to the shift in their thinking apparatus . . ." From there, Komodo began talking about the Greeks, how back in Zeusian days they used to consult Oracles—trees, rocks, and the like—which they believed imparted the vital information of the day. The Oracle read no tea leaf, supplied no print-out; the input was received internally, springing wholecloth into the minds of supplicants.

"They heard the Oracle within their minds and experienced those utterances as the voice of the gods. That was the value of the Oracle—it enabled the petitioner to have *direct communication* with the Beyond. Now how can we account for this in terms of the modern outlook? Is it fair to characterize these individuals as merely primitive, hopelessly superstitious?"

No, Komodo argued, it was a question of biology, the product of a great unfolding cerebral drama. "The consolidation and refinement of the Neo-Cortex was a period of monumental shift," he said, "a process that is now generally called the rise of consciousness." Komodo imagined the Greek mind to be in a state where what *had been* was still fresh enough to be remembered, yet, due to the ongoing cameral augmentation, these "old" thoughts could only be expressed in "new," rational terms. It was a unique juncture: directives once deemed so important to survival were now becoming peripheralized, yet they persisted, echoed. An explanation had to be sought as to the origin of these powerful messages. Therefore, utilizing their newfound reason, these fresh-minted Tricamerals declared the voices in their heads, those that they supposed came from the Oracle, but that actually emanated from the very wellspring of their former existence, to be articulations of the newly conceived notion of Deity.

"Think of it, Ms. Brooks!" Komodo went on, inside that Quadcameral model. "To be relieved of the turmoil of not knowing, to hear the voice of what you took to be indisputable Truth within your own head. Nowadays, of course, this is no longer so. The ensuing years have witnessed the absolute triumph of consciousness. The old voices have faded, are not universally heard. Naturally, many yearn for them still, but this desire is considered more idiosyncratic than paradigmatic. Externalized replacements, faith and prayer among them, are far from instinctual. The psychic record has splintered. Perhaps it is just this condition that has led to the confusion that many experts refer to as the modern spiritual dilemma—"

153

"It's not fair!"

Maybe it was being back in the model again, letting his mind wax contemplative regarding the Quadcam and its eventual purpose within the Evolloo that caused him to go on as he did, but now, hearing Sheila Brooks's shout, Komodo was shocked into silence.

She looked ravaged, crazed. "Why isn't it like that anymore? Why doesn't it do that for you anymore?"

"Excuse me, Ms. Brooks?"

"Your head! Why doesn't it tell you what to do anymore? Sure, it tells you things—but they're wrong. Dead wrong!"

She grasped Komodo's wrist. Her long fingernails dug into his skin. "Now if you hear voices you're crazy. A nut! A schizophrenic! You got to take pills. They lock you up. Is that fair? Tell me, is that fair?" A streak of electricity lurched through the facsimile, whiting out the chamber for a moment. "It's not fair! It's sick!"

Komodo tried to calm her. "But Ms. Brooks, the mind marches on. Its current configuration is neither fair nor unfair. It simply is."

She jumped to her feet, her stark mane oozing into the ceiling of the small neural grotto. A wild look overcame her. "But I don't like how it is. I don't want my brain to be like this. I want to go back—back to how it was!"

Komodo stood up as well. "But that is not possible. Return is illusion. Nothing goes back to the way it was."

"It doesn't have to be back—just out! Out of here!" She looked up, pointed to a trapdoor. "What's up there?"

"Up there?"

"Yeah! What's up there? How come it's got a padlock on it?"

Komodo's face grew ashen. "That's the fourth chamber. The fourth chamber of the Quadcameral."

"I want to go up there," she said flatly.

"But Ms. Brooks . . . that's not possible."

"Why not?"

"Because . . . it doesn't really exist."

"But you said it did!" She began pulling at the lock.

"But Ms. Brooks! It is not finished!"

"I don't care. I've got to get up there!"

"But . . ."

"Please!"

He couldn't refuse her. He pulled a large skeleton key from his pajama pocket and fit it into the lock.

The fourth cameral! Komodo held his breath as he led Sheila Brooks up the small stepladder into that uncharted realm. It was as Komodo said: unfinished. There was nothing up there, just some naked molded plastic, a pile of particle board and sheetrock, a couple of tri-prong outlets. He'd left it like that, a bare attic. What else could he do? He couldn't conceive the inconceivable. True, he'd been inside the *real* fourth quadrant—he'd climbed inside Gojiro's head, banished a hundred million supplications, short-circuited that 90 Series, but that was different. That was an emergency. He hadn't looked around. He'd just cut the wires and left.

"But there's nothing here." Sheila Brooks shouted into the empty chamber. "Nothing at all!"

"I told you it might take generations. Hundreds of generations."

"But I don't have a hundred generations!" Sheila Brooks grabbed Komodo, crushed her long white fingers around his arm. She was a lot stronger than she looked.

"Don't you get it? I'm going crazy!" she cried. "I try my best to do my job, to make up those movies, help Bobby. But it's no good anymore. I start up, thinking it's going to be okay. Like the nightmare's gonna be perfect and all I got to do is tell it. But then it comes! Those pictures, the same ones every time, throwing everything else out of my head, blowing the good nightmares away. Don't you see the trouble I'm in? I didn't dream *Ants for Breakfast,* I made it up . . . *I faked it!* That's why it bombed! That's why they're on Bobby down at the studio. Because of me!"

She began slamming her head with her fist. "That's why I wrote you that goddamn letter!"

Komodo tried to hold her. "Yes, the letter! Ms. Brooks, we must talk about the letter. Those words at the bottom of the letter . . . what do they mean?"

"What words?"

"Bridger of Gaps . . ."

She stood up straight inside that vacant fourth cameral, looked ahead, trancelike. "Bridger of Gaps . . . Linker of Lines . . ."

"Yes!"

"Defender of the Evolloo!"

"Yes!"

"No!" Whatever had come over Sheila Brooks, it left. "I've got to get out of this brain!" All of a sudden she had a gun. A stubby-nosed derringer. It must have been inside her pocketbook. Now she pressed it to her temple.

"Ms. Brooks! No!"

Komodo dove, knocking her sideways. She flew against the side of the Quadcameral model and went through the tear-away fiber, sprung right out of the brain, sure as she was born.

Komodo looked at the hole with an open mouth. "Ms. Brooks . . ."

He couldn't find her for half an hour. He wandered through the giant house, calling her name, but the place seemed deserted. Not even an Atom was stirring. He was about to check the grounds when he saw her in his room.

His room.

It figured that Komodo would pick that room out of the dozens in the Traj Taj. It couldn't have been anything more than a maid's room, a windowless cell where some poor wetback who risked her life to come sweep up might dwell. It wasn't nearly big enough to be a walk-in closet for a midget wrestler. "I don't require much," Komodo said.

No disputing that. Komodo's Traj Taj quarters were a near-perfect replica of his cramped crib back on Radioactive Island. Compared to Komodo, Martin Luther was Liberace, accoutrement-wise. Outside of a small writing desk, there was nothing else in the dim-lit room except that stainless-steel slab where he slept.

When Komodo first came to Radioactive Island, he didn't even use that. He claimed he didn't need any sort of bed. His rationale was, after years of being the Coma Boy, he'd slept enough. Gojiro knew better. He knew Komodo was afraid to sleep, that he feared wink one might cast him back into the paralytic world from which he'd emerged. It became a problem. Komodo looked haggard and lost weight. Gojiro tried to make him take a nap. The reptile brought warm milk, told endless tales of Lavarock, prescribed every variety of pill. But it was no use: Komodo stayed awake. Then, one day, as the two of them stood out by Corvair Bay Beach, that operating table rolled in with the tide. The words "State Property" and a long serial number were hand-stamped onto the bottom of the metal. Who knew how much pain those who had lain upon that slab had suffered, but it didn't matter to Komodo. He salvaged it from the surf and put it in the bedroom he and Gojiro shared down the 'cano.

Gojiro

"You gonna slumberland on that?" the monster asked him. "Don't look like no beautyrest to me."

"Oh, no, my own true friend," Komodo said. "This is very comfortable. You ought to try it sometime."

"No thanks," Gojiro replied with a shudder.

It killed Gojiro that this loathsome operating table was the only place Komodo could rest. "They've made you into a specimen, my own true friend," Gojiro said to himself, watching Komodo lightly snoring on that unforgiving plate, a mirrored overhead lamp blaring into his eyes, a perpetual clench on his face. "I'll get them for this," he swore, "if it's the last thing I do."

Then he reached over and switched off the light. He thought the change might wake Komodo up, but it didn't. Gojiro saw his friend's face loosen, go a little slack. A small sigh came from his lips. Then Gojiro placed the softest kiss he could upon Komodo's forehead. "Perchance to dream, my own true friend, perchance to dream."

Anyway, that's where Komodo finally found Sheila Brooks: in his room, hunched over his tiny desk. Immediately he felt that odd heat. It hit him in the face like a slap. "Ms. Brooks?" Komodo approached slowly, on tiptoes so as to see over her shoulder.

She was sitting there holding Komodo's stereopticon, the picture holder Gojiro had snagged out of the Radioactive Island surf so many years ago. "Are these your parents?" Sheila Brooks asked without looking up, her voice hoarse, barely audible. She'd taken off the repeating glasses. Her eyes were greener than ever, but that fear—it was there.

Komodo stared at the picture of the man and woman inside the old wooden frame. How would he answer her question? The two people in that 3-D picture—the young man and his pregnant wife standing on the lush hillside, beside the crystal lake, before the snow-topped mountain—they weren't really his parents. They were an anonymous couple from long ago whose likenesses had somehow been misfiled into a sack of Fotomat rejects. Yet, they'd been inside that stereopticon for so long . . .

"They're dead, right?"

A vise closed around his heart. "Yes, those people are dead."

"I have one of these, you know. It's exactly the same as this one. My father bought it." Suddenly she sounded a thousand years old.

"Your father?"

"It's weird. I remember that day. We'd been driving . . . for months. We were everywhere, running away. They couldn't catch us. We were too fast, me and Dad. That's what we'd say: hey, hey, nobody's gonna catch us today. Then he said he wanted to go home. Up north, to where he was born. Later I found out it was in Wisconsin. That's where he got it, in a little junk store off the side of the road. I was six. The lady said I was real cute. She asked me if I was from around there. I said, No, but my dad is. She asked me my dad's name, I told her, and she kind of looked funny. Then she took the viewer out from under the counter, told me to give it to him, that it was his.

"The picture inside. . . . It was strange, old, like from the Civil War. A man and a woman and a lot of kids, ten maybe, standing real stiff in front of a clapboard house. There was something awful in there, in the man's eyes. He was looking ahead, but he seemed to be watching everybody, all at the same time. Watching me, too. It got me afraid. I brought it to Dad. Suddenly he looked real upset. What's the matter Dad? I asked. He pointed to one of the kids, the youngest one, said it was him. He was standing right next to his mom. Then he pointed to the scary man and told me it was his father. I don't know what happened then . . . except he made a phone call. And a couple hours later, all those men were in our motel room. They took him away. I never saw him again. Next thing I knew, Victor told me he got sick and died."

Then, without warning, she yelled: "Doesn't this get any brighter? Is this as light as it gets?"

It was a little improvement Komodo had made in the stereopticon system, an external backlight source to accentuate the three-dimensional effect. Now he adjusted it for Sheila Brooks.

"Yeah . . . that's better." She never moved her head, just kept looking. "Then, years later, it came to me in the mail, in a package without a card. The same stereopticon. Bobby said it could have been any one, there were millions of them, but I knew. Except the picture inside was different. It was him, my dad, and my mom. They were standing in the middle of that valley—"

"Ms. Brooks, are you all right?" Komodo called. Her face grew paler every moment; she looked about to faint.

"That's not how it's supposed to look," she screamed. "The background's wrong! There's no mountain, it's rocks. Red rocks and cliffs. There's no lake, no snow. *It's the desert!* Red rocky hills. Dawn light. Red rocky hills. Light!"

She was starting to shake.

Komodo leaned forward. She was seeing something in his stereopticon, something horrible. When he touched her she felt hot. The whole room felt hot, hotter than before. At first Komodo thought it must have come from the small bulb he'd installed, but no bulb could emit such a sear. This was another kind of heat, a terribly familiar fire.

"My glasses! Where are my glasses?" She fumbled about with her hand, trying to locate those black-lensed goggles. But it was too late. Komodo saw those green eyes get big before she screamed: "Mom! No! Dad! Dad! Get Mom!"

"Ms. Brooks! What do you see?"

"Dad! Mom! No!" Her voice—how young it sounded. Small . . . *a baby's cry.*

Then she stopped, sat there a moment.

When Komodo touched her shoulder, it started up again. Except it wasn't a baby's cry anymore. It was her own.

"Dad! . . . *Gojiro!*"

SHEILA BROOKS'S
SECRET

It was almost dawn when Komodo came running out to the Zoo of Shame to
wake Gojiro. "My own true friend!" he shouted. "She has a secret—a terrifying
secret!"

"Secret? Who got a secret?"

Komodo told the still-sleepy lizard what transpired in his room after Sheila
Brooks picked up the stereopticon. "The worst of it," he moaned, "was when
she came to. She didn't remember any of it. She ingested a quantity of pills and
claimed the blackouts to be the result of a breach in her therapy. Then she said
she was late and left as if nothing had happened." Komodo shivered. "She is
haunted by a traumatic image that somehow involves her mother, father, and
you, my own true friend."

"Me?"

"Yes. It is this image that makes her live in fear. We must aid her, if it
is at all possible."

Gojiro attempted calm. "So she got ghosts—all God's chillun got ghosts.
If she needs a celebrity exorcism, let her get Betty Ford to shake some
bedsheets at her."

Komodo slowly shook his head. "If you had only seen her bravery, the way
she charges into the throes of her own terror, seeks to meet it head on. It was
. . . *inspiring*. This is why she wrote us the letter, why she appeared at the
party at Mr. Bullins's house, why she came here last night. She is reaching out
to us. She senses that we can perhaps save her from the horror that stalks her
mind. We cannot refuse the call."

The next few days were filled with numbing run-throughs on that old stereopticon. "All right," Komodo shouted, holding the wooden photo holder in front of his face exactly as Sheila Brooks had. "When I give the signal, turn out the lights."

Gojiro followed instructions, then waited a moment. "So?"

"Nothing . . . nothing again," Komodo reported dejectedly. "Perhaps you would like to try another time, my own true friend."

"No way. I still got spots in front of my eyes from the last time."

Another day, another pit of quicksand. How many times had the reptile watched Komodo stare at the two strangers inside his stereopticon, seen him wish that the unknown couple would step from the confines of their artificial three-dimensionality to truly become his parents, tell him the mysteries of his past? It was a lot to pin on a funky old picture, the monster always thought. Except now Komodo wanted more. "We must see what she sees," the determined Japanese insisted. He went so far as to suggest that whatever hideous nightmare Sheila Brooks kept stored in her ravaged head might actually have significant impact on the Triple Ring Promise. Secret? What kind of secret could Sheila Brooks have—a top secret, an eyes-only secret, an ice blue secret? The monster tried to make light of the affair. But there was no way he could dismiss the fact that, right in the middle of her wacko vision, Sheila Brooks had called *his* name, lumped *him* together with her worldshattering father.

"What a horrorshow," the monster mumbled, stretching out in that old producer's bed to claw through a copy of *Visions in Fission: Private Lives beyond Relativity.* Shig had placed the book in the bedside drawer like a Gideon, curtly imparting that the thickspined tome contained certain "previously unpublished biographical material" on Joseph Prometheus Brooks that "might prove useful" in the development of the upcoming film. "Ain't gonna be no film," Gojiro muttered. However, to his surprise, he soon found himself engrossed in the dry-prose account of Brooks's early life.

"Weird," the monster grunted, noting that the progenitor of the Heater came from a large family. Gojiro never imagined Brooks coming from anywhere; to the monster, the scientist had always been this apparition in black, set down on the earth by demonic forces to torment the planet. But here it said that Brooks was the youngest of ten children born to Mary and Wallace Brooks, a man described as holding strong religious beliefs. The elder Brooks was obviously some kind of nut. After losing his job as a steelsmith in Milwaukee, he moved his family several times, to increasingly remote sections of northern

Wisconsin. Apparently wanting to totally isolate his relations and himself, he vehemently opposed his wife's desire to send their children to school. "However, Mary Brooks, aware of her youngest son's special nature, enlisted the aid of a trusted uncle and succeeded in stealing Joseph away from his ever-watchful father. The boy's obvious gifts were immediately recognized by his teacher, and he was soon passed to the university at Madison. Two years later, shortly after his thirteenth birthday, he was sent to Göttingen, where he was quickly accepted as perhaps the greatest mind of the age."

"A boy wonder," Gojiro snorted. However, as he read the subsection "A Colleague Remembered—Off-the-Cuff Remarks Made by Victor Stiller at the Society of Atomic Scientists' Luncheon, September 1963," a chill traversed the reptile's dorsal plates.

"It was Christmas vacation," Stiller was quoted as saying, "and the school was to be closed. Of course, I would have been most pleased to invite Joseph to spend the holiday with my family, but our home was so dank and cramped, my parents so poor, that this was not feasible. In any event, Joseph had already decided to return home. He loved his mother very deeply and missed her terribly. School officials were against the visit, thinking Joseph, their great plum, still a very young man, might be snatched up by an American institute. But he was determined to go and left after the final day of classes. I am certain he had no inkling of what had happened back in Wisconsin. He'd been with us for nearly three years, without a single piece of mail. The story is horrible to me, even now. From everything we understood, Joseph, traveling alone, did not find out the fate of his family until he actually came upon the site of his former home. His father, a deranged man, had, for reasons known only to himself, bound the entire family to chairs and incinerated them, himself included. The house was burned to the ground; survival was impossible. Of course, it was a great shock to us all. For several months after his return to school, Joseph, our great hope, showed no interest in his studies. I, being his closest friend, was appointed to speak with him and attempt to raise his spirits. I cannot say I had much success. Joseph said little about the events back in Wisconsin, allowing only that the site of his former home was totally overgrown, 'obliterated, as if it had never been there in the first place.' That was exactly what his father had always wanted, he said. I found these remarks cryptic, but in deference to my young colleague's grief, did not pursue the matter. In good time, however, Joseph resumed enthusiasm for his studies, much to the delight of us all."

"Shit," Gojiro said.

"How awful," Komodo added, hushed.

Then the monster turned the page, saw that reproduction, and blanched. It wasn't the first time Leona Ross Brooks's portrait of her husband had that effect on the reptile. The picture was just so oppressive, Brooks standing there, in his black parson's outfit, his arms outstretched, palms up, as if holding an invisible sphere. And those eyes, piercing, searching . . .

Gojiro started to slam the book shut, but Komodo stopped him. "This is the best reproduction I've seen," he said, noting the usual credit: "Used by permission of private collector." Komodo often wondered who this "private collector" was; how he wished he could see the original painting.

"This X-ray style fascinates me," Komodo said, referring to the bold primitivism of the portrait, so reminiscent of cave paintings. "It is an intriguing artistic choice. Why would Mrs. Brooks utilize a Paleolithic technique to portray her husband as he stood on the brink of the New Age?"

Gojiro stole another look at the picture. That X-ray stuff, how you could just about look *through* Brooks, just made it worse. It made the picture seem unfinished, as if it were waiting to be filled in. Except for those eyes! There was nothing transparent about them. They were solid, deadly—so much like they appeared on that imagined afternoon on Lavarock, when Brooks's gaze kept that youngest zardplebe from the Black Spot. The eyes in that picture always got to Gojiro. What was Leona Brooks doing painting his dream?

It was right then that he noticed that strange discrepancy. "Wait a minute. Something's wrong. It don't add up."

"What does not add up, my own true friend?"

"Look at these dates." Gojiro flipped back through *Visions in Fission,* ran a claw to the part about Brooks's supposed abandonment of physics. "The cat is supposed to be blowing in the Hot Club around 1937. That's where they're supposed to have met, right, Brooks and Leona? Well, it says '1934' at the bottom of the painting. How's she gonna paint him before she even meets him?"

Komodo furrowed his brow. "Perhaps it is a misprint."

The monster shrugged. "Yeah, a misprint."

After that, it got kind of boring, watching Komodo stare into the stereopticon, so Gojiro flipped on the old black and white built into the wall in the Traj Taj's wet bar. The joint had long since been drained dry, of course. The succession of shiftless tenants and caretakers had put a serious dent in that old producer's stock, which from the look of it had once been considerable. Too bad, Gojiro thought, he could use a few stiff liquid tons. His 235 stash was running seriously thin.

The call-in born-agains were on again, testifying. Every day these paste-faced yearners appeared to commandeer another channel; it got so you couldn't even get a decent "Rawhide" rerun. It pissed the monster off. In fact, after suffering still another creationist laying down a moldy 4004 rap, the reptile phoned up the show. The heavily pancaked preachercreature had hardly finished saying "Now, what would you care to share with us this fine day, brother?" when Gojiro, identifying himself as "Vinnie from Ped-ro," launched into a paraphrase of an ardent Anti-Speciesist lecture, entailing how Christianity was nothing more than an imperialist sapien self-congratulatory ploy. "I'll tell you the reason your little hustle has gotten over for the past two thousand years. It's because your advance guys were smart enough to savvy how cocky you sapiens were concerning your ascendency to the top of the food chain, like you didn't have nothing to fear from those eagles and bears you'd been carving into totem poles for eons. Hey, no knock on Jesus, but that's your the In-His-Image riff in a nutshell—you're nothing but a bunch of narcissistic pissants recasting the Sacred in dumboized humanoid form. Well, gloat all you want, but you ain't fooling *everybody.*" Gojiro was waiting for one of those pinchfaced Prots to invoke the seven-second delay, but, maddeningly enough, they let him keep talking, finally replying, "Well, praise the Lord for allowing you to get that off your chest this morning, brother. You get back to us, y'hear?" Some people just couldn't be insulted.

But as much as he complained, the monster was hooked on the shows. There was something undeniably poignant about them. Sure, maybe call-in Christians were small-eyed haters, hincty squares who couldn't snag a taste of the millennium if Dolphy blew B-flat upside their eardrums, but you couldn't dog them for buying into a Cosmo, could you? Couldn't dog anyone for that. The dimmest Cosmo had to be better than none; there had to be *something* to hurl into the discord. Then there was the frenzy, the raptured abandon. Sometimes, when those hallelujahs got hot and heavy, the monster felt himself getting swept up, ready to sign on the line when the next prayercloth salesman knocked.

But then he'd catch himself. Because, maybe it's a heck of a space saver, having only one book on the shelf, but which book? Surrendering to the fervor was an endlessly attractive option, but it wasn't as if you wanted to *look bad* doing it. You didn't want to sign up for an all-encompassing creed then read the fine print and find out you had to wear bell-bottoms and tie-dye. No, man, for the Hip zard, it was an intractable dilemma: how to believe and be Cool at the same time.

Depended on your definition of Cool, the reptile always thought. You could be a rigorless nihilista, forever flattening your affect in dim-lit formica lounges, cementing your cute shoes in the staid permanency of the avant. But where was that at? Walking the walk, talking the talk—it's all for sale these days, pick 'em up by the checkout counter, one size fits all. This wasn't to say Gojiro eschewed the facile, that he didn't think someone who dug Clifford Brown wasn't intrinsically a more worthwhile individual than someone who did not. Hip is a constantly whirling Rolodex; one can never neglect the power of the surface. But that didn't mean you should make a talisman of it. You had to go deep.

Seek. Find. Accept. Believe. That was the regimen of the Hip zard. But that was also where the process broke down, in the believing part—that final step. "Be Cool, don't drink the Kool-Aid" had always been the monster's motto. Even throughout his most strident declarations of fealty to the Evolloo, with Budd Hazard inside his head, there was something in him that flinched at the mantle of True Belief. It seemed so final, so unequivocal, so anti keeping one's options open. It was one thing to polemicize, to propose and propound, even to die for an Idea. But to *believe* in it? All of it smacked of goosesteps, crashing kristall in the night.

"I think we are dealing with two visions here, not one," Komodo cried from the other side of the room.

"Huh?"

"She called out twice. First for her mother and father. Then, after a discernible pause, for her father and you, my own true friend. Two related but distinct visions. It is almost as if the first triggers the second. I must note that. It could be a crucial factor. What do you think?"

"Yeah, two visions. Triggered. Very important," Gojiro grunted. Two visions! Why not four? Four hundred visions. Why not four million shards of visions, throw them in a pile, get all the king's kabbalists to stick them back together again? Komodo was going to drive him crazy. The monster wondered: when he finally cashed in that odious Amendment, would it still be listed as a suicide? Probably. There were all kinds of suicides available, whole showcases full of them. Sometimes it's just an open window, a total impulse buy. But most, the monster decided, were drawn out installment-plan deals. Wait it out, he told himself, sit tight.

When he turned back to the television, the Heater filled the screen. At first, he thought it was part of the born-again show. After all, wasn't the Heater the biggest bailout those revelation-mad brimstoners ever got, the government-subsidized cornerstone of their pitch? But then he realized that his tail had accidently brushed that remote control Komodo jerryrigged for him. This was another station altogether.

A Heater station? A station that played only looped billows of mushroom clouds twenty-four hours a day, like the yule log?

Gojiro stared at the cloud on the television screen, wondered which Bomb had made it. Once he'd been on a first-name basis with all Heaters. Mike from Eniwetok, the Russian Joe, he knew them all, the Fat Man's rock and Little Boy's roll. Every Cloud had its quirks, was dense with its particular psychic marrow; none could be mistaken for a nimbus any idiotgrin weatherman ever slapped to a plexiglas map of the lower forty-eight. For Gojiro, shroomic recognition went beyond run-of-the-mill iconography; it was interior, congenital, imprinted like a duck. Once, as sick fun, the reptile got Komodo to project a series of random Cloud configurations on the 'cano wall. Gojiro shouted out his immediate impression of the pattern, Rorschach style. "The spirit of an evil count rising above the smoking ruin of an ancient castle," he screamed. "A manta ray with a thorn in its paw" . . . "Bicarbonate run amok" . . . "Julius Erving's hair." He saw everything in those Clouds. It was like stumbling through the most impenetrable of jungles to come upon a squatting holy man holding a seemingly harmless fungus between his dirty fingers. "Come," the man beckoned. By the third bite the world was white.

It killed the monster, this love-hate relationship he maintained with nuclear holocaust. He wanted his hatred of the Cloud to be complete, palpable. But couldn't hate the Cloud. It was too much a part of him. The Heater, it pulled you by the short hairs, put on you the long stare. *Enola Gay,* the kiss you gave, will it ever fade away?

As it was, the Heater playing right then on that TV wasn't any humdrum cog in the national defense. It was the very first. The Trinity. The Cloud faded away to an old file film taken from an airplane. Below was a large, desolate crater. It might have been the moon. There was nothing much around, just some somber outcroppings of red rock strewn about the scooped-out floor. Gojiro blinked. Where was this place?

A voice-over started up, reading portentous copy about how "this barren, inhospitable stretch of high desert was, for a single yet permanent moment, the center of the world." They flashed a couple of stock photos of the scientists. Brooks was there, Victor Stiller and that Colonel Grives too, the whole crew. "After these cataclysmic events," the voice, now recognizable as that of a local newscaster, continued, "this place faded back to anonymity. For the last three decades the army has used it largely as a weapons dump. But now, a potentially far-reaching lawsuit concerning the title to what has been called one of the most uninhabitable stretches in the world has arisen."

They cut to a decrepit-looking Indian standing in front of a motel by the interstate. Tractor-trailer tires whined in the background. The Indian squinted into the camera. Off his looks, he could have been any age over a hundred. His forehead was deeply lined; the skin on his cheeks hung like mailbags slung over the back of an exhausted pony. A fly buzzed around his head. The unseen newscaster kept talking. He said that Indian land claims on federally held territory were nothing new, "but this one is different due to the historical significance of the land in question and the fact that this man, Mr. Nelson Monongae, is the only living member of the claimant tribe. The only one."

"I am the Echo Man," the Indian said in a timbreless whisper. "Echo Man is the last one. Only he knows what has been known."

Now they showed the newscaster, a pleasant-looking young man whose trench coat blew tight against his body in the wind. "Yes, that's very interesting, Mr. Monongae, but you're just one person. You're claiming more than ten thousand square miles. Why would you need such a large space?"

The Indian's face was full of twitches. "Because I am the Echo Man. I speak for the People. This land is the sacred Land of the Monongae Clan. I speak for all the Monongae Clan. I do the will of the Monongae Clan."

"But what happens when you die?"

"When I die, nothing matters. Now I am still the Echo Man of the Monongae Clan."

"Monongae . . . Does that have a literal translation?"

The Indian craned his weatherbeaten neck. He seemed to be having trouble paying attention. Every so often, as a kind of twitch, the mottled fingers of his right hand reached up to grab hold of a blackish vial that hung from a loose necklace down to the middle of his chest. "Translation to what?"

"English."

"Yeah. Called in English 'lizard.' Lizard Clan. Monongae is lizard. I am the Echo Man of the Monongae Clan."

Gojiro had been about to switch the stations after the Trinity Cloud faded. Only the pictures of Brooks and Stiller had kept him watching. Now he widened his every lid. There was something about that old Indian. A look. It drew the monster in.

Nelson Monongae was twitching worse than ever now. He kept grabbing at the vial strung around his neck. It was black, whatever was inside that vial. Blacker than black. "Monongae Clan people was led to the Valley by my great-great-grandfather, who said, 'The Heart of the World is here. The Blood of the World runs from here.' I am the Echo Man, I must reclaim the Land before there is no memory."

Gojiro drew a deeper breath. "Hey, come look at this," he yelled to Komodo. On the screen the newscaster was stating some charges local residents were making concerning the land case. "People say that you're being used, Mr. Monongae. That, in fact, you have been known to have spent a good deal of the past several years in the county drunk tank. What about that, sir?"

Before the Echo Man could answer, however, a well-tanned man in a silk suit interceded. "Mr. Monongae does not have to reply to these rumors. His case is just and lawful under the Return of Native Lands Act. He will win it. Thank you." With that the man hustled the Echo Man into a gray Mercedes and roared away. Maybe there was some time to kill or something, because the newscasters decided to stick a little coda on the report. Once more cameras panned the redcliffed Valley, the newsman saying, "Here, years ago, time stood still . . ." But he was drowned out by Komodo.

"That's it! The place she saw!"

PAST BERDOO

Gojiro always wanted to see the USA in a Chevrolet. But when he and Komodo left the Traj Taj, they had to go in that fatassed limo. It was Shig's idea and there was no way out of it. Ever since Sheila Brooks's unexpected arrival at the Traj Taj, the severe neoteen had kept an exceedingly close eye on Komodo. So, shrunk down to four feet and peeved, Gojiro threw himself into the wonder-less plush of the limo's ample backseat. This didn't figure to be fun, he decided.

It got worse as they pulled down the dusty path to the Traj Taj gate. Ebi was there, digging by the side of the road, collecting her specimens, making her identifications. She was so busy, then. Every day, it seemed, another sector of the Traj Taj grounds erupted in aerobic and/or anaerobic bloom. Turn around and a dozen new phyla splurted from the sandy soil, came cracking through the mansion walls. One afternoon three separate varieties of barbed-wire vines *(Razorcoilus brentwoodus)* latticed across the back section of the house, cocoon-ing the old servant's quarters with a tighter weave than the gauze across the face of an invisible man.

Ebi was constantly on the go, taxonomically taxed. No sooner would she identify a specimen when two others would begin the herbic creep. She was out in the thicket at sunup, didn't return to the house until dinnertime. Then she'd toil by moonlight on nocturnals.

"It's almost as if she's trying to get it all in before . . ." Gojiro said to Komodo, unable to finish the sentence.

Ebi waved as the limo sped by. Gray dirt smeared across her face, the way it always did. Gojiro loved how, no matter how freshly she'd turn out in her striped party dresses and patent-leather shoes, there would always be a tiny daub of her beloved soil beside her eyebrow, or a slight smudge on her elbow. Komodo pointed it out quietly, unobtrusively, so she would never be embarrassed. He'd wipe the spot away with a moist cloth. Then she'd look perfect.

"Ebi!" Gojiro shouted, pressing himself to the heavily tinted windows, but she never even heard him, the big car soundproofed like a tomb.

They went out the Santa Monica Freeway, through the neon and the neon, the money and the money, the Alpha-Beta and the Alpha-Beta, and the Thrifty Drug too. They traversed the choked inner suburbs, rode past freeway walls covered with the glyphic jumble of bellicose invocations of ethnocentricity and metal bands. "Iran Maidan!" Gojiro squealed. "Morons! Can't they just copy the words off their T-shirts?"

Shig drove the way he always did, fast and reckless. Not that he was alone. The road was full of maniacs. "Asshole!" Gojiro screamed out the window at a Porsche as it whipped in front of the limo.

"Please, my own true friend, get down, they'll see you," Komodo said nervously.

"That bastard cut us off! That one there, the jowly one with silver hair." Then, out the window: "Yeah, you, I'm talking to you. You: Kenny Rogers scumface!" Gojiro could only cackle when the Porsche, its driver stunned by the sight of an accusing lizard hanging out a limo window, skidded into two Ferraris. "And stay over, asshole!"

"Restrain yourself, please!" Komodo shouted in his sternest tone. He pushed the automatic window closer.

"Hey! That hurt!" After this, Gojiro lay in the back of the funereal car, watching the town go by. Really looks like shit, the whole joint, the reptile thought to himself, checking the dense petrochems gumming the horizon. Was this the best the sapiens could do for themselves? Was this their shining City, this pastel smudge? Bah, Gojiro scoffed. Bah and double bah. "Be better if this place was smashed flat," he muttered.

"What?" Komodo asked. A Lamborghini semi-truck swerved into their lane, nearly running them into a Maserati step van.

"Nothing." Komodo wouldn't understand. He'd come swarming with his suffocating Saint Francis dictums about how hate comes from fear and how you have to conquer both. That stuff just made the monster mad. Wasn't it fair to hate them for making you afraid? Looking out the limo window at the line of mirrored buildings (*Mirrors!* Why do they need mirrors on the forty-seventh floor? Do they think the birds are as vain as they are?), Gojiro decided there wasn't anything wrong with the town that a little radicalized urban renewal wouldn't cure.

Where to start? Hmm . . . there were any number of squatty award-show venues that would fit neatly underfoot. How about the Capitol Records building—sure would be a gas to see the faces of those greed-chiseled bad taste purveyors as they watched that payola-layered tower ripped from the ground and played like an accordion. Century City, that could go, left hook followed by a right. Melrose, too, a thousand caterers and their spindly cuisine micro-scorched: watta outage for the power lunch! And what might a brace of well-placed kicks do to the lowslung "charm" of so many wicker-decked hotels? The habitat loss would likely send the burnished clientele jumping back and forth over sagging tennis nets, like mainframe-blown replicants at last having their long-deserved day on the court. Then, just for fun, he'd grab giant donuts from the tops of fastfood joints and ring toss them round the Watts Towers. He wouldn't bust off the points; those steeples were about the only structures in the whole benighted burg Gojiro could tolerate.

"Yes!" the monster guffawed. He'd pry the stars right out of that jerkoff Walk of Fame, sharpen the points, send 'em whirring in through the windows of every morning meeting, really let some heads roll. Could there ever be a name more fittingly up in lights than that Hollywood sign ablaze with Radi-Breath? And who knew, a perfectly placed stomp might jumpstart the ole San Andreas; a little press on nature's reset button. Why the heck not? The place been going downhill since Gondwanaland.

A seethe of excitement came over Gojiro. To be bad! To be *really* bad. To show the sapiens once and for all. To burrow up through the million sediments of their frenzied yet futile repression, to burst loose from the suddenly unquiet graveyard of their past and stand before them: a *true* monster, a destroyer without conscience, a dark shadow across landscapes, dorsals silhouetted in the flaming destruction he wreaked, immune to weapons, beyond the reach of fevered prayers, remorseless, unstoppable. A killing machine, tearing ships from the sea, breaking buses in the streets, ripping bodies between his cutting jaws.

"Dread and horror, horror and dread!" the monster's heated brain shouted. "Lay the black cowl round my shoulders, place skulls and tallow candles upon my bench. Let the bottom of my feet be my heavy gavels. Guilty! Guilty! A hundred years in Hell! A thousand! Justice! Retribution! There'll be some sentencing done here!"

But then, almost immediately, he felt himself deflate. It was the sprawl that did it, that LA whizzing by: the overwhelming sameness, the diffuse repetition. It dulled all passion, doused every fire. Ever spreading, the city was an amorphous sweep without a vital organ or center at which a determined Destroyer could aim. There were no walls round which to drag the vanquished from the back of a chariot, no flag to capture. There was no Empire State to climb, no Eiffel Tower to snap in half; in what amounted to the perfect defense against exactly the attack the monster envisioned, the town had no cherished emblem of itself beyond its very vagueness. You couldn't break its will with a swift and symbolic act. No, killing this city was not the job for a Great Avenger bent on the telling gesture. Only an army of forever-canvassing bureaucrats, Chinese likely, could make a dent.

There was one stop to make before they hit the desert. They were going to see Walter. Walter Crenshaw, Pfc., Okinawa medic.

Walter . . . there wouldn't be a story to tell without Walter, no windswept journey across two thousand miles of sea, no Radioactive Island, no Glazed Days. Walter was there from the beginning. It was Walter's dark, hanging moon of a Carolina face Komodo saw in that hospital room when he opened his eyes for the first time in nearly ten years.

"I must go," Komodo said, through those long-stilled lips. "I have a friend. He lives very far away. He has no one. I must go to him, be with him."

"I know," Walter said.

"You will help me?"

"Yes."

How did Walter know that the poor Coma Boy he'd tended so lovingly had been summoned to an Island no map knew by a terribly lonely giant lizard? Komodo couldn't tell, never asked. All he knew was that Walter had always been there. That it was Walter who told him about the weather outside his dank room, Walter who rubbed his muscles so they stayed alive, Walter who sang to him, Walter who played him the radio, Walter who slapped his leg when the Say Hey Kid hit a homer. That it was Walter who chased the phonies who came to gawk at the Coma Boy, international freak, Walter who was gentle while the others were brusque. That he trusted Walter, completely.

So that night when Walter helped him from his bed, shoved him through the laundry-room window, put him on a metal gurney, wheeled him down the hallway, Komodo knew it was the right thing to do. Faster and faster Walter pushed him down those corridors; above him, the fluorescent lights blurred against the ceiling. Everything smelled of ammonia. Walter got Komodo into black clothes, smeared camouflage paint on his face. Suddenly they were outside. He could see the stars in the night sky; smells of the sea filled his nostrils. How lush it was, how alive! The sand was between his toes, the ocean too.

Then Walter was waving a tiny flashlight, sending a signal through the fog. The boat came, creaking and shabby, a scow run by Korean fishermen. "Two hundred dollars!" the one in the skullcap screamed.

"You said one-fifty!"

"Two hundred!"

"Motherfucker!" Walter dug into his pocket, pulled out the bills, then lifted Komodo onto the slimy deck. Already the first of the searchlight beams were cutting through the heavy air. Walter was waistdeep in the tide, holding the gray box above his head. Komodo knew that box. It had been in his room, always in his room.

Then the drone of the MP boat filled the night. "Mister Crenshaw!" Komodo called, reaching out.

"You gotta go now! Take this!" Walter pushed the box over the gunwale, but the Korean was panicking, casting off. The box was too heavy, Komodo couldn't hold it. It slipped from his grasp, fell into the water. Walter tried to shove it back into the boat, but it fell again, back into the sea. Walter dove down, dragged it up once more. "You got to have it!" But it was too late. The cutter was closing, sirens blaring. The Korean revved his engine, jumped ahead.

That was the last time Komodo saw Walter: in the water, holding that box over his head, helpless in the searchlight's glare. Then he was gone, lost in the fog. Komodo felt as if he were entering another dark world. What happened next, Komodo never knew. Was it a piece of the boat's equipment that struck him, a forearm of one of those petrified Koreans, or was he simply washed overboard as that chasing MP cutter caught up? Whichever, he felt himself fly up, then down, hard, into the cold, fast current. He remembered nothing more until he awoke the next morning—or was it a week later, a month?—in that gray lifeboat drifting, drifting . . . until he crossed the Cloudcover and his life began again.

It was years later, long before the invasion of any 90 Series, that the monster heard a strange voice inside the Quadcamera. "I got talking inside my head!" Gojiro screamed. "Yuke!"

"Yuke?"

"Yuke the Nuke! He keeps calling for Yuke the Nuke!"

"Yuke the Nuke?"

"He says he would have called years ago but they finally let him out of the bughouse!"

"Bughouse?"

"He keeps playing 'In the Still of the Night.' Damn! Am I going crazy?"

Komodo grabbed Gojiro by the supraocular ridge. "How does it go?"

"What?"

" 'In the Still of the Night.' Sing the song, please."

Uncomprehending, Gojiro looked at his friend, but then he sang the first few bars. Show-do and showbie-do.

Komodo's face went pale. "The song he played on the radio! It is Mr. Crenshaw!"

After that, it wasn't long before they knew the aftermath of what happened that night on the Okinawa beach. He almost made it, Walter said, almost got away. He got off the base before the dogs got his scent, pulled him down from behind, near to gnawed off his leg. They never court-martialed him, not exactly. The way Walter had it figured, they could never really bring themselves to believe it, that a boy who hadn't stirred in close to a decade could suddenly get out of bed and escape one of the most heavily fortified bases in the world. It was a lot easier to lie, say that Komodo had finally succumbed to his mysterious malaise, stage that phony tearjerker of a funeral. Not that anybody cared much; by then the Hiroshima Coma Boy was a used-up curio, page-eight stuff at best. Besides, the VA needed the bed space.

"They gave me the shocks, but I never told nothing," Walter said. "Never told them shit. Wasn't their business why I done it. They said I was nuts. They threw me in a bin." Listening to Walter describe his life and times, via one of those early generation of Quadcameral external speakers, never failed to send both Gojiro and Komodo into fits of tears and wailing. It seemed that Walter still thought he was an Okinawa paramedic. He peppered much of his talk with phrases like "Well, let's see what we got here, Yuke" or "I'm telling you,

Yuke." That steady voice, which once had offered comfort amid Komodo's enforced sleep, now jangled, spasmed. More often than not, he'd speak from a cheap hotel room or while walking down a city street, railing at the sky.

"They have driven him mad," Komodo screamed in anguish. From then on, he worked night and day trying to refine his Quadcameral devices. The aim was to construct a transmitter, something that could send as well as receive. "We must contact him! We must help him as he has helped us!" But it was not possible. Great strides in Quadcameral research were made; indeed, the prototype for what became the Crystal Contact Radio was devised at the time. But despite hours of screaming, "Come in, Mr. Crenshaw," Komodo's frenzied messages were never acknowledged.

As for Gojiro, he continued to listen, overhearing snatches of conversation here, a slice of life there. He heard Walter scorn bill collectors, talk back to the TV. Maybe Walter was crazy, Gojiro thought, but much of what said rang true, at least from an outcast's point of view. Once the monster heard him arguing with the mailman, who accused Walter of being paranoid. Walter snapped back, "Man, if you was me, you couldn't be too paranoid." Besides, he still played that good R&B. Yeah, in his way, Walter was a social Budd Hazard; plenty of his worldview found its way into the lizard's lexicon.

There was only one time anything about that box came up. It happened during a period soon after Walter seemed to be doing better, when he went for a job interview at a hospital in San Diego. Walter was excited about "getting back to my proper line of work." But it was a disaster. "They blocked me right out, Yuke," Walter commented later that night. "Said they knew all about me." After that he seemed more discouraged. He bounced around—to Oakland, up to Seattle, back down to Frisco. His communications were often drowned out by the background babel of Greyhound departures and arrivals. Then one night in a fleabag hotel near Delano some migrant onion pickers broke into Walter's room, tore the place apart. They heard he had a machine that talks to dead people; they wanted it. Komodo and Gojiro heard the scuffle, the high-pitched Spanish screams, the ripping of skin with knives. A few hours later, Walter came back in. "They didn't get it, Yuke," he said wearily, all beat-up. "I wouldn't give it up. I never will. Don't worry. I don't regret nothing."

Hearing that threw Komodo into hysterics. The idea that Walter was still protecting him, still trying to hold that mysterious box for him, was more than he could take. But that was the last time they ever heard from Walter. Within months the 90 Series began to crash the Quadcameral. When Gojiro forced

Komodo into the fourth chamber to cut out those supplications, Walter's voice was swept away, along with the rest.

They figured it was a long shot, going by Wilma Crenshaw's house. Once they'd lived together, Walter and Wilma; but then Walter would have a breakdown, wind up on the road again. It broke Komodo's heart to think Wilma's love was still another thing Walter had lost in the aftermath of that fateful evening in Okinawa. Still, amid his wanderings, Walter would come visit Wilma. During those times, with respect for the couple's privacy, Komodo and Gojiro tried not to listen in, but there was no controlling what the Quadcameral overheard. Sometimes yelling and screaming filled their ears, but there were tender moments, too. However, if they were to see Walter, it was worth a try. A quick perusal of the telephone book revealed a W. Crenshaw at 125990 Pollsmoor Boulevard. When they called the number a recording said that the phone had been disconnected. Going over was the only way.

They turned off at Normandie, tooled into the city's outlying regions, watching the color of people's faces change. Walter always said that West Coast ghettos were the worst, since they didn't seem that bad on the surface. You'd get in deep, then it'd be too late. Walter feared this place, Gojiro always felt, and that upset him, the idea of having a home and being afraid of it.

The limo got some attention when it pulled up in front of the house. About twenty or so locals were milling about, debating the alleged intent of such an august vehicle in their sullen neighborhood. When Komodo got out, half the crowd offered to watch the car, for a fee. Shig put the scotch to that, though, slicing his sword through the turbid air faster than any eye could see. "Damn ninja!" was the fleeing cry.

In contrast to the rest of house, which was an amalgam of mismatched siding patterns and chipped paint, the screen door of 125990 Pollsmoor was a spanking-new affair. A wrought-aluminum *C* in its lower panel gleamed in the raspy late-afternoon sun. After three knocks, the inside door opened slightly and the face of a boy on the insolent fringe of teenagehood appeared. Resting his chin on the latched chain, the boy said, with no small belligerence, "My mom's not home."

No doubt this was Trumaine; Walter had mentioned him from time to time. "Bright boy, but he got no frame on the reference."

"I am looking for Mr. Crenshaw," Komodo said, after bowing deeply.

Gojiro

"Ain't no *Mister* Crenshaw. Just be me and my mom." Trumaine's eyes shifted. "You from the government?"

"No. I am a friend. Once, long ago, I knew Mr. Crenshaw in Okinawa."

"My uncle told me about people like you. I know my rights. Let's see your badge." Gojiro peeked out from where he was hiding, in severely diminished form, under Komodo's collar. His eyes immediately went to the back of Trumaine's hand and he felt ill. What had the boy used to gouge that symbol into his flesh—a can opener, a corkscrew? The job was grisly, but there was no mistaking the pattern: three concentric circles. Trumaine Crenshaw was a G-fan.

Komodo didn't notice. "But I am not from the government. It is as I told you: once your uncle was very kind to me. I just want to thank him."

"That what them flowers about?"

"Yes."

"Sure you ain't got no badge?" Trumaine asked, now with some disappointment. Then he said, "Well, don't matter. My uncle Walter's dead. You from the government, you know that."

Komodo's breath stopped. "Dead?"

Trumaine watched Komodo intently, without speaking.

"How . . . ?" Twenty years of grief pressed down on Komodo. His knees buckled.

"Just passed on. About two years ago, right around now."

Komodo bowed unsteadily. "I am deeply sorry and offer my most profound condolences."

Trumaine's face tried to stay hard, but it couldn't. "My mom, she's sorry." Then, swallowing, he added, "Me too." It seemed that Trumaine had given up believing Komodo was from the government, because, without being asked, he told Komodo where Walter was buried.

It was no more than a twenty-minute ride to the graveyard, but it might have taken forever, the misery they felt. The cemetery wasn't far removed from a potter's field. Pitched on a hill behind a giant billboard, it was nothing more than an overgrown array of irregularly sized flat stones sticking from the ground like a stegosaur's plates. An eerie smogfilm hung densely over the graves as mist might cling to a heath in another time and place. On the low margins of the pocked sky, a hardpressed sun plied its lurid wares.

Some of the headstones were inscribed with magic marker, but Walter's was better kept. The top line of his engraved stone said, with a kind of quiet defiance, "Crenshaw—*Husband*." Beneath that: "He fought for his country. Peace at last." Neither Gojiro nor Komodo spoke as they laid a single rose upon the tombstone's jagged top. The rose would bloom for a long time. It was one of the hardy perennials plucked from Ebi's special garden in the Insta-Envir; those things never wilted. As they turned to go back to the limo, they nearly ran into a stout woman dressed in nurse's whites. She carried flowers of her own. This would be Wilma, they knew. They watched her go over to Walter's grave, kneel there. Then she turned and looked at Komodo a second before going back to her silent prayers. Komodo started to speak but couldn't. They'd already intruded enough of Walter and Wilma's private moments.

When they got back into the limo, they just cried. Walter: dead. All the sad horns should be playing.

They went past Berdoo, out to Indio. America gave way to its once and future self. Beyond the Twenty-ninth Palm there was only desert. Even inside that limo, the arid emptiness could be felt and smelt. "Nothing out here, man," Gojiro remarked. "Nothing at all."

"Actually, my own true friend, the desert is full of life," Komodo remarked, attempting animation. "Many interesting species have carved niches in these harsh environs. It can be a subtle and deceptive place. If one is keen to its every nuance, the reward is bountiful."

The monster rolled his eyes. He hated when Komodo went PBS on him. Besides, the reptile wasn't about to concede that a brace of gnarly Joshua trees and a couple of frightwig ocotillos silhouetted against the pinkish sky amounted to any kind of bounty, except to raise the ante of the one Fate had conspired to place upon his head. The night came up fast, took its big gulp with striking suddenness. The blackness assaulted, laughed out loud. Go ahead, it seemed to say, cocky and aloof, fill me up . . . if you can.

Wasn't that the riff when you stared into a vacuum—that there's something in the Universe that can't abide a blank? Certainly it had been so back on Radioactive Island, before their sun, their moon, before Budd Hazard. And how magnificent it had been to respond to that emptiness! To forge, out of nothingness, somethingness. A pure act, as if the creation of Cosmo was reflexive, instinctive, involuntary, Prewire.

But this wasn't Radioactive Island. This was the Mojave, the Sonoran, the Sangre de Cristo. This was a cavity of another kind, a mocking, foreign void.

Gojiro

It enveloped that hermetic limo, flaunted its emptiness. Gojiro glanced over at Komodo. He was sitting there, jotting in his diary, the shadows playing across his sad countenance. The monster was beginning to worry about Komodo; how long could he keep dredging hope from despair, how long would his faith continue to fly in the face of fact? What, really, did he expect to find out here in this alien night? Even if Sheila Brooks had seen something in Komodo's stereopticon, what effect could it have on the Triple Ring Promise? Their great Vow grew from Cosmo, was defined by Cosmo, could only be consummated in Cosmo—Radioactive Island Cosmo. How much could Budd Hazard's philosophy be worth here?

Gojiro looked out the window again, shivered. Sure, they say Ideas spread like wildfire, that there's no containing them once the fever starts. But think about it: how much hay would those padres have hoed without the clank of armor and the come-on of capital's dropped handkerchief? How deep into the heart of Asia would the sultans have swayed sans the scimitar? No, man, the only way to get a square peg through a round hole is with an M-16, and that don't even work most times. Maybe Helen Gurley Brown is coast-to-coast, but Cosmo, stripped down to Thought and Thought alone, don't travel, first class or otherwise.

Cosmo was really a small-town thing, the monster thought, a sweaty hedge against oblivion, a fragile conceit in need of perpetual custodial care. You had to know what your Cosmo knew, what it could do and what it couldn't, never ask it to jump through any hoop it hadn't jumped through a million times before. Back on Radioactive Island, this was easy enough. The Island was a cosmologic safe house, a closed experiment. It wasn't like some wildeyed debunker, some revolutionist contra-Darwin, was about to beagle through the Cloudcover spouting heresies at any moment, crack the tablets of Beam and Bunch. On Radioactive Island, a million questionable checks could be written: the piper would never be coming round, looking to get paid.

But out here, in this mournful desert pressing toward the Arizona line, nothing was safe. Here there were no stage-manageable questions, only the sixty-four-thousand-dollar kind that can turn even the most well-prepped Cosmo into a cow, a big-bottomed bovine standing walleyed in the onrush of an eighteen-wheeler's fog lights.

"Duh."

Komodo turned away from the window. "Did you say something, my own true friend?"

"Yeah. I say duh."

"Duh?"

"You do it good. Like a regular Big Moose. Duh. That's what happens when you twist a Cosmo's arm hard enough. You make it say duh. You turn it into a Duh Cosmo."

"I don't understand."

The monster almost chortled. "You hear that one about those Paiutes. They was from around here somewheres. They looked out on this very nothingness and were spurred to come up with a fully self-sufficient system. They built themselves a millennium over at Walker Lake. Pantheons of gods, the whole scene. Then, zoom, the military-industrial complex is knock, knock, knocking on their bit o' heaven's door. Killing their buffalos and worse. And the Paiutes is freaking out 'cause their Plan don't got a contingency for John Wayne."

"What did they do?" Komodo asked with concern.

"What else *could* they do? Not exactly like you can change central metaphors in midstream. They went into a state of crisis. They pushed their Cosmo to the wall, made it say something, anything. So what's it do? It spits out a Vision. A *secret* Vision. It talks through shaman, says dance all night, call back the ancestors, go out the next morning wearing shirts painted white. Then every Colt's bullets be turned away."

"But what happened?"

"What happened? What do you *think* happened? They got their asses shot off. They don't exist no more. They're out of the picture. Don't even got a bingo wheel to turn. That's what happens when a Cosmo goes past the Duh Point: you beg disaster."

"That's very sad, my own true friend," Komodo answered sincerely.

"Sad? I dunno. It's hard for a Cosmo to keep up these days. The Trans-Amazon be littered with corpses of dead religions. Petered-out cults for days. The Modern World's a hammerlock. Every hour it makes a million macrocosms sing a screechy harmony of duhhhh. Call that sad? Maybe it's just in the way of things. You can't be sad about the implacable."

Komodo looked at Gojiro with piercing eyes. "What are you trying to say, my own true friend?"

"I'm trying to say you can't lay the heavy litmus on a bunch of campfire stories. I'm trying to say that we're out here in the middle of nowhere looking for a needle when we don't even know what a haystack looks like. I'm trying to say I got a bad vibe about this, like we're past the Duh Point, heading into big trouble."

The moonlight was on Komodo's face now, like through a scrim. He seemed different, far away. "I understand your feelings, my own true friend. There is much truth in what you say. But, tell me, is this land really so foreign to us? What is to say that it is not as ingrained in our souls as Radioactive Island itself? Is it not possible that there are Universal landscapes, terrain that is known by all, whether they have actually dwelled within it or not? Could it not be the same with Ideas? Perhaps there are some Ideas that are not hemmed by time or space or country of origin. Is it not possible that, through the vagaries of history and fate, an idea becomes the Idea, the single Way to Salvation?"

Gojiro narrowed his lids. "I don't believe in Ideas like that." Then he turned to look at his friend. Komodo did not return his gaze. "Anyone who does is a dangerous gambler. A potentially crazy man. I think he should think twice before he imagines himself fit to walk on purple carpets, unless he's ready to unleash a whirlwind."

"Perhaps you're right, my own true friend," Komodo said, the shadows deepening his eye sockets. "But what choice do we have?" Then he turned to look forward, into the onrush of the night.

THE BIG PICTURE

When Gojiro first scoped that big picture he figured it had to be the Varanidid. What else could that fabulous beast be, hologrammed against the black velvet night, dancing, shimmering, shifting from ghost to flesh and back again? The V-did! Esteemed Hero of Zards, Peerless Champion of Lavarock! Sometimes, during his recurring dreams of the Precious Pumice, Initiates would speak of the Varanidid, always in hushed and reverent tones. Of course, the conversation was nothing he, a youngest zardplebe—not yet immersed in the Black Spot— could understand, but an essence could be gleaned. He'd been big once, this Varanidid, bigger than big; back in the chaotic times he performed an act of unimaginable greatness, without which the Line could never have come into being. But the details of that matchless feat had faded from the collective brainpan. Not even the oldest and wisest could remember exactly who the Varanidid was, what he looked like, what he'd done. All that remained was the reverence, and the conviction that should the life-giving connection of Bunch and Beam ever again be thrown into the swell of Crisis, the Varanidid would return.

"What big thing did this Varanidid do?" Gojiro once asked Komodo, in those early days. "Think he ranks?"

Komodo looked up from his book, rubbed his chin. "In my readings, I have encountered other figures who are believed to have accomplished an essential service—one Great Act—and then receded from view, leaving only the dimmest memory of their achievement. As time goes on, even that memory ebbs, leaving the knowledge of their feat to burrow ever deeper into the unconscious, where it may be accessed only by the incalculable workings of Myth."

Gojiro lay back, watching the Radioactive Island sky swirl above him like so much creamer spooned into a coffee cup. "A Hero from beyond remembering. Vague, past knowing. I like this Varanidid." After that, the idea snowballed, drawing impetus from the persistent flow of boys' books washing up on the coastlines. Stuffed between dogeared and waterlogged covers were stories of boy detectives, boy world travelers, boys in outer space, Hardy Boys. Gojiro could never get enough of these sagas. "Read it again," the monster called, "the part about how he dedicates his life to be a friend to those who have no friends."

One night, moved by the tale of White Fang's indomitable fortitude, Gojiro jumped to his feet. "I've got it—who the Varanidid is! It ain't like he's any particular masked man, a specific tights-wearing paragon. He is a wellspring of bravery and pluck inside any and all beings. His courage is etched into the heart of those who accept him."

Then, thrusting forward the Triple Rings on his chest, the monster gathered Komodo up in his great claws, looked toward the Cloudcover. "Wherever lurks the black mouth of night, ready to gobble up the slight, I'll be there! Wherever the Heater's scald is near, menacing the infirm with its sear, I'll be there!

"That'll be me—the Modern Age Varanidid. A ronin lonecat, a beacon in the night, fighting for right!

"This is my purpose in life! I know this now!"

Didn't exactly turn out that way, the monster thought, the limo's stale air-con clammy on his leathers. He thought of all the time he and Komodo had spent casting about, looking for the model of the Varanidid he might become. The current heroic landscape was barren, chocked with nothing but screwfaced cops in screeching Corvettes, whisks of hair showing through their open shirts. So they looked to the past, to old Aeneas, who crossed the threshold of the Underworld, dragged his dad on his back, founded the City. In Virgil's weathered pages, Gojiro saw light. To enter a cavern, profound, wide-mouthed and huge, to stride boldly past gods and ghosts, this sounded more like it. "No barking dog keep me back, don't care how many heads he got."

Komodo was hesitant. "But my own true friend," he said, "within the

Evolloo, there is no such thing as an Underworld, no gods with whom to curry favor or defy." Gojiro saw Komodo's point immediately. Maybe once upon a time Persephone purloined a pomegranate beneath the surface of the earth, but if you went down there now it would be nothing but a deserted subway tunnel, a taxpayer's boondoggle crawling with sneering rats and Morlocks. A Hero, the monster realized, could only be a Hero in the context of his Cosmo. Fail to heed that dictum and even the most sharpsnouted of Redeemers might find himself lost in a labyrinth of T-mazes, take a wrong turn, and wind up getting shot by a squinting pig farmer. What kind of swath would he cut across all imagination then?

"Yeah, you're right," Gojiro told Komodo. "Later for Aeneas. We don't even look Italian."

They kept looking for a heroic model, finding every Beowulf and Grendel somehow wanting. The Varanidid's mantle remained unfulfilled.

Except now, out in that desert. Who was that Beast, that spectacular flicker stitched against the night? It was so huge! So magnificent! The way it stood on top of a mountain, beating its fists on a jutting chest spoke of Power itself. But it was a Power tempered with depthless Mercy; you could see that in the crimsony eyes. What a commanding presence! Just beholding such grandeur made Gojiro dizzy.

It was then, however, that he felt that limo door slam shut. "Please stay here," Shig barked. Gojiro wasn't dreaming; he wasn't even asleep. That image in front of him—it wasn't any timeless Varanidid, it was only a picture on a piece of sleazy celluloid projected onto a giant drive-in movie screen. That prodigious being, that hallucinatory champion, was nothing more than the above-the-title player in the idiot film *Gojiro vs. the Enigma-Inking Squid at the Rock of Knowledge.*

"Fuck!" Was there ever a joke he wasn't the butt of? The reptile buried his head in the plush seat. "Desert be a bitch. It even makes a mirage of your delusions."

"My own true friend. You are awake."

"Yeah. I'm awake," Gojiro replied dismally. "Why we stopping here?"

Komodo motioned at Shig, who was walking toward the screen, a large duffel bag slung over his shoulder. It was a box-office check. Shig had been at it ever since they got to America. Every time they passed a theater where a Gojiro movie was playing, the hardeyed martinet marched into the manager's office and demanded to see the books. He knew the nut of every house, kept

a running account of exactly how much each outlet owed. His collection methods exceeded any smashnose thumb-breaker; he tolerated no song, no dance.
Just two days before, he had detected a minor fudge in the figures of the Arcade
Theatre, a wino joint downtown where they doubledated Gojiros with kung fus.
The cigar-chewing manager tried to give guff, but Shig drew his sword and
started slicing up the theater's screen from the back side right in the middle
of the Will Rogers appeal. The cash came. That's where Shig was going right
then, to the box office of the Desert View Motor Cinema, to make them pay.

"Least he could do is bring back some popcorn," the reptile muttered.

Komodo didn't answer. Staring up at the picture on the drive-in screen,
he was choked up. Even after Shig's treachery had been discovered, there
wasn't a single Gojiro movie, no matter how inane, that failed to bring a lump
to his throat. "You look very . . . *impressive,* my own true friend."

Gojiro allowed himself a peek. It was bizarre; he'd never seen the supposed King of Monsters this way before, in his silvery screen natural habitat.
Sure, he'd checked those stolen flickers on the Dish—how could he resist?—
but compared to this, the Dish was a postage stamp. This was tremendous. In
fact, at four hundred feet (a near one-to-one ratio between the actual size of
the star and his representation), the screen of the Desert View Motor Cinema
was the highest point in the whole southeast section of the state. It was the
tallest drive-in in the Free World, at least that's what the theater's original
owner, a former assistant night manager at South of the Border, claimed when
he opened it years before. Even now, with half its listening poles bent to crazy
angles by assaulting fenders, its towering screen pitted by termites, and dozens
of 12-gauge shells pumped through its SWAP MEET EVERY SAT. sign, the Desert
View dominated the otherwise empty skyline. There was no doubt about it,
Gojiro acknowledged—with a head as big as Goodyear blimps, eyes that
whirled like runaway ferris wheels, and a mouth ringed round with razortop
teeth, he cut quite a figure up there. A garish monolith amid all that black, he
was impressive.

Besides, even if he'd never admit it, he kind of liked *Gojiro vs. the Enigma-
Inking Squid at the Rock of Knowledge.* It made him laugh thinking back to when
they shot the film. What a sideshow it was, coaxing that brainless giant squid
up Disinformation Hill, getting it to clutch its deca-legs around the massive
fortune-telling eightball. Komodo didn't have much time for costuming, so all
those "Press" fedoras the Atoms wore were the same size, meaning they were
way too small for the hydrocephalics and fell down over the eyes of the

pinheads. As usual the Atoms blew their lines. It must have taken a hundred drool-showered retakes before they were able to say, "Gojiro, this Squid obscures the Truth with the vile spew seeping from its every eclipsing eye! Please help us! We're on deadline!" Still, Gojiro recalled, it had been exciting, storming up that hill, Radi-frying that squid, affirming freedom of the press by restoring that eightball to the City Room. The only real drag came much later, after Shig's iniquitous dissemination of the film, when Gojiro turned on the Dish and saw that grinning moron of a presidential candidate stealing his best line. "Calamari for the cephalopod!" the scum shouted, raising his pocketpicking hands above his head—as if identifying himself with the King of Monsters would enhance his cheap political person. How the monster longed to make that mother-raper's day—it figured that the thick electorate fell for his act.

Suddenly, it was too close inside that limo. "Think I'll stretch my legs," Gojiro said, pushing open the car door with his snout. Jumping down, his claws sank into the soft sand. Vehicles whizzed by on either side. Shig hadn't even bothered to pull over to the shoulder; he'd parked the limo on the median strip, beside a couple of straggly creosote bushes. The howl of the night wind melded with the clamoring of semis and the racket of low-flying military cargo planes. Gojiro could barely hear Komodo's warnings to be careful lest some traveling salesman pull into Phoenix jittery with a story about the strangest-looking armadillo that ever got sieved through the grille of a Buick Riviera.

It was just time for the next show. Pickups and beater Fords were turning off the interstate, lining up at the cashier's booth, which resembled a checkpoint on the border between two remote and dissolute countries. From the looks of the weatherbeaten marquee—the cracked letters of which spelled out only GOJIRO VS. SQUID—the picture had been playing for some time. "My fans," Gojiro mumbled as he watched a gear-gnashing lowrider chocked with Mexican teenagers skulk by. He didn't know whether to laugh or to cry. It was absurd, watching these poor deluded souls, seemingly from every nook and cranny of the demographic dart board, come like lemmings to sit silhouetted before his elephantine visage. Subteens crawled through holes in the rusted wire fence, grizzled rednecks spit tobacco from their four by fours. What were they doing there? Why weren't they down the road, nursing beers in topless joints? Then came carloads of baggypanted black kids, all fly and feral, their twitchy faces the tableau of every old lady's terror. How'd they get out there? Make a wrong turn at some dread Harlem intersection, get teleported? The monster couldn't figure it; like the spawn of Cadmus's tossed dragon teeth, his fans seemed to spring from the forsaken hills themselves. Plus, there were so many of the fuckers, walking need machines, zealots decked out in the leathery finery of their sect.

Almost everyone carried an Official Embossed-Clawprint Radioactive Island Scrapbook. Those loathsome looseleafs! Not a day went by that the already overburdened Radioactive Island PO box wasn't packed solid with an avalanche of entreaties torn, shag-edged, from these books. The worst of it was when Shig was running those contests: "Write it to Gojiro. Tell him what your scrapbook means to you. First Prize a real scale from Gojiro's own back, suitable for keyring framing!" One particular entry stuck in the monster's mind. It came in from some third-world crudhole, along with a fuzzy Kodachrome of the G-fan's ten-by-ten cinderblock shitbox of a home. "I have no room," the attached note scrawled. "My Gojiro scrapbook is my room." It ravaged the reptile, how it was only when this zardpard stuck his no doubt ringworm-scarred face in his Gojiro scrapbook that he felt free to slam the door, put whatever he wanted on the walls, and play the music loud.

So these were the purveyors of the 90 Series—it was their supplications he'd begged Komodo to banish from the Quadcameral. The monster felt sick. What did they want? Why did they come?

"Because they're lames, geeks, and freaks." At least that was Gojiro's answer back on Radioactive Island any time the subject of his "audience" came up. He made them all desperate dupes, marks for Shig's marketing technique. "Come one, come all! Fun for genetic misfits from six to sixty!" the monster would mock. "I'll tell you, man, these turkeys will believe anything, if you pack it up right. It ain't like they don't know it's bogus, they like it *better* that way. The fakery liberates them, frees them to worship the wrapping." Gojiro always maintained that the popularity of his films would soon wane. "I'm a microflash in the pan," he told Komodo. "By next week the most loyalistic of 'tile-o-files will be hollering for Hulk Hogan to skewer my dorsal plates like so much shish kebab." However, when his fame did not "go to Troy Donahueville" but continued to grow, Gojiro attempted to devise other theories to account for the unending ardor of those who called themselves the "followers of the Greenest Scene."

He presented his thesis at an Anti-Speciesist seminar, under the heading "Twin Totalitarianisms: The Sick Symbiosis of Dish and Heater—A Suicide Pact Within the Sapien Beam-Bunch Relationship?" Simply put, the reptile argued that once the power-mad hominids invented the Heater, they could not resist using it. "Like a dog and his balls!" Gojiro blustered. "Why's he lick 'em? Cause he can!" In their Heater-lust, however, the sapiens confronted a formidable foe: the survivalist imperative of the Evolloo. Doom, after all, is against every impulse of the Blessed Blueprint. "Examine the dilemma," Gojiro intoned. "The Heater is the sapien's crowning achievement, he loves it, craves nothing more than to meld with it as proof of his perverted mastery over the planet, yet his own physical nature forbids the gratification of this passion. So what else is there to do but devalue that nature, gnaw away at all that signifies living as worthwhile, thereby establishing annihilation as a palatable alternative? Why else would they shit where they eat, befoul their every niche? But there's never been a leaking supertanker that left a bigger blot than the Dish Image. That's the sinful duality functioning within the sapien's death wish. The Heater's the end, but the Image is the means."

It was the "ascendency of the easily accessible Image," the monster declared, that robbed the sapien of his ability to be both objective about the past and poetically intuitive about the future. "Check it out. Say you got some raggedy-ass tribesmen in New Guinea, and for two thousand years they've been nursing along some stick figure solar trope about a giant bird hauling a glowing stone up into the sky with its beak. Sure it's weak, a subsistence sort of creation riff, but at least it's theirs. So what happens the first time they see "I Love Lucy"? Little Ricky blows that glowing stone straight out the back of their heads. Their whole world is common denominated to a Havana nightclub. You'd figure they'd catch on. Don't sapiens know Bad Art is like a flag flying upside down, mayday for the Beam-Bunch? But no. They just keep on. Devaluing and devaluing. Grinding those cathodes until they get to the Big Signoff.

"The worst of it," the monster screamed, holding up a lobby card announcing the Midville Manyscreen's showing of *Gojiro vs. the Casey Kasem Beast on a Journey to the End of the Dial,* "is that we're part of it! Right there in the white-hot center of this infernal process!" Then Gojiro stopped talking. He couldn't go on. As cynical as he'd tried to make himself over the years, he couldn't tolerate his own Image, pirated or not, being the consort—the henchman!—of the Heater. It was too bitter an irony.

Yet here, bellydowned on that beer-can-flecked freeway median, watching those ragtag 'tile-o-files, Gojiro felt a shift. Suddenly, it was like that horrible night up on Dead Letter Hill, when he stood beside that oppressive spire.

"Who's it on?" the monster had asked, confronted by the detoured 90 Series's seethe and roil. "Who's got to take the weight?" Komodo shook his head then, said the weight would fall on whoever was prepared to bear it. And the monster wailed, 'cause he knew: face-to-face with all that pathetic longing, the Varanidid wouldn't have turned away. The Varanidid would have gone forth. Because what does a Hero really need . . . but Need? Wasn't all the Need in the world right there, leeching into the ground on Dead Letter Hill? Wasn't that same Need present right now, amid that scrapbook-carrying horde that came to sit at the foot of the big picture in the middle of the blank desert night? "Who's it on?" The question pulled at him, yanked like a billion umbilical cords. It was his Image up there! It didn't matter by what means it got there. It was still his picture. Him.

There was no choice but to come clean, he decided. He would go back into that limo and make Komodo reverse the shrink ray. He would return to his normal size, then break through that Image and expose the *real* Gojiro. He would tell it all. The Truth.

And what was that Truth? That he was a coward. A fake.

"I ain't tough. I'm a wimp. A coward," he screamed out, still beside the roadway. He'd tell those zardpards everything, set them straight on how the movies were shams, how those supposed epic battles were nothing more than setups, tank jobs, fixes. Hero? Bully was more like it. After all, those supposed deathless Opposers weren't even real Beasts. They were nothing but animatron messes of recombinate slime Komodo fudged up in plastic molds. Those sludgicles didn't have single thought in their pseudocellulose heads, much less a diabolic design on how to subjugate Radioactive Island's carefree little crew. Even so, the reptile feared them, quaked before them. He'd cower in his dressing room afraid to come out. Komodo would have to slip him a pill, stick him shivering on his chalk mark. Sometimes the reptile would make Komodo reconfigure the sludgicles on the spot, lop off a head or two, anything to make them less frightening. But then, when he finally did summon the nerve to face the tox-o-masses, he'd whale on them, beat on those bland slabs as if nothing pleased him more than the sound of his fist against insensate chlorophyll.

It was an ugly story, but one that had to be told, Gojiro decided. His fans needed to know all of it, the whole reeking enchilada verde. They needed to understand why he'd turned away their supplications, why he could never be this *thing* they wanted him to be. He was no King of Monsters, Friend to Atoms. He was a reclusive mutant, a vain, spouting, lonely fool. He would tell them every last bit. Then he would throw himself on their mercy. If they felt they should rip him apart, he would allow them to do so. It would be the only decent thing he'd done in his life.

However, as he turned to begin the execution of his plan, Gojiro looked back up at the screen. They were playing the scene where, guided only by the sound of Johnny Hodges's solo on "Star-Crossed Lovers" and the Atoms' mass reading of the retard parts from *The Sound and the Fury,* the monster breaks through the squid's obscurantistic fog, letting there be light. Always kind of liked that part, Gojiro thought. It seemed a shame to interrupt a scene like that. If he was going to set straight the swindle he'd wreaked upon his wretched fans, the apologia's timing had to be precise. There was no need to be hasty, jump the gun. "Give them this last moment of illusion," he said to himself.

But then, as quickly as it had come, the desire to confess fled. What would be gained from it anyway? Would it bring peace of mind to anyone? His sins were beyond any simple act of contrition. Besides, what was the assurance that his fans would accept his word? Why should they? They could take him for an imposter, ignore him, leaving him to twist slowly in the night wind like some moldy warmup act. That would be great, really super. But worse than that— much worse—was that he'd succeed in convincing them he was a fake. Then what? If there was one thing certain as far as those luckless clutchers of Crystal Contact Radios were concerned, it was that Gojiro was the center of their botched universe. What gave him the authority to pull the sun out of their system, just because he happened to be very same merry ole sol? It would be like snatching the last pastry off the plate of a motherloving French memorist, feeding it to just anyone in the street. Where would be the greater good in that? Maybe the zardpards were a dismal bunch now, worshipers of a crooked icon, but to wrest even *that* from them was to remove even the chimera of Hope.

It was an impossible situation.

That was when he heard it: "Please come in."

And again: "Please come in, Gojiro."

It sounded like it was coming from the screen. The monster turned, did a double take. "Can't be!" That great Image was staring down at him, beckoning. *Beckoning to him!* "Please come in, Gojiro! Please heed this humble servant's plea."

"I must be going crazy." The picture was shifting now, closing in on the behemoth's head, drawing a bead on the parietal. Gojiro squinted. He didn't remember that shot. Shig cut stuff out, sure, jumbled it up, but he never refilmed anything. A zoom shot! There weren't any zoom shots in that picture! Cinematically, Komodo admired Ophuls, von Sternberg, early Skolimowski— his *mise en scène* was fluid, sumptuous, eschewing cheap TV effects. Yet there it went, in and in. Closer and closer until the parietal seemed to be right in front of the monster's face, a swirling psychic peristalsis. "Come in, Gojiro . . ."

It was insane, but right then he could have been back on Lavarock, staring down at his reflection in the Black Spot.

"Please come in, Gojiro. Please heed this humble servant's plea."

"I'm thinking about it!" he screamed back at the screen. He wanted to. Bad. He wanted to hurl himself through the air between him and that creature on the screen . . . but there was all that *space* between. He'd have to vault over the rumbling traffic, the wideslung hurdle of the GOJIRO VS. SQUID marquee, a thousand fans in vans—but that would be no problem for a monster who could jump as high as a moon. This was a different kind of space.

"Come in, Gojiro. Please come in, Gojiro, *Bridger of Gaps, Linker of Lines, Nexus of Beam and Bunch, Defender of the Evolloo.* Please heed this humble servant's plea."

"Wha?" Suddenly Gojiro realized the sound wasn't coming from the screen at all. It was closer, right next to him, the voice of a boy. A wild, sun-baked boy. Billy Snickman! Gojiro knew it instantaneously, instinctively. After all, he'd *been* Billy Snickman! He'd lived in the same foster homes, hidden in the same car trunks, eaten out of the same garbage cans. He'd been inside Billy Snickman's head, and Billy Snickman had been inside his.

That night! That terrible night on Dead Letter Hill. "I only got one question," Billy Snickman had said then. *"Who are you?"* Goddamn! What kind of question was that? That question should be banned from speech!

Gojiro reeled about feverishly, trying to get a better look at this boy whose voice he'd sought to avoid for so many years. In the screaming headlights Billy Snickman appeared as a mad, mall-age Moses. His hair was matted and flung itself away from his head in great plaited slabs. His clothes were shredded, the tatters spreading in the wind like flames. He lived in the hollow of the freeway underpass, inside a skeleton of sticks and stretched green garbage bags. It was easy to see why he'd chosen that particular place. The sightline to the giant drive-in screen was perfect, unimpeded. Never once did Billy Snickman take his eyes off that massive Image. He just sat there, repeating that supplication, over and over, into the cool night. A mantra, that's what it sounded like. Billy Snickman, the author of "Forget That House," poet of dislocation, had become a crazed sitting sadhu out there on that freeway, putting his every rhyme and reason into this one unremitting petition.

"Enough!" Gojiro screamed. He couldn't wait another second to find out what Billy Snickman wanted of him. He resolved to confront the boy then and there. But, before he could move, Komodo grabbed him.

"My own true friend!" Komodo shouted through the raging night. "She has been here!"

"Who?"

"Sheila Brooks! I have found this in the sand." Komodo held a small gun. A derringer. "It is hers," Komodo said, his face flushed. Engraved on the barrel, faintly visible in the headlight glare was "From Albie B. to Sheila B."

"A present from Mr. Bullins," Komodo yelled above the traffic roar. "It is identical to the one she had the other night."

Gojiro looked over at Billy Snickman. *Gojiro vs. the Enigma-Inking Squid at the Rock of Knowledge* was over. The last of those phony credits rolled by, the screen grew dark. But obviously Billy Snickman did not consider his evening finished. He kept on, reciting his supplication. Vans and pickups rolled by, heading, no doubt, for squalid dwellings all over the desert country. None of them seemed to notice Billy Snickman. If the boy was a prophet, his message went unheeded by its natural constituency.

Gojiro kept watching Billy Snickman until he heard Komodo once more. "Something has happened in this place. Her gun, it has been fired!"

INTO THE VALLEY

They knew they were close when they pulled into an all-night Fina station and saw the wizened attendant sitting four inches from a television showing *The Day the Earth Stood Still*. The gas station was "For Sale," the house behind it was "For Sale," the half dozen rusting cars off to the side were also "For Sale." In fact, everything around the station was "For Sale"—even the dog, which was a surprise, since it looked dead. It seemed about right for a place called El Callejon sin Salida, which, according to a shredded billboard out on the blacktop, was "the town closest to the site of the first A-bomb explosion."

Even so, they still had a goodly portion of Big Panghorn Missile and Bombing Range to cross. KEEP OUT said the tedious succession of signs posted every few feet along the horizon-piercing stretch of cyclone fence. AUTHORIZED PERSONNEL ONLY. Shig drove the perimeter, then stopped at a shot-up wooden building that had served as the world headquarters of the Deviants MC before that shoot-out with state troopers. They hid the limo behind a lava mound and crawled under the barbed-wire fence. From there they'd have to walk; it was miles to the Valley edge.

In the moonless night, even with Komodo's nite scope strapped to his snout, Gojiro's underneaths were stuck with so many cholla needles he felt like a dimestore voodoo doll dangling from a rearview mirror. "If I knew it was gonna be like this, I would have worn a steel bib," he complained.

Four hours later, they reached the Valley's lip and peered down. Spreading out before them like a vast black sea, the hole was immense, seemingly without bottom. The vista, so huge and hidden, took their breath away, weakened their knees.

The name told it all. El Valle de Encrucijada—Valley of the Crossroads, or Valley of the Ambush, depending on which meaning you took. The monster saw them as the same: to a mutant, every crossroads is an ambush. "Went down to the Crossroads, tried to flag a ride," was how the cheerless song went. "Down the Crossroads, tried to flag a ride, didn't nobody seem to know me, everybody pass me by."

The crossroads was the preserve of the sly and smiling Trickster, sitting on a fence, chewing on a reed. The tired traveler comes up to the crossroads, says, "Hey, you there, sitting on that fence, which way to Chicago?" "Chicago? Been there a hundred times," the Trickster says, pointing. "You got to go that way, you want to get to Chicago." And there you go, down that road, never to feel the wind off the lake on your face, save the gales of Hell. "Went down to the Crossroads, tried to flag a ride, nobody seemed to know me, everybody pass me by." The Heater ruled the crossroads down in that dark pit stretched out in front of him, Gojiro knew. The Heater that tricked a world, turned it to a negative, a ghost didn't nobody seem to know, everyone pass it by.

"Down there," the reptile said, his voice an awed whisper, "that's where it all began, huh? The womb of the Modern World." Komodo nodded. Tears were in their eyes. Standing over that Valley—there was a solemnity in it.

Just then a helicopter came racheting, spraying light across the Spanish bayonet and yucca. Shig grabbed Komodo and the two of them hit the ground beside Gojiro. "The one o'clock patrol," Shig said, as a matter of fact. "In two hours they test the newly commissioned Eleggba III not far from here. The safety cone for this system has not yet been established; it is very erratic. To linger in this spot might be dangerous."

Shig motioned left. "Please come, I have prepared accommodations for the night. It is not far."

Maybe once it was nothing more than a cave, a guano-splattered bat haven, but now the cavern's mouth was a metal door that screwed open with the perverse squeak of an urn lid. Inside was a latticework of rusting catwalks that threatened to give way at any moment. Down and down they went into the consuming gloom, until they reached bottom and walked out into a huge underground room.

Gojiro

"What's this joint, Usher's confessional?" Gojiro murmured. The place was enormous, the strange sheenlike floor at least three hundred yards across. Rocky walls vaulted up as might those of a Gothic cupola, to a ceiling lost in the shrouding darkness. The only available light came from the numerous clusters of candles, their wax dripping down upon multiarmed twenty-foot-tall holders so typical of Shig's interior decoration. A high-pitched sound could be heard, its timbre resembling that of a massive pipe organ set on the sopranomost stop.

"Hey!" Gojiro said with a start. "What you wearing that stuff for?"

Komodo had donned an odd saran wrap–like see-through robe. On his head he wore a visored helmet. Shig was outfitted in a similar fashion. "These are special garments," the pitiless boy answered. "There are high levels of certain potentially corrosive elements here."

"Corrosive elements? What are you talking about?"

"This large cavity has been used extensively for underground nuclear testing. Right now it suits our purpose."

"*A White Light Chamber!* We in a White Light Chamber?"

Komodo hung his head. "Yes. It seemed the best available shelter."

The monster was incensed. "Shelter! How could a White Light Chamber be shelter from any storm? The Beast's own belly—and we got to jump right in it! Auschwitz all booked up or something?"

"I am sorry for the great offense, my own true friend, but there was no alternative. I fear that the shrink ray has proved to be unfortunately unpredictable. I am afraid you can no longer be maintained at a specific height or weight. Here you can be accommodated even at your full dimensions. Please accept my apologies."

"But what if they decide to bust one open down here?"

"My own true friend, have not the Great Powers signed a treaty forbidding such things?"

"You fall for that shit?"

Komodo sadly shook his head. "In any event, it would not happen here. This site has been abandoned for more than ten years. Shig has double-checked these facts with records secured from the Defense Department."

"Damn." How did Shig "secure" information like that? No doubt much intimidation and stealth was employed. The reptile looked across the huge Heater-induced ulcer and saw the whitesuited neoteen running a forklift, moving several crates around. "Now what's he doing?"

Komodo shook his head. He didn't know either.

195

* * *

Originally, the plan was just to stay the night. Until dawn. Then they would emerge, look down into the Valley. "Whatever Ms. Brooks saw happened at dawn," Komodo told Gojiro. " 'Dawn light,' that's what she said. If we are to illuminate her secret we must attempt, inasmuch as it is possible, to see what she sees."

The monster could only grunt. He didn't feel like arguing the point. There was still most of a whole night left to spend in the Heater's haunted house. "Mind if we cuddle up?" Gojiro asked Komodo. "I'm feeling a little . . . on edge."

So they made themselves a makeshift burrow over in a corner of the abhorrent cavity, pushed themselves together, leather to skin, skin to leather. "Kind of like old times," Gojiro said softly. Back in the Glazed Days, they always slept close, a boy snuggled within the soft hyoid of a massive lizard. It was only after Kishi arrived that they took up separate quarters. "I guess I missed this."

"As did I, my own true friend."

They held each other tight. Then Gojiro said, "I know this is lame and all, but I was wondering if you could read to me, you know, like you used to."

Komodo said he would be more than happy to grant Gojiro's request, but he had none of their favorite books.

"It don't got to be nothing special. Could be anything, I just miss hearing you read."

"There is only this." It was a handout Shig had picked up at the gas station: "Prospector Pete's Get-Rich Guide to Panning, Wildcatting, and the Semiprecious Metals of the Jornada del Muerto and Big Panghorn—Revised and Up-to-Date Edition, with Special Section on the Encrucijada."

"Guess that'll have to do," Gojiro groaned.

Prospector Pete's publication, which emanated from 23½ Sospecha Street, Socorro, New Mexico, had the old-timey look of a roadside restaurant placemat, thick with rope letters and rudimentarily rendered Yosemite Sams on the cover. However, a close reading of the smudgy, rexographed pages revealed more than a few salty tales of yesteryear and hobbyist lore. Prospector Pete, who signed every item with his imprimatur of crossed pickaxes, was a polemicist of no small obsession. This was most apparent in a front page "editorial" entitled "More Double-Talk in the Encrucijada."

"I'm sure all you have been following that big stink the Indian Nelson

Monongae's land claim is raising," the editorial began. "Now, the ole Prospector don't have a single thing against a Native American reclaiming what's rightfully his. What sticks in my craw is how, ever since federalizing the land for the Bomb Test, the government has always refused to allow the independent wildcatter a fair chance on sinking a well out there on the Big Panghorn. You ask me, there's some *very serious funny business* going on in the Valley.

"Let me explain myself. Probably you heard about that conference down at the state college about mass extinctions of the dinosaurs. Of course, it ain't exactly news to us rockhounds that the so-called experts have come around to the idea that the earth was hit by an interstellar object of some type approximately sixty-six million years ago, which might have had some hand in the reptiles' demise. What was news was a report read by a professor that there's no place in the world with a higher concentration of iridium at the Cretaceous level than right here in the Jornada del Muerto. As any amateur geologist knows, iridium is the sure sign of celestial intervention—meteorites and so forth. All of which led these experts to conclude that this comet, or what have you, may have come to earth right here in our own backyard!

"It made a lot of sense, since any longtime sandpanner working the outskirts of the Big Panghorn doesn't need a conference to tell him that the Jornada del Muerto has one of the widest assortments of dinosaur fossils in the world. You want triceratopses, we got 'em. Allosauruses? You name it. Well, Prospector Pete got to putting all this together back at the ole assay shack. I did a little checking and found out that the Encrucijada Valley itself— which is really no valley at all but a meteorite-type crater—has an iridium count *more than one hundred times higher* than the already high surrounding area. Which leads me to go out on what I feel is a very short limb and say the Encrucijada Valley is the actual site of the comet fall!

"Now hold your horses all you panners and wildcatters. Maybe you think the Prospector's gone off the deep end with all this talk about comets and dinosaurs. I just want you to ask yourself one question: *What's fossils mean but fossil fuels????!!!!!!* Let me tell you, if that comet really did hit out there in the Encrucijada, don't that make it potentially one of the richest fields ever? And let me say one more thing: I'm willing to bet I'm not the only one who ever came to this conclusion. Fellow rockhounders and roustabouts: how long are we going to let the federal government and Big Oil tell us we can't seek our fortunes in our own backyards on account of they once shot off an Atom Bomb out there?"

When Komodo stopped reading, a shocked silence enveloped the White Light Chamber.

"Shee-it," Gojiro finally whistled. "He saying that the saurs bought it right out there, in the Encrucijada?"

"That is what Mr. Pete seems to intimate, yes."

The monster shook his head. "The Heater born in the same place where the saurs died . . . that's heavy."

"It would be a remarkable coincidence, an astounding confluence."

Gojiro shuddered. "Talk about your fearful symmetry."

"It is an eccentric notion to be sure," Komodo said tentatively, rubbing his chin. "Yet . . ."

"Yet what?"

"Oh, it's probably nothing, but seemingly unrelated items synchronate in my mind. The first, of course, is Mr. Monongae's contention that the Lizard Clan came to this spot because his great-great-grandfather felt 'the blood of the world' was here. Secondly, there is Ms. Brooks's mother's portrait. That X-ray pattern, it's so . . . paleontological. Then there's Mr. Zeber's statement that she insisted the Trinity Bomb be exploded here and nowhere else."

Gojiro gave Komodo a sidelong glance. "What are you getting at?"

"Oh, I don't know, it's probably silly," Komodo sighed. "It's just that I was recently reading a book that touched on the discipline of geomancy. The author, in an unfortunately unscientific manner, expressed the belief that there are places in the world—he referred to them as power spots—where extraordinary events seem to occur over and over again. I only mention this now because if this Valley proved to be one of these power spots, then perhaps *more* extraordinary events could transpire here—which gives me renewed hope in regard to our Solemn Vow."

The monster was feeling sick now. "Hey look. This is giving me the creeps. You mind if we don't talk about it right now?"

Komodo nodded sharply, the animation draining from his face. "Of course, we must get our rest. We must be up at dawn. Tomorrow is potentially a most consequential day." Then Komodo extinguished the last of the candle clusters, plunging the White Light Chamber into darkness.

He couldn't sleep, couldn't stop his mind. Listening to Komodo's quiet breathing only made it worse. For the millionth time he felt he didn't deserve such

a loyal friend. That loony riff about the Encrucijada being a power spot, whatever that meant—it just proved it all over again. Maybe Komodo was a terminal
pollyanna, forever naive, but at least he was throwing his heart and soul into
their sworn quest to fulfill the Triple Ring Promise. How the monster despised
himself right then. So he didn't believe for a minute that business about Sheila
Brooks having a secret—wasn't it still his duty to offer Komodo more than
flaccid, reluctant assurances of support? The Triple Ring Promise was pledged
between them, ostensibly of equal importance to them both. Yet as Komodo
scoured the landscape for every clue, however unlikely, what did Gojiro do?

Withhold evidence.

It was worse than a lie, the reptile knew, not informing Komodo of that
business with Billy Snickman on the freeway. After all, in the investigation into
Sheila Brooks's alleged secret, it seemed a significant piece of evidence. How
else could she have learned of that mind-bending supplication, if not from Billy
Snickman? Telling would have been so easy. When Komodo came over with
that tiny gun, holding its barrel gingerly between two fingers, fingerprint-squad
style, Gojiro could have said, "Yes, she *was* here! I know it!" He could have
pointed to that wild boy right then, let Komodo listen to the mantra he spoke.
It could have come out right then and there—what happened that night on Dead
Letter Hill, the reason for that terrible operation, all of it. Except he didn't say
a thing. Those phrases: Bridger of Gaps, Linker of Lines, *Defender of the
Evolloo*—they intimidated him, kept him silent.

"Shit!" He got up, paced in the joyless gloom of that White Light Chamber.
What an abominable place, how huge and hideous! Some major megatoning
must have been done down there to have gouged so grotesque a vacancy into
the earth, the monster thought. He was flipping out! Jagged images of the past
few days tumbled through the Quadcam, cascading like an all-night game of
fifty-two pick-up. He saw that Indian, the Echo Man, who he said his Lizard Clan
owned the Valley. That vial round his neck—that black vial!—what was it?
Then, in rapid succession, there came Albert Bullins, flying low in a Superfortress. And Bobby Zeber's mournful smile, and Wilma, walking away from
Walter's grave, Victor Stiller with his martini; what did he want? And Sheila
Brooks, of course, Sheila Brooks.

"Stop! Leave me alone!" Seeking refuge, the leviathan reached out for any
tool to tamp the raging furies. Then he thought he saw it. Those boxes Shig
had been pushing around—they were Dishscreens! Beat-up Philcos and Admirals, B&Ws bought from a secondhand store in Alamogordo, a bank of video

sanctuary. But when he turned the screens on, every one of them got only one picture. A large, murky landscape filled each screen.

"What's this? 'Sunrise Semester' for the deforested zone?" Then the monster saw those red cliffs and knew: this wasn't regular programming. It was monitors! That's what Shig was doing with those forklifts—setting up monitors to scan the Valley outside.

The cliffs were redder now, color slowly infusing them. Dawn! It was dawn—time to see the secret. "Hey! Wake up," the reptile shouted as he twirled dials to clear the picture. In the incipient daylight, the redrimmed crater shone. Encrucijada was a near-perfect circle, at least five miles across, three deep. That nut bag prospector was right; it could have been caused by a foreign object, a great ball driving itself into the earth, leaving, all those eons later, a bare, somber hole.

It took a moment to realize there was a house sitting in the middle of a vast bowl. It was stone, a sprawling affair, with several additions. The roof was gray slate, the chimney was smoking. The monster gulped. Someone was home in that house!

Then Gojiro saw him, standing behind the stone fence. A man in black. A man in black.

A tall man, a tremendously old-looking man wearing a black hat, his face obscured by the brim. Staring out, staring out.

Then it was right there. The face. It was looking out of the monitor, right into Gojiro's face. Those eyes! Those black eyes. Searching, connecting, locking on.

"It's Brooks! He's alive!"

PART

THREE

ALONE IN HELL

The desert sun was edging above the red cliffs when Komodo walked out into the Valley. Rock gave way to sand and then to a sheet of glass, a greentinged sheen stretching for hundreds of yards in every direction. It was the Heater's legacy, Komodo knew, the glass cracking beneath his feet like the brittle bones of a past made forever obsolete.

Up ahead, a dark ghost shimmering in the rising heat, was Joseph Prometheus Brooks. Joseph Prometheus Brooks! Komodo fixed his path toward the blackclad figure, did not waver from it.

With him, he brought only the *fumetti*. It was a gift, a token of esteem. "We cannot approach him empty-handed," Komodo told Gojiro back inside the White Light Chamber. Not that the *fumetti* could be compared with a fountain pen, or even the key to Radioactive Island. It was just a twenty-eight-page aggregate of thick-grained snapshots festooned with bulbous dialogue balloons in the manner of an Italian comic book. Still, Komodo considered it the perfect offering. It represented Truth—at least a certain kind of Truth.

"Our *real* story, told by us." That's how Gojiro referred to the *fumetti* in the frenzied days immediately following the discovery of Shig's skullduggery regarding the King of Monsters, Friend to Atoms movies. The monster's original intention was to restage the events of their lives, from the founding of Radioactive Island to the creation of the Cosmo, up to the current scene. Bound on full disclosure, the reptile rejected Komodo's proposal to show the story in a series of abstract drawings. "The whole Truth and nothing but," the monster demanded, insisting on photography. "No touch or retouch."

203

Gojiro's plan was to print up a limited number of *fumetti*—five hundred, a thousand tops—then place them in strategic positions around the globe, one in a telephone booth on Forty-second Street, another in a bush at the Everest tree line, a few shoved into crannies in the Great Wall, etc. Publishing millions, muscling them onto every newsstand, all that smacked of the official denial, the monster declared, the totalitarian and parental. That was no way to dislodge Shig's narrative from the impressionable minds of G-fans. Truth could not arrive blustery and bullying and expect to be accepted; it had to creep subversive, like rumor, legend.

The scheme, however, was never executed. The 90 Series headed it off. Everything got put on the back burner after that. So there was only one *fumetti* in existence, the paste-up prototype that Komodo now held in his sweating hands as he walked across the Encrucijada toward the slate-roofed house where Joseph Prometheus Brooks stood.

The *fumetti* would help, Komodo thought, the early morning sun already hard upon his forehead. It contained the only existing photo of the King of Monsters and Coma Boy together, a shot of the two standing on Corvair Bay Beach. Showing it to Brooks, Komodo thought, would immediately make the predicament clear. Every moment counted; the vicissitudes of the Triple Ring Promise had to be presented as quickly as possible. Mastering the rudiments of Quadcamerality, deciphering the mysteries of Reprimordialization would likely be child's play for someone like Joseph Prometheus Brooks, Komodo surmised. But then again, who could predict the workings of genius? It operates on its own schedule, does not square with the nine to five. All he could do, Komodo thought as he made his way across the giant Valley, was to impress the urgency of the situation upon the great scientist.

He got within a hundred yards of the house before the image became clear in his mind. The way Brooks stood there, gaunt and stiff in his worn parson's coat, his huge hands thrust out before him, palms up, spiny fingers spread as if he were cradling an invisible sphere—it was identical to the pose in Leona Brooks's X-ray portrait. It was as if the picture had come to life, right there in the middle of the Valley of the Crossroads.

The recognition wobbled Komodo, made him weak. For a moment he thought he'd pass out, faint right there on the Heater's greenish sheet, but he gathered himself up, pushed on.

"Mr. Brooks?" he called into the parched air. "Please forgive this oppressive intrusion. I am Yukio Komodo. If I may approach and speak to you, I will restrict my altogether insignificant questions to the barest minimum." Brooks offered no acknowledgment of Komodo's presence. He just kept looking, staring out into the Valley. It was just a matter of asking the perfect question, Komodo thought, bulwarking himself. If only he could frame the exact right query in the exact right way, the incisive force of the interrogatory itself would compel Brooks to reply as any great man-of-science must when confronted with a problem worthy of his mettle. But what was that question?

"Mr. Brooks, I come to you with a serious matter that represents a potentially . . ." The words caught in his throat, would not clear his tongue. Komodo berated himself. To be granted a moment like this, to stand face-to-face with the great and terrible Brooks, to petition his help in resolution of the Promise, and not be able to utter a single intelligible phrase! Not a comprehensible point! It was madness.

"Mr. Brooks, please listen . . ." Those eyes! Dark and glowing from within the deepset sockets of the physicist's cadaverous face, they appeared to blaze an unassailable path across the empty landscape. Komodo felt himself wilting before those bituminous orbs.

"You see," Komodo stammered, holding out the *fumetti,* "my friend and I . . . we live on an Island, it's not near here. In fact it is quite far. We were hoping you might pay the smallest attention to our paltry dilemma . . . Perhaps you might chance to glance at this modest work, so as to get a better idea . . . Please, Mr. Brooks, there is not much time."

Then Komodo felt that sudden gust pierce through the previously calm desert air, pulling the *fumetti* from his hands. Caught in an updraft, the old comic first rose straight into the azure sky, then blew across the Valley floor. "Oh no," Komodo gasped. Then, as if on cue, came that glare. The popping of a flashbulb—someone was taking his picture! And Komodo was running, back across that Valley, away from Joseph Prometheus Brooks.

Gojiro watched it all on the monitors Shig had set up down in the White Light Chamber. There was nothing else he could do, not after that unfortunate incident following his positive ID of Joe Pro Brooks. "Not dead?" the monster convulsed. The corrective could be applied to that, forthwith, no sweat. "Rarrr," he roared, long-fermenting bile bubbling up, overflowing. He tail-slammed the Chamber walls, looking for the bust-out. Only Komodo's quick string and zing of that stun-tipped harpoon stopped the lizard, sending him to

Crash Gordonsville. When he woke up he was outraged to find himself trussed like bedlam's mummy in a straitjacket the size of which no Big and Tall ever sold. But still he promised. He swore he'd stay inside the Chamber and not interfere with Komodo's attempt to engage the seemingly resurrected Brooks on a high-type scientific plane.

Now, however, Komodo was back in the Chamber, crying. "It was horrible. I couldn't speak. Then I lost the *fumetti*, and that flash . . . Oh! How shameful. I panicked, I ran away. Mr. Brooks is our Promise's last chance, and I failed to communicate with him. Can you ever forgive me?"

Gojiro tried to comfort his friend. For sure, he didn't care about the jerkoff *fumetti*—his only reaction when Komodo pulled the thing from the pocket of his black pajamas was, "Don't you ever throw anything out?" Besides, who was he to blame Komodo for running away? Komodo was the bravest, truest, most reverent. Clean, too. "Hey, man, anybody would've bugged out. Cat's eerie. It's scary enough just seeing him on them monitors." That was so; for a dead guy who suddenly turned up alive, Brooks still looked pretty dead. Talk about your timeslips, what *was* Brooks doing out there, still posing for a picture that had been painted decades before? It was too strange, especially when you considered Brooks was supposed to be six feet under at Arlington. Hadn't it been giant, Brooks croaking? Gojiro watched the old newsreel at least a dozen times—the flag-draped coffin, slide rule tossed into the open grave, the whole twenty-one guns. A full complement of the rogue's gallery had been present, Fermi, Lawrence, and the rest, a double row of spaceheads. Victor Stiller himself served up a real heartrending eulogy, his East Euro brogue never smoother as he talked of his "godlike" friend. John Foster fucking Dulles threw dirt on the fluted box, for chrissakes.

Brooks was supposed to be dead. Yet there he was—the dead man, alive, smack in the middle of the Valley of Death.

Gojiro looked at the monitors, studied the unmoving form. "I dunno, maybe he *is* dead, maybe we're all dead." Wasn't Komodo the Coma Boy, and wasn't the Coma Boy supposed to be dead, expired after "a nine-year fight to cling to a life he hardly knew." And what about a certain supposedly imaginary five-hundred-foot-tall star of sleazoid screen and cathode ray? "Never alive"— didn't that add up to the same as dead? Maybe that's what this so-called Valley of the Crossroads was, the reptile thought, a limbo land, a halfway house for them between states and stations. "I say we blow this popstand. Ain't nothing here for us."

Komodo did not reply. He just stood still, watching those snowy Philcos and Admirals, studying Joseph Prometheus Brooks. "Look at his eyes! How they stare ahead. My own true friend, what do you suppose he's looking for?"

"Who knows? Who cares? He's one zoned hombre. Bonked. Total."

Komodo drew closer to a monitor, held out his hand, lightly touched its sheer face. "It was awful, being out there. I thought if only I could get his attention, then I could make him understand. But he wouldn't look at me . . . no, that's not right. He did look at me. But it was as if he wouldn't *see* me. He looked right through me, as if I wasn't there at all."

Gojiro was up, pacing. "Just what I'm saying. The guy is nuts. Mindblown. Look man, we gave it a good shot, coming here. But it's a dead end. Besides, someone took your picture out there. This gotta be some sickass CIA shit. Makes my blood run more cold and clotty every second."

Komodo did not look up. "I sensed that he was searching for something . . . something he *had* to see. Perhaps that's why he wouldn't see me. Because somehow, I was . . . *wrong.*"

Then Komodo turned away from the screens, faced Gojiro. "I must go."

"Go? Where? Back out there?"

"No. To her. She must be told her father is alive."

"But . . ."

Komodo rubbed his face agitatedly. "I spoke with her about her mother's portrait. She said she'd never seen it. 'I don't want to see my mother's dreams'—those were her very words. Yet she *does* see what her mother saw." Komodo reached into the pocket of his black pajamas, drew out his stereopticon. "She saw it in here! Think, my own true friend, of Ms. Brooks's mother's portrait. The background is a blaze of white, but there is no detail, no physical features that identify the land. It was Ms. Brooks who provided those details— 'Red rocks!' she called out. 'Red rocks and cliffs!' Oh, my own true friend. Do you not feel the gratitude we owe her? We came to this foreign land hoping she might provide us with an insight into her father's thinking. Has she not done better than that? She provided *him!*

"Now we must reciprocate. We must seek to alleviate her torment—free her from the spectres that haunt her."

The monster interrupted with a scream. "I don't think we should be messing with stuff we don't know nothing about. Whatever's happening here— it ain't our business."

Komodo frowned at the reptile's outburst, then peered intently at the stereopticon. "So many times I have wished this photo would spring to life. That somehow these people would step from this holder. But it has not been possible; my prayer has never been answered. Yet, that night, when she looked into this very frame, she saw her father. It was as if by seeing him, she has snatched him from Death."

Komodo turned to look at Joseph Prometheus Brooks. "Perhaps it is strange to say, but through Ms. Brooks's vision—it is almost as if my own father has been returned to me."

A tightness seized the monster. His head felt as if it was about to shoot off his shoulders. It was one thing to propose that a picture in an antique viewer found on the beach of a mutant's island might somehow qualify as an area of transference, a smallest rectangle where every needy soul might come to petition love, and that the love found there might be interchangeable with all currencies of the heart. But including Joseph Prometheus Brooks in that exchange. Wasn't that going off the cognitive map? Brooks as Komodo's dad—as *any* dad—it was insanity. Still, the monster knew there would be no arguing his friend out of telling Sheila Brooks that her father was alive, if not kicking, in the Encrucijada. "Okay, you win. Let's cut. Don't want to knock the service, but this joint was getting a little old."

Komodo looked at Gojiro resolutely. "I feel it would be better if I went myself."

"What?"

"It would only be for a short while."

"You want me to stay in this spook house by myself? You crazy?"

Komodo threw some clothing in a bag. "You will be safer in this contained environment. Your thermoregulation has been fluctuating. It will be easier to maintain a proper temperature here. Also, there is the shrinkage problem."

"Screw the shrinkage, I ain't stayin'."

Komodo bit his lower lip. The words were hard for him. "I desire to go to see Ms. Brooks . . . by myself." The tortured expression on his face begged Gojiro not to protest.

"Oh."

Fifteen minutes later, Komodo was ready to leave. "This time will pass quickly. Perhaps this separation will be a good thing. As Budd Hazard says, 'In the pursuit of True Identity, one must sometimes follow his own road not taken.' "

Gojiro grunted. Komodo was too much! Quoting Budd Hazard, at this latest date, extrapolating the Muse's mumbo jumbo about the solitary path to self-knowledge. Not that the monster denied the principle. Even on Lavarock, where each was everyone and everyone each and the Line linked all, there remained a crucial moment when a zardplebe had to walk alone, make his decisive plunge into the Black Spot by himself. But what could these sentiments matter now, inside this fearsome Chamber?

"I'm trying to be brave, but . . . I'm afraid."

Komodo hugged his friend. "Me too, my own true friend. Me too."

Then he threw a sack over his shoulder. "Please do not think me impolite, my own true friend, but you must be . . . *Gojiro.* Be *Gojiro,* then you won't be afraid."

Was there anything that couldn't happen to a mutant zard in this crazy, mixed-up world, the monster wondered, the singular prisoner in the Heater's own Spandau.

There wasn't anyone to talk to, if you didn't count Brooks. The old worldshatterer was on every one of those Philcos and Admirals, gray blue and hoary, that black-eyed stare boring from his lanternous head, his vampire hands clutching at that phantom ball. "Dude looks like Max Schreck on the Stillman diet," Gojiro shuddered, wanting to turn away but not quite managing it. *What was it with Brooks?* Why was it always like this with him and his stare. Years ago, in a dream, that same look kept the youngest zardplebe from the Black Spot. Even now, with the physicist reduced to seemingly nothing more than a loony desert anchorite, Gojiro was appalled by his own powerlessness to resist the man. Again and again, he'd try to escape the lure of his wizened nemesis, only to succumb once more. Those eyes! Peering out, searching.

"Hey Brooks! What the hell are you looking for?" the monster yelled at the bank of monitors. "What do you want to see?" Why did he have to promise Komodo he wouldn't mash the scientist, scatter his frayed helixes across the windswept plain?

Frustrated, the monster catapulted himself across the foul cave, pounced down on a transistor radio Komodo left for him. "Got to get some sounds!" But all that came out of the box was that cruddy forty-five he cut on Radioactive Island, back when he was trying to put a little slink into the Atoms' funkless step. "Get Up Offa That Levi-a-thang" by B. Hemoth and the Cosmic Rhythm Kings: it wasn't nothing but a thin Soul Bro #1 homage, a synth-sampled, drum-tracked demo, never supposed to seep neath the garage door. But Shig copped it, put it out. The flacks did the rest. Now a digital-voiced deejay was saying the platter was top ten for the fifty-sixth straight week.

"Goddamnit!" The reptile smashed the box with his fist, knocked it clear across the Chamber. When it came down it only got one station, the Kountry Kousin out of Alamogordo, an endless pelt of flat licks about how hearts be broken in a plastic-paneled station wagon. Well, at least those peckerwoods made no bones about being dumb.

How could Komodo have left him stowed away in this hellish abscess? Some friend! "Be *Gojiro,* he tells me," the monster spat, "as if I'm supposed to know what that means. What I should have said was, Sure, I'll be *Gojiro.* All you got to do is be *Komodo.* Be *Komodo* and you won't be afraid!"

But then the monster stopped himself, because he knew Komodo *was* afraid. The fear on his face when he said he had to see Sheila Brooks by himself told the whole story. He looked the way he did the night Albert Bullins's Bearcat blew up and he found himself in that zone with Sheila Brooks. But it wasn't the kind of fear that makes you run and hide. Rather, there was an awesome expectancy in that look. Gojiro thought he'd seen it on his friend's face before, a long time ago, as he walked with Kishi on the Radioactive Island shore.

Bang, bang, the monster crashed his massive skull on the Chamber wall. "Can't take this no more!" Again and again he bashed himself. Then, without warning, large slivers of the vault's roof rocketed downward, glancing off his supraocular ridge. "Ye-ow!" He'd loosened a cascade of dagger-shaped stalactites from the cavity's upper reach. They rained down like the arrows of a vengeful tribe. Shielding his eyes, the reptile peered up. It was weird how the rocks appeared to have tracers on them, luminescent contrails.

Soon enough, the deluge ended. Stacked around him, like kindling, lay a glowing hillock of fallen shafts. Cautiously, Gojiro picked up a medium-sized stone, inspected it. "Hmmm," he said, giving the rock a quick lick, "what have we here?" It figured, really, the joint being a nukish shooting gallery, that there'd be some hardcutting 235 about. "Some spoons been fried down this crib, no lie," the monster commented, goon-eyed. Then he popped a rock into his mouth, gobbled it down.

The jolt and glide brought him far and wide. The next several hours floated by in the most vaporous of hazes. Blue lights bubblegummed, and all about wove a spidery net spun by the hottest and blackest of widows, the arachnid's raunchy, bursty belly moving to the low-slung bleat of the baritone saxophone. His viscera, so long seized up, let go, his every joint rolling in its socket like an outsized ball bearing in a honey pot. Sometimes he'd catch a dose unpleasantly alloyed with the rank ardor of 238, or some other contaminant. Then he'd put on his Lugosi accent and say, "I never smoke . . . strontium 89," breaking into hacking fits of hilarity at his joke.

A new broom of mental floss swept through the plaquelike polar cap of his hates and fears. His thoughts became farflung, speculative. He meditated on the White Light Chamber, imagining it not a vile blast hole, but a sad pocket, a tear-shaped bead in the vast sea of earth. "They had to bring the Heater down here," he thought, "to hide it. It's like how they shut up their brilliant but antisocial children, never allow them to see the Light." Then he shook his head, a silent comment on the sapien species, magnificent in so many ways, a race with the power to invent a second sun—but a Bunch forced to bury that sun inside a hole in the ground, after they found out its artificial heat could do nothing except melt their all-too-waxy wings.

What about Brooks? The madman was still out there, staring, even as the moon began to rise above the Encrucijada. Didn't he sleep? Fortified with fallout's brand of oblivion, the lizard engaged the worldshatterer's glare, looked back into the black eyes. And, right then, a wild idea crossed the Quadcameral transom. It sounded like something Komodo might come up with—the notion that, like his daughter, Joseph Brooks also had a secret, a consuming enigma that haunted him, and that the old man would stand there until the solution came to him. The nutty part was how the monster decided the trajectory of Brooks's stare could be traced, plotted in space, and, at the end of that line, the key to the worldshatterer's secret could be found. After that the idea just got sillier, because Gojiro thought it was possible to repeat the process with Sheila Brooks, abstract the path of how she looked into Komodo's stereopticon, prolong it, see where it went. Then, suddenly, there were more lines, more desperate stares extending outward from eyes—a million lines, a million million lines, all starting from different places, going in different directions, lines that could never meet, never cross, except somehow, they did; a million million lines extending from a million million eyes, every one of them connecting in the same place, at the same time, nexusing there in the Encrucijada, at that very spot where Brooks looked. And somehow, in that collision, each gaze would glimpse what it hoped to see.

"Geez! I must be stoned."

So he forgot about the nexusing lines, ebbed them from his addled mind. He lay back on his dorsal crease and looked up at the luminous ceiling of his abode. Like some ancient movie palace, all varieties of heavenly bodies could be seen up there: orions, dippers, great bears, and dogs, a Milky Way of stars etched into the black stone heavens. Some gleamed so brightly he took them to be supernovas, flaming out in the most spectacular of finales. Others were so faint he couldn't conjure the necessary zeros needed to calculate their distance from him. It was the Heater's firmament, a nebula of rocks, innocent and dense, made bold and noble by fusion's brush. Gojiro looked at them and saw jewels, glittering and precious, diamonds and pearls.

He proclaimed the gems to be his horde. "Ain't this the postmod's perfect dragon lair—and who could that dragon be if not me, and what's a dragon without a horde?"

It was exactly then, as he lay back to behold his riches, that he felt that sear in his brain. Right off, he knew it came from deep.

A BEAM

The flux took him, sent him. His eyes went blind; only the parietal saw light—light of day, then night. But not the next night, or the next day. It was yesterday's sun that set and reset, with hastening repetition, yesterday's and the one before that. Hands of clocks whipped around backward, faster and faster, the counter-flying friction melting their faces. Pages of calendars uncrumpled inside wastepaper baskets, sailed across rooms, refastened to walls. Every Sunday became a Saturday, each November an October, 1955 turned to 1954, then '53—a hundred years of backflashing montage.

"Whoa!" Gojiro screamed, but the flow kept on. Outside the parietal window, the history's half gainer withdrew its savage splash, swooped upward, landed its merciless feet once more upon the platform of malign design. Every army marched in retreat, cavalries choked on their own dust, ships of conquerers denavigated, returned to port, were dismantled board by board. Romans disappeared, followed by Greeks, and a hundred hairy tribes beat back to caves, their fires fading to black.

No landscape or life form was untouched. Butterflies became caterpillars, frogs lost legs, turned back to tadpoles. Those that spent a million generations inching from the muck so they might walk on land now regressed, slipped back into the swamp, submerged beneath their own bubbles. Ice fanned down from poles, froze solid, melted to vast pools, froze, advanced again. Old mountains, weathered and rolling, gathered themselves up, shot jagged and virile into the skies, then fell off the map altogether.

"On some crazy rewind here," the reptile yelled, his panicked shouts fading in the whooshwake, each syllable left a hundred years behind the next. It was like being inside an endless, retrorunning pneumatic tube. Eras whizzed by, too quick to see; ages were swishpans. It was insane! Wasn't forward motion the Big Wheel of the Universe? What could drive him against that most immutable grain?

It hurt, too. Blasted face-first into the teeth of the tide, the monster felt his snout contort, his leathers smoke. He looked down, was aghast. First he had scales, then not so many scales. His tongue forked and reforked. No configuration lasted very long. Four toes! No, three! Two! "Going Gumby here!"

Then, all of a sudden, he felt himself slow down. Out of the distorting warp came faces. Zards! A million zards, maybe more. A forever flipbook of zards. Lavarock! Was the strange force nothing but another wooly detour into the same old recurring dream? The monster couldn't say; all he knew was that he was the youngest zardplebe once more, basked out amongst the great carpet of his fellows upon the Precious Pumice. But it wasn't just an ordinary day in the seemingly timeless sweep of the Bunch's realm. The buzzy telepathies calling assembly denoted that. The youngest zardplebe looked up, saw the grizzled hisshonkers—Initiates all—begin to gather. Immediately he knew why. It was Ritual of the Molt—gala among galas, the most sacred day on the herpic calendar. For weeks Initiates would ready themselves for the ceremony, speaking in hushed tones of magic words like "renewal" and "reconnection." A particularly elderly fullgrown, the wisest of the wise, described what would take place: "Together we whirl, from the First Moment to the Last, from then to now, and when it's done, we're ourselves again—One." As for what actually happened during the mystic moment—no more than an imperceptible split second—the youngest zardplebe never knew. The Ritual of the Molt was closed to those who had not yet immersed themselves in the Black Spot.

To Komodo, the Ritual of the Molt seemed central to the Reprimordialization process. "Based as it is on the shedding of old skin and the celebration of the new, the ritual affirms the eternal cycle," the thoughtful Japanese observed. "Yet what is the medium by which the group collectively whirls 'from the First Moment to the Last'? Could it not be the Beam?"

Once Gojiro scoffed at this notion. But now, swept up in this coercing pneumatic force, Komodo's words took on a new resonance. *Beam.* The word seared through Gojiro's brain. Could that be the source of this insane backdriving energy . . . *a Beam?*

Not that there was time to consider this incredible possibility. Because right then, water filled his mouth. He was swimming—swimming for his life. But swimming backward—away from Lavarock! Back across the sea. "Wait! Wrong way!" With every fevered stroke his Hallowed Homelands grew smaller on the retreating horizon until they disappeared altogether. Then the sea itself was gone, and he was back inside that roaring retrogressing tunnel.

Until: bump. Like being thrown out of a truck. "Owww."

When he opened his eyes he saw an immense jungle. Even at his zardplebe dimensions, he knew this place was gigantic. Crenelated swirls of elephant-eared leaves fanned out twenty feet or more. Moss-draped cypresses rocketed upward to a canopy so thick no sky could be seen. Branches heaved under the weight of swelling, redbellied fruits. How lush this world was, how imposing. There was nothing in Radioactive Island's hysterical thicket to match this majesty. Ah, the monster marveled, instantly drunk—finally a country pitched at a proper scale! Beam or no Beam, that strange flux had snatched him from the hellish White Light Chamber, checked his bags straight through to EDEN.

That was when the ground began to shake. Something vast and terrible was crashing through the primeval, smashing flat the undergrowth, crushing boulders like candyrocks. It was coming closer. Closer. The lizard took a deep breath, watched the forest fall away above him. Then he saw him: a Rex. A T-Rex! Gojiro's jaw hung slack.

It was a dirty secret, the monster knew, a chauvinistic fleck on his otherwise impeccable Anti-Speciesist politics, but he'd never been able to reconcile saurs within the egalitarianism of the Evolloo. To him, saurs had always been *different*—another class, unclassifiable—a presence too grand to be hemmed by even the infinite boundaries of the Magnificent Matrix. The saurs were rulers. Masters, Doms. True Doms.

It was pathetic, Gojiro would remonstrate, the way sapiens pretended to the exclusivity of the Sauric summit. Them—Doms? What a laugh. It was one thing to Attila over everything, smash it flat, squeeze it dry, and another to *rule.* No saur was ever up in the morning and out to school, taking care of business, working overtime. Saurs were Titans, kings, gods. Maybe books say they once ranged across every continent, but Gojiro had difficulty accepting that the great beasts had ever sullied their claw bottoms with the same wretched terra firma over which sapiens now claimed to lord. Full of bluster, he'd charge that when it came to saurs, paleontology was nothing but a hoax. "Ever wonder why UFOs don't leave hardware?" he'd badger Komodo. "It's because they know some dumb Okie just gonna pick it up along the highway, nail it to his garage wall alongside the plates off his dead Plymouth. It's the same with saurs. Why should a God leave a mandible for some museum clod to fit into his tinkertoy vision of times gone by? Fossils! I sneer at fossils!"

This didn't mean there was no relationship between the sauric and sapien crews. That was clear enough in the way children loved their dinos, took the stuffed effigies to bed. It made sense that younger humanoids, more in touch with the most primal levels of their cameral mentalities, would retain true love for that most transcendent element of their own nature. When they got older, though, watch out. Grown-ups—vicious, insecure—spared no propaganda in their endless effort to demean the so-called Terrible Lizards. Slow-witted, lumber-footed, brains the size of a walnut—was there any misinformation the temporary arbitrators of reality hadn't spread?

Gojiro looked up at the snarling, gleamtoothed T-Rex, felt his pulse race. Could there ever be a creature more magnificent than this? A more perfect predator? So often, morphologically dim reviewers likened the diffident star of the King of Monsters, Friend to Atoms movies to a T-Rex. Fools! Imbeciles! There was no way the regal beast now towering above that great jungle could be crammed within the deprecating confines of a movie screen. The thought came to Gojiro that he should run, hide. But he dismissed it. If that backscanning energy was a Beam and it brought him to this place for no other reason than to be served up as a tiny hors d'oeuvre upon this master's table, the monster had no kick. It would be an honor to be torn asunder by those magisterial claws. The monster looked up in tribute; if he had a hat, he would have taken it off.

But right then, Gojiro saw the twinge, that crimp of confusion across the sheen of the beast's unchallenged ascendency. It was awful to watch, like a cut across the eye, a dirty print in fresh snow. Something was happening to that T-Rex, something the saur could never guess. How could he? Until that instant he'd been invincible, the most ultimate of weapons. By what means was he to respond to that stab of doubt, much less deal with the dambreak of fright that followed it?

Gojiro, of course, knew the sensation only too well. "Oh, no!" But there was nothing to do, nothing to say. The Rex twitched once more, staggered a moment, fell out of the frame.

Then came the holocaust. Hadros, spinos, a thousand birdy dromis, spunky parkies, bonehead pachycephals, saurs of every kind, pantheon members all, stumbled through the near impenetrable haze, gasping as if the air itself was poison, then tottered, thumped down. "They're dying! The gods are dying!" the monster screamed out. The worst of nightmares: paradise crumbling, descending in flames. The ground shook. Towering treetrunks splintered like so many arthritic femurs, bushes curled and shriveled, the jungle's shielding canopy slid away to reveal a sky not unlike Bayonne's own. Crevasses ruptured the land, opening hideous gullies running for miles, mass graves for the thundering herd.

"It's the End! Death's knell!" the monster shouted out. He felt he should plunge into one of those voracious chasms, that if the mighty saurs should succumb, certainly he had no business living. But he couldn't make himself. Something made him go on. Forced him on, toward the steaming hillside looming before him. Up and up he went, over the ruined hulks of allosauruses, across fields of heaving, doomed ultras. Then, at the top of the hill, he could look down to the other side. "Oh, wow!"

Even through the consuming murk he knew these hills, that sky. "The Encrucijada!" But it wasn't the same Valley he'd just left, not the Heater's birthplace, that stark, moribund place where Joseph Prometheus Brooks stood and stared. It was rockier, raw and seething. And, somehow, the monster knew there was no choice for him but to cross that terrible bowl, to pass the falling bodies of former kings, to traverse extinction itself. His course was set, immutable.

"Death behind, her ahead." The message blazoned unconditional in his head, driving him on. *The pheromone!* Here, as he journeyed, no bigger than a zardplebe, across a world's killing fields, the pheromone had returned to him.

"Wrong!" He screamed out the mistake, tried to explain that he'd treaded this exact path before, through this same redrimmed Valley, that it had led only to disaster. To that horrible whirlpool and Kishi's death. "No! This is not for me!" But the pheromone wouldn't listen. It kept pushing, as if the whole force of the Evolloo were behind it.

Then, up ahead, in the center of the Valley, he saw a figure, blurry, too far ahead to make out . . . "No!" he screamed again.

But it didn't matter, because then, as if some unseen, all-powerful hand had reached down and plucked him from his path, the monster was lurched backward once more.

The trip wasn't long. A local hop, less, even. But there was a finality about it. This, he understood, would be the last stop. Like the sidewalk springs up on the absentminded jumper, he saw a wall ahead, knew there would be no dodging. He girded for the splat, but it never came. Instead, a viscousness enveloped him, a warmness, wetness. He found himself in a very small, completely curved room, enclosed in a diaphanous darkness. He expected death, a final crush, but it wasn't that at all. He felt safe. Safe and new.

All he heard was the steadiest of rhythms. Thump. Thump. Thump.

Thump. Thump. Thump. Gojiro thought he could listen to that sound forever. It was like nothing he ever knew, being in that dark, feeling the generous dampness about him, listening to that beat. That . . . heartbeat. The beat of the purest heart!

Thump. Thump. Thump.

Is it possible that the womb is so safe and sure that no child would ever want to leave it, and, to make certain the world continued, the Evolloo felt the need to invent some measure to make that most perfect place somewhat less than perfect? Gojiro would say yes. He would say that once one hears that beat and realizes what it is, whom it belongs to, that perfect place becomes a prison. Because in there, the child cannot see the mother's face.

"Mom!" It was absurd, biologically impossible. How could that thump come from his mother's heart? The maternal zard lays eggs in a burrow, moves on. It's the Law, an affirmation of the all-succoring power of the Line. For a zard, to be secure within the bosom of the Bunch—that's mothering enough. Yet what was that sound?

Thump. Thump. Thump.

"Mom!" The audacity of dreams!

He used his special hooking tooth, the one included with his morphological set-up for this task and this alone. He slashed through the leathery shell, nudged a nose out, triggered his fresh-issued claws to dig up through the sand.

"Mom!" Four to six inches—that's how much ground the schedule said he had to get through before he hit the surface. It's all right there, spelled out in the program: the proportion of how deep a zard's eggs have to be buried so as to afford the freshouts protection against sniffing mammalians while not be so deep as to exceed a newborn's strength to burrow up.

"Mom!" Four to six inches? He'd already gone eight and still it was dark as night. He thought he couldn't make it, that his new-issued body had used up all its energy, that he'd suffocate before he ever saw the light of day. *Before he saw her face!*

"Mom!" She'd dug her eggs too deep! How could she make a mistake like that? *His* mother? "Mom!" His limbs were too heavy, he couldn't make it. He was sinking down. Dirt filled his mouth. Birth and burial—all before dawn!

But then, air. Light. Another swipe. One more.

"Waaaa!" The breath of air and his cry together—his first ever cry, his Freshout Cry—echoed in his ears. Alive!

When he felt the heat he thought it was her, her body warming him. "Mom!" He pried loose his lids. Her face! To see her face! But there was only the falling rock. Black and obscuring. Then, the whitest of lights.

THE THINKER

If only he were coming to tell her about her father's death, then he'd know what to do. Komodo knew Death, was accustomed to its somber nuances, its terrible finality. But someone coming alive? What words were right to herald the rolling away of *that* stone? Should he charge into the oceanside Turret House blurting, "Wonderful news, Ms. Brooks! Your father is alive!" Or should he approach quietly, matter-of-fact, so as to minimize the potential shock? Besides, what assurance was there that Sheila Brooks would deem news of her father's continued existence to be "wonderful"? Komodo felt ill. The idea that his unending bungling might cause Sheila Brooks more pain was a dagger in his heart.

As it was, however, he never made it to that brooding Turret House. There was no time, Shig informed from the driver's seat, his comportment tighter than the whole KGB. They were already late for a "very important meeting." As was clear from the thick document prominently displayed in the limo's magazine rack, Shig had exercised the power vested in him as the sole bargaining agent for King of Monsters, Friend to Atoms Productions and finalized a deal with Hermit Pandora Productions to make *Gojiro vs. Joseph Prometheus Brooks in the Valley of Decision.* Eyes glazing over, Komodo thumbed through the legal sheets. Nearly every item was crossed out, the wholesale deletions reducing the once lengthy contract to a few sparse paragraphs. The heavy editing came as no surprise. In business, as in all else, Shig, ultimate man of few words, pursued only the short and (not) sweet. Should he meet with any resistance, the neoteen wasted little time puncturing the old saw about the pen being mightier than the sword. But what struck Komodo about the contract were the initials "OK—BZ" scribbled next to every obliterated clause and subclause. Bobby Zeber had agreed to every change.

Komodo stared uncomprehendingly. The possibility of actually making a film entitled *Gojiro vs. Joseph Prometheus Brooks in the Valley of Decision* never entered his mind. The most unsettling item, however, appeared on the contract's final page. There, in Shig's clipped hand, was written: "Existing footage, if any, is to be destroyed if said movie is not completed to the absolute satisfaction of ALL concerned within ninety days from the date of contract completion."

Ninety days? Komodo counted quickly. *August sixth!* His birthday—the date the Triple Ring Promise Amendment fell due!

The whole thing seemed incredible. There was no time. Why, they hadn't even begun casting yet. Bobby Zeber would have to know that. But he'd initialed this last clause as well.

Before Komodo could inquire about any of this, however, Shig had the limo spitting gravel up the wideflung oval of Albert Bullins's Bel Air driveway. "You are awaited in the garden," said a Filipino super-Jeeves in a sarong, ushering Komodo up a marble staircase. Circumnavigating the outside of the house with numbed obedience, Komodo was led between a series Macedonian columns, which according to the antique dealer had once resounded with the plinkplunk of Apollo's lyre. From there he walked out onto a splendid terrace overlooking a great lawn dotted with low conical shrubs that could have started moving at any time, like gumdrops in a Czarist ballet.

"Komodo! You son of a Jap. Come on down!" It was Albert Bullins, the mogul's voice staccatoing through the heavy haze of honeysuckle and other aromatic transplants. He was wearing a nineteenth-century British field commander's uniform and had a pearlbutted rifle slung over his shoulder.

"Mr. Bullins," Komodo said, bowing.

"Bully bitchin' you could make it over!"

"Mr. Bullins, it is to my great shame that I have as yet to apologize to you for the destruction of your beautiful automobile. I will do everything in my power to make proper restitution—"

"What? You kidding?" Bullins bellowed. "Haven't had so much fun since I shot Hemingway in the ass by mistake back in Rwanda. You see all those jackasses run for cover? You couldn't duplicate that in million years." Bullins turned and landed a heavy arm over Shig's linen-clad shoulder, eliciting a bloodcurdling sneer from the odd boy. "Duke here and I been discussing an honest little test of eye-hand coordination. So if you'll excuse us, I understand you and Bobby have some business."

Bobby Zeber was seated at a white wrought-iron table wearing a washed-out burgundy sweatsuit and dirty running shoes. "Something to eat, Mr. Komodo?" Zeber offered, gloomily indicating several large wooden bowls on the glass tabletop. "Designer lettuce, all organic. Grown from custom seeds by formerly codependent dirt hippies up in Mendocino, flown in daily."

"No, thank you, Mr. Zeber," Komodo said, patting the pocket of his black pajamas. "I have packed a sandwich."

"Good idea. It's smart to bring your own. It establishes control. Isn't that what everyone wants, control? I shouldn't be eating this stuff either." He chomped on a radicchio leaf. "No one should. It's like what you said at the party."

"Pardon?"

"About Gojiro—'The green that men have created.' I've been thinking about that."

"You have?"

"It makes a lot of sense. You know that expression 'You are what you eat'? Really, it should be the other way around: 'Eat what you are.' And what's that? Snails and puppy-dog tails?" Zeber laughed mordantly. "Nah, I think we're lower, much lower. If there was real justice, we wouldn't be allowed to eat anything except totally chemical foods—not one natural thing, only stuff squeezed from tubes, ejected by fluorocarbon aerosols. That's the proper diet, all we deserve. Men's food."

Zeber stopped, put down his fork with a sigh. "Then maybe you're wondering why I'm eating this, if that's how I feel. Because it costs, Mr. Komodo, that's why. You see, I'm a prisoner of my class." Zeber laughed again, took a drink of his mineral water. "You read over the contract?"

Komodo felt dizzy. "Well, just briefly."

"Funny thing. You know, we—Sheila and me—we've never done business with outsiders. But still, I had that contract made up—just in case. It's a ball-breaker, too. Half of it is just in there for spite. That's the game here: speak glibly, carry a bigger dick. Maybe that's why it was so liberating to cross all those clauses out."

"But, Mr. Zeber, didn't you tell me that such a project was not possible before—"

"Before I said a lot of things. Let's just say, when the right deal comes along, the *exact* right deal, you've got to go for it. Your arrival here has put a whole new outlook on things."

Across the vast lawn Albert Bullins raised his rifle. "Pull," he shouted, blasting several clay pigeons from the sky.

The gunfire only served to underscore Komodo's discomfort. "My arrival? I'm not quite sure what you mean, Mr. Zeber."

Zeber watched Bullins shoot a few targets, then turned to Komodo. "Have you ever felt trapped, Mr. Komodo? Like somehow you're all knotted up and there's no way to get out? It's an awful feeling—you're just there, suffocating, and you don't know how it happened. Or maybe you *do*. Maybe you even saw it coming. Maybe you walked right into it with your eyes open, maybe you even *liked* it for a while. Except one day it dawns on you that the lies you thought were necessary weren't necessary at all. That this thing you've built, it isn't good and it isn't safe, that everything you thought you were protecting . . .

"You don't have a clue about what I'm talking about, do you, Mr. Komodo?"

"I regret to say that I do not."

"But you care about Sheila, don't you?"

Komodo's throat cramped. "Yes."

"You'd like to help her? That's why you answered her letter."

"Yes. I want to help. I must see her, tell her that—"

"Tell her what?"

Komodo never got to answer. Right then, Zeber's head spun around. "Oh, shit."

Victor Stiller, spiffed out in a natty seersucker suit, his gold-rimmed glasses and Rolex glittering in the sunlight, was coming across the rose-bedecked garden. With him was a large man with a blond crew cut wearing a silk suit tailored to stretch across his wide shoulders. Komodo started to get up, to go into his bowing routine, but Stiller cut him off with a curt show of palm. "So happy to see you again, Mr. Komodo. A beautiful day, isn't it?"

Komodo nodded vigorously. "Yes. Not a bit hot."

"Usually I retreat to the mountains at this time of year, but this is quite wonderful." Stiller leaned over, sampled one of the exotic fruits piled in one of the wood bowls. He made a small appreciative sound. "These papayas are perfect."

Bobby Zeber looked at the large blond man standing impassively on the grass, his bulky arms folded in front of him, then turned to Stiller. "They keep issuing you bigger and bigger models, huh, Victor. I should have known you'd turn up here."

Stiller smiled. "I like to keep abreast of my major holdings." He indicated the copy of the contract lying on the table. "Bobby, you can't be serious about this."

"Never more," Zeber said tartly. "As I was telling Mr. Komodo here, I'm a go-for-it kind of guy. Hermit Pandora's a go-for-it kind of company. When you see daylight, you run to it. And this particular project, Victor . . . it's *talking* to me."

"Bobby, I think you've—"

"No, it's hot . . . in this business, you've got to go by feel. And I can *feel* this—like, for instance, you walking in right now. Could anything be more perfectly timed? Your input could be invaluable. After all, you knew him, you were his *only* friend. The only one he ever *trusted.*"

Stiller reached for a rambutan, dropped the hairy fruit into a bowl in front of him. "What do you think this is going to prove?"

"Prove? I'm not trying to prove anything. We're in business to make movies, create product. And this is *the* product. Sheila's masterpiece. Her life's work. Decades in the making."

Stiller frowned. "Let me see the script."

"Not written yet."

"If you were thinking of her, you wouldn't be playing out this impotent charade."

"You're one to say that."

"Someone has to look out for her interests."

"I suppose that's you?"

"Don't you care about her at all?"

"You're really a sick bastard, Victor."

"Please stop!" Komodo didn't realize the words were out of his mouth until he saw both Stiller and Zeber staring at him. He hadn't meant to say anything. Back in the White Light Chamber, Gojiro had told him to forget trying to make sense of why Joe Pro Brooks was alive when he was supposed to be dead. The apparent subterfuge was no doubt the product of "some Tri-Lateralistic trickeration," the monster maintained. There was no percentage in trying to sort out the cross-purposes. Even the shortest walk in that thickest forest was bound to lose an unsuspecting zard or boy in that house of mirrors that is the naturally selected habitat of spooks. No doubt Stiller was in on it, the reptile remarked. But why? To what end? "Who knows, the old fuck's got more twists than a barrel of psychotronic pretzels." Did Zeber know too? Komodo couldn't bear to consider the possibility. Zeber was the keeper of the safe place; how could he withhold such information from someone he loved? But then again, Komodo thought, who was he to make judgments on the responsibilities of love?

No, he hadn't planned to speak. But he couldn't stand to hear Stiller and Zeber argue about Sheila Brooks, bandy her name about in some clandestine tug-of-war.

Stiller looked up, regarded Komodo. Suddenly, he was the genial grandfather again. "Mr. Komodo, I must tell you how much I enjoyed our conversation the other day. If you only knew how invigorating it is for an old man to hear such impassioned talk. I sense you are a man who seeks to temper the metaphysical with the rational and vice versa. Therefore, I am certain that you are well aware of the dialectic between magic and science."

Immediately, Komodo returned to the role of the eager student. "Why, yes, I find it a fascinating topic."

"Of course you do! Then I'm certain you'll understand what I'm trying to say. You see, for me, enlightenment stretches out as a great grid, an endless chessboard, each square a Chinese box, the contents of which are unknown and unexplored. There are two separate entryways to these boxes: one belongs to the magician, the other to the scientist. Most often the magician will arrive first. He is the psychic adventurer, the sorcerer touched by otherworldly insight. He uses his special capacities to shed a private, incorporeal light. This affords him Power—for what he knows can be known only by him. However, for progress to take hold, the magician must be followed by the scientist. It is the scientist who seeks knowledge on behalf of the society at large. He is a social man, a democrat. He makes accessible the magician's gift, creates from it a public boon. It is from his work that civilization is established.

"To me, Joseph Brooks was both a magician and a scientist. He stood alone, astride a specific juncture of history, possessed by the supernatural, yet determined to exercise the democracy of science for the good of all mankind. That is the image I prefer to keep in mind of my great, dead friend."

Zeber hooted, banged the table. "What a performance, Victor! You'll say *anything!*"

Stiller shot Zeber a hard look, turned back to Komodo. "It is for this reason, Mr. Komodo, that I will do everything in my power to keep Joseph Brooks's name from the soil of exploitation."

"But—but—I would never do anything like that." Komodo felt sick.

"Of course you wouldn't," Stiller said reassuringly. He reached over, grabbed the sleeve of Komodo's black pajamas. "You have such a willing, open face, Mr. Komodo. I feel you may be one of the few people who really knows how to listen. It is an indispensable trait, Mr. Komodo. I don't know how you came upon it, but you should treasure it. Listen now, Mr. Komodo. It may be said that technology purchased in a dimestore or received in a movie house also serves to merge the forces of magic and science. But that is faulty thinking. There's nothing there except the mediocre fantasy of the mob, a carnival for the rabble. Mr. Komodo, I appeal to you, do not reduce that moment when Joseph Brooks stood alone, pushing together the twin hemispheres of knowledge, into what Bobby refers to as *product.*"

Zeber drummed his forefinger into the contract for *Gojiro vs. Joseph Prometheus Brooks in the Valley of Decision.* "Signed, sealed, delivered! Komodo, don't let him hustle you."

Stiller's gleaming eyes never left Komodo. "We are kindred spirits, Mr. Komodo, hungry souls, men of science. We revere Mr. Brooks's contributions in life. We must be respectful of his death. Let the man rest in peace."

Komodo thought he was about to hyperventilate. "Mr. Stiller, your argument is quite moving and no doubt bears the ring of Truth. However, there is a problem—"

"Problem? In the pursuit of the sublime there are many problems."

Zeber pounded the table again. "Come on, Victor, it's only a movie. Let the American public see the Great Man in action. Let's bring him back. Let's *resurrect* him!"

"Resurrect . . ." The word stopped Stiller. "Resurrect . . ." Suddenly the debonair former neutron basher seemed to come unstrung. He cocked his head, stared at Komodo.

"I *do* know you . . . I'm remembering now."

Komodo braced himself. From across the lawn came the sound of Albert Bullins's pump gun as he blasted clay targets. Blam, blam, blam. "Nineteen of twenty, Duke. Beat that, beachboy! Your brown ass is grass." It was Shig's turn now. He stepped to the line and drew out a small plastic pistol. "What's that, Duke?" Bullins bellowed. "You can't shoot skeet with a goddamned watergun, Duke!"

Stiller narrowed his eyes, bored deeper into Komodo's skull. "Yes, it was long ago. After the blast in Japan . . . my God . . ."

Shig fired. It seemed that he'd instructed Bullins's gun bearer to send up twenty-five pigeons at once. When they were all in the air, a noiseless yellow streak sprang from the short plastic barrel. The ray pierced the uppermost target, chain-reacting with the rest, igniting a dazzling rainbow of light above the lush lawn.

"My God," Victor Stiller said again.

It was a good thing Shig had that laser pistol turned up past "ultra intense." Anything less wouldn't have induced the blinding flash that allowed Komodo to slip from the patio and out to the limo where the odd boy was waiting to drive him back to the Traj Taj.

What an upsetting afternoon! Still rattled after returning to the melancholy mansion, Komodo sought to collect his thoughts with a brisk stroll through the Insta-Envir. Besides, he wanted to see Ebi. He'd been worried about her all day.

Ebi would be inside her thinker. She was always in that cellulose sanctum around twilight time, codifying her taxons. Thinker time was an essential part of Ebi's day, ever since the colossal tulips first appeared in the Insta-Envir. First, it appeared that the twenty-foot-tall flowers might be useful as birdbaths for the Flying Dutchman-following albatrosses that sometimes swarmed out by Past Due Point. But the plants wouldn't stay upright. The narrow stems bent under the weight of the bulby tops. The flowering cups then attached themselves to the semifirma with an epoxylike seal, thereby creating six-foot round domes that could be entered by peeling back several pseudovinyl petals. Most of the Atoms used the tulip heads for forts—clubhouse kind of stuff. However, they soon grew tired of the photosynthetic cells, trashed them, and went back to hanging out in the rusting Chevy hulks that ringed the shoreline like yesterday's asteroids. It was only Ebi who possessed the calmness of spirit to take advantage of the plant's real utility. She withdrew into the flower's isolation and thought. It pleased Komodo and Gojiro, knowing Ebi was in her sanctuary, apart from the upheaval and pain of Radioactive Island, the pollen gently falling from the inverted stamens, dusting her beautiful black hair like fine gold.

It hadn't been Komodo's intention to eavesdrop. He'd never do that. He just meant to pass by the pink flower (it had to be pink if it was Ebi's). However, the variety of thinker produced by the Traj Taj soil was cramped and thin-petaled; Komodo could hear Ebi's lissome voice through the anemic flower. Ebi often entertained herself with a singsong recitation of her findings, an endearing habit, both Komodo and Gojiro agreed.

This time, though, Komodo detected an unusual tension in the little girl's tone, an impatience he'd never heard before. "Please," Ebi was saying, "you must try again. Concentrate. This is very important. One more time now." Through the translucent thinker sides, Komodo could see her standing up, holding a long vinelike object in her hand.

Then he felt heat. A match was igniting. "I gotta smoke, okay?" said a whiny voice. "I can't think right now, I told you that." Someone else was inside Ebi's thinker!

"Please." Ebi seemed anxious, pleading.

"I don't know. Chicken-wire ivy?"

"Taxonomic title?"

"*Cluckbuckus perdueus* number two?"

"Right! Oh, Ms. Brooks! I knew you would be a fast learner. I knew from the moment we met that you had a feeling for the earth."

Sheila Brooks in Ebi's thinker! Komodo could not believe his ears.

"Now we must move on to fungi."

"Fungi?"

"Yes. Please identify and distinguish between the types I've placed on this table."

"Hey, I don't know, this is like school—you stick wires to the dead frog legs and watch them jump."

"Please."

"Okay. This is the metallic-spore group here. That's the *Mylarius*. This one makes the lightning in the microwave, the *Tinfoilus reynoldus*." Sheila Brooks went on like that, making every single identification.

"Wonderful! You have an affinity, I knew you would!" Ebi sounded so pleased.

"Just lucky. Lucky guesses."

"No. You have an excellent memory."

"You think so? I think I always had a good memory. Like there was this time, with my dad. We were driving along, the way we did, and we must have stopped at a truck stop or something, because usually it was only us. Anyhow, this man asked me what I did all day. I said I kinda watched the road, counted the telephone poles. The guy must have been a real jerk because he said it was dumb for a little girl to spend all day counting telephone poles. My dad got mad. I remember how his face twisted up. He said, 'How many telephone poles between here and Tulsa, Sheila?' I knew. I just had it in my head. 'Three thousand five hundred and sixty-two, buster,' I said. Could be they changed it now, but then it was three thousand five hundred and sixty-two. It shut that guy up, anyhow. And my dad, I think he was a little proud of me, especially the 'buster' part. I guess I always did have a good memory."

"Memory is important. Really important! But you'll need more than that to become a good taxonomist. You have to use the past as a step to the future. That's what taxonomy is all about, establishing foundations, building on them. On Radioactive Island, the tide is plentiful, the recombinate possibilities infinite. A taxonomist can never rest. Ms. Brooks—should a creeper-vine plasticineus merge with a strand of razorcoilus, what might be the result?"

Sheila thought for a moment. "Let's see . . . you have to consider the antecedents. Snapping plasticineus are amalgams of *Bullwhipus gatlinburgus* and California lawn *mulcheratorus* first sighted on Cathode Cay . . . so you could call it *Razorcoilus plasticineus,* gatlinburgus mulcherator type, but that's too long. Consequently, I would say the best designatory tactic would be specify the locality. I'd go with *Razormulchus vineus,* Cathode Cay variety."

"Oh, Ms. Brooks! You have a gift! It is as if you have been taking samples your entire life."

"Wow . . . thinking this way—it's like A's not for apple anymore, B's not for boat. Like a whole new world I've never seen is inside my head . . . and I *like* it."

Ebi shut her notebook gleefully. "I feel so much better now! I was worried about the work—that it would not be carried on in the proper way."

"What do you mean? Why couldn't you do it?"

"Oh, nothing. I'm just so happy."

Then they started dancing around. Sheila Brooks was holding Ebi and swinging her. She was far too tall for the thinker, and her head kept hitting the stamen that hung down like a showerhead. It didn't matter, they kept on dancing.

Komodo stood there, tried to keep his composure. Off in the distance, he could hear some of the other Atoms fighting, issuing harsh threats. Someone was about to get hurt. Komodo knew he should go to them, break up the fight, tend to the wounded. It was his responsibility. But he couldn't move.

"Would you care for some cake, Ms. Brooks?" Ebi asked.

"I don't know. I'm on this diet. My biospheres don't converge harmoniously. I've got to hold little bags of pills under my tongue until they burst. Every pellet does something different. It's all written down, somewhere."

"I made it myself, from my garden. It's pharmfresh."

"Well, I guess that's okay. Sure. Sounds good."

Ebi went to a corner of the small thinker and returned with a thickly iced cake. Stuck into the cake, lighting up the semigloom of the thinker, were eleven burning candles.

"Today your birthday? Why didn't you say so before?"

Ebi giggled. "It's not exactly my birthday."

"A not-exactly-your-birthday party, just for the two of us?"

"Sort of like that," Ebi said, softly. "Like your cake?"

"Great! Totally terrific! Best I ever ate!"

"Ms. Brooks, what's your mom like?"

"My mom?" Sheila Brooks sounded stricken. "My mom is dead."

"Mine too."

"Really? That's sad."

"Yes. She died the day I was born."

A quiver came into Sheila Brooks's voice. "Mine too."

"Do you remember her?"

"That's crazy. How can you remember someone who died the day you were born?"

"I remember my mom," Ebi said, as sweetly as she ever said anything in her life.

"Come on."

"I really do. It was in the water. Water was all around, mad and angry. But I could still see her, looking at me, smiling. She liked me, I could tell. Except then, she flew away . . . just went, into that water." Ebi paused a minute, then went on as cheerfully as ever. "You know, Mr. Komodo once told me that I am the only Atom ever born on Radioactive Island, but it's not true, not exactly. I was born offshore. I could correct Mr. Komodo when he says that, but I don't. It's better that way, I think."

"But that's impossible. You must have dreamed it," Sheila Brooks said, her voice cracking. "How can you remember being born? It can't be done."

"Is it that unusual? It has always been so simple for me. I just sit here and *think* about it. I wouldn't say so if it wasn't true. If I concentrate hard enough, I can do it right now."

"Right here?"

"Sure. I'll do it."

A moment went by with no sound. Outside the thinker, Komodo thought his heart had stopped. Then, piercing, undeniable: "Waaaa!"

"Ebi! Are you all right?"

"Yes," came a small voice. "Okay. I'm sorry if I alarmed you, Ms. Brooks. But it makes me so happy—happy and sad—to recall that moment. I bet you could remember too. I *know* you could—*absolutely*. You have such a good memory."

Sheila Brooks was over by the wall of the thinker, her large, spidery hands pressing against the elastic sides. Komodo could see the bony fingers right above his head. "I think I try to. Sometimes I think it's all I ever do. But I can't do it—it doesn't work. Sometimes I think I'm getting close, and then all this other crap, those stupid movies and the rest, they come in and block everything up . . ."

Komodo could hear Sheila Brooks weeping then. She cried for a minute or so until Ebi said, "I think you'd make a great mom, Ms. Brooks."

"Me? No way. Bobby—my husband, Mr. Zeber. He's wanted children for so long. But that's not for me. I'm a mess. Everyone knows it. I read it in the paper, they say I march to the beat of a different drum machine. I'm lucky they don't have me shut up somewhere, in a bin. It's where I belong, you know. Not out here. I don't fit in. Look at me. I can't even dress right."

"But I *like* the way you dress."

"Get out!"

"I like it and I think you'd be a great mom!"

"I could never be anyone's mom, it wouldn't be fair."

"You could be my mom, if you want."

Sheila Brooks let out a high-pitched laugh. "But Ebi . . . don't you think it's a little late for that?"

"No!"

"You're sweet."

Komodo couldn't see, but he knew Ebi's face must have been big, open. "I'm serious. What do you think about Mr. Komodo?"

"What about Mr. Komodo?"

"You know, if you and Mr. Komodo could . . . then it would almost be like . . . well, maybe you wouldn't *really* be my mom, but I could pretend that you were, for a little while."

Sheila squealed like she was a teenager and this was girl talk. "You think me and Mr. Komodo should . . . that's crazy."

It was about then that Komodo fainted, fell onto the petals of the thinker, and pulled the whole thing down around Sheila and Ebi's heads.

FIELDWORK

"Furballs!"

They pounced unexpected from the underbrush, rapacious warmbloods, their red rat eyes beady streaks in the greasy moonlight. Onward they surged, flaring bucky incisors, breath hot and clutchy, closing ground. He ran from them, skittered over the mossmuck on hopelessly stunted appendages.

No chance. Not a prayer. Furballs can't be outrun. It's Prewire's instinctual decree, you could look it up: "when confronted by the sudden presence of superior-sized woodchucks and worse, freeze! Make yourself a pithy twig, a braided root—never run away." That's because, as any garden skink knows, furballs eyeball peripheral, crosshair on motion. They work in packs, ply canny angles. Plus, they've got the speed. They'll chase you to a corner, rend your leathers gnash by gnash.

So why was he running? Because Prewire's impulse told him to! "Haul ass!" it screamed. Prewire . . . wrong? How could that be? When Prewire fails, the system's junked. Termination, over and out. But what was there to do? Nothing overrides Prewire: it impulses, you obey, there is no next question. So he was running, to what he knew was the deadest of ends.

Then the pain was in him, a million electric ants charging up his spinal column as the malignant chomps serrated through to the bone. Rodents to the left, rodents to the right, there was no escape. It was madness! To die here— eaten by shrews in this unknown place, who knew how many million years from home. But then, from across all time came a familiar voice: "Swing your tail!

Clout 'em out! Only shot you got!" He knew that voice, recognized those words. They were his own. Well, not exactly his. Rather, they came from that moldy King of Monsters, Friend to Atoms. He'd said them during a curiously similar situation in *Gojiro vs. the Gigantor Prairie Dogs down the Burrow of No Return.* It always pissed the monster off, the way little snatches of pathetic dialogue from those movies stuck inside the Quadcameral like resistant disk viruses. But here, backed against that primeval wall by Prewire's bum steer, Gojiro was happy for the cue.

Across a hundred ice ages, the message decoded. A body coiled, a tail lashed: a reflex born. Thud! Thud and thud! Furballs flew through the air, yowling clumps of hair. Vertebrae bent and broke against the bark of new-sprung pines, the swamp echoed with their thrashing death throes. What sweet music those last gasps made!

But it wasn't over. Still they came, endothermic, viviparous, a horde of hyperbolic metabolism. The swinish New Order: there was no turning back the tide, the tyranny. The Empire of the Saurs was diasporized, vanished from the earth. Those coldbloods who remained—suddenly subalterns within the new, harsh hegemony—would have to adapt, become a different race. Without the reign to roam, they required a reconfigured scheme, an updated operating manual. They'd have to accommodate themselves in cracks, get canny in the crannies, never forget they were living in The Man's world.

A bittersweet moment: to feel power slip from your kind, to become a refugee in the place you once ruled, yet to know that through change, Life goes on, that's the way of the Evolloo. For no more than a moment later (or was it a hundred thousand years?) in another forest (on which drifting continent?) that same little lizard was again surrounded by gnawing shrews. Except this time he didn't need input from a melancholy movie star to make good his escape. Now he didn't run, didn't give himself away. He couldn't. "Play dead," the Prewire commanded. "Play dead or be dead." Change had come, instinct imprinting the proper course. Without backtalk or precondition, the zard submitted, made himself colder than any stone, breathed not a single breath. The misdirecting fecal pellet, that was a nice new wrinkle, a little extra something to flummox the vaunted sniffer now standard in mammalian snouts. Soon enough, they gave up and skulked away, off to pilfer the young of their brethren or however furball bastards filled their days at the dawn of primate times.

Gojiro

A Beam? Could that strange compulsion that overtook Gojiro inside the White Light Chamber truly be a Beam? The very word roused the deepest longings. The reptile tried to wrap his battered mentality around the idea. "It's like I go where I been but I ain't been, do what I done but I ain't done, know what I know but I don't know. Like the ghost's inside me and I'm the ghost . . . a schizoid for all seasons."

It couldn't be a Beam, could it? Beams sprang from the Eye of the Matrix itself, in them flowed the soul of the Mainstem, the cohering force of Life—why would anything like that suddenly root inside his rueful head? The monster rolled himself into a tight ball. What was happening to him? All he knew was once that bizarre pneumatic force clamped its pirate frequency across the Quadcameral dial, back he'd go, through Time's netherways, stopping off here and there as if to sample a bit of life and cuisine in every cene—Pleisto, Plio; Eo, too.

It ended in that egg. That confounding egg! "Mom!" Then he'd be digging, upward, through hard black dirt. "Mom!"—a glimpse of her face, that's all he wanted, a picture to remember, treasure. But there was only searing light and a cry. *That cry!* "Waaaa!"

Bleary from his all-era blue jaunt, the reptile split lids, expecting to see Komodo. Every other time he'd woken up wailing, Komodo had been there to soothe and steady, to say it was morning now and the wild things were away. But now there was only Joseph Prometheus Brooks, eight times over, electronic gray and hoary on those Philcos.

Brooks! Riveted to his spot in the middle of the Valley where the Heater came to life, just as the forbidding Ahab once stood beside the mast where he nailed the Whale's bounty. Brooks . . . staring out . . . staring out.

It seemed like the best thing to do at the time: wipe away all emotionality, declare Brooks an object, a neutral item suitable for study, clinical use. It was only fair, Gojiro decided, recalling the humiliation he'd felt as he pored over those field studies that constantly turned up on Radioactive Island beaches, monographs with titles like *Soma-sensory Pathways in the Medial Lemniscus and Related Structures of the South Sea Varanidae.* How hideous it was to think of those safari-suited bio-boys smugly aggregating scats, pulsing strobes, dropping zards into infernal obstacle courses. Criminals. Who appointed them experts on the 'tilic life? By what license did they suppose their reports to be definitive? Nevertheless, Gojiro couldn't keep away from those master theses. Bereft of Bunch and Beam, he felt he had no choice but to grab whatever shred of secondhand self-knowledge came his way, even if it came interred within the provincial sapienspeak of Order, Class, and Phylum. Now, however, he resolved to apply the same torpid criteria to Brooks. Joseph Prometheus Brooks: specimen. There was justice to it.

As might be expected, the reptile's initial inclination was toward the ultra-invasive, the noggin nip, neural removal. And why not? Wasn't Brooks's brain legend, totemic? "The most powerful mind in the history of mankind has stopped thinking!"—isn't that how they hyperbolized in that newsreel of Brooks's phony funeral? But really, the saga of Brooks's brain was only beginning, what with all the legal hassles regarding which scholarly institute might be granted access to the scientist's supposedly defunct mentality, not to mention those tabloid stories about Israeli graverobbers selling cuttings of the vaunted cogitator on the black market. Brooks's brain could stand a little demystification, the monster decided. An image invited: the mythic mind sitting like a Jell-O mold in the middle of an open, upraised claw and then squeezed tight until it oozed from between every leathery digit, electrostat tests to be made on the runoff.

How the great reptile would have loved to set Brooks down in a T-maze, raising and lowering his thermoregs at irregular intervals, then harshly grading the scientist's performance in various motor skills. However, owing to the promise he'd made to Komodo barring such hands-on intervention, Gojiro was forced to reject that methodology. He would have to restrict his analysis to mere observation.

Off the surface, there wasn't much to see. It was amazing how little Brooks did and how standardized those few actions appeared to be. Every morning, two hours before sunrise, the old man would appear in the doorway of that windswept stone house and walk stiff-gaited, as if on wooden legs, to the same place—exactly six feet to the right of the arched gate—where he assumed his singular posture. Then he'd just stare, motionless, his eyes fixed on a single spot, his cranelike neck upright, unwavering. At the start of his investigation, Gojiro could barely stay awake. "Talk about being out in the sun too long, this dude is pickled," he yawned. But then, as the hours wore on, watching the stationary scientist turned hypnotic, a visual mantra. How he kept *looking!* There was a withering fortitude about it, an indomitable willfulness. The reptile's conviction of Brooks's madness began to slip; with gathering uneasiness he allowed the possibility that there *was* something out there—something the worldshatterer wanted to see. The monster labeled the old man's behavior "the searching position."

Substructured within this enigmatic trait was the equally puzzling "cradling" mannerism. Gojiro made these notes: "As if performing a sensory exercise in a beginning acting class, the Subject displays open, inclined palms, thereby giving the appearance of cradling an absent, rounded article of indeterminate size. Subject alternately holds this object close to his abdomen and then, with a small careful motion, appears to face it outward, in the general orientation of the previously described searching position. Inquiry into the striking analogy between this self-presentation and the portrait executed by Subject's deceased wife, Leona Ross Brooks, approximately forty years earlier invites numerous textual interrogatories. Recommend close reading of this apparent coincidence at some later date."

Gojiro filled several looseleafs in this manner. However, with each scrupulously recorded twitch of Brooks's prominent Adam's apple, each cross-referenced foot shuffle and hat rearrangement, the monster grew more impatient with the limitations that the same midshot from those fuzzy Philcos imposed upon his investigation.

"Got to get in tight."

It wasn't exactly going against his word, Gojiro rationalized, frantically rummaging through Komodo's black bags. He'd sworn he wouldn't leave the White Light Chamber to mash Brooks up. That was the last thing he wanted to do now. This was research, this was for science! Komodo could have no quarrel with that. Still, it was no party pushing that syringe, its needle fatter than Minnesota's bluetipped cue, through the parietal, coursing that shrink fluid into his system. Dosage was a crap shoot—a drop too much and Alice's dormouse wouldn't know him from a swimmy paramecium. Through luck and little else, however, he managed to stabilize himself at approximately fourteen inches, a tolerable dimension.

After a monumental struggle with the passageway door, the miniaturized monster made his way out into the Encrucijada. From the beginning it felt like a mistake. Mutant or no mutant, noontime walkabouts in the desert heat were contraindicated. If his blood boiled over, bubbled from his panting mouth, he would have no refuge, no remedy, no excuse. But when he felt the Valley floor beneath his clawfeet, its sand turned to glass by the Heater's fury, he knew there could be no turning back.

"Brooks!" Fifty feet from the unmoving old man, the shout came out before it could be properly suppressed. It wasn't his intention to make contact with Brooks. This fieldwork was supposed to be noninterventionist, impersonal. But who was he kidding? How could anything between him and Brooks be impersonal? The two of them went back too far.

"Brooks! Remember me?

"Brooks! Out of the multitudes, why me?"

It was useless, pointless. Maybe, amid the chiaroscuro of a rubberized volcano, deep in the fevered fantasies of a half-mad lizard, a man in black with heart-stopping stare could be made to answer for his crimes. But out here, beneath the blaring sun, every accusation desiccated to dust, blew away on the swirling Valley winds. What did Komodo say—that the old man looked *through* him? Now the reptile knew what his friend meant. Brooks's demeanor did not invite smalltalk; it looked like you could snap a popper neath his jutting nose and he'd never raise an eyebrow.

But it was more than that, Gojiro realized as he drew closer. There was a trajectory problem. Given the near-imperceptible tilt of his dark eyes within their deep sockets, there was no way Brooks could see him, or any other object so close to the ground. "Subject's field of vision assumes an elevated aspect," the reptile noted. "Will attempt calibration."

Cursing the lack of instrumentation, Gojiro nevertheless protracted the incline of Brooks's sightline to be between thirty and forty-five degrees. The scientist appeared to be focusing on a distinct sector of sky that the monster estimated to be between two hundred and eight hundred feet above the Valley floor. "Weird," he said to himself, peering into the empty blue. "It's like Brooks is waiting for something to show up in that spot." Not that the reptile was able to continue this train of thought, for right then he felt that hot breath on his neck.

"Yike!" It was that basset hound! He'd seen the bejowled canine during his earlier surveillance but had paid it little mind, understanding household pets to be a typical sentimentality-cloaked sapien expression of dominion. Even obvious tangentials like Brooks might have a dog; he probably needed the mutt, there didn't seem to be anybody else around. Now, however, the monster found himself looking up into the dark hollow of the pooch's yellowtoothed business end. It turned into a pathetic little chase, the stupid dog gaining all the while. Finally, the shrunken leviathan flung himself under the raised house, just beyond the reach of that wet black snout. "Fuck you, Fido! Rat basset!" Cornered by a flabfaced hound who for sure never caught a rabbit, what kind of format was that for the King of Monsters, Friend to Atoms to find himself in? What a day! First furballs from prehistoria—now this! The reptile was disgusted. It seemed like hours before that idiot dog got bored with his scent and he was free to move around again.

He figured he might as well reconnoiter the immediate environs so as to better fix Brooks in his habitat. Ardent scholar of Heater-related memorabilia and minutia that he was, Gojiro had long ago identified the ramshackle complex as the McDonald Ranchette, a foreclosed homesteader spread taken over by the Feds after the decision to use the Encrucijada as the test site. It was here, in the tumbledown stone house that now served as the scientist's abode and the several outbuildings, that the Bomb was conceived and assembled. The place was indelibly documented in those same eight or ten photos that appeared, over and over again, in every tome ever put out about the Project. The shot of laundry hanging outside the quonset huts; the one of Victor Stiller smiling behind a fake mustache as he sang in what was always described as a "New Year's Eve bash talent show in the makeshift dance hall"; another of Colonel Grives's bulk silhouetted against the desert twilight as he examined the tower where the Heater was to be installed; and, of course, the famous picture of Brooks himself carrying the box containing fissionable materials on a Coca-Cola tray, placing it on the backseat of a '42 Dodge parked at the front gate— these were the official, defining images, the visual record of the Heater's gestation and birth. No others were ever released. It was all top secret. During the war no one was even supposed to know such a place existed. Then, some years later, came the report that the ranchette buildings had been burned up in a lightning storm, the remains eventually bulldozed flat. Yet here it was, at least some of it, along with its solitary resident. Some way to treat a shrine of the Modern Age, Gojiro snorted, padding about the dilapidated property. What a waste of potential tourism. Where was the line of school buses, the concessionaires hawking "I lived through the Trinity" T-shirts?

One structure in particular drew the monster's attention. No more than a shed, freestanding behind the collapsed wood barn, the reptile first dismissed the structure as an abandoned outhouse. But why would an old crapper need that kind of security? The splintered door was slapped with at least a dozen heavily oxidized padlocks. Hundreds of nails were driven, scattershot, through haphazardly affixed shutters.

Looks like somebody wanted this place closed up pretty bad, the lizard thought, making his way along the bowed walls of the hut until he found a hole big enough to squeeze through. "Pee-yew!" Filled with swelling cans of army C rations, useless plumbing fixtures, yellowed ledgers and maps, a pile of Jeep distributors, the shed reeked of formic acid and must. Gojiro was about to leave when he noticed a small desk tucked behind sections of a smashed wind gauge. On top of the desk, leaning against the wall behind, was a blackboard.

The shock surged through him, a dorsal undulate from tailpoint to cranial dome. The chalk scrawls on that dusty blackboard, those numbers and letters, vectors and inversions—the monster knew them. By heart. They were blazoned into his brain sure as the Triple Rings were etched onto his chest. That blackboard . . . it was *the* blackboard.

Maybe to some it might have looked like a child's toy. But as far as Gojiro was concerned, that slate, and the figures written on it, represented the end product of all hominid aspiration. "Their entire history leads there, from Olduvai on!" the monster exclaimed whenever the topic of that blackboard came up. "You see them faraway looks in the faces of the Pekings and the Cro-Mags? You think they're puzzling the hunt, the gather? No way. Even then, inside those dimmest mentalities, they was figuring how to bombard the nucleus, accelerate the particle. From the start, all their seemingly unrelated eurekas was aimed at a single goal: what's written on Joe Pro Brooks's blackboard."

Szilard blinking in front of that London stoplight, Rutherford and Cavendish, Fermi's exponentials, Urey's heavy hydrogen, Bohr, Born, Meitner, Heisenberg and the rest, everything Einstein knew—to Gojiro all of it was nothing but the feverish last lap, concluding linkages in a harrowing chain. But it took Brooks to write it down, to bind the final fusion. The Heater's recipe!—that's what was on that blackboard. Gojiro felt weak. How hideous it was to stand before that old slate, that tablet of the New Dark Age.

That night . . .

The reptile often thought of those events as another private nightmare. After all, how could any version of that night—of those final months for that matter—claim to be definitive? The saga of the Heater's birth—so filled with awe and terror as to be intolerable in the naked realm of fact—had been reimagined so often, from so many points of view, as to scuttle any attempt at universal certainty. The story had escaped to the public domain, that sub-jectivized zone where each and every one was free to enter a personal rela-tionship with the billowing Cloud. That's how it is at the moment of holocaust, when meaning is exploded and all expectation shattered: facts become story and stories fact, mix and match, say anything, history's play-doh in our hands.

So, write in on boxtops if you know better, about that night.

Tell if the Reich, its every chinstrap in place, every boot shined, wasn't marching across the land. Tell if Civilization's supposed last, best chance didn't rest in the hands of a cabal of vague longhairs, feyish Jews and worse, watched by uniformed keepers who had no choice but to trust them. Except it wasn't going good. The gadget stood inert, stalled in Fate's midstream.

Say if it wasn't then, with the sun disappearing behind those red cliffs, that Brooks put down his clarinet and told them all to get out—that he, and he alone, would forge the Thing. That he would do it that night, be finished before dawn. Impossible, the chorus rose, no one could encompass the Big Idea all by himself, certainly not in a single night.

Go ahead, swear that Brooks didn't face them and then say he would do it by himself because that's what he was *born* to do.

Say if it's not so: that Joseph and Leona Brooks didn't walk off together at nightfall, go deep into the Encrucijada, not to return until well past midnight. Tell if Brooks didn't then walk into that very shed where Gojiro now stood, and, before the sun rose again, set down on that blackboard the sum total of all his kind had ever known. And tell if, exactly nine months later, the Loom was not upon the land.

Joseph Prometheus Brooks's blackboard . . . the monster took a deep breath. Once, in a perverse moment, he'd urged Komodo to stick a "fabulous production number" into one of those cheesy movies. "Line up ten rows of Atoms, ten abreast, all in black, give each one a pointer, stand them in front of a chalkboard scribbled with the fateful formula. Then I'll come out, in tie and tails, announce the show—'Ladies and gentlemen: 100 Brookses! 100 black-boards! Come on, worldshatterers! Go into your dance!' "

Now, however, face-to-face with Brooks's real blackboard, the monster could only cower. Indeed, it was only his application to his fieldworking tasks that kept him from cutting and running, scuttling back to the White Light Chamber, lighting up a heebiejeebie-quieting hunk of the hardcuttin' 235.

He was trying to calm down when he saw those paintings. They were stacked face-down, twenty canvases, maybe more, on an old workbench. Snout-flipping the top one over, the lizard did a double take. It was all there: the X-ray style, that peculiar depthlessness, as if the paintings weren't on canvas at all, but rather petrogylphs on a cave wall. The technique was so similar, there could not be any doubt—whoever painted these pictures was also responsible for the portrait Joseph Prometheus Brooks was aping even then, right outside that very shed.

But that wasn't what got to the monster, not first at least. It was the mastodon. That mastodon on a savannah, and the first time you look you think everything's fine, the wooly thing is just grazing—but then you see the gash on the side of his leg, the rip in the belly. And the sabertooth, off to the side, waiting.

"I seen that mastodon before . . ."

Fainting, the lizard fell off the table, knocking the paintings onto the packed dirt floor as he went. They piled down on top of him, a rain of oversized playing cards. That's when he saw the T-Rex. The same T-Rex, towering above the jungle canopy, and on its majestic face—that first hint of fear. There could be no mistake. It was the same T-Rex he'd seen inside that Beam!

"Wait a minute!" Feverish, the reptile clawed through the paintings. There they were, the giant shrews, the needlenosed fish with the quizzical looks . . . and that giant stone, hurtling down from the sky! What was going on? There wasn't a single one of those pictures the monster hadn't seen before, hadn't lived through in that retrorunning influx. Each one was signed Leona Ross Brooks, dated 1934. The same year she painted that portrait of Brooks . . . three years before she was to have first laid eyes on the man.

It was insane. How could Sheila Brooks's mother paint *a Beam?* None of it made sense, but right then the monster didn't care. If Leona Brooks saw everything else, then maybe she saw . . .

"Mom!" Desperately, he cast aside one familiar scene after another. Depictions of mountains rising and falling flew left and right. "Mom!"

But he never got to her. He never got past that Echo Man, that Indian, the one he'd seen on television. Nelson Monongae, who said his Clan—*the Lizard Clan*—owned the Encrucijada and everything in it. They were talking about him again the other night, on one of those funky Philcos Komodo had switched over to outside reception. The Echo Man was missing, they said, he'd disappeared right in the middle of the trial proceedings, hadn't been seen for days. A search was on, in every flophouse from Gallup to Grants, up to Shiprock and down to Socorro. The Indian's fancy lawyers denied their client was "off drunk," instead claiming he was engaged in a secret religious ritual sacred to the Monongae Clan. They asked for a continuance on that basis. The State protested, said their anthropologists knew of no such ceremony. The judge looked tough. "Find the man," he decreed.

Now, there he was, that same Echo Man, in an X-ray painting by Leona Ross Brooks. But he wasn't that wizened toothless man from the TV screen. This was a young Echo Man, a teenager, strong and straight, dressed in an elaborate costume. And around his neck, that vial. The same vial he wore around his neck the other night, on television. There was something about that black vial!

"Come in!"

The monster looked around. "Who said that?"

"Please come in!"

"Oh!" Suddenly Gojiro was traveling again, whooshing away. Except it didn't feel like that Beam. No, it was more like . . . "Oh shit!" . . . that 90 Series!

He went like he'd gone to Tyrone of Philly, to Abdul of Beirut, to Billy Snickman. He went the way he always went, before he forced Komodo into the Quadcameral, demanded that his great friend short-circuit whatever wiring brought those clutching supplications into his harried head.

And, just as he'd inhabited the souls of all the others, Gojiro became Nelson Monongae—a young Nelson Monongae, no more than twelve, at the edge of puberty, sitting inside his father's hogan, with stretched skins all around, cracked and tearing. Outside he could see the drawn faces. People hungry, dying. In here, surrounded by somber elders, his father was chanting, trying to rouse the spirit. Praying to a Beast—a magnificent Beast who once upon a time set a world in motion, but had long since withdrawn, his memory fading from the minds of men, save a few. It was the job of these men to petition the Beast, to beg its return so the world might begin again.

"Come in," they summoned, Nelson's father leading the prayer. "Come in!" They called the Beast to rise from the earth, which is where He lived, deep in slumber.

Then they were dressing him, decking him with leathers. Off came his loincloths, the bands around his waist and arms. On went the scaly headdress, a great ridge of dorsal fringe down to the ground. When they were done, he looked into his father's face, so sick and worn—the greatest shaman of the Clan, dying before forty. "You will be the Echo Man, you will awake the Beast," his father said. Then he reached up behind his head, pulled, broke a cord. The vial! The father took it from his own neck, tied it around his son's. "Blood from underground. *His* blood," the dying man said. "Take it, bring Him back to us." That's when, reflected in a piece of polished silver, Gojiro caught sight of himself, how it looked to be young Nelson Monongae at that moment. He saw those snaking dorsals, reddish comb on top, the glittering eyes: the image of a great zard so much like himself, yet with a critical, indefinable difference. Instinctively, the reptile knew: here, in this place, in the body of that boyish Echo Man, he was looking at a true vision of the Varanidid.

In the hogan the grave men were chanting again. "Come in! Please come in!" Except that youngest Echo Man wasn't there. He was outside, in the night air, scanning the dark shadows of the surrounding hills. Gojiro scoped the Encrucijada geography immediately. That campfire was burning in the same spot where Joseph Prometheus Brooks would come to stand all those years in the future.

Then there was a noise. Someone was coming out of the dark, climbing down from the hills—a young girl. A young white girl in an odd billowing dress. She was coming down from the red-rimmed hills, walking right toward him. Closer. Gojiro blinked inside that Varanidid costume the Echo Man wore. Those eyes! He'd heard Komodo talk of those eyes. Verdant, like an isle of pines, he'd said, describing Sheila Brooks's eyes. But it wasn't Sheila Brooks coming toward him.

What had Zeber said about Sheila's mother—that she chose the Encrucijada as the site for the Heater's debut because she'd been there before? Been there before she ever met Joseph Brooks? The monster was trying to figure it when he felt that Echo Man begin to move toward Leona.

And the way he went: it was as if he saw her and a million more like her. A billion more, as many as could be seen in as many opposing mirrors, an unbroken chain of her, a snaking double file of her, queued to infinity. *The pheromone!* That's what drove that Echo Man toward Leona Brooks right then.

2 4 4

The pheromone . . . *pulling* that boy in Varanidid leathers onward, ever closer. To her.

Instantly, the monster knew. "No!" he shouted. "It's wrong! You're not the one!" But he never knew if his host heard his warning, heeded it. For right then, whatever force had reconnected that 90 Series to the Quadcameral gave way.

MALL DARTERS

She said she was sorry about the speed. She had to go fast, keep the scenery blurry, imprecise. It was part of her therapy. A single sharp image was enough to trigger the Dystopic Reflex. Then Wilmington oil refineries would be transformed into pestilence-crammed flotillas of black freighters sailing into frightened harbors. Empty meadows would clog with shabby condos, power lines falling on the flat tar roofs, sparking electromagnetic plagues. Speed was the only remedy—velocity and those blinder goggles.

"My dad used to let me drive," she said, pushing the little red Corvette up past eighty. "He'd sit me up on his lap, put my hands on the wheel, let me steer. Except sometimes he'd fall asleep. I'd be driving the car for real. It was crazy, only three years old and driving. That was before interstates, too. It was just those skinny blacktops, big trucks coming the other way. But then Dad would wake up and smile. He said it didn't matter, because I was a good driver.

"We slept in the car. We'd park in a grove of trees, or under a railroad trestle. He let me sleep with my head in his lap. Then he'd wake me up, say we had to go. They were after us again. They were always after us. We never could rest. He said we were wanted in forty-eight states—every other country, too. What did we do, I asked him, rob a bank? He laughed, told me not to worry, because we weren't guilty. Not like *they* thought. It was hard to understand, he said, but someday I would know. Then he'd stop the car and play his clarinet. My mom really liked that, he said."

Komodo gripped the door handle, tried to keep smiling. Maybe in the Encrucijada, Joseph Prometheus Brooks remained a brooding, unrevealed symbol, but inside that speeding little red Corvette, the famous worldshatterer was a gently grinning man who took his daughter to Daffy Duck cartoons, pushed her on swings at the state fair, won a panda bear.

"Ms. Brooks . . ." Why couldn't he speak? What was this autism that overcame him, precluding straightforward elocution? "Ms. Brooks, there is something I must tell you . . ."

But she kept on, explaining how this wonderful man always stopped at Perkins' Pancake houses because it was her favorite place, especially the peach rollups, how he let her have seconds, even if he never ate a thing.

The shame of it! Why couldn't he simply say her father was not dead but standing in the middle of that same Valley that haunted her dreams? What a coward! "Ms. Brooks . . . ," he'd begin, only to stop once more, slump back into his bucket seat, sit watching her. How smoothly she piloted the sports car, deftly darting in and out of the freeway traffic, her spindly arm hard on the downshift. Brooks was right: she *was* a good driver.

Tell her now, he screamed to himself. But he couldn't bear to break the mood. Had her hand lightly brushed his? He stole a glance. Were those thinnest of lips formed into the faintest smile?

Back at the Traj Taj, after Ebi's thinker fell in, he tried to tell her. They were in the kitchen, waiting for the tea to steep. Recalling the scene was torture. Why did he have to pull that packet out of the pocket of his black pajamas, pour the contents into the steaming water? Couldn't he have guessed how silly it would seem, those massive heart-shaped balloons flying out of the tea cups like some Lawrence Welk extravaganza? "Magic flavor crystals," he called them, with an asinine giggle. But he couldn't stop himself. The sunlight was streaming through the calico curtains of the breakfast nook, spreading across the wood plank table, and Ebi was sitting there between them. The glorious normality seduced him, sent him into a revel of domesticity. A kiss on the cheek, out to work and play, presents under the tinseled tree. Husband. Father. The words themselves made Komodo weak. *The shame of it!* Sheila Brooks—another man's wife, a married woman!

What was Ebi's role in this, Komodo wondered. Who else could have concocted a walk through the Insta-Envir guaranteed to lead them past that brand-new growth of giant roses, which just happened to burst into full bloom as they approached? What scenario was Ebi attempting to arrange in her supposedly guileless head?

Komodo looked at the kudzu-banked freeway and replayed the day, his confusion mounting, turning to dread. How could Ebi know? How could she have remembered what happened that awful day by the Cloudcover? He'd been so careful to keep the horrendous events from her. Yet there was no doubt— Ebi knew! The reference to being surrounded by "water everywhere"—that might have been a guess, a poetic invocation of the womb. But what of her insistence about being born offshore and the description of going around and around? The details were there.

Fool! Komodo berated himself. How his previous sins returned to mock his current ones. Why hadn't he told Ebi? Would it have been so difficult to drop the guise of the overbearingly cheerful benefactor, to tell the Truth, allow her the joy of calling him Father instead of that tortured Mister? A decade of useless, heartless deception, only to find out that she knew it all along. Recalled every last bit! She remembered her mother's face . . . *Kishi's face.*

"You okay?" Sheila Brooks asked, throttling to eighty-five.

"Some dust has flown in my eye."

Could Ebi actually remember her Freshout Cry? It seemed impossible, but she wouldn't say a thing like that unless she believed it to be true—unless it *was* true. Ebi was a scientist, a follower of the most precise of disciplines. She cared little for illusion, less for fantasy. Yet to remember one's own Freshout Cry, to be able to summon it at will, to know exactly who you were, from the beginning to now—Komodo staggered beneath the immensity of the idea. "Waaaa!" How long had he searched for the merest hint of that same scream?

The Freshout Cry! The yelp from a blueskinned child, held upside down, slapped on the backside, the shriek of birth across the savannahs—the bugle blast of all beginnings, the clarion of Life itself. The most sacred of sounds. That's how Budd Hazard described the Cry all those long, long, and lonely nights ago. Except that the Muse spread his net wide. According to Budd Hazard, the Freshout Cry was the Evolloo's clapboarding cue, the common squawk that announced the fuse of Beam and Bunch, the confluencing clamor of which every baby's first shout was nothing more—or less—than a celebratory echo.

To Komodo, the Freshout Cry was the soundtrack of Reprimordialization. He bugged the Fayetteville Tree branches with multidirectional mikes, pressed his stethoscopes against the curved glass enclosure. "If only we can record this Cry and gain the means to reproduce it," he told Gojiro, "it might prove a tonal beacon, an aural clue toward the fulfillment of the solemn Vow." He didn't know what to expect. Who knew the tenor of things inside that crease in Time and

Space—that Instant where Beam and Bunch came together and only Throwforwards dared to tread? Komodo was forever refiguring his gains and gauges, running them through oscilloscopic speakers so no woof or tweet would remain unexamined. Anything to catch Blip One. But, just as his cameras failed to grasp even the merest phantom of Change, Komodo's tapes stayed blank. "Just one more tree fell in the forest we know not where, huh?" Gojiro commented one morning after still another newly minted Bunch of chickadees sat preening in the Fayetteville Tree. To which Komodo could only nod sadly.

Yet, inside that thinker, Ebi screamed "Waaaa!" Furthermore, she said she could do it "anytime"—that Sheila Brooks could do it too! *Absolutely* she could, Ebi said.

Komodo looked over at the Hermit Pandora. She was still talking about her father. Except now her mood was anguished, wrought up. Her words came in gulps, halting spasms. "Then they were after us, closing in. It seemed like every time we turned around there'd be that car, the gray one, following us. That's when Dad started to get strange. Days went by, he wouldn't talk, not a word. I thought he didn't like me anymore. Then he said we had to go to Wisconsin. He had to see what was left, if *anything* was left—that's what he kept saying, over and over—he had to find out if there was any *trace*. It was fall, nearly winter. I was so cold. He wrapped me in blankets, told me to be brave. We drove up icy roads, farther into the country. It was where he was born, he said, where he grew up—before they found out he was a genius and sent him to Europe.

"Finally we got to this overgrown field. He stopped the car and got out. It was real early in the morning. Dad just stood there, not saying a word, looking at the field for hours. 'What are you looking for?' I asked him. He turned to me with the saddest look on his face. 'Nothing to offend His eyes,' he said. 'Nothing for Him to see. As if we've never been here at all.' He told me that's what his father always said. Then he started tearing at the weeds. Ripping them up. It was awful, I thought he was going crazy. Then he picked up this charred board, held it in his hands, and started to cry."

She turned toward Komodo, her mouth twisting beneath her grotesque glasses. "He killed them . . . my father's father. He killed his family. He did it because he thought God was disgusted with the world—that we didn't belong in His sight! He burned the whole place to the ground so it would seem like they'd never been here, not even a trace. That's crazy, isn't it? That's wrong, isn't it?"

"Ms. Brooks . . ." She was going faster now, almost a hundred. She wasn't watching the road, not at all.

"Tell me!"

"What?"

"That it's wrong."

"Yes, Ms. Brooks."

"Yes what?"

"It's wrong!"

"How do we know?"

"Ms. Brooks! Your father is . . . here! Look!" Komodo reached into his pocket, pulled out the page he'd torn from that *Visions in Fission* book. "Your mother painted this. It is exactly how your father stands, even now. Look!"

Sheila Brooks grabbed the reproduction of her mother's X-ray painting. Instantly her hands came off the steering wheel, flew up to her face. "No!"

"But it is so! It is him."

"No! It's wrong!"

"What?"

"My mother saw it . . . wrong!"

There was nothing else to do once the little red Corvette began veering into that pickup with the NRA stickers. Komodo had to reach across her body, grab the wheel, flare the car up that off-ramp, out to that wide and mirthless boulevard. A few missed turns later, they were forced to squeeze left, into the underground parking facility of a huge shopping complex. That's where they got surrounded by all those demonstrators.

"Save the Mall Darter! Transcendental lies must be thwarted!" the crowd chanted as they snake-slalomed between parking meters in the monoxide-thick garage. One seriously overweight teenager draped with shawls that looked to be back numbers from Madame Blavatsky's tag sale, crammed a leaflet through the Corvette's open window. Skimming the literature, Komodo was quick to recognize the issues in the Mall Darter controversy. Apparently, the managers of the Oversoul Mall, a wholly owned subsidiary of the Transcendental Corporation of the Southland, in attempting to create "an ecospherically correct shopping environment" had stocked the complex's interior waterway with several varieties of fish, primarily strains of the Mid-American snapnosed scooter and the bluetipped rock tummeler. These two animals crossbred, which caused quite a stir, especially after a team of naturalists validated Oversoul as the lone habitat of the new species, popularly referred to as the Mall Darter, owing to its propensity to lurch in either direction in response to the stimulus of fast-pitched pennies. Initially, this development was hailed by the mall owners. But the prodigious breeding capacity of the Mall Darter soon proved a problem. Cramped in their poured-latex tub, thriving in the chlorinated water, the fast-growing fish developed a cannibalistic trait. The steady accumulation of mauled and bloody darter carcasses kept customers away, resulting in the pullout of several key tenants. When another mall, the Gary Owens Presents, opened just one exit over, the parent company, seeking debt restraint, opted to restructure the property as a dual-use industrial park/pitch and putt.

As shouts of "Maintain the Habitat!" filled the parking lot, Komodo felt his mind wander. He thought of the darkened shopping center, its filtered air acrid with ammoniated floor cleaner, nothing moving save the rise and fall of the gently snoring night watchman's chest . . . and then, in that undersized pool, a single snapnosed scooter, following an incomprehensible yet imploring compass, moved forward toward a lone rock tummeler. And then—resounding through the silent sneaker stores and shuttered game parlors: "Waaaa!"

Komodo's reverie was soon shattered, however. Sheila Brooks was pushing a ten-thousand-dollar check, hastily made out to the Mall Darter Must Live Fund, into the hand of a young punker with chain saws tattooed onto his shaved head. "That okay? Can we go now?" she shouted hoarsely.

"Sure thing!" The stunned boy's eyes bugged. He was beginning to clear a path for the Corvette but then stopped. "Hey, wait a minute. Shit! We got Sheila Brooks here!"

Almost immediately the plight of the Mall Darter was forgotten. Placards were abandoned as a swarm of protesters lurched forward, a crush of black leotards and gypsum cheeks. Everyone in that indoor parking lot had a terrible Apock Vision they wished to convey to the Hermit Pandora herself.

The chain-saw-headed boy tore up Sheila's check. "Doesn't matter!" he screamed, his features twisted against the Corvette's windshield. "What good's money with no banks? No banks, no stores, no nothing! Year Zero! That's what I see: Year Zero! Fire and flames! Fire and flames shooting out of eyes like blow-torches! Sheila Brooks, listen! I see the End—every night!"

Her lipstick-smudged mouth was contorted into a frightful oblong. "Go away! What you think—it's wrong! We're *better* than that!" Still the crowd forged ahead, a sea of harrowed faces.

"Oblivion!" they shouted. "Oblivion!"

However, when Komodo turned back to Sheila Brooks again, she no longer seemed affected by her fans' hysteria. She was looking into a stereopticon. It must have been in her purse, fallen out in the tumult. Komodo studied it. What she'd said back at the Traj Taj seemed accurate: her stereopticon was remarkably similar to the picture holder Gojiro snatched from the flotjet tide all those years ago. Except, of course, for the image within. It wasn't of a mom and dad on a lush hillside, beside the bluest lake, before the towering mountain with the diamond sparkle of snow upon its crowning top. No. This picture showed Joseph Prometheus Brooks and Leona Ross Brooks standing together. They were in the middle of a Valley. A Valley surrounded by red craggy hills, beneath a wide-open sky. And they're smiling, happy. Brooks's hand is on her belly. She's pregnant!

Komodo's head spun. Sheila Brooks . . . inside.

The crowd surged on, desperate to unburden their Doom upon the Dreamer of the Sad Tomorrow. But in the car there was only silence. Silence and heat. Komodo felt it, that terrible, familiar fire—until she started to scream.

Then: Varrooom. She gunned the motor, squealed the tires. The Sheila Brooks Club members flew away. In the distance, Komodo could still hear them yell. "The End . . . I've seen it . . ."

They were back on the freeway now. She didn't need the speed anymore. Whatever potential terror might pass by, it could never get to her. Behind those forbidding goggles her eyes were fixed, straight ahead. Komodo sat beside her, said nothing. There was nothing left to say.

On they went, past Berdoo, out to Indio, Desert Center. Komodo felt as if his heart was about to break, watching Sheila Brooks's hands tighten about the steering wheel. How awful, to see that terror on her blanched face, to watch it bully her across the landscape, yet remain aloof, unnamed, out of conscious range, never be to acknowledged or exorcised. Komodo thought he'd seen expressions like that before, many times, always on his birthday.

Every August 6, he'd sit by the Dish, watching the *hibakushas*. One by one, the stolid Bomb survivors rose from their folding chairs, stood behind the podium, bore their witness. The pointylipped woman said, "The sun was before me, but then there was no sun. It was a red ball of wax. I was seized, inexplicably, with the need to see if it was raining. I held out my hand and a drop of the sun fell on my palm, like a bloody tear." Then came the man with the dark glasses, the one with the tic. "My fingernails were ripped out. They flew across the room like darts." Another woman told how she saw her own shadow burned into the wall.

By that time, Komodo would be weeping, his head in his hands. "Why should I escape while they suffer?" he asked Gojiro. "Why am I not on that platform, sharing their pain?" The monster would respond, as was his reflex, with rage. "Every year the same stories! Ain't there a Dean Martin roast on or something?" But then, more tenderly, the reptile would hug his friend. "You wouldn't like it. They'd make you dress up, wear itchy clothes. You know how you hate itchy clothes. Come on, turn it off."

But Komodo couldn't. He had to keep on watching, looking at the faces from his devastated hometown, hoping for a clue as to who he was. One survivor in particular stuck in his mind; she was different, not a regular. She was younger, no more than forty, which would have made her a child when the Heater hit—six, no more. Yet she looked older, wearier than the rest. They put pancake makeup on her haggard face to cover the keloid scars, but that only made her look more ghastly. Speaking in a grinding monotone, she said she'd wanted to be a teacher, to "create a world where a child would feel happy. A pretty world." But then the Bomb fell, so that was over, of course. "I saw something I knew I wasn't supposed to see. I saw Hell. I shall never leave it."

Komodo watched that woman's face and found it impossible to imagine her saying anything else. The Heater had stolen all her other words. This seemed the greatest horror of the Bomb, Komodo sometimes thought, the way it consumed the minds of the living. It was as if the agony of the dead had been transferred to the minds of the survivors, remaining with those *hibakushas* to see, and resee.

So many times Komodo wished he could find that *hibakusha,* snap his fingers before her eyes, throw open the doors of that Hell in which she dwelled. But there was nothing to be done. The sad woman never returned to the Dish, no matter how many of Komodo's melancholy birthdays passed by. Now Komodo peered across the interior of that little red Corvette and felt the same appalling impotence. Sheila Brooks was in Hell, and there wasn't anything he could do about it.

The most hideous thing was that he wouldn't, even if he could. There was no way Komodo would lift a finger to alter the course of that speeding sports car. The Triple Ring Promise prevented it. *"She has a secret, a secret that she may not even know herself."* That's how he'd pled his case, trying to convince Gojiro that Sheila Brooks's dilemma might overlap their own, that light shed on one might illuminate the other. Now the words resounded with an awful irony, for there was no turning back. What was sworn was sworn in blood and fire. If Sheila Brooks was driving straight toward the Encrucijada, Komodo understood that he had no choice but to go along for the wrenching ride. He could not, would not, stop her. It was his most sacred vow.

The shame of it! Gojiro was right, Komodo knew then; there were limits to Cosmo, boundaries to self-dramatized Order. He had no business being in that little red Corvette. What was happening now was a private thing. It was between Sheila Brooks and her father and her dead mother. If he had any decency he would jump from that speeding car and dash himself against the black slab highway.

At least that's what Komodo was thinking when he noticed that car behind them again. A gray Mercedes. Komodo thought he'd seen it earlier, before they turned off at the Oversoul Mall, the large, sleek Germanic automobile effortlessly keeping pace with the frantic accelerations of the Corvette. Now it was trailing them again, not particularly close, but there nevertheless.

". . . Every time we turned around there'd be that car, the gray one, following us . . ."

It was just then, with the moon rising higher in the giant sky, that she slammed on the brakes. Sand flew as the Corvette hairpinned across the median, hurtling between yuccas until it cracked into the wooly trunk of a Joshua tree.

"Ms. Brooks! Are you all right? A good thing we were wearing our seat belts. Their effectiveness in the reduction of highway fatalities cannot be overestimated. Did you swerve to avoid an injured animal?" Sheila Brooks did not answer. She'd already left the car.

When Komodo got out all he saw was the towering screen of the Desert View Motor Cinema. *Gojiro vs. the Enigma-Inking Squid at the Rock of Knowledge!* A long shot now: the leviathan bellowing, beating his withery foreclaws on his Triple-Ringed chest. Komodo paused to watch. It was involuntary. From the earliest of times, even the slightest glimpse of his friend would cause Komodo to stop, be stirred.

It was in the reflected light of the reptile's image that Komodo saw Sheila Brooks. Again, Komodo stopped, stared. In her red gravity boots and tangerine sundress, he thought he'd never seen her look more lovely. But then, as a tractor-trailer truck blared by, his quavering heart turned cold.

She was holding a gun to her head!

Komodo leaped. His jump was long, loaded with apogee, laced with hang time. He beseeched Newtonian dispensation so he might come down in time. He impacted feet first, harder than projected.

"Oof." The gun flew one way, Sheila Brooks the other.

She was lying on her back when he got to her, looking up. Her goggles were up around her hairline. He stared into huge green eyes. "I try," she sobbed. "I try . . . to get there. But *he* stops me." She pointed toward the drive-in screen where that giant squid clamped on Gojiro's head like a helmet of slime. "I can't get by him . . . it's driving me crazy!"

That's when it started up, with the two of them on the freeway, looking up at Gojiro. She felt it first. "That time at Albie's party," she said slowly, "before the car blew up. I don't know . . . I looked at you, and there was like a click. It's like, weird, but it's happening again."

"Yes," Komodo concurred. *The pheromone!* It was infusing, right on that beer-bottle-strewn median, just as it had under that smoky big top. Only now there wasn't a hundred yards to cross, or even a hundred feet. It was inches— inches between their lips.

"Ms. Brooks . . ."

"Mr. Komodo . . ."

The wind ceased to blow and the sound of speeding trucks was sucked out. Then, just as it was beneath Bullins's birthday tent, all time and space fell away. Again, they could have been anywhere. Atop the great ice floes, upon the endless pampas, racing down the long, mirthless hallways of a Paris office building. They were in a zone of their own, moving forward, according to the pheromone's irrepressible pull.

"Ahhh," Komodo said.

"Ahhh," Sheila Brooks said.

Closer, closer, across that fearsome gap.

But then Komodo sensed it, things blowing apart, her lips receding, swirling away like blown leaves into the vast desert night. Something was coming between them, driving them apart.

At first it was far off, then nearer. "Come in, Gojiro! Please heed this humble servant's plea! Please come in, Gojiro, Bridger of Gaps, Linker of Lines, Nexus of Beam and Bunch, Defender of the Evolloo! Please come in!"

That strange supplication—someone was chanting it! Komodo whirled to the sound, saw a boy. A wild boy, dressed in rags. He was coming closer, singing all the while. But then that lone voice in the night was joined by another. It was Sheila Brooks, picking up the boy's refrain.

"Ms. Brooks!" He reached for her, but she staggered away.

That was when Komodo felt the cold steel against his ear. "Federal agent. Don't move. A derringer is a lady's gun, but at this range, it'll still make a hole." Cologne sheared through the diesel fumes. Farther down the median, another man was knocking that wild, chanting boy to the ground. "Please come in Gojiro! Ow!"

"Wait—"

"I said don't move!" The gun jammed harder into Komodo's skull. "Ms. Brooks, please. There are orders to return you to your home. Your husband is worried about you." Komodo could see the man now. He was huge and wide shouldered, with a blond crew cut, wearing bubble shades.

"Bobby? Worried about me?"

"Worried out of his mind."

"But what are you going to do with Mr. Komodo?"

"No problem. He's an alien. His papers are not in order. He needs a medical briefing." Right then an ambulance pulled up. Out got three heavyset men in white coats. They walked closer, carrying a straitjacket.

"But—"

"If you'd just step into the car, Ms. Brooks." The rear door of that gray Mercedes, which was now parked beside the little red Corvette, swung open. The man who'd been kicking the wild boy came over to help Sheila Brooks into the backseat, slammed the door behind her. It was hard to see through the tinted windows, but Komodo was certain someone was raising his arm, greeting Sheila Brooks. On the screen above, Gojiro was vanquishing that squid, flinging it around by its tentacles.

"Ms. Brooks—" Komodo pitched forward, but the blond man was too strong. No doubt the recipient of much special-forces training, he nonchalantly brought a knee up into the small of Komodo's back, sent him to the ground coughing. "You're supposed to be dead, so if I kill you it won't matter much, will it? Be a good Coma Boy and go with these guys. You're way overdue for a checkup."

"What's a fucking Coma Boy anyhow?" asked the man with the straitjacket, grabbing hold of Komodo.

"He was big once," said the blond.

"For what?"

"For sleeping."

"Sleeping?"

"Nine years."

"Jap Van Winkle." The man gave Komodo a kick. "Hey, asshole, how come you were so tired?"

"You'd be tired too if you got hit on the head with a A-bomb."

"No shit? That's rough."

"Yeah. Strap that thing on him, tuck this Coma Boy in nice and tight. We haven't got all night."

They were grinding Komodo's face into the cold sand when half a dozen vehicles pulled up in a rush. Blocky men with video cameras swarmed out, followed by several elaborately coiffed women teetering on unsteady high heels and brandishing microphones.

"Mr. Komodo! Channel Seven," a cool brunette yelled. "Is it true that you are the Coma Boy?"

"Mr. Komodo! Channel Two. Is it true that you escaped from Okinawa in an open boat and the government has been covering it up all these years?"

"Mr. Komodo! Channel Eight. Are the Gojiro films based on your experiences?"

"Why are you wearing that straitjacket?"

"I-I-I," Komodo stammered. The blond and his henchmen were no longer in sight. They were in that ambulance, tearing down the freeway, followed by the gray Mercedes containing Sheila Brooks. "Ms. Brooks!"

The newscasters jumped. "Sheila Brooks? Was Sheila Brooks in that car? Is it true that you've signed a deal with Brooks-Zeber to make a picture about Joseph Prometheus Brooks? Can we confirm that, Mr. Komodo?"

Then, through a megaphone, came Shig's voice. "Mr. Komodo cannot answer your questions now. A full statement will be forthcoming on this spectacular revelation. Whatever you have imagined about this fabulous Coma Boy case, the actual truth will be far more astounding. I repeat, no questions now."

The newspeople were in an uproar. "You said we'd get coverage for the overnights. You can't shut us out now!"

"Mr. Komodo is still subject to recurring bouts of comatosis, due to the cruel, inhuman, illegal, and morally unauthorized experiments done on him while he was held prisoner by the U.S. Army on Okinawa," Shig announced through his bullhorn. "Please respect that condition. A detailed account of the lawsuits now being filed will be forthcoming at the news conference soon to be held."

"You fuckin' geek! You promised exclusives! You promised on-cameras. One-on-ones. Up-close-and-personals. We need morning-show coverage. Drive-time supplements."

"No further comment!" Shig barked. Then he grabbed Komodo, led him to the limo.

The reporters pushed forward, their flashblubs popping like microwave corn, but it was no use. The limo was already barreling away.

VISITORS

It was the sun that woke him, the brutal desert rays hard on his loose-slung leathers.

"Fuck!" Through sleepbound eyes, he saw the metallic creature, its gleaming jaws closing for the kill. Where was he now? In some hideous mecho-world ruled by knife-toothed insect robots? What to do? Instinct offered no advice, substantive or otherwise. He girded himself for ravaging. But then, just as the fiend had approached, it receded, its steely head rising up into the arid blue sky. That's when the shrunken reptile caught the true nature of this most recent would-be assailant. It was a pumper. One of those ever-nodding petrol plumbers, set out on a desolate stretch of salt flat.

He couldn't move. He was stuck, caught in a circle of thorns. Immediately, the pathetic scenario came clear. Obviously, while in the throes of whatever Quadcameral invasion had catapulted him back into the person of that youthful Echo Man, he'd been snared by a clump of tumbleweed and cartwheeled across the Valley floor, eventually blowing to rest against the side of this lone pumper. "Damn!" Rolled random inside a wind pollinating thicket—was there no end to humiliation?

Extricating himself from the dry thistle, the reptile sat up and panted. No wonder a hundred lost wagon-train leaders dubbed spots like this Devil's Furnaces. If he was an oven stuffer roaster, his pop-up button would have blown long ago. The monster looked around. It was hot, all right. Hot and empty. What was an oil rig doing in the middle of nowhere? And why was it covered up with sand-colored canvas? Evidently, someone was trying to hide it; there wasn't supposed to be any drilling on the Big Panghorn Missile and Bombing Range. Ole Prospector Pete, that paranoiac rockhound, would give his left ball to get the goods on whomever was working this little claim, for sure. Not that the monster cared. Whatever sleazebag graybeasts stole from one another was no nevermind to him, Gojiro thought lying there, watching the pumper pump.

Up. Down. At first he figured it was the heat, the way he got caught up in the cadence of the metal head's rise and fall. Up. Down. Hypnotic, like the swing of a carny's silver-plated watch. Up. Down. Diamond shafts thrusting, piercing sand and shale. Up. Down. Biting, screwing through. Up. Down. Not rock now, but skin. Up. Down. Slashing, sharp on sinew. Up. Down. Muscles severed, bones shattered. Up. Down. Pounding, a stake into the heart.

"Owww!" The pain shot through.

Something's down there! Eyes bulging, Gojiro staggered toward the well, looked down into the hole. He saw the black dot coming, but not in time to move away. It splashed up into his face, seeped into the parietal. A smallest glob of crude, belched from down below, it blinded him for a moment, knocked him back.

If it was oil, why'd it feel like blood? *Blood . . . blood from the earth.*

Rearing up on his shrunken hindclaws, the monster reeled away. It was almost his last step. Because right then that engine started up and the lizard came within a hairsbreadth of being gut-crunched by the sandspewing quartet of Michelins. The car must have been parked on the other side of the well; Gojiro never noticed it. "Motherfucker!" Over and over he rolled, dust cramming every orifice. He tried to get a plate number, but the big car was going too fast. All he saw was the fuzzy gray shape disappearing into the heatstreaked desert air.

His stride diminished along with the rest of him, it took nearly two hours to find his way back to the center of the Encrucijada. Thirsty and beat, the monster planned to check Pro Brooks, jot down a few cursory fieldwork notes, then scuttle back to the White Light Chamber to wait for Komodo's return. But that changed when he saw the gray car again, parked in front of the worldshatterer's crib.

The reptile squinted, took a breath. Victor Stiller was there, standing beside Brooks. Stiller and Brooks! Stiller—in his summer suit, gold cufflinks

Gojiro

reflecting in the sunlight. Brooks—severe, parched, unadorned in his parson's outfit. Brothers in fusion, together again in the Valley of Doom.

Arms spread, fists clenched, Stiller wasn't his usual impeccable self. He looked all pent-up. He was yelling in Brooks's ear. Brooks did not appear to acknowledge his longtime colleague. He kept his gaze firmly ahead, maintaining the searching position. Immediately recognizing the potential behavioral bonanza inherent in Stiller's attempts to alter Brooks's display, Gojiro moved in.

Stiller placed his ringed fingers on Brooks's angular shoulder. "Joseph, this is a serious matter. Your continued presence here is in jeopardy." He reached into the inside pocket of his suit and drew out what looked to be a snapshot. "Do you know this man?"

Brooks did not answer.

"Look at the picture. He was here. He spoke to you. What did he say?"

Again no reply.

Gojiro swallowed hard, remembering how Komodo had reached out, seeking to explain the Triple Ring Promise to Brooks, and then—a flash. *A hidden camera!* Gojiro was certain this was the origin of the photo Stiller was pushing into Brooks's face, blocking the blackclad scientist's searching stare. "View impeded, Brooks blinks," the monster duly noted. It was a first. Until then, as far as Gojiro could tell, the worldshatterer's ever-forbidding eyes had remained wide open in a steady, uninterrupted gaze. But with that photo thrust before him, Brooks blinked. Then, in one quick motion, he snatched the photo from Stiller's grasp, crumpled it, threw it to the ground.

Stiller picked up the picture with glum resignation. "Why are you testing me, Joseph? Haven't I always cleared the way for you, secured for you everything you've ever wanted? How much trouble would it be to answer a simple question?"

That's when those army jeeps roared up and that booming voice echoed across the yard. "Damnit, I knew you'd be here trying to tip him off!"

"Colonel Gaylord Grives, military head of the Project . . ." That's how he was always referred to in those newsreels. Grives, regulator, crew cut amongst the longhairs, a hardhead to reign over the spaceheads, charged to keep the Bomb commonsensical, American. Black-and-white images cascaded in the reptile's head. Grives in the Valley, after the Heater's debut, white booties on his feet, inspecting the shattered tower site. Grives in front of Congress giving testimony, a general now, his medals shining in the TV lights. Grives at Komodo's bedside, looking faintly embarrassed, his large rough hands placing a teddy bear on the pillow of the Coma Boy. Then Grives at Brooks's funeral, refusing to speak.

And, always, in his Black Spot Dream: Grives slogging toward the Lava-rock shore, screaming at Brooks, pushing the worldshatterer into the surf, swearing what happened before would never happen again.

He had to be near mandatory retirement, Gojiro guessed, watching the bulky general hoist himself from his jeep. But even with his considerable girth and the sweatspots radiating from under his hammy arms, Grives retained a reigning presence. He looked strong, alert, ready.

"Gaylord! A pleasant surprise," Stiller said jauntily.

"What are you doing here?" Grives spat back.

"Visiting an old friend. Joseph is alone out here now. He is entitled to some companionship."

"Cut the crap, Victor. It's over."

"Over? What's over?"

Grives held out a thick booklet. "The evidence."

Stiller raised his bushy eyebrows.

"Proof, Victor! Proof of what's been going on out here. And before I'm done, everyone is going to know about it. Everyone in this poor, beloved, deluded country."

"Illuminate me." Stiller was calm, superior.

"You'll find out—if you don't know already."

Gojiro drew closer. It was crazy how the two harped on, talking right past Brooks's face as if he were not there at all. Brooks didn't seem insulted. Returned to his searching position, he just kept on staring.

"I never realized you had this flair for melodrama, Gaylord."

"You won't be able to bluff your way out of this. I've got the goods."

Then something strange happened. Suddenly, Grives and Stiller weren't yelling at each other anymore. They were standing stock-still, one on either side of Joseph Brooks, locked into a bizarre tableau, looking out . . .

Searching! The three of them had assumed the position, their sightlines honed to that exact spot. The reptile scrambled to obtain a frontal view. This was a breakthrough, corroboration. Something *was* out there!

Grives was the one who broke it off. "No!" he screamed. "I won't stand here, not in this spot—never again!"

Then he turned and went into the house, followed by Stiller and, much to the monster's surprise, Brooks, as meek as any lamb.

Gojiro

*   *   *

It was no snap, hanging upside down, suckfooted to the varnished rafters of that ranch house. He wasn't a fussy little tree frog, there was nary an arboreal indication to be found in even his most strangled helix. Besides, he didn't have any practice. Try finding a branch from which to drape when you tip in at fifty tons. Now that he was up there, however, Gojiro appreciated the benefits of ceiling-sticking. Shrunk down to a couple of inches, the monster could imagine himself inverted upon on the Sistine Chapel ceiling, bridging the breach between the outstretched hands of Man and God. Also, you couldn't beat the vantage; who was to notice an anonymous little house lizard, a bug on the wall?

Scanning down, Gojiro wondered about Brooks. Did he function biogenetically, take a dump, make any kind of mess? In contrast to the ramshackle exterior, the inside of the house was as neat as a 4-H pin. Nothing seemed to have changed. The Pueblo rugs on the wall, heavy plank floors, leather easy chairs, the cow skulls above the giant stone fireplace—the reptile had seen it all before in those pre-Bomb shots of convivial fissionist smokers, the flannel-clothed spaceheads puffing on greenpack Lucky Strikes and drinking highballs, as if they were nothing but congenial collegiates in a rathskeller. The only new item was the army-issue cot pushed against the wall, its wool blanket stretched tight with crisp hospital corners. Brooks slept there, the reptile surmised. The grayframed bed couldn't have been more than six feet long, not nearly long enough.

Grives was all the action, strutting about, his belly straining against his khakis, waving his report. "I got some very strange geologic findings in this area. Very strange," he thundered in the brusque baritone of his Kentucky coal-town origins.

Stiller leaned back in his chair, filing his nails. "Get to the point, General," he said with exaggerated impatience.

"I didn't come to talk to you," Grives barked back. "I came to talk to him." The general walked toward Brooks, tried to catch his eye. But Brooks did not look back. He stood motionless in the middle of the room, his shoulders slumping, like a man waiting for a bus that had long since stopped running.

"Come on, Mr. Brooks, let's put a few things on the table here. Fr' instance, I'd like to know why there's been a mess of seismic irregularities in the area of the abandoned test sites. Also, I'm wondering about the two-

263

thousand-percent increase in radioactive levels in that same twenty-mile radius."

Stiller stood up, surprise on his face. Obviously he'd been expecting another kind of data. "Gaylord, where do you get these numbers from? Why wasn't I informed of this study?"

"And have you squash it like every other one? This old soldier isn't that stupid, not yet, anyway."

"Let me see that report."

"Not so fast."

"But it sounds like testing." Stiller wiped his forehead with a silk handkerchief. "There's not supposed to be any testing out here."

"Now, isn't that a fact?" Grives glowered.

Stiller regarded Brooks with widening eyes. "Joseph, if there is something—"

"I'll do the interrogating!" Grives was right next to Brooks now, his eyes slitted, saliva flying. "You're cooking something up out here, aren't you, Mr. Brooks? I want to know what it is, and I want to know now! Talk, you—" Grives's hands rose in front of him. For a moment it seemed as if he was about to take hold of Brooks, throttle him.

"Gaylord! You know his condition."

"Don't give me that. You can hear every word I say, can't you, Brooks? Confess, or I'll have my men rip this place apart."

Gojiro looked down from his suctioned perch, acknowledged the irony of the situation. Here was Grives blaming Brooks for those shaking seismatics and big fallout numbers when it was obvious enough who was freaking the Geigers. "Little old me." It was no surprise. Hadn't Komodo warned the reptile to stop pacing around the White Light Chamber and belching those gratuitous blasts of Radi-Breath?

Yeah, it was a real scaleslapper okay, Brooks taking all that heat. Probably, once upon a time, nothing would have tickled the monster more. Except now he wasn't laughing. Gojiro knew the hate on Grives's face; it was the same hate he himself had once felt toward Brooks. It was an ugly thing, wiping away all mirth.

"All these years of spending money to protect this madman, when all along we should be protecting *against* him!" Grives signaled to his men. "Go to it boys. Whatever he has out here, we've got to find it."

"That is not your decision, General!" Stiller was on his feet now. "You have no authority when it comes to Mr. Brooks."

"I'm taking the authority, Doctor."

"On what grounds?"

"On the grounds of national security. On the grounds that it is the right of every human being on this planet to be guaranteed a chance to live their lives free of whatever this man has inside his head. On the grounds that it is incumbent on every right-thinking individual to oppose Evil."

Stiller rolled his eyes. "Not *that* again!"

Grives leveled his gaze. "Victor, tell me one thing. Have you ever lost a night's sleep over what he did? Has it ever ruined a single meal for you? Have you ever been sitting with your wife, relaxing, watching the Early Show maybe, and suddenly you have to drop her hand and run to the bathroom because you get sick just thinking of it? I bet not. I bet it doesn't bother you at all. Well, it bothers me. I remember . . . what he did!"

That's when the monster went off, riding the sound of those voices he'd heard so many times before, at night, in his sleep. He rode those voices all the way back to Lavarock, bellydowned amongst his type, watching that silver plane land on the water. And again, the three of them were walking through the surf: Grives and Stiller, then Brooks. His old dream, the back pages of a life he always assumed to be of his own writing. Never real.

Below, he could still hear the argument, the rising volume.

Grives: "We saw what he did here, yet we took him to that island, gave him another chance."

Stiller: "These things happen in science; mistakes are made. We've been over this a hundred times! It was a miscalculation. A twenty-five-year-old miscalculation."

Grives: "As if the passing years could ever dull the crime! Twenty-five thousand years can't erase what he did. Forty-seven times the prescribed payload—forty-seven times! That was no mistake, that was murder! Premeditated murder. The only miscalculation was that he didn't kill us all—which is what he wanted to do!"

The monster heard this on a separate track. The rest of him was back on Lavarock, a youngest zardplebe once more, trying to heed the Black Spot's call, kept from the mantle of age-old Identity by Joseph Brooks's gaze.

Below, Stiller and Grives kept yelling. But on that ceiling, Gojiro was leaping . . . higher and higher . . . to the apex . . .

It was Brooks who brought him back, his voice low, like a sound from down a well.

"That was no miscalculation."

Gojiro looked down, watched Brooks grow, his lank body unfolding in hinged segments like a massive insect burst from an invisible wrapper. It was incredible the way the old man's neck seemed to unfurl, pushing the great white face, suddenly infused with blood, high into the air. He's schagging, the reptile noted with dazed wonderment, making clinical reference to the lizard proclivity to body inflation. *Schagstellunging* was the teutonic term those biologists used; nothing wrong with that, but if you believed their monographs, you'd conclude schagging was an everyday occurrence, invoked liberally by zards for everything from turf war to amour. Gojiro knew different. His dreams of Lavarock told him that to schag was to step out, announce yourself, make a statement of your own. This was no little thing for those who lived within the aegis of the Bunch, sanctified in the collective flow of the Magnificent Matrix. For them, to differentiate was to challenge the sacred uniformity of the Line. To go against every grain. You schag, you better be serious. You schag, you better be right.

"That was no miscalculation," Brooks said again, growing bigger every second. "Technically it was perfect, in every aspect of planning and execution. The error was one of commitment, not performance. I believed forty-seven times the projected yield to be sufficient. But it was not. The payload was too weak."

Brooks shifted his raven gaze toward Stiller. "You never understood that, Victor. You never understood any of it. We failed."

For the first time, sweat beaded on Stiller's forehead. "What do you mean, Joseph? How did we fail?"

"He didn't notice. That's the goal. It always has been. To make Him look at us. So we might see His face."

Grives exploded. "Madman! Blasphemer!"

Brooks kept on. "Forty-seven times the projected payload was not enough. I understand that now. If it had been a hundred times it still wouldn't have been enough. There is only one thing we can do to get His attention. We must threaten *all* creation. We must harness the power to extinguish every light, to obliterate every blade of grass. Ultimate destruction is the only path to ultimate redemption. He will show His face when everything is at stake, and only then."

The monster felt a shiver, nearly lost his grip.

Down below, Brooks was done. His statement made, he seemed to deflate, go limp once more. A sickly silence overcame the room for an instant. Then

Grives screamed, "I'll see you burn, just the way you sent her out to burn! Your own wife!"

Gojiro looked down, watched the ruckus below with curious detachment. For when Grives ran at Brooks it might as well have been happening on a beach slated for destruction, before a crowd of unsuspecting lizards, in a dream. Except this time, instead of driving Brooks into the soon-to-be-poisoned surf, Grives knocked him out of the ranch house door, into the air of the Encrucijada.

Gojiro released himself, fell fifteen feet, scurried after them. When the monster reached the dusty yard, Grives was on top of Brooks, pounding him with a fist. With his free hand, the general pointed to the horizon. To the very spot where Brooks always searched. "I close my eyes at night and I see it!" Grives screamed. "Right out there! How could you let her do it?"

Then, his face a mask of anguish, Brooks emitted a single word. "Wrong!" With one great spasm, he flipped Grives over, throwing the heavy man onto his back.

Brooks stood up straight, brushed the grit from his black suit. "She did what she thought was right. She thought she was going toward Him. But she was wrong."

Brooks turned away, stood again behind the stone wall.

Gojiro skirted along the rocky ground to his observation spot in front of the ranch house. Brooks was searching, as always, but now a tear ran down his face.

THE ESCAPE

Komodo buried Ebi on the lee side of a hill behind the Traj Taj. There was no question about where the grave should be. Ebi picked the spot herself, about a week before, in her elegant, offhand way. The two of them were taking a walk, stealing for themselves one of those moments during which nothing was ever said. In the absence of those words only love, implicit and fiercely tender, poured forth.

They walked the back acres, where the Insta-Envir thrived, through the loams of chemofragrance, the exuberance of the neo-fecundity weaving its particular luxuriance about them.

By and by, they came upon a bald spot where nothing grew. Ebi bit her lip and stopped. "This place seems neglected," she said, momentarily pained. From anyone else it might have been an idle comment, but Komodo caught the quiet purpose in Ebi's words. He understood her bond with the misbegotten soil in which she toiled, the way she thought of herself as extension of the earth, interchangeable with it. And how, if a place was barren, she took it as a personal mission to make it bloom.

He dug her grave with a rusted shovel from an old tool shed. It was unorthodox. On Radioactive Island, when an Atom died, the procedure was to call everyone together, light candles, make a procession of banging drums and tinny trumpets, a loud yet stately composite of a New Orleans secondline and Chinese New Year. Still, Komodo found the ceremony's unchanging repetition irksome. Death should be as idiosyncratic as life, he thought. But on Radioactive Island, there were so many funerals. It was better, making them all the same.

That's how he should have buried Ebi, Komodo knew. He should have followed form, called assembly, rung the somber gong, let the wailing fill the night.

But, in this final act, he couldn't treat Ebi as he had the rest. "I'm weak, selfish and weak," Komodo sobbed, digging Ebi's grave, alone, unwitnessed save by those wretched residents of the Zoo of Shame. Glassy-eyed, they stood, watching Komodo cover Ebi's coffin, never making a sound.

It wasn't but a few moments after he'd packed the soil flat and hard that the first green sprigs peeked through. Komodo bent down, grasped one of the resinous sprouts and named it: *Shaft grassine ebius.* It was not the practice to utilize names of Atoms in the taxonomic process, but Komodo felt Ebi would not mind. Continuity, not the labels themselves, had always been her great concern.

Right then, a lancing mother-in-law tongue pronged from the Insta-Envir, tearing through Komodo's black pajamas, nicking his skin. Strange, he thought, looking at the dot of blood on his fingertips. In all the years he'd spent in the thicket, no plant had ever caused him harm.

Then Shig was by his side. The two of them stood together for a moment, without speaking. They turned, exchanged a glance. Was there a bit of softness in the rigid boy's eyes? Komodo wanted to fall into those wintry arms, but Shig pulled away. The glance was all he would allow. "There are many people outside, seeking information," he said. "Your safety here is no longer assured. Contingency plans have been initiated." Shig then said that Komodo had a midnight appointment, that he would have to leave immediately, by the back way.

Bobby Zeber was waiting for Komodo in a nondescript Toyota secreted behind a clot of plastic shopping carts at the far end of a Ralph's Supermarket parking lot.

"I feel like I know you," Zeber said, sending the car onto the vapor-lit boulevard. He was wearing an old leather jacket and a pair of jeans torn at the knee. The uneven light gave him a furtive aspect, deepening the pocks scattered across his cheeks.

"But you do, Mr. Zeber," Komodo replied with cautious good will.

"No, not like that. From long ago. I wrote you a letter once. You know, letters to the Coma Boy. It was a class project, from the *Weekly Reader,* in between the articles about what to do about communism. The teacher said mine was the best letter in the class. It was very compassionate, she said. I had just gotten this new electric football game—I wanted you to come play it with me. I never understood why you didn't write back. Stupid, huh?"

Twenty minutes later, at the bottom of Neptune View Lane, Zeber stopped, flashed his headlights twice. A parked car returned the signal. Then Zeber went ahead, turning at the Turret House gate. A broadfaced man with Latin features leaned out the window of the other car. Beside him, a stout black man dressed in a nylon jacket said, "So far, so cool."

"Need some more coffee?"

"No more coffee, please! But you can empty this bottle." The Latin held up a container filled with a yellowish liquid.

"You guys are disgusting," Zeber smiled. "Appreciate this, man."

"No problem."

"Cops," Zeber exhaled as he drove through the open gate. "If they think you've got the Power, you can get them to do anything." The house was dark. Zeber led Komodo around to the beach side, past the contorted statues, and out onto a cement dock. At the end of the pier, they turned, looked back at the house.

Komodo gasped. Up there, a shadow framed in the same picture window where he'd first seen her, was Sheila Brooks.

"Beautiful night, huh, Mr. Komodo?"

"Yes, it is a full moon." His breath was coming quickly.

Zeber lit a cigarette, leaned against the railing. "I come out here a lot when there's a full moon. Moon, rhymes with swoon . . ." Zeber let out his sad laugh. "You think the moon's the same, even after Buzz Aldrin crunched his rubber boot across its face? You think Shelley could still write a poem about a place that's got a plaque on it signed by Richard Nixon?"

Komodo watched that window. She was out of the shadows now. A light fell across her face, a small, roundish pool of illumination. The stereopticon! She was holding it in front of her, at arm's length.

"What do you think?" Zeber asked again. "Do you think that by obsessively following our aspirations, we inevitably wind up defiling what we most revere?"

Komodo's eyes stayed on the window. "I think the heart's space is infinite, ever changing, and that Inspiration, no matter how battered, can adapt even to regions thought to be most defiled, leeched of Light. Yes, I believe there can be poetry, even in a world on which Nixon wrote his name."

Then he felt the heat. It was beginning, up in that window. "Ah!" came her first shout.

"The Hermit Pandora of Hollywood at work," Zeber said quietly. "But you know that already, don't you, Mr. Komodo."

Komodo began to stammer, but Zeber waved him off. "It's okay. You don't have to say anything. I know. I know that you know, anyhow. I have, ever since that night she was at your house."

Zeber dragged hard on his cigarette. "It's pathetic, you know, all these years those idiots said I ruled her, that I made her do what I wanted. But it was always her. Her idea . . . from the beginning. That's what she said when she woke up that first time, talking about the Tidal Wave—'Wouldn't this make a great movie?' She had it all down—the whole plot, the dialogue, even the pitch. A total package.

"Hey, don't get me wrong. It's not like she had to twist my arm. Sure, I could have stayed in New York, been a starving artist. But it was a different time. I had the idea that movies were going to change the world. I put my Bolex in my backpack and rode across the Brooklyn Bridge thinking, I'm going to change the fucking world. Nebraska, Colorado, Nevada—I never noticed them. Then there she was: this incredible creature, falling right into my lap, saying, Please take these dreams, make Art out of them—real Art. Get rich and famous while you're at it. Do it, or I'll *kill myself.*"

He laughed again. "Out of all the sweaty little careers in Hollywood, she's got to walk into mine."

Sheila Brooks was beginning to shriek. A terrible high-pitched scream. Komodo began to go toward her, but Zeber grabbed his arm. "Don't."

"But . . ." Komodo tried to break free.

Zeber gripped tighter, drew Komodo's face close to his. "Nothing you can do now. She's getting close, closer all the time. That's how it works. You have to know that. All those movies, those millions of dollars—it was just repression. Substitute images. You see, there's something in there. She looks at it, and it looks back—whatever it is. Except it's too big, too much for her to take in all at once. So her head invents something else. Tidal waves, rocket ships full of doomed executives, anything to throw into the breach. But now, she can't avoid it anymore, can't think of anything to protect herself. It's too close."

Sheila Brooks screamed again. Komodo jumped. "I can't just sit here!"

Zeber pushed Komodo back. His face was full of rage and sorrow. "How do you think I feel?"

Then, quieter: "I always hoped she'd wake up one morning and it would be gone. Like a bad cold. Then, maybe we'd stay here, become regulation Industry scum—eat lunch, buy West Hollywood real estate. Or maybe we'd get on the bike, blow out to Phoenix or Little Rock, buy a doublewide, sit in front of the cable, twelve-packs and cheez snacks, bounce checks, have bad teeth. Be happy. But that'll never happen. It won't go away."

The heat seared Komodo's cheek. She was screaming louder. "Mom! Dad!"

Zeber kept talking, his dark eyes boring into Komodo's head. "There was no chance, until now. Until you came along, Mr. Komodo."

"Me?"

"You said it yourself, at Albie Bullins's party. About the Way Out. The earned arf. What more can anyone hope for in this life? For me, Mr. Komodo, you're the earned arf."

"I don't understand."

"Sure you do. I love her, but I can't help her. You love her and you can."

"But Mr. Zeber . . . you are her husband, that is a devout bond."

Zeber's voice rose. "There's no time for that shit now. This is *important!* Look man, I don't know what your trip is, or where you're from, or how you got here—none of that matters. All that does is that you help her. Listen, it was slick bringing out that Coma Boy stuff when you did. Without that, you'd be dead now—roadkill by the freeway. A little item in the *Times,* three days later it'd be all over except for the liability adjusters. You bought some time, but that won't stop Stiller. You make him nervous. He's going to try to crush you. And he's dangerous. You have no idea how dangerous."

Zeber pulled a tarpaulin off the Triumph motorcycle parked on the pier. "Look, if there's anything you want to ask me, do it now."

Up in the window Sheila Brooks was still screaming. "Mr. Zeber . . . did you know about Mr. Brooks?"

Zeber kneeled, checked his chain. "That was Victor's thing, something only he could think of. The National Security Council probably gave him a medal when he came up with the idea. I mean, consider the problem: you're trying to justify dropping the Bomb, you're building up a war chest of the fuckers because you claim it's the only sane thing to do, and the guy who made it—your National Hero—is totally out of his mind. Completely crackers. How do you think that plays in Peoria? 'We trusted the fate of the world to a guy we knew was crazy, but you should keep on believing what we say anyhow.' It wasn't exactly like they could get rid of him, either. Who knew what the Russians might come up with? Who knew when the home team might need Joseph Prometheus Brooks's special talents again?"

Zeber stood up. "That's where Stiller came in. You see, Victor knows how to handle Brooks. He's been doing it for years, way back to their school days. The 'indispensable interface,' that's what he calls himself, the middleman between Brooks and us mortals. Victor said why not just pretend he's dead, hide him somewhere, put him in mothballs? Kill every bird with one stone. Only a truly cynical mind could have come up with something like that."

"But why would Mr. Brooks go along with such a plan?"

"Victor says he's just crazy. That his mind blew out. But I don't think so. There's something out there—in that Valley. It's got to do with Sheila and her mother and her father and who knows what else. But it goes back, way back. Before the Bomb. Back to whatever happened to Sheila's mother when she wandered into the Valley. She *saw* something there—some kind of vision. Sheila sees it too. I don't know what it is, or why it's in her head. But that's her life, trying to get back to the Valley—to whatever's there."

Zeber grabbed Komodo's arm. "Listen, man, maybe I'm weak. But I'm not a scumbag. *I'm not a scumbag!* I told her about her father—don't think I didn't. I couldn't love her and not tell her. I told her a hundred times. But she didn't *hear* it. I even put her on the bike to take her out there—to show her. They stopped us, Victor and the rest. But you know what? It didn't really matter. I could have put her right down next the old man, and I don't even know if she'd have noticed—at least not when *I* showed her.

"Tell me, what else was I supposed to do? Except protect her—keep her safe until whatever time she was ready? Ready for what? Who knows? So we just stayed here, getting richer and richer, and then, one day, I open a letter from Victor Stiller telling me he owns eighty percent of National Pictures, has for years, that he's pleased with my 'effective management of the company's major asset.' "

Zeber kicked down on the bike with an ear-splitting rumble. In the window, Sheila was writhing. Zeber watched her, yelled above the noise. "There's something different about her. Something strange. She's not the same. Maybe it's biological. Maybe you know."

He arranged the rucksack on his back. "Coma Boy and Zombie Girl— together again, for the first time. I like it."

"Please . . . Mr. Zeber."

"Go to her, take her with you. Make the movie. For chrissakes, make the movie! *Gojiro vs. Joseph Prometheus Brooks in the Valley of Decision*—it'll be hot, I know it."

Upstairs, Sheila Brooks dropped the stereopticon, collapsed against the windowpane.

Zeber reached over to embrace Komodo. "Take good care of my wife, keep her safe," he said and roared off.

The voices came oblique, as if bounced from derelict satellites, diffused through water. They were talking about him, he knew, but the sense of what was said remained out of reach. He opened his eyes, tried to see. Tried to get up, walk around. Nothing worked. Where was he? Hands moved against his temples, warm, succoring, working with a purpose, removing the cloth stretched across his forehead. Nice hands, he thought, so much like . . . in the hospital. His mind raced. Okinawa! Room 227! Walter!

Then: light streaming in. Iris shock. The first thing he saw was Joseph Prometheus Brooks in the middle of the Encrucijada, his raised palms extending away from his body, his black eyes elevated, looking up. The great worldshatterer towered above him. Except he wasn't all there. You could see through him, like an X ray.

"Ah, there you are," Victor Stiller said, his not unkindly face coming between Komodo and Leona Brooks's portrait. Wearing a casual white pinstriped jacket over a forest green turtleneck, Stiller's eyes looked moist behind his metal-rimmed bifocals. "I've been watching you sleep. I hope you don't mind. It recalls so many memories for me."

He was sitting on a sandcolored Danish modern couch in a large, sun-filled room. "Of course, you would not recall, a young child in your condition, but I often visited you back in those days. Usually this was for propaganda purposes, to illustrate concern for your plight in the scientific and military communities. However, many times I came on my own. This surprised me. I am not a sentimental man by nature. Also, I despised that hospital, so shabby, with those officious little doctors. But I came anyway. It was your look that attracted me. Dead, but not dead—somehow beyond death. I think you made me feel hopeful."

Komodo couldn't move. Gagged, his hands and feet bound, he lay at the base of the wall where the painting hung. It all came back now, standing on that pier as Zeber rode away, then the picture window going dark, empty. And running—up the switchback stairs behind the beach house. To her. Except there were shouts, men screaming in the night. Gunshots. A dull slap against the side of the head.

"I see you are admiring Leona's portrait of Joseph," Stiller remarked. "A great work, don't you think, Mr. Komodo? A legend. It has been in my collection for some time. The longer I keep it here, under lock and key, the more the legend—and value, of course—grows. Such a shame Leona did not create more works of this nature. The Brooks family has always been so good to me."

Stiller watched Komodo struggle a moment, then let out a long sigh. "Yes, hopeful, that's what it was. You made me feel hopeful. It's remarkable how little you've changed. There's something that's still very much the same." Then he called across the room. "Mr. Henderson, please untie Mr. Komodo."

Henderson, the large blond man who'd beaten Komodo on the freeway median, was now swathed in navy blue Gore-Tex. He got up from the bottom step of the spiral staircase, came over, undid the ropes. "But you got to be good," he said, displaying much perfect dentition.

Unbound, Komodo coughed and fell into an Eames chair. His throat burned, he thought his collarbone might be broken. He was in what appeared to be the living room of a mountain chalet, the sort of sleekly appointed A-frame corporate raiders might rent for ski season.

"The Sierra foothills. A pleasant environment, don't you think?" Stiller indicated the luxurious view from the soaring triangular windows that made up the impressive west wall of the house. It was already afternoon, Komodo noted. But which day? He'd been drugged, shot up with something, he could feel it in his knees.

"Upon occasion I bring friends here and tell them I enjoy the air, that it reminds me of my boyhood in the Carpathians. But that is a lie. My father was a tailor. We lived in a disgusting hovel in the ghetto. I never saw a mountain until I was sent away to school. Still, it is a comfortable lie. People seem to enjoy hearing it."

Stiller handed Komodo a glass of carrot juice. "Mr. Komodo, I sense you are a deeply subversive spirit, a revolutionist of the most radical bent. Now, of course, I myself was once a revolutionist. Turn the world upside down, that's what we longed to do, back in Göttingen. And didn't we succeed? We achieved a catharsis greater than a billion Bolsheviks could ever have dreamed. Did it make things better? Who's to say? Change was the mandate, and change we made.

"I am no longer a revolutionist. As dreary as it is, there's no escaping: in my old age I've come to like things more settled. So indulge an elderly gentleman with a late-ripening passion for Order, Mr. Komodo. Explain something to me. That night on Okinawa? Tell me how a boy who hadn't moved or spoken in more than nine years suddenly got out of bed and managed to escape dozens of MPs and navy cutters. Please. It's been on my mind."

Komodo swilled the thick juice down his parched gullet, tried to get his voice back.

"I'm sure you can imagine the difficulties your disappearance caused. The embarrassment. As acting head of the Project, you fell under my jurisdiction. Mine and General Grives, of course. I personally questioned that man, that black nurse."

Komodo's tongue finally loosed. "Walter."

"Walter? You remember his name? How curious. A most disagreeable individual, very uncooperative. He wouldn't volunteer a thing, resisted all reasonable attempts to establish the course of events."

"Walter Crenshaw."

"Yes, of course. Perhaps we were a bit zealous in our questioning. The man became delirious. He seemed to be under the impression you would contact him on some kind of a radio. We never found any such device. Do you have any idea what he was talking about?"

"No."

"I didn't think so. The man was obviously mentally unstable. Completely mad."

"Poor, sweet Walter."

"What's that, Mr. Komodo?"

"You made him sleep in bus stations, walk down mean streets, hurl insults at the sky. You hounded him, tortured him . . ."

Stiller's cheek twitched. "They found the wreckage of that Korean fishing scow. All the men were dead, drowned, half-eaten by sharks. The seas were quite heavy, if you recall. A typhoon arose, out of nowhere, a most unusual occurrence. There was no chance of survival. Yet here you are. How is that possible?"

Komodo stared back at Stiller. "Are you certain it's me? I saw you on television, saying I gently slipped away in my sleep, died as peacefully as I lived."

"Don't be flippant with me! How did you get away? Where did you go? Where have you been all these years?"

"I've been behind the Cloudcover. In the contours of Corvair Bay Beach."

"What?"

"In the dense forests of Asbestos Wood."

"Talk sense!"

"Standing in the stiff wind of Past Due Point. In the grottos of Dead Letter Hill."

"Shut up!"

"I won't say what Walter wouldn't."

Stiller's face was red now. He stood up in front of the portrait of Joseph Prometheus Brooks, reached into his jacket, produced a creased photograph, and slammed it onto the coffee table. "You are a filmmaker, you know the camera does not lie, so why does it show you here, talking to Joseph Brooks? Two dead men—alive! What do you want, why have you come here?"

Komodo stood up, leveled his gaze at Stiller. Anger gripped him, but a great sorrow as well. "It wounds my soul to say this, inasmuch as I have long admired your achievements in particle acceleration and the development of heavy isotopes, but I can no longer respect you, Mr. Stiller. You speak exquisitely of the dichotomy between science and magic, but your words are hollow. You have forfeited all moral authority, violated a most solemn trust. Men capable of sublime thoughts must possess a sense of honor that is incorruptible. You do not. You are no man of science. Your Order is a false Order. In its way lies only cruel self-interest. Nevertheless, the crimes you have committed against me, I can forgive. But what you have done to Ms. Brooks can never be condoned!"

Stiller's hand lashed out, slapping Komodo across the cheek. "Ms. Brooks is no affair of yours! She is a sick woman. She cannot be told the truth. It will kill her!"

"A child should know her parents."

Stiller stopped yelling now. He looked tired, weary. He sat down on the couch, breathing hard.

"You signing off on this, Doc S.?" Henderson inquired, hovering close. Stiller said nothing, turned away.

Thus cued, Henderson jammed a pistol butt into the back of Komodo's neck, smashing him face-first to the floor. Then the large man picked Komodo up again, flung him into a chair. There were several other men in the room now, all clad in brand-name athletic garb. Komodo recognized them as the strait-jacket-wielding ambulance drivers.

"Let me introduce the team, Mr. Komodo," Henderson said with affable menace. "Bill. Frank. Sammy. Sergio. Over there, we got Mohammad K-Paul, he's the Pakistani of the group. I'll explain the problem, Mr. Komodo. I just got off the phone with my brother agents in L.A. They tell me the local police are engaged in a pitched battle with about five hundred people attempting to converge on your house there. These people—they're dressed as lizards. They keep screaming about something called the 90 Series. Would you have any pertinent information about this, Mr. Komodo?"

Komodo felt stunned. "The 90 Series . . . but how could that be? The supplication has been disconnected from the Quadcameral."

Henderson squinted. "Whoa! Back up here a minute. The suppli-what?"

"What's he talking about?" one of the others said. "A quadriphonic? I had one of those. Wound up throwing it out with the eight-track."

"That's enough," Henderson interrupted with a withering glance. "Let's get basic, Mr. Komodo. Why were you in the Encrucijada? What do you want from Joseph Brooks?"

Komodo did not answer. Henderson slapped him.

"Are you and Brooks involved in some kind of nuclear project?"

Again, no answer and a slam.

"Look, we know something is going on out there. The facts and figures are on the table. If you're smart, you'll help us. What's between you and Brooks?"

Komodo shook his head, felt a cracking as Henderson's foot landed in his ribs.

"Why did you come to America?"

"What's this supplication? What do you want?"

"Talk, you fucking Jap bastard!"

Then they knocked him to the ground, ripped his black pajamas, exposed his chest. "What's these circles here? What do they mean?"

"That goddamn monster in the movies got the same circles!"

"What do they mean, asshole?"

Again they kicked and punched him. Komodo felt a bubble of blood precede his words. "I fell down on a waffle iron."

"What?"

"Someone seared me with a car cigarette lighter."

How happy Komodo felt right then, even as Henderson smashed him with karate blows. For he remembered that day, so many years ago, when Gojiro first emblazoned the Triple Rings on his massive chest and their great Promise was sworn. "We'll never tell how we got 'em, or what they mean," the monster declared, his fists clenched, emotion rising in his voice. "Don't matter what nobody does to us, we won't say. We'll tell them something like . . . I dunno . . . like we tripped on a hot manhole cover or something." What a joy to be able to follow his great friend's suggestion now, Komodo thought as another foot crashed into his side. There could be no greater honor than to be true to his friend and their Vow.

Henderson was getting ready to hit Komodo again when Stiller waved him off, pointing to a manila envelope lying on the couch.

"Right," Henderson said, taking out a gray file. "Mr. Komodo, we'll return to the previous line of questioning in a moment. We like to pursue several avenues of discovery at once. Media management, as you can well imagine, is a major concern. In that vein, I thought you might be interested in the story we're currently seeding in certain newspapers. To summarize, you are no longer the Coma Boy. In fact, your entire story is a hoax. You weren't found in any pit after the Bomb blast. You've never even been to Hiroshima. You were brought up in Tokyo, a fair student in several schools. Your father, now deceased, was a bank clerk convicted of embezzlement. Your mother is a sometime travel agent in Kobe whose virtue, I'm sorry to report, is somewhat questionable. You had a brother, but he was killed in a drug deal about two years ago."

"What are you talking about?"

"I'm talking about *you,* Mr. Komodo, who you are." Henderson took out a picture of a grade-school graduating class. One head in the middle row was circled. "That's you, at ten. You can't see it that well, but we'll have better pictures by tomorrow. I got one of your mom, though. You want to see it? She's kind of hot."

"No!"

"Hey, don't be so ungrateful! We're giving you a whole different identity here and you don't even have to apply for a new Social Security card."

"This is horrible! Unspeakable!"

Henderson turned to the other men. "I hit a nerve here or what?" Then, to Komodo, "Yeah, this new you is going to be front page, along with how you dreamed up the whole story to save your sagging movie career. Your operation is in deep financial trouble, has been for some time, if you don't know. That's why you lied to Sheila Brooks about being the Coma Boy. You wanted to play on her guilt about what her poor, dead dad did to you back at Ground Zero. A cunning Jap plot, inscrutable as shit."

Komodo tried to get up, but Henderson knocked him down. "Mr. Stiller! How can you allow this?" Stiller had turned away to rearrange his outfit.

"That's not the end of it, Mr. Komodo. Oh, no. There's more. Much more. You're a child abuser. A mutilator, too. We're running checks on all those kids you had up there at that house. It looks bad. Real bad. Grieved parents from Somalia and whatever other third-world hellholes will be coming forth in droves to tearfully testify how you stole their kids and threw them into your freak-show movies. But the worst of it is probably the murders. How you kill them when they get too old to be in the pictures. We found that grave, you know."

"What?"

"Hey Joe! We get a name on that kid in the grave yet?"

Joe, blowdried and heavyset, looked up from the *Penthouse* magazine he was reading. "Yeah. Ebi. Little girl. Horrible, just horrible. Tears your heart right out."

"You're a ghoul, Mr. Komodo. The American public needs to know that. We got a disinterment order on that grave. We'll dig her up, find some very graphic things in the autopsy, I'm sure."

"Ahhhhh!" Komodo's shriek came from the bottom of his soul, welled up, sprang him forward. He flew across the room, knocked Henderson aside, and went for Stiller. He got his hands around the old man's withery neck, began choking.

They pulled Komodo off, threw him against the fireplace andirons. Then Henderson was there, with his .45. "Just the way it has to be, I guess. We confronted you with the proof of your inhuman activities, you went berserk, attempted to do bodily harm to several officers, were unavoidably shot dead. Kind of too bad. I saw a couple of those Gojiro movies. Lots of laughs."

It was right then that red water balloon crashed through the chalet window and exploded against Henderson's forehead.

"Ughhhh!" The agent went down immediately, his body covered with what looked to be hundreds of leeches and lampreys, all immediately burrowing through his jogging suit and into his skin.

"What the fuck?" The others whirled their guns around from combat crouches, only to be met by a barrage of balloons. It was a regular Republican convention in that chalet, the way those shiny red, white, and blue spheres poured in through the windows and filled the living room, each one packed with a payload of slime and squirm.

Komodo rolled under the coffee table, hid there. He knew those leeches, the slugs and maggots, too. After all, he'd made them, modeled them after mescal worms for that wooden zard scene in *Gojiro vs. the Vulgarians of Troy at the Seven-Layer Siege of Ahistoricism.* The pseudobeasts were programmed to skintunnel upon impact with any living tissue in the 98.6 range. Of course, in the interests of safety, the minisludgicles only had a half-hour lifespan and left no lingering slimetracks, but Komodo was not about to tell Henderson and his crew that.

Then there were footsteps on the stairs outside. Shig was deploying the more mobile Atoms. Each carried a snaploaded crossbow, ten balloons on the shaft, two more at the ready. Wing, wang, zing, they fired, sending the agents screaming hysterically through the room, eel simulacra extruding from their every orifice.

"We have rescued you, Mr. Komodo!" It was Bop, that saddest Atom, attempting to keep up with the others on his prosthetic legs. He smiled wide, showing that bottomless hole, no tongue or teeth. Suddenly, Bop's banty chest exploded. That Henderson! He shot Bop in the back!

Shig sprang as if jets were in his boots, sword drawn. With one crescenting slice, he hacked off Henderson's arm, the blood spraying across the portrait of Joseph Prometheus Brooks. But Henderson, his face so thick with worms as to look like a shag-rug remnant, wasn't done. He staggered up, pumped a bullet into Shig's side. Blood blotted the neoteen's white linens and he fell. Henderson reached over, grabbed Komodo, and using him as a shield began to make his way out of the room.

"Get back you little bastards or he gets it," Henderson called out through maggot-teemed lips. With his still-extant arm, he managed to pull Komodo onto the chalet's deck. Komodo felt himself go numb. He had no doubt that the big man planned to kill him, break his neck right then. Down below, a gray Mercedes sped down the dusty road. Stiller was getting away!

That's when Komodo sensed that blast of heat go past his ear, felt Henderson's clutch release. It was Trumaine Crenshaw, standing there, holding the laser gun Shig had used to blow clay pigeons from the sky at Albert Bullins's house. Henderson made one last lunge, trying to take Komodo with him, but he missed and fell off the chalet deck, making the three-hundred-foot plunge into the pine tops by his lonesome.

"Damn . . ." Shaken, Trumaine wiped his brow with his Triple-Ring-tattooed hand. "I wasn't meaning to shoot nobody, but . . ."

Komodo got up, put his arm around Trumaine. He could feel the boy's heart beating. "But how could you know?"

Trumaine spit a few times. "My Uncle Walter, he made me swear, 'Yuke the Nuke comes to call, do what you can for him.' "

THE NEW EQUATION

Crypted up once more amid the macabre expressionism of the White Light Chamber, Gojiro lay numbed and bummed as the Coma Boy coverage splayed before him. Garish stills of Komodo tipsy under Albert Bullins's big top split-screened with delicate black-and-white shots of a small boy sleeping on a stainless-steel pallet in Okinawa. "Is this the same man?" tightbootied tweet-tones from here to Tonopah intoned.

Of course there was no proof, no evidence. The "investigation" turned up nary a matching hair fiber or corresponding swirl of thumb. Cops in smocks potted busts depicting what the Coma Boy was supposed to look like today, but as for the likenesses they produced, they might as well have been trying to hang a rap on Charlie Chan. No obstensible principle was talking. The army put forth the tersest of no comments. At Hermit Pandora Productions, the phone had been off the hook for days. The only one who'd speak for attribution was Albert Bullins, and all he said was, "Cut off my nuts and fry 'em on a redhot skillet if I know a thing about any Coma Boy. I thought he was a surfer."

But once the tabloid reflex locks and Luce's sluice flings loose, who needs proof? The tale's a torrent, cresting over every levee, each stonewall. It's no coincidence that "journalist" and "jerkoff" start with the same letter, ditto "reporter" and "retard," the monster fumed as he watched the story roll on. No angle was too obtuse, no slander too low. "The coma guy's gotta go," a hamfaced gaffer's union boss bellowed into an obliging mike. "He brings in these little freaks and lights that don't got no plugs. I say, Hey Frankie, this AC or DC? They say they're running the stuff themselves. I say, Hey Frankie, get the bats, nobody turns on a nightlight in this town unless it's us. But they start shining those crazy floods on us. I got three fellas that still can't read the big *E* on the chart. That coma guy, he's a lowlife union breaker. A gook scab from outer space." Killed Gojiro, hearing that. Komodo was a good union man! How the monster longed to Radi-Breath those teamsters' slack skin—fry that jerky beef like a Bikini Bar-B-Q. Assholes! They all should sleep beneath Hoffa's sheets.

It didn't stop there. One after another, leering, sneering faces tossed in their supposedly sensational tidbit. Some third-banana character actor who owned the estate down the road from the Traj Taj was all shook up. Eyebrows arching for the sky, greased and powdered for his first TV shot in years, he told how he woke to find a "hideous beast" in his swimming pool. What a moron—it was only that toothless, harmless giant sloth, escaped from the Zoo of Shame. On the talk shows, Pacific-theater vets kept calling to warn that Komodo was the ultimate of Jap cave-dwellers, surfaced at last to banzai his emperor's most nefarious bidding.

Gojiro listened with growing helplessness. Komodo = Coma Boy had captured the nation's imagination; it was an idea on the move! With every replay of those suddenly ubiquitous Okinawa newsreels, each repeating crescendo of the announcer's booming question—"This boy, is he our witness or our judge?"—the concept lurched forward, reaffixed itself to long-dormant mythic wiring, struck submersed chords.

Then: Extra! Extra! They were going live remote to the Traj Taj. The videoboys had busted in, were steadycamming down the empty corridors, zooming in on the devastation. The place looked as if it had been ransacked by a column of Crusaders searching for their car keys. House plants were ripped from pots, their roots still twitching. The dining-room table was hacked to pieces; china lay shattered on marble floors. Fires burned in shower stalls, mysterious dark fluids ran from beneath doors.

It was insane; Komodo would never have stood for that sort of mayhem. Certainly he wouldn't have allowed the slashing of those paintings the old producer had made of his beloved starlet. Komodo would rather die than see true love's expression desecrated. There was only one explanation: it was a set-up. Komodo was in trouble! The monster summoned all his strength. Komodo in trouble? Help was on the way!

Upward Gojiro soared, bent on breaking the Chamber's miserable confines. But just as quickly, he thumped back to the cavern's unforgiving floor.

"If Komodo's in trouble," he puzzled, "how come I don't know about it?" How come he wasn't already on the scene, battling alongside his friend, a fabulous avenger wreaking inconceivable destruction on whatever Opposer dared threaten the most elemental provinces of the Triple Rings? It was supposed to be automatic, Prewire.

It core-quaked the monster, made him wail. "Komodo in trouble and I got to find it out from the Dish like some barroom lug listening for a ball score!" What was happening? Why didn't Komodo call out for him in the night, send his plea across all space? Then it came to the monster: maybe Komodo had called him—tried, and failed!

"Oh, no!" Did that Beam interfere, blot out his friend's SOS? "Fuck!" the monster anguished. "Komodo invokes the great Oath, and I'm not around to take the call—'cause I'm in an egg, a sixty-six-million-year-old egg!"

Then: "Come in, Gojiro! Please come in! Please heed this humble servant's plea."

"What?" The monster looked up, saw them on the Dishscreen. G-fans! Hundreds of them. A thousand 'tile-o-files, more coming all the time according to the traffic choppers. They were converging on the Traj Taj in their scruffy, makeshift leathers, carrying scrapbooks, Crystal Contacts on their juggy heads. "Why are you here?" a newsman asked a zardpard, son of a Salinas migrant worker, caked with dirt from his all-night hitchhike. *"Why?"* the G-fan retorted, the homemade parietal swirl strapped to his forehead glaring in the sunlight. "Because *he's* here."

"The Coma Boy, you mean?"

The 'tile-o-file looked at the microphone man with disdain. "No. *Him!"*

"Him?"

"Him—*Gojiro!* The 90 Series! It's happening *now!"*

The reptile reeled, fell backward, crashed down. When he looked at the Dishscreens again, the G-fans were gone. All around flickered images of Joseph Brooks. Immediately the monster relaxed. Anything was better than those screaming 'tile-of-files. But there was more to it than that. It was different now between Gojiro and Joseph Prometheus Brooks.

The turning point had come just hours before, as he hung from the ceiling of that old ranch house, watching Stiller and Grives scream. That's when the monster saw that old photo lying on the mantel of the stone fireplace. It was two pictures actually, side by side on a single card—a stereopticon photo now minus its holder. Not that the monster needed the viewer to make the 3-D come alive. One look was enough. He saw the whole family there, ten kids at least, dressed like pioneers in patches, hand-me-downs. The mom stood behind, severe, frightened. The dad was off to the side, his eyes dark with dread, piercing. And in front—a boy, the youngest one. What an odd, faraway look he had on his face. From his perch, Gojiro tried to meet that boy's eyes, to see things from his point of view. That's when it started, when he felt himself begin to be transported, just as he had been so many times before. And suddenly he wasn't suctioned on that ceiling anymore. He was waistdeep in a Wisconsin snowdrift, running toward his mother's call.

"Joseph!" Her dress was gingham, her brown hair done up in a bun. How big and white *(his skin!)* she looked, how soft her hands felt around him when they hugged. Then she said it was time to go, his trunk was packed, everything arranged. He was different from his brothers and sisters, she said, suddenly stern and practical, her pale blue eyes firm and dry. He was different from everyone. He would understand that someday. Thu-wap! His father was out behind the house, cutting firewood. She put her hand across his lips. There could be no good-byes. The wagon was there, waiting, that tired horse and the man with the hat pulled down. "My son," she said, pushing him up into the seat, kissing him one last time, an icy oval on his cheek for a moment, "please, help us. *Redeem* us."

Then through the snow . . . crying, shrieking . . . a nine-year-old boy with a freezing nose going to the university, incredible ideas inside his head. Even the professors receded from him, made timid by what he knew. Then he was on a ship, great waves rolling, and in a carriage, riding through black forests to Göttingen, to be with Stiller and the rest. Even there, feeling the sting of their envious, scheming glances, he was an aberration, different. How he hated their glibness, their minds so fluid, their hearts so empty. Then he escaped to the club . . . the music hot and slick, the terror in his mind funneled out through the end of a licorice stick. Except the saxophone player, whom he hoped would understand, could only shake his head and say, "Joey B, sometimes you go way *outside.*"

Only she knew. Leona. She came over after he played "In a Mist," looked up at him with her green eyes. "I know who you are, I've *seen* you . . ."

They left the club immediately, ran through the rainy streets, up the flight of stairs to a small room. She took the sheet off the easel, showed him what she had made. He went closer, touched the canvas, saw himself in his parson's clothes, standing by a fence, hands outstretched looking out.

"But it's not finished," he said. "You can see through it."

She looked at him, beaming. "You will finish it."

Then they were in the desert—Brooks and Leona in the Encrucijada! It was dawn and they were walking across the sand. Walking toward the tower where the gadget hung. The Heater! Dead ahead. What was that in Brooks's arms? The monster strained to see. But now the worldshatterer was yelling, "No! Leona! It's wrong!"

That's when the reptile grew weak, when his tears fell from the ceiling of that ranch house, splashing down unnoticed amongst the screaming men below. Brooks was right, Gojiro knew then: Grives and Stiller *didn't* understand, they never would. They'd never know the apartness, the illimitable separation, what it was like to be without a Beam, without a Bunch—to be an Atom.

Could Joseph Prometheus Brooks, father of fingers on buttons and red telephones, be an Atom? An Atom just like that melancholy crew from Radioactive Island, like Tyrone from Philly, Abdul from Beirut, and those thousand G-fans wailing in the night? Yes. There was no question, Gojiro decided. After all, it took one to know one. Years ago, when he was a lonely mutant stuffed inside a foreign world, he cried for help across all time and tide. And then, from the mind of a Coma Boy came the words, "You have no friends? . . . I will be your friend!" Komodo came for him. Who, Gojiro wondered, would come for Joseph Prometheus Brooks?

But then the monster's mood shattered yet again. It was what Brooks said about that hot afternoon all those years ago, about the mistake he made, why forty-seven times the projected payload was still not enough. Because "He did not show His face."

He. *Him.*

On the Dishscreen they were showing the scene outside the Traj Taj again. "90 Series now!" a thousand G-fans shouted. "90 Series now!"

He pumped half of Hanford into his throbbing head, sought to seal himself up in the hardcuttin' 235's special glow. But it didn't work. No stupor was thick enough to keep him from looking at those monitors, to deflect the probe of Pro Brooks's stare. At least until he noticed that the worldshatterer wasn't in the position anymore. "Shit!" The monster fumbled with his fieldwork notes. "Subject's gaze alters . . ." Brooks's basic stance hadn't changed, but the trajectory of his gaze had lowered. He wasn't staring into that same spot of air above the Encrucijada. He was watching something straight ahead of him. Something getting closer all the time.

"Pull back! Give me a wider angle," the reptile screamed at the unresponsive monitor screens. But it didn't matter, because right then the Echo Man stepped forward into the picture.

It wasn't easy, measuring a mess of that shrink potion, shooting it on the run. But there was no time, he'd have to shrivel in stride. Back in that courtroom, the Echo Man's slick lawyers were obviously just stalling, trying to explain away their client's disappearance with that obvious fiction about a secret religious ceremony. As if they could have known, or cared, what Nelson Monongae was doing out in the middle of the Encrucijada, dressed in the same leathers—the Varanidid's leathers—he wore the night he met Leona Brooks all those years ago. And around his neck, that vial. The Echo Man had returned to the Valley to stand before Joseph Prometheus Brooks. Gojiro had to know why.

However, when the monster reached the Valley floor, the Echo Man was gone. There was only Brooks, back in his standard position, searching as always. If the Echo Man's presence had made a difference, the old scientist exhibited no evidence of it. "Where'd he go?" The reptile pivoted every vertebra, scanning the darkening horizon, but there was no sight of the Indian. "Shit, shit, shit!" he screamed, pounding his foreclaws into the hard sand.

Then, from the corner of his eye, Gojiro noticed the approaching tumbleweed. At first, it seemed just one of millions bouncing through the sagebrush. It wasn't until the thicket snagged against Brooks's leg and the old man tried to flick it off that the lizard saw the flat green object caught up inside. Again Brooks sought to free himself but still the tangle wouldn't move. Finally, he reached down, grabbed the snarl, examined it. Then he shoved his hand inside and pulled out the green item.

It was a book. A comic book . . . the *fumetti!* The story of Radioactive Island, saga of boy and lizard, lizard and boy. "A practical gift," an eloquent statement of the situation at hand; that was how Komodo had described the *fumetti* when he left the White Light Chamber to beg for Brooks's help in the solution of the Triple Ring Promise. Except it had blown out of Komodo's hands, whirled up into the cloudless sky, undelivered, until now.

Brooks started reading, thumbing through. There was no sound, no rush of sand, no insect's creak, nothing but Brooks's fingertips upon the yellowed

288

pages. Gojiro sat motionless, breath bated. He'd envisioned the *fumetti* as a corrective to Shig's purloined tracts. "The Truth—our version, at least!" he called it. But really, he wanted it to be more than that. He wanted it to be hopeful, as hopeful as Komodo was. That's why he'd insisted on that single shot of the two of them together, his monster's arm around his friend's shoulder, the two of them looking out to the unseen Cloudcover, brave, forthright. "To the future!" said the white balloon hooked to the reptile's mouth.

The reading was over now. Brooks closed the *fumetti,* let it drop to the ground. He was looking out again, but not as before. He was looking down, to the Encrucijada floor . . . his eyes sweeping over the sand . . . *as they had across Lavarock* . . . passing over every other animal and bush . . . *as he'd scanned the multitudes, a thousand zards, maybe more* . . . until he came to that shrunken lizard . . . *that youngest zardplebe* . . . Him. *Him and him alone.*

As Gojiro had felt Brooks's stare in his Dream, he felt it now.

Forty-seven times the payload! Still not enough!

Those dark eyes, boring in. The reptile turning, returning the stare.

Forty-seven times, still not enough . . . the job unfinished . . .

Man and Beast—their sightlines fused.

Then Brooks wasn't at his spot anymore. Nothing was there except that old *fumetti,* caught in the draft of a late-afternoon dust devil, rising upward, its pages detaching from their rusted staples, flying every whichway.

Brooks was running now, past the house, toward that decrepit shed. When Gojiro got there the old man was pulling away the wooden shutters from the door with a crowbar. He cut his hand, bright red blood deltaed across the stark white of his skin. But it didn't matter, he kept ripping at the pitted boards. Then he was inside, madly tossing objects from his path, kicking at old machine parts, tossing aside piles of ocher envelopes.

The blackboard! He was going for the blackboard.

Brooks stood in front of the equation he'd written so long before and spit. His saliva ran down the board, taking figures with it. He wiped away the rest with his sleeve. Gojiro felt it in his stomach. It was as if a carpet was pulled out from beneath his feet, sending him swirling to midair, a slow-motion somersault, and down below, no ground on which to land. "He killed the Heater, wiped it away."

The screeching started. Chalk on slate. A squeal of agony.

Brooks's hand moved like a ghost's. Numbers, vectors, variables settled upon the blackboard like a print in a photographer's solution, as if they'd been there all along, waiting only for the great worldshatterer to summon them to visibility.

Gojiro scrambled for an improved vantage point. The world was shifting; he struggled to memorize its new configuration.

Then Brooks stopped, regarded what he'd written: several lines of figures, a board full of symbols and signs. His hand returned to the board, drew an equal sign, paused again.

Gojiro swallowed.

But there was no last stroke. Instead, Brooks laughed. Loud. A boyish, rollicking kind of laugh. Then he dropped the chalk and walked out of the shed.

PART

FOUR

GODNOOSE

The noose had been tightening around Gojiro's neck ever since Komodo, tuckered and worn, made his way back to the White Light Chamber and saw those figures etched on the wall. "What is this, my own true friend," he inquired. "A gylph? A legend inscribed upon these forsaken walls by an unknown and neglected people?"

The monster did not remember writing it down. He hardly recalled any of what happened after he staggered, purblind, away from Joseph Prometheus Brooks's blackboard. Even now, those clawed gouges looked like chicken scratches left by a haywire polygraph, the sheet music of a mad Stone Age composer.

"Oh, that." He thought he'd make up a story, something about how if you locked enough monkeys inside a cave and gave them enough chisels, sooner or later they'd chip out a petrogram that resembled a scientific equation. But Komodo was already writing the numbers into his notebook, so the monster had no choice but to tell how Brooks erased the Heater's birth formula from his blackboard and wrote this new thing in its place.

Komodo sat down on a high stool, hunched over his tiny desk like a black-pajamaed crab, and, with the candlelight stretching shadow against the rugged Chamber wall, went to work. "Spectacular deduction," he purred, his fingers hot and light over the calculator keys. "Magnificent induction." Every vector, each differential was cause for celebration. For Komodo, to commune with the elegant mentality of Joseph Prometheus Brooks was pure ecstasy. He took special pleasure in the fact that the old scientist hadn't finished the equation, that for some mysterious reason the right-hand side of the equal sign had been left blank. It seemed an invitation, an opportunity for collaboration.

However, as the pile of crumpled paper grew beneath his dangling feet, Komodo's mood changed. The deeper he delved into the labyrinthine intricacies of the formula, the more he felt himself surrounded by an arbitrary, chaotic violence. Far from the quiet certitude he'd expected, a serene landscape where Ideas might reveal themselves wholescale, as immaculate as Bach, the terrain of Joseph Brooks's thought seemed afflicted, demon-ridden. The swell of tortured calculations threatened to consume Komodo, drown him in a sea of cinder.

"I believe it to be a vacuum problem of some type," the haggard Japanese finally said, after twenty-four straight hours of deliberation. "A nuclear vacuum problem on a massive scale . . . the dimensions are enormous."

"Super," Gojiro grunted. "An Electrolux to intake Texas. Where you gonna get replacement bags for the sucker? If Brooks thinks he can go door-to-door with that, he better get himself some encyclopedias."

Komodo only resumed his math, murmuring of sorption, torrs, and thermosublimation pumps.

Then: "Nothing."

"What?"

"Again . . . nothing." Komodo's voice was full of anguish. He slammed his fist down onto the desk.

"Nothing what?"

"Nothing! Nothing at all. My sum . . . I continually arrive at nothing. Zero."

"Zero?" The monster shifted his weight.

"Nothing. Everything is dispersed. Obliterated." Komodo leaned back in his chair. His eyes were sinkholes, his face ridged with lines as deep as Baikal.

"But that's not possible. Matter can never be created or destroyed—that's the Law, ain't it?"

"Yes," Komodo said, his voice low, dazed. "Physics teaches us of the indestructibility of matter. Yet Mr. Brooks appears to attempt the repeal of this dictum."

"Who does he think he is? There's always got to be *something* left over."

Something left over . . . For Komodo and Gojiro, the concept went beyond any temporal weight and measure. It was basic to all they believed. After all, they'd both been besieged by the Heater's holocaust, had everything they ever knew taken from them, yet had managed to survive; however altered, they were *left over*. This was the essence of the Continuum; even in the face of absolute annihilation, something would remain, even if it was nothing more than a single pair of cells. For from a single pair of cells, a whole new world can arise.

But now, facing the emptiness beyond the equal sign of Joseph Prometheus Brooks's equation, Komodo appeared lost, without direction. "I see nothing here."

"Don't get pent-up. I must've remembered it wrong," the reptile offered. "You know, inverted when I should of diverted, botched a variable. I could go back, check it again."

Komodo bit his lip. "No. Mr. Brooks's logic is difficult but inexorable. These are the correct factors. The fault must lie with me. I have blundered somehow. What a fool I was to presume I might make sense of Mr. Brooks's work."

"Hey! You ever stop to think that maybe *he* got it wrong? That maybe the great Brooks has lost a step, gone south in a leaky seabag? Look at the guy, standing there in the hot sun. Some genius!"

Komodo didn't even hear Gojiro. "I must find a solution to this problem. Suddenly, I fear *everything* is at stake."

That clinched it, Komodo using that same exact expression as Joseph Brooks had thirty-six hours earlier, with Grives and Stiller. *"He will show His face when everything is at stake."* Brooks's phrase throbbed through the Quadcameral, brought a deeper winter to the monster's blood. With that objective in mind, what else could the worldshatterer's equation add up to? "Nothing!" Each time Komodo said the word Gojiro felt a deeper winter in his blood, another gallows trapdoor opening beneath his feet.

It was insane. For years the monster had railed against what he labeled Shig's "master plot." Stealing the movies, corrupting the Cosmo, distributing the Crystal Contacts, the culminating invention of the 90 Series—to Gojiro, it was all directed to a single goal. "He's got me fitted for the Fallgod, some bogus Eye in the Sky," the reptile charged, teetering beneath the weight of those unremitting supplications. Shig's motive was revenge—a relentless program of retribution to make him pay for what happened to Kishi out by the Cloudcover. At least that's what Gojiro always supposed. But what was happening now was beyond anything even Shig could conjure. This was a load no Atlas could carry.

The conspiracy was huge, multi-angled, a vast entrapment aimed at hustling him into a singular, unwanted destiny. That Beam—if he was correct in calling it that—was part of it. A key cog! Because: if it was a Beam, then where was the Bunch?

"Beams for Bunches, Bunches for Beams"—wasn't that Cosmo's copacetic combo, Budd Hazard's Inviolate Binary? Wasn't that the clarion with which Lavarock Initiates summoned themselves to the Molt, so they might "whirl from the First day to the Last, to Attach ourselves to What We Are." It was supposed to be paradigmatic—each one everyone, everyone each, a Line integrated in body and soul, indivisible, a fabulous collective. But what happened when that so-called Beam entered Gojiro's head? Sure, he'd spun back through every eon, but throughout those repeated passages, had he ever felt the succoring commonality of the group? Had he ever—through the nightmare visions of Sauric death, the muggings by furball marauders, or even during the relatively sedate eras of basking and burrowbuilding—felt himself woven into the magnificent tapestry of the Zardic Bunch? The answer was no. Not for a single moment. All the way back to that bizarre egg his existence remained unique, apart. Everything he did was as a loner, a solitary figure.

A Beam for him and him alone? One of a kind? What sort of hand was that to play across the boundless reach of Time?

But who really was to blame? Once he'd railed against the sapiens' "malignant megalomania," warned how their steroid-puffed self-esteem threatened to split the seams of the Magnificent Matrix. "We call their sin Stallonism because they delight in inventing wholly specious cosmologies with themselves at the self-aggrandizing center," he'd preached. Now, however, that rectitude soured in the harsh light of his own Ptolemaic hallucination. It reminded him of something old Jung once said, how just because flying saucers turned up on radar scans it didn't mean they actually existed. Rather, the wily Swiss suggested, the signal was a product of the *psychic desire* of those who so ardently wished to see something in the sky; their longing, coalesced in a single spot in the heavens, became palpable and therefore detectable by electronic means. Gojiro had always scoffed at such notions, but now he wondered. Although not about those yearners on the ground. He thought about the imaginary saucer itself. Did that incorporeal disc appear on those blipping screens through a sheer craving to be seen?

With each new thought the nightmare grew: the unshakable sense that somehow he'd rigged it, wished the whole thing into existence, that he was caught in his own trap.

Gojiro

That night on Dead Letter Hill, when Billy Snickman's supplication came into his head . . . what made him answer as he did? What could have possessed him to announce himself as "the Bridger of Gaps, Linker of Lines—*Defender of the Evolloo*"? The monster didn't know. He'd never known.

Behind him, he could hear Komodo still wrestling with Joseph Prometheus Brooks's equation. "The vacuum properties create a medium of artificially induced excitation of molecular bonding, thereby stimulating excessive transmutation . . ."

Lost in thought, the monster paid little attention to these arcane murmurs. However, Komodo was soon yelling, his voice a mix of discovery and terror. "Why, it's remarkable. Incredible!"

Gojiro looked up warily.

Komodo was sweating. "Of course, it seems highly unlikely that Mr. Brooks could have intended his formula to read in such a manner, but it appears to speak quite specifically to the question of Reprimordialization, pertaining to the overstimulation of mutation. Why, if this equation was enacted at the proportions Mr. Brooks cites, it would institute . . ."

Komodo stepped back from his paper-strewn desk, his face the color of sulphur. "My own true friend, according to my calculations, if Mr. Brooks's formula was to be brought to fruition, it would usher in an All-Inclusive Crisis of the Evolloo!"

Once the phrase left Komodo's mouth, Gojiro knew his friend had solved Joseph Prometheus Brooks's equation. An All-Inclusive Crisis of the Evolloo— what else could put *everything* at stake? An All-Inclusive Crisis, that was game. Endgame.

The idea had come up years ago, in the midst of a desultory post–Glazed Days Budd Hazard session. "As the Muse has indicated, 'Change is Crisis, Crisis is Change—all Change is Risk,'" Komodo said, holding forth in his academic mode. "But let us try to place this koan in the context of Reprimordialization. After all, are not great risks incurred each time there is a reconnection of Bunch to Beam? That is the drama of the Reprimordial Instant—the Throwforward's heroic journey into that realm where Eternal Equations switch from $P + AT = I$ to $P = I$ and back again. The renewal of Life always carries the possibility of its dissolution—as we have seen in the Zoo of Shame, not all Bunches can be assured of continued existence, at least in the form to which they are accustomed. Molecular bonds can be torn asunder, atoms flung from configuration. This is the Crisis of Change. And, if the Evolloo is to be thought of as one encompassing symbiotic entity, then a Crisis for one Bunch must be considered a Crisis for All. So we see that the Evolloo is composed of a great chain reaction of such Crises—risks—and that in this eternal cycle, we may find the engine of Life."

The monster sat back, snorted. "Okay, sure. But suppose every Bunch in the world goes into Reprimordial Crisis at the same time. Then what happens? Don't that overload things, blow out the systems?"

Komodo grimaced. "An interesting thought, my own true friend. Change unbalanced by stasis becomes discord. If every single Bunch was to enter the Reprimordial realm simultaneously, it is possible that a measureless entropy could be unleashed, mortally wounding existence as we understand it. Yet this potentiality must be considered exceedingly remote. Amid the infinity of Creation, there are uncountable Bunches fusing with an equally uncountable number of Beams. Each of these units operates according to its own autonomous agenda, its own separate Reprimordial schedule. Therefore, I believe, the dilemma you describe is all but precluded by probability."

"But it *could* happen, right? All Bunches could go into risk behavior at the same time, therefore affecting all Beams. It could be an All-Inclusive Crisis of the Evolloo. I ain't saying it's *gonna* happen, but we're making Cosmo, right? And who ever heard of a Cosmo without a last-things scenario? Everywhere you look they got apocalypin' Rongaraks, a hundred blue-in-the-face, multi-armed exterminators. Them seven seals been barking for so long, someone ought to throw 'em a fish already. I'm talking story here—beginning, middle, end. You got to think of the symmetry of the thing. What's wrong with an All-Inclusive Crisis of the Evolloo? It'll round everything out a bit."

Komodo swallowed deeply. "An end to the Endless Flow? This is a shocking idea, difficult to accept. Something impossibly polluted . . . unthinkable."

"It's *supposed* to be unthinkable," the monster smirked.

Now, however, inside the White Light Chamber, Gojiro could hear Komodo softly weeping. How piteous! To witness the mourning for an innocent vision of a world without end. The reptile couldn't take it, tried to immerse himself in the Dish. But there was only Brooks, searching as always, in the center of the Encrucijada. Except he looked different, somehow more relaxed, as if his urgent seeking had been replaced by a patient expectancy.

Gojiro lashed out a foot, smashed it into those Philcos and Admirals, got the outside transmission back. With any luck at all he would have picked up a hockey game, or maybe a marathon of heavy metal videos. But there were only G-fans.

"The PA and the 90 Series are one," a dough-faced 'tile-o-file announced to a reporter.

"PA?"

"Personal Appearance, man. The PA is the 90 Series made flesh."

Made flesh . . . the monster's head rolled back. You know you're in deep when they start restructuring the standardized millennials into fresh syn-thotext. By what manner did his would-be flock presume he'd satisfy this PA? Did they want him to show up at the mall, sit at a bridge table, sign autographs?

Things were out of control, going by themselves. They kept showing that overhead shot of the Insta-Envir, commenting on the "bizarre pattern." It was bizarre, all right; the way he saw himself posed, vigilant, in deep mantis stance, Gojiro might as well have been looking at one of the Atoms' potholders. Except that this was no foot-square rag easily held in a single claw. It was real size, an image sculpted into the Insta-Envir, visible only from above, as if it were the work of a wretched agri-tribe trying to catch heaven's eye. In all taxonomic history, there was no record of the Insta-Envir simply *growing* like that.

Luckily, it was at that point that the dishscreen unhinged its vertical hold once more. When it came back, "Mister Ed" was on. That prattling gluepot! Once, under the banner "Down with Dolittle and Frances too," Gojiro had declared war on the chatty palomino, along with every other talking animal. "A Dom plot!" he blustered. "Who are they to stuff delicatessen slang in the mouths of chewy equines?" Now, however, the reptile gave thanks at the sight of the wheedling nag. Mister Ed was having trouble reading the fine print on an insurance policy, prompting his keeper to suggest he wear glasses. Vain, Mister Ed refused. "Contact lenses, Wilbur!" he kept demanding in his anthro-implanted baritone.

"Some funny shit on here," Gojiro shouted to the bereft Komodo. "Really! It'll cheer you up. Haw, haw, haw."

A moment later, the reptile felt a presence at his shoulder. He thought Komodo had stopped his sobbing and come over to laugh about a horse who wanted contact lenses. But it wasn't Komodo. It was Shig.

"A package has arrived," he said stonily. Freshly turned out in crisp white linens, showing no sign of his wounds, the austere boy stood next to a steel-mesh shopping cart. Inside was a squarish object covered in coarse burlap. "It came to the former residence, brought there by one Ms. Wilma Crenshaw, mother of Trumaine, controller of Gojiro Crystal Contact Radio #2766669. She had been holding this parcel in trust for Mr. Komodo."

The monster rose, slackjawed, and looked down at the package in Shig's cart. A handwritten note was pasted to the side. "Keep for Yuke the Nuke."

Komodo nervously cut through the burlap with his pocketknife. Inside was a steel gray square, a foot and half around. Komodo stepped back, wiped his brow.

"It is the box! The one Walter wished me to have that night! The one that fell into the surf!"

Eyes big, Komodo reached into the cart. But the cube was too heavy. It slipped from his grasp, just as it had all those years before as he lay across the bow of that Korean's fishing boat. "Oh, no!" The box crashed to the Chamber floor, cracked open.

Gojiro was aghast. "Shit! It broke!"

"That is only the casing," Shig said sharply.

Then they heard the sound of metal scraping across the stone floor. A rounded piece had come loose from the box and was rolling on its edge.

It stopped right at Komodo's feet. He picked it up. It was round, three concentric circles welded together by a thin connecting rod. Komodo grasped the metal bands, held them up in front of his face. Then, without speaking, he ripped open the top of his black pajamas, exposing his hairless chest and the three rings emblazoned on it. He laid the metal circles over them.

"My own true friend!"

INSIDE THE BOX

The Triple Rings!

Komodo and Gojiro were struck dumb. Could that cracked cube sitting on the White Light Chamber's killing floor actually be the wellspring of their Promise?

"Looks like an art deco boom box," Gojiro nonplussed.

"A radio of some type, certainly. Here is the speaker." Komodo probed the malleable surface stretched across one side of the lead parcel. The mesh was blackened, fire-singed. At its center, like a negative's shadow, lay the bleached outline of three concentric circles. Komodo picked up the metal rings he'd held to the scars on his chest, pushed them against the mysterious markings. They aligned. "These rings appear to have been originally constructed as a decorative grillework for this machine."

"Grillework . . . geez." The monster had never let on, but blazing those concentrics onto his own chest had been no simple grin-and-bear waterfront tattoo job. He never felt a thing, of course, but the look and smell—the charring leathers, the curl of branded flesh—it was all he could do not to shout out, faint dead away. How then could it have been for Komodo, who had no two-inch-thick hide, no pony express ride between nerve endings? Mercifully, Komodo did not recall. He recollected almost nothing prior to the moment in Okinawa when Gojiro's voice came into his head. All the rest was lost to him, blotted out and gone.

"We must get inside," Komodo said breathlessly, pulling a longstemmed

301

screwdriver from the pocket of his black pajamas. "We must see what is within."

"Yeah, within . . ." A foreboding overcame Gojiro as he watched Komodo work to loosen the rusted screws. If the contents of that box were to be a revelation, suddenly the monster had no desire to witness it. What a foul, incognizant thing he had become, he thought, fighting the urge to turn away. It didn't seem so very long ago that he wished only for more perfect eyes to lead him about a world where there was ever more to see. That was when unknowing was polemically equated with slumber, and lethargy a sin. But those days were long since past; now Sominex was the only shot the reptile craved. Sheila Brooks had the right idea with those blinder glasses, he thought. After all, what was the big bitch against repression? Repression seemed one of the singular triumphs of so-called civilization. Why should anyone be so concerned about where they'd been? Did they suppose it was less dreary than where they were going? Memory's an elephant in the china shop, only amnesiacs are truly free, the lizard thought, stewing that funky chestnut about not forgetting history so as not to repeat it. It was exactly the opposite. In a world paralyzed by dumb choice, to remember an event was likely to imbue it with the force of a self-fulfilling prophecy. Let sleeping traumas lie, that's my motto, Gojiro decided.

Komodo was grunting now. He had a wrench, had braced himself with his foot, was pulling like Dr. Pain, and later for the Novocaine. What was next? A jackhammer? Depth charges? The monster was assaulted by a fresh attack of doubt. Opening the box suddenly seemed profane, a spiritual suicide. Weren't the Triple Rings the spokespinning hub of their creaking conception of the Wheel of Life? Didn't they represent the perimeter of Cosmo's last stand, the arc of wagons pulled tight against the Unknown's remorseless reclamation? The Triple Rings were Symbol, encoded by an anonymous author, their origin lost in the primal mists, untouchable, immune to despoiling consciousness. That was how it was! How it had to remain! What was Komodo doing, opening that box? What was he hoping to prove? Why not just dig up Christ's Cross, rip it from its place inside a billion souls, slat it to a suburban deck? Wood's wood, right?

But what choice was there? That box was sitting there on the White Light Chamber floor, tangible in all dimensions. It couldn't simply be ignored, turned into a planter or smallish coffee table. This was the very object Walter Crenshaw deemed so crucial that he dragged it into the surf that night on Okinawa. "Take this," Walter screamed even as the MP boats approached. "You got to have this!" For years Walter carried the box around, protected it in cheap hotel rooms against shivs, zipguns, and worse. Walter believed in this box. He held it apart from Stiller and the rest, let them drive him mad rather than reveal its location. He made it his legacy, entrusted it to Wilma and Trumaine. There was no way Gojiro could turn his back on that.

"Uhhh," Komodo strained as he slid off the top of the box, sending it clattering onto the floor. He hovered there for a moment, not speaking.

"So?"

Komodo's incredulity turned to excitement. "Amazing! It is a transmitter and receiver of the crystalline type. Yes . . . a crystal-based radio . . . with four distinct elements . . . Oh, my God."

A haiku occurs, about a painter of perfect pictures who is never happy because none of these pictures was the one he wanted to make. The painter dies, made crazy by the painting he never could paint.

So often Gojiro feared that might be Komodo's fate. For years the monster watched his friend toil over the beakers and bunsens, only to turn crestfallen, proclaiming his beautiful creations to be worthless, having "no business being invented." What woe it was to think that the one invention Komodo really wanted to make was the one that remained beyond his reach. Yet here, down in that forlorn White Light Chamber, Komodo was pointing at a water-damaged box and whooping Eureka! "Finally! After all these years!"

"Lemme see!" The lizard lurched forward. It figured, he exulted. He and Komodo were in the biggest of fixes, that Amendment's razored pendulum swinging low above their heads like a not-so-sweet chariot—and who comes up with the last-second save by the railroad tracks? Walter! Walter Crenshaw, Pfc.! This was some kind of high-five from beyond the grave, okay.

Drawing a breath, Gojiro peered into the battered box. Immediately, elation became confusion. "Wait a minute, this ain't nothing but a couple of corroded connections. It looks like a Crystal Contact Radio. In fact . . . it *is* a Crystal Contact Radio! A crappy old Crystal Contact Radio."

Komodo's joy continued. "So many times I imagined this very device, and now here it is: all I ever hoped to attain."

"A Crystal Contact?" Gojiro was enraged. To have his hopes dashed like this was near to unbearable.

Komodo was weeping. "At last . . ."

"It's the Rings," Gojiro sputtered, "seeing the Rings. Yeah, that's what got to you. You're just bonked, strung out, too excited."

"No!" Komodo shouted.

"No?" The uncharacteristic vehemence in Komodo's retort took Gojiro by surprise. For a moment he felt like grabbing his friend's head, bouncing it off the steely box. "But this is a goddamn Crystal Contact Radio, the same shit Shig sent out all over the world to drive me insane! You said so yourself—they didn't have any business being invented!"

"This is different!"

"Don't look no different to me. How do you know it's different? You ain't done no schematic, no shakedown. It's a Crystal Contact. A five-dollar hustle, like a million others!"

Again, Komodo did not appear to hear the reptile. "Walter must have known . . . Somehow he knew . . ."

"Knew what?" Gojiro's brain was too-tensing, seizing up. "What? What did Walter know?"

Komodo opened his mouth, was about to say something, but the reptile never heard it. For it was right then that the whooshing Beam once again invaded the Quadcameral.

"Ohh . . ." Gojiro moaned as he felt himself beginning to be thrown back through time. He staggered about the White Light Chamber. The last thing he saw was that box, closer and closer. He fell right onto it, its sharp corner crashing through his parietal.

It started like always. He was hooked and yanked, slingshotted headlong through innumerable diurnals, as many nocturnals, back through the increasingly familiar blur of bygones and bygones. Zam went the mastodons, zim went the sabertooths. Good-bye Cenozooey . . . hello Mes-o-zo!

When Gojiro opened his eyes, however, he wasn't one step ahead of an encroaching glacier or in a Sauric killing field. He was on a lush hillside, beside the bluest lake, before a towering mountain capped with snow gleaming like diamonds. Stretched out below was a magnificent City.

"Smile!" someone called.

Straight ahead of him, Gojiro saw a man focusing a camera, his face obscured beneath a black cloth. What kind of double-wirecross was this? That crazy Beam had catapulted him into the Opening Sequence!

But right then Gojiro heard, "My own true friend, can this truly be happening?" Komodo? What was he doing here?

"Smile!" the cameraman said again. Then he emerged from the dark cowl, started forward. The monster gasped. The man—a Jap!—was running toward him, reaching out to straighten his school tie, telling him to look into the camera. And on the other side of him, Gojiro heard the soft rustle of satin. The monster turned to the sound . . .

But he was carried away, moving again . . . to a field of brown grass. "Look!" Komodo's voice again!

The man who'd taken the picture was in the field, pulling a cart over the rough terrain. In the cart was a leaden gray box . . . the same box with Triple Ring grille that sat even then upon the floor of the White Light Chamber, its corner jammed into the reptile's head! The man pulled the cart into a grove of trees beside a river. He stopped, plugged in a wire, and began speaking into a microphone.

"Come in, birds! Come in, trees! Come in, snakes! Come in, sky! Inishiro Komodo calling. Please come in! Inishiro Komodo calling. I am human. I wish to speak with you, for you to tell me of your lives. We are all alive in this world! Come in, please!"

Gojiro heard Komodo's voice, all welled-up. "My own true friend . . . it is my father."

The picture scrambled, reassembled in a small bamboo house. The man Komodo said was his father was standing beside a young woman wearing a maroon kimono. Gojiro didn't have to be told who she was. Her skin was fair, like a china plate, her hair jet black. They were huddled together, Komodo's mother and father, clutching each other. There was a crash. That box! It was falling, knocked from a wooden table, hitting the floor.

"Talking to birds again! Dreamer!" It was a man in a uniform, screaming. He was squat, strong, terrifying. Behind him were more soldiers, rifles cocked and ready. "You have not been at work! The war grows more difficult every day. Japan needs aircraft."

Komodo's father drew himself up to his full six foot height. He was young, proud, indomitable. "I am a scientist. I struggle forward accordingly. My work is for the living, all that have lived, all that will live."

"I remember . . . I remember this." It was Komodo talking. Just as the monster had been inside the far-off heads of a thousand supplicants, their distant troubles suddenly becoming his own, the process was repeating with Komodo. He saw through Komodo's eyes, the eyes of a child cowering in the corner of a paper house.

The soldier hit Komodo's father, drove him down to the floor with a wooden stick.

"You can beat me, but I will not give up my search! I will not make planes for men to die in. I dedicate myself to Life!"

The soldier hit Komodo's father again. His mother's screams filled the room. Gojiro could hear his friend crying. And crying.

They were moving again. Gojiro could feel it, that decisive closing push.

Darkness now. Tears and darkness. Screams and tears.

Thump . . . thump . . . thump . . .

"Mom!" Gojiro sceamed. He was inside that egg again!

Thump . . . thump . . . thump . . .

"Mom!" Hatching out! Coming alive . . . burrowing upward . . . to the light! Except he wasn't alone. Someone else was bursting from the same egg, the two of them hatching out together, straining toward the light.

"MOM!" Did he hear an answer? Finally, an answer? An affirmation? His own mother, answering his call?

But it wasn't his mother. It was Komodo's—his mother's screams and tears. And his father, shouting too, exhorting her. Their faces came into view, blurry, wet. Then, clearer.

And there was a cry. "Waaaa!"

"My own true friend!" Gojiro heard Komodo shout. "I am being born!"

"Waaaa!" It was the Freshout Cry, Komodo's Freshout Cry!

And, at that exact instant, that lizard burst through, saw light.

"Waaaa!" Gojiro heard that same cry he'd heard before, the beginning bleat of a tiny lizard, sixty-six million years ago.

"My own true friend, we are being born together!"

A lizard and a boy, who so longed to merge themselves, had finally succeeded. A lizard and a boy were born, sixty-six million years apart, yet together. "Waaaa!" The sound of their Freshout Cries converged into a common squawk, a harmony across all Time.

Gojiro

* * *

But then they were being pushed again. Forward this time.

To that hillside, beside that lake, with a gleaming snowcapped mountain behind. Now, however, that hum was in the sky. The hum that becomes a buzz. A drone, a dull gnash, a ripping, tearing sound. But it wasn't the same . . . no. The boy's eyes don't go up.

Remember? . . . in the Opening Sequence, how the Mother and Father stand still, looking ahead, smiling, never knowing? *(He worked on it for days!)* But the Boy's eyes go—up into the sky?

Well, that's not how it was, not this time. This time it's the Boy whose eyes stay straight ahead, smiling, never knowing. The Dad's the one who peers up into the sky, sees the Superfortress. Then he turns back to the Mom, and they both put their hands on the Boy's shoulders . . . the Boy, smiling, never knowing.

Then they were running by that same brook where Komodo's father tried to talk to every other living thing in the universe, carrying the boy in their arms. They ran into their house, pulled aside a straw mat, threw open a roundish trapdoor.

The boy was crying now, holding his mother tight. She grimaced, gripped his body, held him away from her. Her arms were thin but strong. "My son," she said. "Someday, in another world, perhaps you will succeed where we have failed. Long be your line, my sweetest son."

Then the rope was around Komodo's waist and he was going down into the hole. It was like a well, narrow and deep. Round and round Komodo went, down and down. It was like looking into the opposite end of a telescope, his mother and father growing smaller in the pool of light above. Then he heard a scraping sound and that light began to disappear, like the waning crescent of the moon.

"Parents!" Komodo shouted when his feet touched bottom. "I do not understand!"

"Take this," came his father's voice as he lowered that gray box into the hole. "You must have this." Then he slid the lid across, closed the trapdoor on top of it.

And the monster shook, because it was like being in that egg again, smoothsided and complete. Except it was not an egg. It was a crypt, black and sightless, and there was no sound of a mother's heart. There was no sound at all, save the hum. Which became a buzz . . . and a drone . . .

Roar and heat. A world splitting in half.

Then Komodo saw the front of his father's box begin to glow, three rings—the Triple Rings—unthinkably incandescent, coming toward him, a screaming target.

A MUTANT'S GAMBLE

The tourniquet inside the monster's head squeezed, dripped fluid. But then, all at once, the gauzed layers of lament, the swaddled sorrows, gave way. In his tortured sleep, an escape route appeared. After all, what did Joseph Prometheus Brooks's equation *really* boil down to? What was it but a few chalk strokes written on a blackboard by a man long ago adjudged to be dead and buried?

"We can erase it!" the monster screamed, rousing himself. "Plugpull that All-Inclusive Crisis. Blot it out. What the Continuum don't know can't hurt it, right?"

Komodo, however, never heard Gojiro. He was over at the other end of the White Light Chamber busy with the Fayetteville Tree. It was quite a scene, too, the twelve-foot-tall bottled tree sitting on that floodlit scaffolding, a gangliatic web of multihued filaments pasted to its glass sides. Komodo was climbing a ladder that leaned against the Fayetteville container, a royal blue velvet pillow balanced on his outstretched palm. In the middle of the pillow lay a single inch-long golden capsule. At the top of the ladder, Komodo picked up the highly glossed oval and inspected it. Then, in a lightning motion, he opened the top of the jar, dropped the pellet in, slammed the lid tight.

Gojiro recognized that goldplated pill, remembered the day, not so very many years before, when it rolled up onto the beach at Spandex Shore, one of several set inside an elaborate handworked snuffbox. Game for any drug, he was about to submit the pellets to his raging gastros when Komodo stopped him, pointing at the ornate funeral robes that had washed up along with the case.

"Arsenic," the prudent Japanese said after opening the curious latching seal at the top of each capsule and performing chemical analysis. "Odd . . . such a strong poison inside a pill of twenty-four-karat gold." The riddle was solved by a note found inside the case. It explained that the pills were once the property of Lieutenant Yajima, a flyer in the war, a kamikaze. Yajima's great-uncle, a metallurgist by trade, concocted them "in veneration" of his nephew; in the event that he failed in his mission, the young flyer was to ingest the poison to avoid the "shame of living." However, Yajima was blown off course and crash-landed on a small island inhabited by people who nursed him back to health, therein creating what the airman called "an inextricable tangle of obligation." To commit suicide would be a hideous affront to his gracious hosts, but how could he go back on his oath to die? He cast the pills into the sea, Yajima wrote, "in hopes that others can die with the honor I find lacking in myself."

Gojiro always figured Komodo destroyed the pellets—passed on their offer, so to speak—yet there he was, tossing one into the Fayetteville Tree bottle. The reaction was next to immediate. The chickadees, 122 wholly separate genophenic groups according to the last Bunchic census, lingered momentarily in quickly dissipating afterimage, then were gone. Gojiro's jaw dropped. It didn't make sense. If Komodo had, for whatever non-sequiturous reason, picked this time to sharpen the sleight-of-hand he sometimes utilized to pacify the more unruly Atoms, you'd figure he'd experiment on one of those pathetic Zoo of Shame creatures Shig had insisted on bringing into the White Light Chamber. Why didn't Komodo dematerialize that mopey dodo, then bring him back as the daffiest of ducks swinging in a Napoleon suit from a chandelier? What was he doing messing with the Fayetteville Tree, center of all Reprimordial research?

"Hey, what's up?" the monster croaked, his throat dry.

Komodo turned quickly. "Oh, my own true friend, you are awake."

"Yeah, I'm awake. The trick's great, but why don't you bring them birds back now, okay? Gives me the willies, looking at that empty jar."

"Well . . . you see . . ." Komodo sputtered.

Like a plexuskick, the monster got the picture. "Oh, shit!" he screamed, bolting toward the vacant vessel, pushing his snout to the cool glass. "Chickadees? You in there, chickadees? Oh, no . . . they're gone. Completely gone. Nothing is left, *nothing at all.*"

Komodo did not answer, only looked away.

Gojiro dropped onto the hindlegs, slammed the White Light Chamber floor with balled claws. "BROOKS'S EQUATION . . . YOU DID IT!"

Sure, there'd been times through the years when they'd roughhouse, roll around on the 'cano floor, but that was all. It wasn't until right then that real violence came so close.

"Just couldn't leave well enough alone, huh?" the monster seethed, stalking forward, a fire in his brain. "It wasn't but a doodle, scribbles on a slate. It could've stayed like that forever, at least until the termites ate through. But no! You had to intervene. What's the matter, couldn't resist the itch? Technically too-sweet for you?"

Komodo edged away. "My own true friend. Please listen, it was necessary to understand—"

Gojiro lashed out a foreclaw, the breeze of which was enough to knock Komodo down. "I should've known. Once a Dom, always a Dom. Never trust a sapien, no matter the patter!"

"It was imperative to demonstrate the equation within a closed environment."

"Criminal! Hypocrite!" The monster launched a bolt of Radi-Breath, shearing off a chunk of the Chamber wall. "You're no better than a whitecoat spinal fractionator!"

"There was no other way. I had to determine the potentiality of comprehensive Permanent Dispersal—"

"Permanent Dispersal? That's a good one! Peddle your techno-euphemisms somewhere else. You iced those chickadees! Zapped 'em! And why? For what? You loved those stupid birds."

Komodo was standing behind the vacant Fayetteville container now. "Yes. I loved those birds. What I did can never be forgiven. It was a terrible transgression, a sin against Life. But there was no choice. Our Promise is paramount, it must be fulfilled, no matter the cost."

"Leave our Promise out of this." Through the jar's thick glass, Gojiro saw Komodo smile. It was crazy. Komodo, who'd been known to break down at the sight of a wounded aphid, had just synthesized a means to the world's end, used it to murder his cherished Fayetteville chickadees—and he was smiling his ass off. It took the baleful wind out of the reptile's sails, that smile. "What have you got to be so cheery about?"

"I am sorry, my own true friend, but I cannot help myself. It is just that my heart is so filled with joy and anticipation. Our future has never been brighter."

"You're out of your mind. Our future is all used up."

"That is not so. Do you not sense how close we are? It is almost as if we can reach out and touch Identity even now. Oh, my own true friend, to have traveled with you back through all history, to days beyond remembering, to witness images seen and unseen, to peer into the very soul of the Evolloo itself. The sound of our own two Freshout Cries becoming one, two entities springing from a single source. Is this not what we have always sought? A Beam! A confluence of souls, a common beginning, a conduit to a New World!"

The behemoth sat down, hung his head.

Komodo went toward his friend, his arms outstretched. "Have we not been guided, as if by an invisible, benevolent hand, to this place and time? Why else would we have journeyed to this strange Valley, if not to fulfill our solemn Vow, to become who we truly are. For it is only here, my own true friend, that a shy and frightened reptile might rise to become a Bridger of Gaps, a Linker of Lines, Nexus of Beam and Bunch . . . *the Defender of the Evolloo!*"

The monster buried his head in his claws. "So . . . you know."

"Yes. Now."

"About Dead Letter Hill, about Billy Snickman . . . and all that?"

"Yes. All of it. Everything is in the Beam."

The monster began sobbing. "Shit, I'm sorry. I knew I shouldn't have lied, shouldn't have kept it from you. It was a terrible thing to do. But . . ."

Komodo held the reptile. "Do not apologize, my own true friend. Destiny is a daunting thing. We cannot be sure if it is something we create for ourselves, or whether it is thrust upon us. But we must acknowledge that it is unavoidable."

Gojiro was wailing now, his tears flying. "Yeah, but what am I supposed to do? How am I supposed to bridge gaps, link lines, nexus Beams and Bunches? I mean, this is me. *Me!*" The monster grabbed hold of his saggiest leathers, pulled them away from his body. "Me, a skel of a zard! A cinematic charlatan, scared of a sludgicle's shadow . . . bogus to the bone. How am I supposed to be this . . . *God* thing everyone wants me to be?"

Komodo peered into the emptiness of the Fayetteville jar, did not speak.

"Look at that, man," Gojiro despaired. "Not one chickadee left, not a single one. You said it yourself—Permanent Dispersal. We're talking about an All-Inclusive Crisis of the Evolloo here, for chrissakes. How can you stand in the way of that kind of Power?"

When Komodo turned toward Gojiro again, he had *that look* on his face—the glowing optimism that sheared through every doubt. "Think of that song Budd Hazard once sang: 'To find Identity, you've got to jump into the Mystery.'"

Gojiro shook his head. "Cosmo. That's just Cosmo—dreams and illusions percolated by a lizard and a boy on some unknown Island. You still don't get it, do you? We're not walking the broad beaches of Corvair Bay now, we're in some awful hole in the ground, beneath the Sunbelt's sprawl. Up there they got George Jones on the radio. They drive to shopping malls, try to balance their checkbooks, and if they don't, the bank comes and takes the doublewide. This ain't our world. It never has been, never will be. You can't jump into a Mystery that ain't *your* Mystery."

Komodo's eyes widened. "What else can we do? There is no other path for us but to rush toward Identity. Our Promise demands it."

Gojiro backed away, horror on his face. "You'd risk the world to fulfill the Triple Ring Promise? That's crazy . . . a madman's gamble, a mutant's gamble."

"But my own true friend, is it not a gamble every time a Throwforward answers the call of the pheromone, each time a Bunch attempts Reprimordialization? All Change is a gamble. Budd Hazard says, 'Change is Crisis, Crisis is Change.' Does it not follow that the greatest of Crises offers the greatest Change?"

At that point, Komodo appeared about ready to restate, with a forthrightness that was his alone, his allegiance to the halcyon Universal, to once again assert his trust that an Idea born in the minds of a lizard and boy inside a forlorn volcano might indeed resonate around the globe. But he never got there. He began to tremble, pressed his palms to his cheeks.

"What's the matter? You all right?"

Komodo grew rigid. "Ms. Brooks is approaching! I must go to her!"

Komodo never said another word, not good-bye, nothing. He just left, as if seized by an invisible, undeniable force. It was the pheromone that took him, Gojiro knew. He'd seen it happen a hundred times in his dreams of Lavarock, the way Initiates would simply drop whatever they were doing, heed the summoning. That was how Komodo went, involuntary, like Prewire.

So, again, Gojiro was alone inside that White Light Chamber. He thought of the last time Komodo went to Sheila Brooks, left him there. "Be *Gojiro,*" Komodo said then. "Be *Gojiro,* then you won't be afraid."

"Be Gojiro," the monster said aloud. All of a sudden it was a tremendous joke. "Be Gojiro!" Like it was snap. No hassle at all. Great peals of laughter poured from his outsized voicebox, echoed through the cavern, the shockwaves of his howling roar sending a seismo-smashing tsunami of mirth right through to moho. It was hilarious, a riot. After everything, that's what it came down to: "Be Gojiro." After all, who else was he supposed to be?

"Okay," he screamed out. "I'm Gojiro."

Was this the way those fate-pressed, strawgrasping Paiutes felt? the monster wondered. Them and a thousand other societies living on the rubber chit of borrowed time, accelerating toward the end of the tunnel, seeing no particular light there, but still going, going on, armed with nothing more than the same slagheap of half-baked ideas that had brought them to the brink to begin with? Probably. Because, really, what other option's open? How else is there to feel? You crash past the Duh Point, cross your fingers, and hope.

That's what Gojiro was thinking when he realized that goony dodo was standing beside him, shuffling its webbed feet against the White Light Chamber floor.

"Something I can do for you?" the reptile asked.

The dodo raised its mica chip eyes, looked at the monster, and dropped the gilt-edged box from his cracked beak. It was that snuffbox, the one Lieutenant Yajima's uncle had made. Gojiro picked it off the floor, opened it. Inside was a single gleaming Goldplate Pill.

It came on slow. Like the creep of a coaster up the first rise, or maybe how a window washer feels, sixty stories up, when the first of the supporting strands begin to unravel: a catch in the throat, a subliminal pang of peril.

He could watch it happen—see himself as if he were a pyramid on a supermarket shelf, the centermost can pulled out. Then, like those Fayetteville chickadees before him, he shuddered, shook, and fell. Fell right through the floorboards of reality's suspended solution. *Slurp.* The noise was unmistakable, he'd heard it a thousand times before, whenever they opened a can of freeze-dried this or dry-roasted that on the Dish. Vacuum packing, one of those 1939 World's Fair promises of the utopian morrow. Except here the process was reversed. Instead of Gojiro swallowing the Goldplate Pill, it was swallowing him.

His entire fifty tons was being sucked into an inch-long pill! Komodo's rough treatise on the dual-stage workings of Joseph Prometheus Brooks's equation appeared accurate. First it intook, packed every molecule tighter than a junkyard press, then it blew it out, spewed forth every deconstructed atom. Maybe it was like those stories about the traveling salesman—you know, he pulls the old Delta 88 off the road, walks into Hopper's diner, orders coffee, a buttered roll, but before the paper's folded back, wham, he's hit by the spontaneous combust and nothing's left but dust and the spinning stool.

Eyeless, the monster blinked.

Which of those tiny specks sheened across the blackest firmaments had been what building block of his former corpus? Gojiro couldn't know. Broke loose of him, they all looked the same: a shower of anonymity.

OVER THE
EQUAL SIGN

Komodo went out into the immense American night, behind the wheel of that pink plasti-car. First devised as a soapbox racer for automotive-minded Atoms to crack up in around Dead Canon Curve, the balsa-weight vehicle was in no way street legal, but it went 150 and that was all that mattered.

He found her where he knew she would be, on that strip of freeway across from the Desert View Motor Cinema. She was wearing the same fuzzy pink bathrobe she wore the first time he saw her at the Turret House. That same fear was on her face. She was in Hell, Komodo knew, still in Hell.

Komodo looked at her and understood what his parents had done for him on that exceedingly bright morning in Hiroshima; and how he'd unknowingly sought to repay their act of love in the Opening Sequence. They put him in a hole so he wouldn't have to see. See: It. Their efforts were rewarded. His life had had its ups and downs, Komodo thought, but it had always been his own. Not for a single instant had he ever been in Hell.

He could hear her screaming now. "Out there!" she yelled, her long, white finger pointing east. "That's where I've got to go. But I can't get past here!"

In an instant he was beside her. "That's why I've come, Ms. Brooks, to help you. To take you on." He held out his hand, clasped her bony wrist. Then they were standing, facing each other. And it started up again.

"Ahhh," Komodo said.

"Ahhh," Sheila Brooks said. Closer, closer, across that gaugeless gap. But before their lips could touch, Komodo stiffened, pulled away.

A shadow passed over them. It was Billy Snickman, ward of a dozen foster homes, author of "Forget That House." The wild boy stood beside Sheila and Komodo, an oddly cherishing smile spread across his exhaust-streaked face. Komodo knew that look. He'd seen it on Ebi's face, only hours before she died, as she sat in the Traj Taj kitchen, watching her share a pot of tea with Sheila Brooks. "We're just a family," Ebi said then, so sweet.

"Ain't supposed to be on now, you know," Billy Snickman said in a soft voice, gesturing toward the print of *Gojiro vs. the Enigma-Inking Squid at the Rock of Knowledge* filling the giant screen. "Usually, show's over at midnight. But not now. Not anymore. The fans got into the booth, chased the manager out. They're gonna keep playing it. Until He comes."

The sun was verging over the jagged peaks. Dawn was coming fast. Komodo hadn't noticed before. But now he felt a tension in his head, a pile driver through his brain. The early morning light was diffusing the picture on the movie screen, bleaching it out. Gojiro was fading away, becoming a ghost. "Oh, no!" Then Komodo was pulling Sheila Brooks, dragging her toward the plasti-car. "We must go!"

She was asleep when they arrived at the edge of the Encrucijada, curled up beneath that silvery space blanket Komodo had tucked around her to guard against the desert cold. Looking into the Valley below, Komodo felt an awesome portent. The elements, so long assembling, were about to go critical in that ancient bowl.

"Where are we?" she groaned as he gently shook her awake. One glance at the Valley was enough to snap her neck back. "Oh . . . here."

They made the rest of the way on foot, Sheila Brooks's red designer galoshes against gnarled ravines, over the pinnacle rocks. It was the long way around, but with the sun now rising in the sky, they couldn't risk cutting straight across. Komodo thought they were home free when they reached the salt flat. But then, no more than five hundred feet from the Chamber door, Sheila Brooks grabbed his sleeve and gasped.

The figure shimmered across the white ground like a mirage. Komodo breathed deep as the great scaly ensemble lurched closer, the reddish comb of its cranial dome stark against the blue sky.

"What is it?" Sheila Brooks screamed, clutching tighter.

"It's . . . the Varanidid."

"The what?"

"A myth, walking."

Onward it came, claws glinting in the sunlight, across the rapidly heating sand.

"It's looking at me!" It was so. The approaching beast's eyes were fixed on Sheila Brooks.

Then, when it was close enough, it said, "You have returned. I knew you would when the time was right." The voice was a rasp, a croak.

Komodo thought she would run, but she didn't. She stepped forward, toward the Varanidid. "What are you talking about? I've never been here."

"Yes you have."

"Never—not until now."

The Varanidid seemed unsteady now, but still it came ahead. They were almost face-to-face. "But . . . you came as you came before, over this same ridge. Walked as you walked before . . . to this *very spot!*"

Komodo said nothing; what was playing out was beyond his intervention.

"Don't be upset, Leona. Today is a great day. After so long, you have returned."

"Leona? I'm not Leona."

"Not Leona? But you are. I can *feel* it."

"Leona was . . . my mother."

"Your . . ." The Varanidid reeled back; when it straightened up once more, the Echo Man was poking his wrinkled face from beneath the scaly mask. There was an unbearable silence as the Indian studied Sheila Brooks with narrowing eyes. Then, without warning, he shot out a clawhand, grabbed hold of her goggles.

"Hey! What's the big idea! Lay off!"

The Indian would not let go. He pulled at the glasses until the heavy elastic came loose with a loud snap. The glasses flew from Sheila's head, rose up into the blue heat of the Encrucijada sky, and fell back into the Echo Man's hand. "Let me see your eyes."

"Get away!" she screamed. But the Echo Man held her tight, peered deep into her face.

Then he released his grip, stumbled back. His Zardic regalia was askew now, ripped and hanging, his wrinkled head fully visible. He looked older, sadder. "Years ago, she came to this place. I always knew, someday, she would return. But instead, it is you." A tremor ran through him as he spoke. No longer the mythic Varanidid, he once again seemed to be the fleabitten Nelson Monongae, just another whiskey-drinking Indian haunting the plasma banks.

But he recovered, straightened up. A light suddenly in his eyes, the Echo Man closed his leathery palm around the black vial hanging from his neck. With one sharp pull he ripped the rawhide strand. Then he reached over and placed the vial in Sheila's hand, folding her long white fingers around it. "Your eyes are her eyes. See with them. See what she did not."

Sheila Brooks looked down at her fist. "What is this?"

"Blood."

"Blood? I can't stand the sight of blood." She opened her hand. "It's *black.*"

"Blood from the earth. *His blood.* They're stealing it, draining it away. You take it. Use it—I have kept it for you, all these years."

Right then Komodo felt that horrible pounding in his head once more. Except it was worse now. "Gojiro!" He grabbed Sheila Brooks, and they started running, away from that Echo Man.

"My own true friend, I have returned! Ms. Brooks has accompanied me."

Komodo called again, only to hear his voice once more reverb and fade away in the highest reaches of the White Light Chamber. There was no reply. He turned to Sheila Brooks. "Perhaps he has become shrunken once more, the result of the potion I described. Shrunken down and somehow wedged in an unforgiving nook or cranny. My own true friend! Indicate your presence, please!"

Sheila Brooks looked around in numbed stupefaction. With that transparent antirad protection suit taut over her fuzzy pink bathrobe and titanium lamé pantaloons, she looked shrinkwrapped.

A desolation overcame Komodo. So many times—across unfathomable gulfs—he'd followed love's radar, arrived in the nick of time to snatch his friend from the brink. But now, his heart straining until it ached in his chest, he felt nothing.

It was a violation of their Promise, he knew, bringing Sheila Brooks into the White Light Chamber without first asking Gojiro's permission, but what choice was there? Things were different now. The monster was right, they weren't on Radioactive Island anymore. They were in a new world, with new rules. The Triple Ring Promise was no longer their solemn secret, between them and no one else. Others were involved now; who knew how many? He turned to watch Sheila Brooks stagger about the ghastly Chamber. There was so much he longed to tell her, so much she would have to know! But where was Gojiro? A mere glimpse of his great friend would explain so much of what he could not put into words.

That's when she screamed. "Over there!"

Komodo wheeled to see the dodo. The unfortunate former extinctive was sitting in the middle of the Chamber floor, seemingly engaged in a poignantly vestigial nesting activity. The sad bird met Komodo's gaze and emitted a deep sigh. Then it got up and waddled away, leaving behind a shiny pellet. That dodo had been sitting on a Goldplate Pill—as if it were its own egg.

Komodo was hovering over the gleaming capsule when it came to him. At first the sound was no more than a scratchy whisper from behind a thick wall, so faint he thought he'd only dreamed it. But then it came again, no less undeniable for its imperceptibility. Komodo's mouth dropped open. "There is Quadcameral activity here—I can *feel* it! Oh, my God, Ms. Brooks. Gojiro—he is inside this Goldplate Pill!

"My own true friend, can you hear me? Please, come in. Acknowledge reception!"

Sheila Brooks was beside Komodo now, staring down at the pellet. "But, how . . . I mean . . . it's so little and he's so big . . ."

She extended her index finger. Then, just as he'd seen her push her extended arm through the parietal loam of that massive Quadcameral model, Komodo watched Sheila Brooks's bitten nail travel through the dank air, toward that Goldplate Pill. When her fingertip touched the polished metal, her eyes rolled back in her head.

"Ms. Brooks . . . you sense it too!"

With a sudden spasm, she pulled away. "No! I dunno! Shit! Why'd that goddamned Indian have to steal my glasses?" She reached out for Komodo, grabbed him hard. "I'm begging you, tell me what's going on here—I'm not a fucking idiot."

Once again, the shame flooded in. He wanted to bring her into the Valley, to show her the man standing at its center, to somehow liberate her from Hell. But Gojiro was in trouble, and there was no time. He took her hand. "Oh, Ms. Brooks, if I had only been honest, forthright. It is to my great disgrace that I have not revealed this earlier." He reached out, flicked on that bank of monitors. Blue-gray light filled the Chamber.

"Dad." She took a step ahead, then looked back over her wingy shoulder. Help, she seemed to say—help me now. But Komodo could not help her, not then. Gojiro was inside the Goldplate Pill!

Komodo projected his Quadcameral overlays onto a ten-foot-square foldout Dishscreen. Years before, Komodo envisioned those transparencies as a first step toward a comprehensive mapping of the monster's fabulous mentality. The plan was to chart the energy of each neural coupling, fix their positions as one might the constellations in the night sky. But the Quadcam was simply too big, too varied. Komodo's astral-neural maps were pocked by empty spaces, barren patches, great black holes. Whole cortexial partitions remained unexplored. And, after the 90 Series incident, the task had been abandoned altogether.

Now, however, those woefully insufficient charts seemed the only chance. Gojiro was alive—the Quadcameral activity inside that Goldplate Pill proved that. If the still-viable sectors of the reptile's brain could be pinpointed, then insight might be gained into his condition.

Connecting the Dishscreen to a keyboard, Komodo sat down and began to punch deck like a Dexi-driven dictaphonist. The music would point the way. It always did. To Komodo's trained ear, each separate pair of neural connectors and its accompanying synapsial spark struck a distinctive tone. "The infinite symphony" Komodo called it, back in the Glazed Days. How thrilling it was to press his ear to his friend's frontal plate and hear the majestic interplay—the low, earthy bass lines of the most ancient reptilian wards underpinning the skittish cadences of the limbic rock, those two blending with the allegro fleet of the neo-cort, all of it topped off by the angular clash of the uncharted fourth realm, that dissonant, offcentering careen of the New.

Now, however, the Quadcameral soundscape offered no ever-redefining swell, no dazzling aggregate of hue and timbre. The track Komodo heard was more minimal than a Tibetan trancer's demo, nothing but a solitary Om, a lone high-hung hum. The tone penetrated, louder and louder, vibrating inside his head like a hardstruck, razortonged tuning fork.

That sound! He recognized that consuming, bell-shattering note. He'd never forget it. Once, he'd fixated on that same drone, tracked its soul-shearing

pitch throughout that terrible descent into Gojiro's head. Oh, appalling memory—how he kept going deeper into the Quadcameral's sacred fourth tier until
he found that single neural pair, short-circuited the electricity there. Could it
be? That out of the great mentality's boundless ensemble only one tone remained—that same pulse to which the 90 Series once adhered? Komodo sat
stunned, attempting to make sense of things. How could that 90 Series coupling, receptor of those desperate supplicants, be back? Every indication
pointed to the unregenerative nature of Quadcameral cellular material; once the
cortical matter was destroyed, it did not—would not—grow back. He told
Gojiro as much on that long-regretted day. Time appeared to bear out the
prognosis. After the operation, supplications no longer swamped the monster's
mind. Never again had he been transported into the despairing consciousness
of the pleading Atoms, G-fans, and the rest.

Until now. Until they came into the Valley.

Komodo felt chills when he heard that other noise. It had been there all
along, thrumming low behind the tremulous tonality of the neural signal, but
he hadn't made much of it. There was no reason to. The sound was clearly
external, a stray byte, not Quadcameral in origin, no part of the infinite symphony. But now it grew louder, dominant. That whoosh . . . the howl of wind
roaring through a tunnel.

"The Beam! It's inside his head!"

Komodo keystroked feverishly, desperate to locate the impulse on his
overlays. It didn't take long. When he saw it, Komodo gulped. Once that 90
Series receptor had been just a single neural coupling, one among billions, but
now it stood by itself, a sole, tiny blinking star amid the blank. Komodo
amplified the pulsating image until it filled the Dishscreen. It didn't look different from the usual Quadcameral neuron: a pair of opposable cerebral stan-
chions, topped by the jagged sear of synapsial energy. But it was—radically,
remarkably—different.

"My God," Komodo said softly, "the Beam has refastened the 90 Series
neurons. It has taken the place of the truncated synapsial force. It's all that's
left of him. The only thing keeping him alive."

First he saw pi, a ruthless irony. There was a time he'd spend whole days, even
weeks, happily employing that useful Hellenism, extending it dozens of decimal
places beyond the standard 3.14 so as to more precisely compute the circumfer-

ence of the Triple Rings upon Gojiro's chest—the chest that no longer existed. But that Beamically supplied energy reconnecting the monster's last neuron was no fixed thing. Bonewhite phosphor amid the lusterless steel gray of the Dishscreen, it roiled, refigured, bisected. What did it look like now? Two tildes over a wayward n? Twin lightning strikes between radar towers? These items came to mind. But then Komodo settled on one imprint and one alone. "The Equal Sign," he murmured.

Years before, Komodo had tried to convince Gojiro of the relevance of the Equal Sign within the working of the Instant of Reprimordialization. "In considering the properties of the eternal equation Prewire $=$ Identity, we would make a grievous error to assume that the equal sign is nothing more than a mathematical convention, a simple conduit to be taken for granted. On the contrary, it represents a terrible chasm, a yawning breach. Oh, my own true friend, Reprimordialization is no easy thing, no walk in the park. It is Belief, personal decision. To view Identity from across the river is not enough. We must seize it, immerse ourselves in it. In my mind, this is the significance of the Equal Sign. It is Faith. That is the leap we must make. The Leap across the Equal Sign!"

Peering up at that quivering image on the Dishscreen, Komodo felt only despair. It was like being back on Radioactive Island, watching those seemingly endless reruns of Gojiro's Black Spot Dream. "Leap!" he screamed then, urging that vacillating youngest zardplebe to plunge into the dark pool—only to see him go up but never come down. Now the whole thing was repeating itself, Komodo thought. Once again a youngest zardplebe, in this case disguised as a five-hundred-foot-tall King of Monsters, Friend to Atoms and goaded by a hopelessly idealistic, terminally foolhardy friend, had attempted to leap—only to be wrenched, yet another time, from the world he knew. This was the futility of that lone idiogram on the Dishscreen, Komodo decided; it was possible that even at that moment, his friend was waking up lonely and afraid inside another volcano, on another charred island, and calling out for another boy. Komodo put his head down on the keyboard. Once that Equal Sign had represented so much promise to him. But now it was nothing more than a pair of horizontal prison bars, a hideous limbo.

"Oh, my own true friend! I should have listened when you spoke," Komodo sobbed. "You were right. There are lines that should not be crossed. Mr. Brooks's equation should never have been touched. Mine *was* a mutant's gamble, the result of which now stands before me. You are caught up in a realm out of time, out of space . . . like a coin forever on its side."

"Wrong!" The word rang through the White Light Chamber, sheared through Komodo's sobs.

"Wrong?" He'd almost forgotten about Sheila Brooks.

"Wrong!" She stood in front of that bank of Philcos and Admirals, her palms pressed to her pasty cheeks. "It's not right, not what it's supposed to be!"

Komodo raced over. Joseph Brooks was on those monitors, in his searching position, as always. Now Sheila was backing away from the picture. At her feet was her stereopticon. Komodo bent down and examined it once more: Joseph Prometheus Brooks and Leona Ross Brooks standing in that Valley, happy. And why not? They were soon to have a baby. The Echo Man had it right, Komodo noted. Sheila did have her mother's eyes.

"His arms are *empty!* They're not supposed to be empty!"

Komodo turned to the monitor. "You refer to the cradling position, Ms. Brooks. A most enigmatic—"

"It's *wrong!* That's not how it is in . . . in . . ."

Komodo came closer now. He could feel her struggling, trying to battle her way from Hell. "Not the same as in what?"

"As in *Gojiro vs. Joseph Prometheus Brooks in the Valley of Decision!*" The words flew out in a solid stream.

Komodo peered at the monitors again, then back at the stereopticon. Now he understood. It had started when Leona came across the country, heading for Los Angeles with her mother. Except their train broke down. Then she wandered away, found her way into the Valley. She met the Echo Man there—the poor, sad Echo Man, hope of a dying Clan. He thought she was the one who would help him fulfill his mission, renew his kind. But he was wrong. Instead, she saw the Beam and painted what she saw, in that X-ray style. That part was easy enough, Komodo thought, rubbing his chin. But what about Joseph Brooks? He wasn't in the Beam. No, that was different. Brooks was Leona's contribution; she *put* the scientist in the Encrucijada. Somehow, in the unknowable workings of her artist soul, she understood that the Beam was incomplete, that it needed a *catalyst,* someone to set the Power into motion. Then, in a Paris bar, she saw her vision playing "In a Mist" on a clarinet and convinced him of his destiny.

Komodo looked over to where Sheila Brooks stood, still yelling that her father's searching position, the same stance her mother had foreseen in her X-ray painting, was wrong. This was not exactly accurate, Komodo decided.

"Unfinished" was a better term. The notion that any idea—any vision—was the product of an individual practitioner, or even a single generation, struck Komodo as presumptuous. More than likely it would have to be passed on, like a baton in a relay race, to the next visionary, and the next—sifted and simmered through who knew how many generations of brains before it came into perfect focus.

"His arms aren't empty!" she screamed again. "He's holding . . ." She stopped now.

"Ms. Brooks! Tell me what you see!"

"Victor! What's Victor doing on television?"

Komodo turned to the monitors once more. Those extra surveillance cameras, part of Shig's exhaustive security apparatus, had preempted Joseph Prometheus Brooks. Victor Stiller was there instead, standing beside his Mercedes, relentlessly dapper in a summer suit. Several men in overalls milled around what looked to be a camouflaged oil rig.

A man was yelling, motioning everyone to stand back. "Gonna rip!" The rig shook, black liquid surging out.

"Owww!" The pain came simultaneously with that gusher, a thud between his eyes that knocked Komodo off his feet. He tried to get up but fell back down again.

"Are you all right?" Sheila Brooks asked.

"A momentary balance problem." That's when he saw what was happening on the Dishscreen, the way the Equal Sign was flickering, arcing like a poorly screwed-in bulb. Off, then on, off again. "My own true friend!" It was like watching a dozen deaths, a dozen resurrections. With the pumper's every gush, the signal grew fainter.

Amid the ensuing panic, one phrase stood out: "What do fossils mean but fossil fuels?" That was the riddle of the Encrucijada, Komodo understood then, the reason Leona Brooks brought Joseph Brooks there to make the Bomb, the reason a lizard and a boy had come from so far to seek their Identities in that sandy, comet-made bowl where the dinosaurs perished.

"The Beam! It comes from oil!"

On the monitors, the well spurted again, black fluid spewing to the stark sky. Stiller's plan was all too plain: he'd used his position and the secrecy surrounding Joseph Brooks to quietly pilfer the Valley's lode and then got his lawyers to trump up that specious Native Lands Act case on behalf of the Echo Man as a fallback, so he could keep on stealing. An ingenious scheme, to be sure, but a scheme nevertheless. In the end, just another tawdry caper. Even at this late date, Komodo could not help but feel sorry for Stiller. Why would a man who once seemed capable of undertaking Life's great gambits settle for something so paltry? What base instinct could have possessed him to dispassionately siphon the Beam itself from the sacred geologies, to shunt it into profane refineries, brand-name pumps, and combusting engines so that Hope might be blown choking and pointless out the ends of a billion exhaust pipes? Kleptomancer! It was difficult to imagine a more heinous crime.

Komodo looked at the Dishscreen, watched that Equal Sign dissolve. "He's murdering my friend!"

Except then: boom! On the monitors all that could be seen was the flying debris, those roustabouts staggering through the dust, their faces dusked like Jolson. Stiller got it bad. His hair standing on end, his suit shredded, he groped through the swirling grit like a demented pilgrim, irredeemably lost in the maelstrom of his own making. Probably he never even saw those crazy Atoms running back and forth, yowling triumph. They always loved a good explosion.

"Too late!" Komodo cried, turning back to the Dishscreen. The Beamic energy sustaining the monster's lastmost neural coupling flared one last time, embered, faded away. Stiller's offending shaft had pierced through the Beam's heart, dealt the Font a fatal blow. "My own true friend . . . you are dying. I cannot help you."

Except right then, Sheila Brooks came lurching across the White Light Chamber. "That Indian, he told me I would see! He said this would do it. Take it!" She crammed the black vial into Komodo's hand.

Komodo held the Echo Man's flask up, watched the dark fluid inside flow from side to side. "Blood . . . *blood from the earth!* The Varanidid's blood—the Black Spot."

"What?"

"Something he always dreamed of."

Komodo wedged the cork stopper from the small container, set it down beside his beakers and bunsens. With the utmost care, he grasped the Goldplate Pill between his fingertips. The pellet fit perfectly within the mouth of the vial. Komodo guided it down until it was completely immersed in the black fluid.

"Leap, my own true friend . . . leap into the Black Spot."

It took a moment, a horrible forever. But the image bled back onto the screen. That 90 Series neuron, short-circuited so long ago, had been resuscitated yet again. Komodo turned to embrace Sheila Brooks. But she wasn't beside him anymore. She was back in front of those monitors, staring at her father.

"It was fun, you know, riding around together. I didn't make that up. We had a lot of fun before they came and took him away . . ." She was crying now. "He looks so lonely out there, all by himself. Why didn't he try to . . . call me up or something, you know? I could have kept his secret. Nobody had to know. Damn it!" She began beating on the monitor screens with her fists.

Komodo came near to comfort her, but she pulled away. "You don't know what it's like, not to know who you are . . . where you come from."

"But I do."

She was crying harder now. She looked back at her father. "Why's he out there? What's he trying to see?"

Komodo put his arms around her, held her tight, tried to make her feel safe. "What *you* see. That same thing."

"But what's that?"

"Ms. Brooks, please listen. There are certain things I must tell you." Komodo glanced up at the Equal Sign now blazing on the Dishscreen. "You see, once, very long ago, my friend had a Muse, who we called Budd Hazard. In our beginnings, when we were all alone in a cold dark place, Budd Hazard pointed the way for us, turned us toward the Light. However, it is only in the past few days that I have come to truly understand much of what he said. For instance, the Tenacity of Genes and Dreams: 'Dreams and Genes, it's them that stitch the seams.' That's what Budd Hazard said. Ms. Brooks, did you notice that crook in Ebi's eyebrow?"

Sheila Brooks blew her nose, nodded.

"So many times, over the years, I would steal a peek at that crook. There was a special angle to it that gave me so much pleasure; I never knew quite why. Ms. Brooks—once I was like you. All that I knew was taken from me, everything that I was. These things have now been returned to me. I've reached back to my beginnings. And now I know the source of that crook in Ebi's eyebrow. It came from my own mother—all those years, without knowing so, I saw my mother in Ebi. Somehow, across the great abyss, an exploded generation, that crook persisted."

"Ebi's dead, isn't she?"

"Yes. She was my daughter. I could not say that before."

"I knew it. I don't know how, but I did."

Komodo squeezed her tighter. "Ms. Brooks, there is much that must be accomplished in a short time. We must adhere to Budd Hazard's teaching, we must demonstrate the Tenacity of Genes and Dreams. We inherit more than the simple helix coil from those who gave us life. We take on their aspirations, their hopes and wishes . . . their delusions as well. Ms. Brooks, your mother came to this Valley and dreamed of your father standing at its center. Just as he is right now. That same vision lives inside you—it always has. Your mother's own unfinished vision! You are the only one who can complete it. We must get it out of your head. It is the only chance—*Gojiro vs. Joseph Prometheus Brooks in the Valley of Decision.* The movie must be made!"

Sheila Brooks wailed. "But how? What do you want me to do?"

"Are you afraid of needles, Ms. Brooks?"

"You mean shots?" Suddenly, there was a wariness to her voice.

"Not exactly." Komodo reached into his pajama pocket and pulled out a four-inch probe. "I'm sorry I've not yet developed a more sophisticated method. The hookup will be subcutaneous in the parietal."

"The what?"

"The forehead."

"You're gonna stick that knitting needle in my head?"

"Just under the skin. It would be a three-way process, a line between the Goldplate Pill, yourself, and this machine."

"What's that?"

"This is a radio. Quite an old one. It was designed by my father, in Hiroshima. He believed it might enable him to speak with other species. I am not certain if he ever achieved his goal. I think not. He bequeathed it to me before his death. However, some time later, I lost it. It has only recently been recovered. Ms. Brooks, nothing remains of my friend save a single neural coupling. The function of that coupling is to receive cries for help. Supplications. There is one supplication, a special one, the one you wrote at the bottom of your letter summoning us here, that I believe is essential to my friend's survival. I think this machine contains unique properties that will enable you to reach him."

Sheila Brooks ran her stark white hand over the box's singed surface. "Your father made it?"

"Yes, he was a great inventor. I am but a mere shadow of him. I feel by using his invention in this way, I am satisfying his quest."

Then she looked away, to the monitors. "But what about *my* father? What's it gonna do for him?"

Gojiro

*   *   *

She made a joke before it started. "Kiss a sleeping lizard on the lips, make him a prince? Why not? It's all in a day's work for the Hermit Pandora of Hollywood." Then she lay down on the White Light Chamber floor, alongside Komodo's father's radio and the vial containing the Goldplate Pill.

"Are you ready, Ms. Brooks?" Komodo asked, handing her the stereopticon. She nodded, squeezed his hand. How he wished to embrace her then. But there was no time. As soon as she glimpsed the image inside the viewer, the vision started up.

Komodo was at the Dishscreen, checking for signs of Quadcameral activity, when he heard it. His father's radio—its crystal connections were hissing, spitting. One after another the heavily corroded inner workings began to pop. The stress was too much for the old transmitter. It was burning out.

Sheila Brooks's vision was starting. "Mom! Dad!" she shouted, her face a mask of familiar terror. Stunned, Komodo watched the smoke pour from his father's radio. Should he unhook her from the box now, right in the middle? He couldn't decide. On the Dishscreen, the 90 Series neuron was becoming unstable once more. Komodo tore at his face. "I'm going to kill them both!"

But then he felt the heat. The Triple Ring grillework he'd reaffixed to the radio's speaker was starting to glow. Komodo peered at the fiery concentrics, stood in their light.

It came back to the Triple Rings, as everything always did.

It was a funny thing, too, because when they left Radioactive Island to come to America, Gojiro asked Komodo what he would do should they be unsuccessful in their quest to fulfill the Promise. "Like, if we don't get Identified, and after I'm snuffed." Komodo thought for a moment and said likely he'd enter a life of contemplation.

"Just think? About what?"

"About the Triple Rings," Komodo said forthrightly.

It was a vocation Komodo sometimes considered, disappearing deep within Asbestos Wood to become an itinerant monk. It would be a quiet but fruitful life, he imagined, meditating upon the Evolloo and the role of the Triple Rings within it. Now, however, he rejected this option. He could never allow the Triple Rings to recede to mere abstraction. He needed those perfect arcs alive. He needed them raw, savage, burning into his flesh.

The Triple Rings opened an aperture amid the gloom of that White Light

Chamber. Komodo peered through. Again, he saw what the Beam had shown him—what happened on that clear, warm morning when his parents put him in the hole. He saw it again, and this time understood what his mother meant when she said, "Long be your line, my sweetest son."

The Triple Rings told him what he needed to know. They told him he'd done more than survive that exceedingly bright morning the Heater ripped through all continuity. When those Rings flew toward him, they brought a new logic, another way to be. No wonder he'd slept all those years. Transfiguration can be arduous, it takes time to assimilate.

The words passed Komodo's lips: "I am a Quadcameral. I have always been. Quadcameral and Throwforward."

It would, of course, change everything. It already had.

Then Komodo bowed to the Triple Rings. He thanked them not only for the revelation of his destiny, but also for the repose with which to perceive it. For no matter how byzantine and beleaguered the antic Cosmo became, the Triple Rings remained the center of the cyclone, the crystalline, unshakable eye, steadfast against the encroach of Chaos. To return to them was to touch home base, affording the assurance and courage to go on.

Komodo went on. He looked at the singed hulk of the radio his father had made and smiled. The gray box had come a long way, but now its work was done. Gently, Komodo moved it from its spot and lay down in its place. Then he took the two wires, one that led to Sheila Brooks and one attached to what remained of Gojiro, and forced the strands into his forehead.

THREE RINGS

Was he dead? Was death what the Goldplate Pill dealt? The monster couldn't
say. He had no claim to know dat about Dis. Sure, the poster nailed on the
sheriff's wall says "Wanted: Dead or Alive"—no paying off on in-between. But
who's to tell where one stops and the other starts? Is the demarcation hard and
fast, so that a degree either way—212 or 32—pushes you to water, steam, or
ice? Or is it possible to be in several states at once, like a zard poised at the
fourcornered point where Colorado, Utah, New Mexico, and Arizona collide, a
claw across every line? Could it be that "living" and "dying" are just bureau-
cratic shorthands, syntactical shams invented by quota-driven medics itchy for
the bag and tag? Tell me: they slam the morgue drawer behind your head, does
that mean you're dead? Who knows? Bigger than Life, Death, hard to get the
specs on.

Not that the monster had wads of time to spend on these questions
subsequent to submitting himself to the Pill. The reaction was too rash and
blitzing, a sensurround to shock every scope. It's a bit o' schizo, okay, tom
peeping at the Big Bang of your ownself. The reptile saw the ever-expanding
array and said, "Geez, a Milky Way of me."

It didn't hurt, not a bit. Throughout his molecular diaspora, all Gojiro felt
was release. Indeed, if a mutant's nothing but an endless stalemate on Mendel's
tic-tac-toe board, the Goldplate Pill took the role of a tentyard preacher; it broke
the crutch of yesterday's paralyzing paradigm across a knee and screamed,
"Walk!" To long, skinny molecules mashed flat and coughing in the sootcaked
smokestacks in Birmingham, it said, "Run free!" To particles shackled white

331

and glossy within PR sheets handed out by flacks, it shouted, "Liberty!" To polyester nodules needlerammed in the sweatshops of Guatemala City, it said, "Don't look back!"

"Adiós arm," the monster remarked with particular detachment as his withery upper-right appendage vanished from his ebbing torso. "Check you later, leg."

It was easy, letting go. What else was he to do? Ride herd on those fleeing elements, hound them back into his in-no-way-OK corral? He had no right, no claim. Unbolted from that Superfortress of his unending misery, those atoms became free agents. He could not deny them what the Goldplate Pill offered: the clean slate, the new deal.

Going, going, but still not gone. Because, really, what's the big deal to lose a body? Nine out of ten spiritual professionals agree: the body is the rent-a-car of life. Crash it into the side of a semi-truck, leave it in flames, who gets bent out of shape? Hertz? No. It's the soul—the soul you got to shake! The soul's the Continuum's Krazy Glue. You want to bust the bearings of samsara's ever-churning treadmill, you've got to take the soul off the Line.

Except Gojiro didn't believe in souls. Never did, wasn't about to start now. Still, looking through nonexistent eyes and seeing nothing, he wondered: why am I still here? Something was holding him, lashing him to his next-to-defunct self. But what could it be? What part of himself would cling resolutely to Life when the rest was so pleased to leave?

Suddenly, he was moving. Being pushed. Back. That Beam! The monster didn't get it. How could the Beam take hold of what did not exist and hurtle it back through time yet again? Then he heard the thump; a heartbeat across Eternity. Thump. Thump. Thump.

"Mom!" He was inside that egg again, hatching out, burrowing up . . . But wait, there were others there beside him—two others! One on either side, fighting through the blackness with him, fighting to the light.

And then he heard that Cry. The Cry that pierces sleep, that can't be shut out. But not one . . . three! Three cries! "Waaaa!" Three Freshout Cries together!

Someone was talking now. "Ms. Brooks! Can you see yourself?" It was Komodo, again in Hiroshima, again being born. But what was he doing talking to Sheila Brooks?

"Wait a minute," Gojiro called. But there was no waiting, no stopping. He could feel himself slipping down, coming out, then looking up, through blurry eyes, and seeing faces above him. Smeared and blotched at first, but then clear. Brooks! Joseph and Leona Brooks, smiling down at their daughter!

Then there were more voices, dry, authoritative. "To the New Era!" Victor Stiller said, a champagne bottle exploding in his hands. The rest were cheering now, those European faces—wintery even here in the desert, in the middle of July. They all wanted to see the baby, the child whose entry into the world came at the stroke of midnight of such an auspicious day, to such auspicious people.

After that they went away, because they were very busy. There was so much left to do, so little time in which to do it. Just the two of them remained. Brooks (had he ever been that young?) and Leona, the great pitch of reddish hair framing her green eyes. "Sheila," she said, her voice both soft and thunderous. *Her name! Hearing her name for the first time!* "You've come in time. You will see . . ."

Then it was dawn and they were standing in the desert chill. Leona was wrapped in her bloody sheets, barely able to stand, and Sheila, in her father's arms. *Cradled in her father's arms!* They were walking across the Valley floor, to the dark tower ahead, the gadget hanging down.

"Get those people out of there!" came the call. It was Grives, screaming in terror. Then another shout. "Sir! It's Mr. and Mrs. Brooks . . . they're leaving the forward bunker."

Grives again: "Brooks! You're crazy! Get out of there!"

And Victor Stiller: "Leona! Joseph! What are you doing? Go back! . . . My God! They've got the child out there with them!"

She remembered it—now it all came back! She looked up into her parents' faces, what bliss. What was all the shouting about? Wasn't this the most normal sight she'd ever hope to see: her parents kissing, embracing, looking down at her with pride? She was only six hours old.

She remembered it! The terrible wind across her face, the fire, her mother's eyes raising up, a tremendous glow upon her forehead. "Yes . . ."

Gojiro tried to turn away, but there was no choice. He was in her body, he'd have to see what she saw: her mother walking, stumbling ahead, forward to that seethe.

"Leona!" It was Brooks's voice, shouting after her. "It's *wrong!* That's not Him, not Him at all!" Then the monster felt Brooks's arms tighten, trying to pull his daughter's eyes away. Away from It. Away from Hell.

But the shock knocked him backward, his grip slipped. She flew up, out of his arms. It wasn't more than a second before he grabbed hold of Sheila again, managed to shield her eyes. But she'd already seen too much. She saw her mother walking ahead, into the flash, a melting silhouette.

"Mom!"

Hers to relive again and again.

"Mom! Dad! . . . No."

Then there was only the Cloud, billowing up. The Cloud, and the weeping.

But that's not where it stopped. Not that Beam. For, right then, it rolled back once more, back and back, to the day that Valley was born, to that smoking comet, the saurs falling in its wake. And again, Gojiro was inside the body of that tiny lizard, traversing the killing fields. That's when he understood who the Varanidid was and what he did. And why the memory of his Great Deed was lost in the faded mists. After all, the Varanidid wasn't a fierce and powerful T-Rex, or even Radi-Breathing star of stage and screen. He was just an ordinary zard, a funky-looking one at that, and his only act of heroism was the commonest of acts. He followed the pheromone, kept himself alive until he found his mate. And together, amid that Death, they forged the first link of the Line.

It was the most monumental of destinies, easy to confuse, claim for yourself. Gojiro, a lonely mutant, had succumbed to the lure, imagined himself to be what he was not. He went ahead, caused that terrible whirlpool. The Echo Man, his people dying out, made the same error. But this time there was no mistake. This time it was as it was meant to be.

"Sheila!"

"Yukio!"

Twisting, writhing stegosaurs fell beside them, but it mattered not at all. Their mission was singular, without provision for detour. The straightest path to the purest goal.

"Yukio!"

"Sheila!"

Is it the pheromone that directs hearts, or hearts that drive the pheromone? They didn't know, just pushed ahead, closing distance. They came as they had under Albert Bullins's smoky tent, as they had out on the freeway median. They came like two elegant butterflies living deep in a jungle no saw's ever seen. They came the same as two roaches in a kitchen, knowing that they alone possess that one confounding gene to set back pest control another ten years. They came like Mall Darters in a derelict shopping center, like so many chickadees on the branches of a glassed-in Fayetteville Tree. They came like every pair of Throwforwards who ever homed to that unremitting cry: *"Adapt! Adapt or Die!"* They came like all who would make New Life must, shining, full of Hope.

They met on top of the smoking Comet, the stone that dropped from the sky to announce the passing of an Age. It didn't matter if their feet got hot. They lay down and made love right there. They made love through the ages, through sixty-six million years of time, until the Comet turned to dust and there was nothing there in that Valley but themselves. They made love until the Heater came and turned the world to white. And when it was gone, they were still there, making love.

It was about that time the monster heard that shout echo through the void of the Goldplate Pill. "Come in, Gojiro!"

"Wha?"

"Come in, Gojiro! Please come in!"

The supplication? What was it doing inside this place where even Bird's solo didn't sound?

"Come in, Gojiro! Please heed this humble servant's plea!"

"An afternoise," the monster supposed. "Residual electricity. Like what makes Frank's chickens get up and dance funky in the grocer's bin even though they got no heads."

"Come in, Gojiro! King of Monsters, Friend to Atoms, Bridger of Gaps, Linker of Lines, Nexus of Beam and Bunch, Defender of the Evolloo. Please heed these humble servants' pleas."

It occurred to him to deny. Dummy up, ignore the call, as he had every other 90 Series supplication, except for that one crazy moment with the wolf boy, Billy Snickman, out by the spire on Dead Letter Hill. But the chant kept on, louder and louder until it sounded like a billion voices, a booming noise to shake the stars, tear the plaster from the walls of space.

"Can't you see I'm dispersed? Gone."

Again the supplication came. Again and again.

"I can't. I'm afraid!"

Then, amid that gnawing tumult, the monster heard his friend's voice, sweet and reassuring as ever, whispered in his ear just as if the two of them were about to cuddle in their burrow during the earliest of times. "Be *Gojiro,*" Komodo said, "then you won't be afraid."

"Gojiro . . . I *am* Gojiro."

That's when he saw the foot, floating down there, where before there was only dark. A familiar-looking foot. A foot with a gnarly tuber, the result of a hundred stubs against the doorstep of a vulcanized volcano. A zardish kind of foot. His foot, that floppy old size two thousand.

It was the supplication that summoned back those parts of him. The words themselves: "Come in, Gojiro . . . Come in." Each syllable wielded its own specific gravity, its own particular pull. From behind the moon came his craggy dorsal plates. From south of Saturn, his belly hit him like a medicine ball. Those arms, which he always cursed for being too short to change a channel, boomeranged back, fused to his sides. The great tail came twisting through the black, the supraoc, too. Then he sensed it, far off at first, a tiny speck in the black—his face. His face coming across space. Fast. Bigger and greener and closer until: clang! Clang and clamp, the screws tightening down with airgun squeals.

Then he was back, all of him. But it wasn't done. Not yet.

Komodo was right. Reprimordialization is no walk in the park. Identity is not handed out by a gruff man with the nametags behind the Ellis Island counter. It is will, decision. You've got to declare it, you've got to *want* it—*Leap into it!* So the monster listened as the supplications came in. Millions and millions . . . Dick from Londonderry, someone put a bomb into his daddy's car, Okoye from Tanzania, whose truck was buried in a landslide, Pablo from Peru, they took away his brother in the night . . . Denise from Pittsburgh, Ali from Dhaka, Anatoly from Kazak, Mzwakhe from Soweto . . . Loud and clear they came, their yearning echoing through the Quadcameral.

More and more . . . until he was ready. Then he schagged himself up and broke through the confines of that tiny Pill, shattering the stifling bonds of his own ambivalence.

"Yes!" came his shout, sonic cross the heavens.

"I, Gojiro, King of Monsters, Friend to Atoms, Bridger of Gaps, Linker of Lines, Nexus of Beam and Bunch, Defender of the Evolloo, am here! To do what I must!"

0.0247 SECONDS

Through the predawn murk of the Encrucijada, Gojiro saw the cameras on the hillside. Maybe that Shig was a lot of things, but he wasn't a welcher. He'd signed a contract with Hermit Pandora Pictures to make *Gojiro vs. Joseph Prometheus Brooks in the Valley of Decision* and he intended to deliver. Not that Gojiro would require much direction. You don't when yours is the role you were born, or reborn, to play.

Ditto for Joseph Prometheus Brooks. With that two-foot golden sphere cradled in his previously empty palms, he stood in his spot, eyes fixed ahead, as always.

That was how they faced each other, Opposer and Defender, bound by a common, solemn purpose.

If it had been a day earlier, a week, or a year, Gojiro wouldn't have been able to keep a straight face. What were the two of them trying to prove anyway, he'd have asked, an old man and a mutant zard playing a high-noon game in the middle of a Valley already steeped with the maudlin sediment of crumbled symbols? The whole thing was absurd—didn't they know that all the good archetypes have already been taken, beat flat of meaning?

That's what Gojiro might have thought, before. But this was now. Now, across the Equal Sign's great divide, the monster's sense of his own ridiculousness was obliterated. Here was only Identity. Identity and Action. For there could be no question as to the contents of Brooks's glowing globe. It was annihilation, pure and simple, a hand-held All-Inclusive Crisis of the Evolloo. *Everything* at stake.

From his vantage point five hundred feet above the sand and creosote scrub, the monster's view was comprehensive, unrestricted. He could see Sheila Brooks come running. It was a heartbreaking scene, really, the way she tried to tell her father she knew everything, that she loved him anyway. Heartbreaking, too, that she knew nothing could make her father put down that golden ball—that he wouldn't even look at her, much less hold her in his cradling arms again. After all, she'd seen this scene unfold before, hundreds of times. But still, knowing everything, she kept on, petitioning for her father's love, because that's what daughters do.

Gojiro could not be moved. To him, Komodo and Sheila Brooks were nothing more than faceless, antish figures, a black-pajamaed guy and his girl, like any couple you might see on a bus or in an airport terminal. Strangers. None of his business. Nothing mattered now except what was between him and Joseph Brooks and that golden sphere. What started sixty-six million years ago would be settled now, once and for all. That's how it is on the other side of the Equal Sign.

It was General Grives who set it off.

Some might say he snapped, that after so many haunted nights it just got to him. Poor ole Grives, he never could convince those snide Beltway boys about Joseph Prometheus Brooks. *Evil,* they snickered when he left their offices; Grives thinks Brooks is *Evil.* How much easier it was for those prep-school cynics to swallow Stiller's lustrous line. Gojiro, though, had no quarrel with the chunky soldier. Grives had his excuses. He'd seen the Heater, been marked by its Power, felt its horrible Revelation in his fundamentalist heart. He wasn't a bad man, just dumber than a stump. In fact, taking into consideration typical sapienistic prejudice, you could say that what Grives did was only human, especially after he saw Brooks standing in front of that looming, leather-wrapped, red-eyed Beast.

"Satan! I'll send you back to Hell!" the bejowled general shouted, snatching a rocket launcher from the shoulder of a gunnery sergeant, and bouncing a volley off Gojiro's Triple-Ringed chest. A pointless, misinformed gesture, as any G-fan knows. Nevertheless, it is difficult to tell what might have happened if Stiller hadn't shown up right then.

"Joseph! You've done it again," the former cyclotronist shouted, stumbling from behind the stone house. His once elegant presence ruined by that exploding oil well, Stiller was carrying Brooks's blackboard. "It's remarkable," he raved, a wild look on his singed face, "your greatest work. Do you have any idea of what this is worth? Billions! Trillions! Something like this will turn the defense industry on its head. I must contact the president immediately!"

At first Brooks paid Stiller no mind, but the ravaged Hungarian pushed forward. "Is this it—this globe? You have created the prototype already? Let me see!" He reached for it.

"No!" Brooks growled, flinging an elbow at Stiller.

The movement threw the worldshatterer off balance. Pitching forward, he tripped on a protruding rock. The gold sphere flew out of his hands and into the air.

Up. "Ah!" Sheila Brooks screamed.

Up. "Oh!" Komodo yelled.

Grives's voice pierced the morning silence. "Beelzebub's ball!" He drew his pistol, squinted, and fired.

The bullet inched through squares of air.

Lips pursed, eyes grew tight. Joseph Brooks looked up at the apexing sphere, then to Gojiro.

There was no sound except the distant click of film through a shutter's gate. Up in the hills, Shig was getting it all.

Regarding what happened next, let's say it came down to something the monster never could get straight, which is what makes a Hero. What do the latest polls say about swordswinging lone cats making their way through the arcane's labyrinth? Does Courage alone spur them on? Gojiro would say no, nobody's that brave; he'd say Great Deeds can never be predicted or precognitioned, that Saturday's Hero is no Hero unless he does what he does in a week that Saturday doesn't come. (For, truth be told, Sheila Brooks's scenario for *Gojiro vs. Joseph Prometheus Brooks in the Valley of Decision* was really nothing but a premise, a concept limited to bringing the key players together. What happened after that was an empty reel waiting to be filled in.)

No, Gojiro would say, if a Hero knew, a priori, what it took to be a Hero, Olympus would be an empty tract. The Deed must lurch like reflex, Prewire. And that's how it was, a moment later, when, like automatic, he tonguespeared Joseph Prometheus Brooks's wounded sphere from the desert air and jammed it through the parietal, deep into the Quadcameral.

Techwise, Brooks's golden ball functioned in much same fashion as Komodo's Pill, albeit on a larger scale. First it effected total vacuum intake; then, as a second stage, it exploded the matter within the source receptacle. Count one-Mississippi, two, if you want to imagine how it looked: a solid streak aimed between your eyes, a mystery train, a billion coaches long, clackety-clack into your head. Suffice it to say that the planet, and everything on it, was vortexing into Gojiro's parietal, atomizing inside the Quadcameral.

Sometimes he saw faces, could pick out individuals. Some he knew, like Albert Bullins stunt-flying his mint-condition kamikaze, and Bobby Zeber on his Triumph, heading east. But then there'd come Tashkent and Mexico City, all in a lump. There were mountains, some Holy, some pincushioned with ski lifts. Oceans, too, the swell of mighty currents suddenly rerouted to a single downhill torrent. Forests, no earth beneath them to sink roots, coursed forth as so many densepacked Birnam Woods-come-to-Dunsinane, like straight out of Macbeth's real bad trip. Australia zoomed in, a jagged frisbee. The planet peeled like fruit along the lines of longitude. All perimeters collapsed, no center held. Nothing was turned away. There was room for Everest, space for the frozen poles and lonely prairies. The noise was incredible, the ear-splitting creak of a giant wooden ark. The world churned, a molecular stew in the most bubbling of cauldrons, the fourth tier of the Quadcameral.

Then it stopped.

Gojiro opened his eyes and saw only the Encrucijada. The Valley hung there, alone. Beyond its red-ringed hills was nothing, only the blackness of space.

No sound. Except: "My own true friend!"

Good old Komodo, alive! Such a comfort to hear his voice. He was down there, with Sheila Brooks, standing at the monster's feet. Them and no one else, save Joseph Brooks, still in his spot by the stone fence.

"Are you all right?" Komodo asked.

"All right?" Gojiro considered. "I guess so. I feel like the Statue of Liberty after closing time and they forgot to tell the tourists. Be okay, long as they don't start banging on the windows."

Komodo looked down, read from a piece of paper. "I have compiled some calculations that may aid you in what you must do next, my own true friend. I am afraid they are quite rough."

"Rough?" That Komodo, what a guy! He watches the world sandstorm into a hole in his best friend's head and he's still counting the quantums. Stick him in Vegas, doubledown, and no house would be left standing.

"Based on the rate of vacuum influx effected by Mr. Brooks's device, it is my opinion that the Instant of Reprimordialization will become available from 0.0239 seconds to 0.0246 seconds. 0.0246 seconds—that's the maximum period, from the time of total engorgement."

"Total what?"

"Engorgement. The point at which nothing is left in the world . . . nothing except yourself, that is. Only 0.0246 seconds, no more. Beyond that point, Permanent Dispersal will take over."

"Then what?"

Komodo bit his lip. "Good luck, my own true friend . . ."

That was when Joseph Brooks spoke, his voice low and rumbly. "Sheila . . . forgive me."

Tears streaking her parched face, Sheila reached out, kissed her father. "It's okay, Dad. I love you." They held each other, a dad and daughter who'd ridden the highways together, only to have their road return to this desolate and fateful place. Then they said good-bye, Sheila Brooks returning to Komodo's side. And like that, the two lovers were gone, sucked into the Quadcameral.

Gojiro looked around, saw Shig. The froze-eyed boy was still in the hills, his camera running. Weird kid, nothing fazed him, not even the sudden disappearance of a Universe. Even now, he gave Gojiro the creeps. But zap—he went in there with the rest. Too bad he'd miss shooting the climax, but that's just the way it went.

Now the Big Throwdown could begin.

They stood there—Brooks and Gojiro, worldshatterer and King of Monsters, Opposer and Defender—etched out in a field of nothing, two to do the dance of the Evolloo. Twice before, their gazes had collided, fused, locked on. On Lavarock, they'd been a famous scientist and an unknowing zardplebe awaiting the confirming plunge into the Black Spot. The second time, just a few days ago, it had been between a dead man and a depressive movie star.

Now, the third time round: scramble the riddle of the chicken and egg in a teflon pan and ask, who between them, Brooks or Gojiro, be which piece of

Paracelsus's puzzle? God makes Man?—Man makes God? That's your toss-up question, Teachers' State. Slap that buzzer down—either way, it's no news.

Strange, Gojiro thought, how much he once hated Brooks—hated him more than hate itself!—and how that passion had turned the full 180. From Lavarock's seamless quilt of zards, Brooks had chosen him. Made him Gojiro. Now the monster would repay what he owed.

The leviathan bent down, opened a clawfist. Brooks stepped onto the giant palm, stood there as the reptile raised him up. Up and up, so high that Brooks could look around and be sure that the task he set for himself had been accomplished: he'd vanished a World, and before him stood the Being whose calling was to Restore it.

Brooks smiled now. His eyes, freed from their search, almost twinkled. They were kindly, boyish. Brooks nodded to Gojiro, and Gojiro nodded back, proof their deal was done.

Then Brooks began to schag. He arched himself and jumped. Higher and faster than you'd figure an old man could, he flew through the still air, into the hole in the monster's head, and was gone.

You know what it's like to be alone, completely on your own, and in your head . . . a Zone? To have a billion Beams, a billion Bunches, every Line crisscrossing between your ears? Do you know how that feels? Of course you don't. How could you? If you did, you'd be Him.

Maybe, someday, an old clipping will appear in Corvair Bay's mucky surf, a report from an extraterrestrial reporter. A column inch, no more, it'll say, "At 5:48:34.9089 pan-stellar synchronization, earth, stone 3 of solar system #9078A, was removed from orbit and replaced by a mutant reptile of the varanid type. Cause of the occurrence is unknown at this time." Next to this item, there'll be a splotchy photo, a shot no clearer than those of the long-necked resident of Ness, a likeness of a shellshocked zard plying Kepler's oval, desperate for an aspirin to soothe that one biggest headache.

Until then, rely on this. How it looked: the Void, where there was nothing to see. And how it felt: Apart. The Eternal Present, where no past image lingered on, where there was no future to foretell. The numbing evernow.

Amid all that black, the monster asked one question. He wanted to know how come, if he'd truly become Eternal, a circle without circumference, a point without extension or duration, then what was that ticking?

"Damn!" Gojiro screamed. 0.0245 . . . 0.0244 . . . Komodo's sums! Even here, the countdown never stopped. What good was Infinity if it came strapped to your back like a time bomb?

0.0236 . . . 0.0235 . . .

A horrible idea crossed the monster's overstuffed mind. He couldn't have been the first, could he? There must have been others before him, other would-be, conveniently forgotten, Defenders of the Evolloo—those who went forth to bridge gaps, link lines, those with whole planets crammed between their earwhorls, dudes that didn't get over. Maybe that was the real origin of the primeval swirl, Gojiro thought. Maybe the Big Bang wasn't nothing but shrapnel from a great Zardic cosmohead gone blooey.

"Keep cool," he told himself. No need to flip out. Plenty of time, 0.0130 seconds left. All the time in the world.

"Be positive." He thought about Ebi, what she always said while she did her taxons. The Evolloo was not only impossible to anticipate, Ebi said, it was silly to even try. The real joy was in the expectation, waiting to see Life's new gift. The monster sighed. Here, now, thinking of Ebi. How she would have loved to be alive to stick her labels on a world makeover. Now someone else would have to do it.

Not me, Gojiro knew. He understood the limits of his mandate. Like Moses of old, if a Reprimordialized Promised Land lay on the other side of his yet unaccomplished Deed, it would not be revealed to him.

0.0050 seconds left. Beyond that, the Continuum cracked, the fiber tore. Permanent Dispersal—flatline till the next Year Zero.

"Listen up," he yelled to all the diffusing molecules within him. "This be your captain speaking. Answer me this: how come the Cosmo crossed the road?"

"Give up? Because it was the chicken's day off. Little levity, courtesy of the Atomic Comic. Lighten things up a touch, you dig?

"Okay! Let's get this party started! Fasten your seat belts! Reprimordialization is no walk in the park. Who knows how many of your past lives is gonna pass through your eyes? So stay loosey, stay goosey, when I say—move out!"

0.0016 . . . 0.0015. Counting down, counting down.

"Okay! Now! Rock and roll!"

There was no movement.

"Hear me? The gates are open. You're free! Git! Peel rubber! Return to Walden. Make with the Rousseau scene!"

Still nothing.

"Come on! We only got 0.0006 to Permanent Dispersal here. No loitering! You want to become another asteroid belt? Reprimordialize! Get out of me!" The monster torqued the muscles in his head, tried to get a reverse peristalsis going in the parietal tunnel.

That's when he thought he saw that dodo's face. That dodo and all those other residents of the Zoo of Shame. They were just hanging there in front of him, spectral gnats swarming Gojiro's Learish noggin, as if to remind him it wasn't every citizen of the Evolloo who blissfully volunteered for passage to the Next Notch. Komodo's speech about the Equal Sign held true: Identity is not preordained, it can't be ordered in. It must be sought, seized. The monster's brows rose in terror. He remembered that he himself had been less than zealous about taking the critical plunge. But it was one thing for a lone zardplebe to equivocate before the Black Spot. This was worse. This was a World Balk.

"Leap, you fuckers!" Had Existence become so disaffected that the world had devolved into a society of dodos? Could Life be so despairing of the future as to reject its own Continuance?

"No, I won't allow it!" As the gongs of Doom clanged with barbarous persistence, the monster readied himself. There was no other choice. Identity determines action; when you're the Defender of the Evolloo, you do anything you can to Defend it.

"Come in," the monster cried to the planet he'd ingested.

"Come in, please heed this humble servant's plea."

"Come in, all Bunches, all Beams! This is Gojiro, King of Monsters, Friend to Atoms . . . Bridger of Gaps, Linker of Lines, Defender of the Evolloo. The world is full of Hope! You will see!"

Then he began to feel it: the kick inside, the coalescence of desire, a universe yearning for renewal.

But the wait had been too long. The remorseless timer's hand slashed into the monster's heart. The 0.0246 seconds was up. The moment that Komodo predicted for Permanent Dispersal, the point of no return. All that had begun to come together, pulled apart. It was the greatest pain: the strain toward entropy.

"Aggggh." The monster slapped a claw over his parietal, held his splitting skull together with the other fist. It was agony, but the leviathan held fast. He would not allow the world he loved to scatter into nothingness.

How long did a single mutant zard safeguard the planet with the sheer force of his Love and Duty? One ten-thousandth of a second? Even less? Still, it was the True Eternity.

Then came the deafening sound, the roaring cry. And it's funny, with all those ringing voices, those many tones and timbres, you'd figure they'd run together, become a slurry holler. But that's not how it was. Each call was distinct, beautiful and unique, just like Ebi's newborn voice at the edge of the Cloudcover.

"Waaaa!" The common squawk, the confluencing call. A whole world's Freshout Cry inside that reptile's head.

Then: zam. A moment's rush, and everything was as it had been. The red sand, the blue sky. The scrubby brush. Peering over the mountains ringing the Encrucijada, the monster could see the rolling hills, the majestic desert, the vast forests beyond. He saw the magnificent and the spoiled, the great oceans and the city full of smog. He saw every zard flicking out a pink tongue and every fly he caught, he saw the hustlers in the candy stores, guns glinting from those that drive by. He saw everything he loved and everything he hated, all of it returned to where it'd been. And still, he hated what he hated, loved what he loved. He hadn't gone softheaded, convinced himself to love what did not deserve to be loved. But his despair was gone. Because he knew: Change was possible.

At his feet, Sheila Brooks and Komodo were looking up. Grives and Stiller, too. The soldiers also, scratching their heads. Something had just happened, but what?

Then he heard a scream. "Dad! Where did you go?"

It was Sheila Brooks.

Gojiro's eyes went to the stone fence where Joseph Prometheus Brooks had stood searching, but saw no one. No old worldshatterer to return his stare.

END NOTE TO FANS

So: yo! Still snakin' and shakin', zealous zardpards? Continually contacking, top 'tile-o-files? Yesireedy, be yours for-true truly, crystallizing via the spire, cooking the cool connection, over the foremost frequency for all G-mungous G-fans—till all hours.

Well, that about knock the docket when it comes to this particular adventure of the big Green Machine? Let me check the files.

Nada más, unless you need to know about the fabulous escape from the Encrucijada, how Komodo Queequegged Gojiro with one of those shrinkage harpoons and everyone hightailed it to the harbor, where Shig had that SS *Adamski* stoking, and, suddener than Jack Robinson, the Cloudcover was looming from the gloom. A final chase scene like any other. De rigueur, Morty. Fill in the blank, Frank.

Other than that, this sector's just about talked out. Call it colonic, I dunno, but having told thees, it fades, just fades away. A life in the rearview, ever more smaller down the highway.

Just yesterday I asked Komodo if he remembered any of what went down during that 0.0247-second slice of Time out of Time, Space out of Space. "No," was all he said. Neither did Sheila Brooks. As far as they knew, one moment they were standing there on the early morning desert sands of the Encrucijada, and the next moment they were still standing there. Not that either one of them was tremendously put out by the jump cut on their tape. On the contrary, they loved the idea. Komodo said the very fact that he and Sheila couldn't remember what happened made them certain that it had. That was the joy in it, Komodo said, having *faith* that my story was so.

That word again—it's supposed to make you a spiritual millionaire. But even here, this side of the Equal Sign, it's hard to buy without looking at the prices. Things get crazy. Know what Komodo's saying now? That what happened in the Valley is likely going to cause "a revolution in cosmologic thought." You should hear him, he's so excited. Every day it's some new revelation. Just this morning he was sliding down the 'cano pole to tell me the latest. "The Encrucijada Incident may not have constituted an Instant of Reprimordialization in the classic sense," he said, "but rather served to effect definitive terminus of an existing condition." It's Komodo's current theory that the world at large had been laboring under the heavy yoke of a slow-acting All-Inclusive Crisis ever since Brooks first committed the Heater's equation to his blackboard back in '45. That act instigated a period of hypermutation causing too many Bunches to acquire too many new traits too fast, thereby threatening Beamic configurations and, eventually, the Evolloo itself. Noting the growing emergency, the Blessed Blueprint, ever lousy with contingency plans, came up with the sequence of events which fall loosely under the heading of *Gojiro vs. Joseph Prometheus Brooks in the Valley of Decision.* To hear Komodo tell it, Brooks's desire to see the face of the Deity served as "the dramatic embodiment of the Matrix-wide yearning of all things for a return to the $P = I$ paradigm." The Personal Appearance of the King of Monsters satisfied this Reprimordial longing.

"Mr. Brooks opened the window of Change in 1945," Komodo says. "Gojiro closed it."

"That's a heck of a long time to leave a window open, you catch a death of colds," I told Komodo, trying my best to maintain the oppositional stance. Mostly, though, I just listen politely. Right now, Komodo's going on about how memory, like matter, can never be absolutely destroyed. He's repeating, yet again, his conviction that it might take a dozen generations for the recollection of what happened in the Encrucijada to bubble up through the subconscious, but that it will, eventually. His idea goes back to Budd Hazard's Tenacity of Genes and Dreams concept, Komodo says, how visions carry on, make their myths, coalesce to Cosmo and finally, Truth.

The process is already underway, Komodo contends, handing me a copy of what Billy Snickman wrote. The wolf boy stowed away on that SS *Adam-*

ski—maybe I forgot to say. You'd figure Shig would've thrown Billy overboard, but the froze-eyed martinet only slapped a plate of slop in front of the wild child as if he were just another Atom. Sheila Brooks remembered Billy from those nights on the freeway, so it was kind of a party. Anyway, as soon as the boat came through the Cloudcover, the kid ran off the gangplank, graffitied his poem on the palisades of Past Due Point. *"Came far on a boat, not planes or trains. / To the world of four brains."*

"The poets know it first," Komodo points out, indicating that Billy's couplet more or less confirmed what he already suspected, that Quadcamerality will be the taxonomic differentiation that will come to distinguish the New Bunch he's certain will arise on Radioactive Island. It's only a matter of time until the adaptation is recognized and consolidated, Komodo says. You just have to wait.

But, to tell the truth, I'm not much in the mood to wait. I'm not much in the mood to do anything these days. Feeling kind of dragged, tired. Probably something I ate. Komodo says it makes sense, feeling pooped, tough ruckus I been through. Relax, he says.

So I'm relaxing. Taking a load off, kicking back. Watching the Dish.

Some little trip about Grives and Stiller, huh? Ole Grives finally getting the mandatory retirement for going round screaming about a five-hundred-foot-tall Devil turning up in the Encrucijada—that was kind of sad. What happened to Stiller was better. Did you see that crazy scene in Times Square, how cops found him wandering up and down Forty-Deuce street all vacant-faced and gnarly? He was yelling about an equation he claimed would put the Universe's "ultimate power" in his hands, except he forgot what the formula said. "One moment it was there, the next, it was gone," he said, over and over, his finger screwed against his temple. But best of all was how Stiller's lawyer kept pressing that Native Lands case and wound up winning the whole Valley back for the Lizard Clan. They showed the Echo Man, grinning his toothless smile from the window of his brand new four-wheel-drive with the longhorns bolted to the hood. "Oil," he said, in his airy whisper, "oil here? Worth billions? Sure, it's a nice surprise." Then he ordered the TV boys off his land. But not before they got a shot of Brooks's ranch house, deserted and forgotten, a decayed wreck. "Home to science's greatest mind," they said, "until his untimely death years ago."

Goes around, comes around. Satisfaction in that, sense of loose ends tied.

Yeah.

Komodo was down again, all wowed about the New Beam and the New Bunch. You should see the glow in his eyes.

I told him anyway what I decided. I told him I couldn't be happier about how it all came out, but I just didn't see where I was going to fit in on this new, improved Radioactive Island.

Komodo tried to protest, but I cut him off, made him hear me out.

"No," I said, with only love inside my heart, "I've been a mutant zard too long. I've done what I've come to do. The next world is the one for you and Sheila to live in, not me." I told Komodo that even though the Triple Ring Promise had been fulfilled, I was asking him to stick to the terms of the Amendment, to snuff me according to the contract.

Komodo took it as best as he could. "If that is your wish, my own true friend, I will try to comply. But the Amendment falls due tomorrow. I will have to make tests, to determine methods to circumnavigate your invulnerability . . . there might not be time."

"Don't think it'll be a problem," I said, picking a crashed Coke bottle off the 'cano floor where I'd thrown it during who knows what stupor. I raked the jagged edge cross my leathers and heard Komodo gasp. He couldn't believe how the glass cut through and my blood flowed. "Been happening ever since . . . you know. Some kind of side effect, maybe. Anyhow, I ain't what I was. All you got to do is stick me on a raft, float me out toward the Cloudcover, the thermoreg'll take care of the rest. Okay?"

Komodo nodded. His face was white as Virgil's empty sheet.

"Sorry."

Komodo bowed. "Do not be sorry, my own true friend. Your wishes are always respected by me."

"No, I mean about tomorrow, it being your birthday and all."

So, Green Scene Fiends—this comes off the hottest press yet. Up to the minute, dateline August 6. Like I said way back in the beginning, I can hear Komodo's hammer banging, ballpeen to the bamboo. Happy birthday, great soul.

Final thoughts? How about: if you're on your bike tonight, wear white. I dunno. I guess all the choice yocks have been picked over. I'll just say, G-fans . . . my fans. I love you more than I will ever let on.

Now the hammering's stopped, the raft must be ready. Up top, the 'cano cover is scraping, the crescent shaft of light descending. It's Komodo, come to get me for the final walk. He never misses an appointment.

"My own true friend!"

What's this? Outside there's all kinds of commotion.

Some Atom's crying from the crow's nest atop the glassine pines ringing Corvair Bay. "Land ho! Land ho!" Another chunk of ravaged earth is flotjetting through the Cloudcover, ready to merge with what was once just ours, ours and ours alone.

"My own true friend! You must come see! It is incredible!"

I see Komodo now. I thought he'd be so somber, but he's smiling. Ecstatic. Sheila Brooks is with him; they look great together, they really do.

"Please, come to the beach with us."

I'm trying to get up, but it's hard. I must be half-dead already. I feel so sleepy.

"You must see." Sheila and Komodo—they're picking me up! How are they doing that, two skanks like them lifting a behemoth like me? Man! Been so out of it, I didn't even realize I was shrinking. Can't be more than a couple feet long now.

"Look! Look, my own true friend!"

I'm trying, squinting every lid. But I only see the sea.

"There!"

Now I see it, I do. A piece of land coming in.

That promontory . . . it looks familiar. Yes, it does. What's that covering it—a carpet of 'tiles? Zards from wall to wall?

I feel Sheila Brooks stroke my shaggy leathers.

And the Atoms screaming, cheering.

"My own true friend, it is so!" Komodo's shouting.

Could it really be my Hallowed Homelands, returned to me?

LETTER TO A FRIEND
LEFT AT LAVAROCK
PROMONTORY,
RADIOACTIVE ISLAND

Please forgive this intrusion of your privacy. On this day, however, four-teen years since we last were together, I was feeling quite lonely for your presence. It was Sheila who suggested we make this journey, inasmuch as today, as you might remember should you care to retain such trivial details, is also my birthday—another August 6—the forty-sixth in my altogether in-sufficiently productive life.

The boat trip has been pleasant. The waters off Past Due Point were calm, unlike our last voyage, when we came quite close to capsizing. Today we have had perfect weather. Our sun still shines, more brilliantly than ever, I am proud to say. Its warming glow has guided our trip.

The children have been insistent about coming ashore. Little Ebi, who has just reached six, wants very much to pet you. When I attempted to ex-plain that you were perhaps not the petting type, she broke into inconsol-able tears.

Joseph Jr. has taken me to task for my prohibition. It is their right to go onshore, he says, citing a recent case brought before the Budd Hazard Court in which the residents of New Cognition Village, many of them new-comers, pressed for a measure limiting access to Lavarock, seeking to en-shrine it as a Landmark of the Evolloo. This was in deference to your residence on the Promontory. I opposed the initiative, arguing that you would have resented such special treatment. I trust my statements, mod-eled on a speech of yours given before the Anti-Speciesist Tribunal stress-ing "the bogusity of personality cults, Zardic or otherwise," continue to coincide with your true stance. Now Joseph Jr. has thrown these words back at me, claiming that as legitimate organisms of the Realm he and his siblings should be given free access to all niches. Furthermore, he asserted, it has never been established that you are "not the petting type."

Joseph Prometheus, Jr., only thirteen and already a sage of Quadcameral Law!

(Can you see him? Is he not a strapping boy? Nearly as tall as his namesake already! I dare think his mind may be as fine, but that might be a father's pride.)

Stumped by young Joseph's eloquence, I am forced to retreat into parental authority: "You'll stay in the boat because I say so!" This outburst, which I repeat for your amusement, incited great peals of laughter, nearly tipping the vessel. Even tiny Walter, who last month enjoyed his second birthday, found his father's attempt to point a stern finger to be exceedingly hilarious.

Still, they have stayed in the boat, much more for your sake than mine. After all, they are aware of your once-stated fondest wish "to be seen from the sea and not seen, to look no different than every other zard ever seen from the sea."

By now it has become a little game. We paddle in, close to the reptilian tangle basking on the Great Rock, near enough to see the seams in the carpet of your fellows. Then the children shout, "But mom and dad, which one is he? They all look alike . . ." From there they begin their refrain: "One hundred yards at sea, / Which one is me? / Which one is me?" To which they reply, "It's me! I'm Gojiro!" Things generally grow somewhat raucous at that point, everyone screaming, "No, it's *me! I'm* Gojiro!"

They carry on until Sheila calls a halt with an extension of her hand. "Silly," she says so softly *(so lovingly!)*. "You're all Gojiro."

Then everyone sits in the rocking boat, quietly, simply looking, for they know you are in them and they in you.

Oh, my friend, life does go on.

In the beginning, soon after our separation, I felt a terrible weight on my shoulders. It was only then that I glimpsed the terror of responsibility that must have haunted you. I felt as if a New World was dawning and I, being already resident, needed to set a certain standard, one of which I could not be sure. It was a dark time, full of doubts. But, somehow, in my self-obsessed despair I managed to raise my head, take a bearing. I saw I was not immobile, not cemented in a vault, but was moving, that the Evolloo was carrying me along, in spite of myself.

Ours is a wonderful world, my friend. You would not believe its splendor, the great range of its treasures. I walk with Sheila into Asbestos Wood, sit silently as she records her taxons much as Ebi did, and I am amazed. Overnight five new species have hybridized. I pause to breathe that air, let it fill my lungs. Creation!

Myself, I work. You'd never recognize the laboratory. I attempt to further penetrate the studies we once undertook together, although I must say, without a Budd Hazard to lay planks over the unfathomable, illumination is an elusive thing. I plod. A new Fayetteville Tree has arrived to replace the one that was lost. The vessel is larger; 209 species thrive within it at the latest count. Despite my greatest efforts, I still have not been able to reproduce the Instant of Reprimordialization. Shig, however, I must report, has filled in the 0.0247-second missing sector in *Gojiro vs. Joseph Prometheus Brooks in the Valley of Decision.* The film continues as a worldwide hit, but somehow I have no desire to see it in this "augmented" version.

Yes, life goes on. Sheila is pregnant once more. We are quite excited, since it will be the last one. Sometimes, when we are feeling giddy, we imagine our lives beginning that moment in Encrucijada, but we know we are much older than that. Are we too old? we ask ourselves. Only time will tell.

We must leave now, the children say they're hungry. The Island's so big these days, it's a five-hour sail back to Corvair Bay.

(Remember when I sat upon your shoulders and we'd go from here to there in as many giant steps?)

I still sing "Heartbreak Hotel" at bedtime, you know. I can't be late.

(Remember that first time, your eyes alive with fire, me with slicked-back hair?)

(Remember . . .)

I throw this letter on the wind, from the speeding ship, that it may come to you.

Long be your Line, my own true friend.